Hopeful He

Vicki Beeby writes historical fiction about the friendships and loves of service women brought together by the Second World War. Her first job was as a civil engineer on a sewage treatment project, so things could only improve from there. Since then, she has worked as a maths teacher and education consultant before turning freelance to give herself more time to write. In her free time, when she can drag herself away from reading, she enjoys walking and travelling to far-off places by train. She lives in Shropshire in a house that doesn't contain nearly enough bookshelves.

Also by Vicki Beeby

The Women's Auxiliary Air Force

The Ops Room Girls
Christmas with the Ops Room Girls
Victory for the Ops Room Girls

The Wrens

A New Start for the Wrens
A Wrens' Wartime Christmas
Hopeful Hearts for the Wrens

VICKI BEEBY

Hopeful
Hearts
for the
Wrens

CANELO

First published in the United Kingdom in 2023 by

Canelo
Unit 9, 5th Floor
Cargo Works, 1–2 Hatfields
London SE1 9PG
United Kingdom

A CIP catalogue record for this book is available from the British Library.

Print ISBN 978 1 80032 429 9
Ebook ISBN 978 1 80032 428 2

This book is a work of fiction. Names, characters, businesses, organizations, places and events are either the product of the author's imagination or are used fictitiously. Any resemblance to actual persons, living or dead, events or locales is entirely coincidental.

Cover design by Lisa Brewster

Cover images © Colin Thomas, Depositphotos, Shutterstock

Look for more great books at www.canelo.co

Printed and bound in Great Britain by Clays Ltd, Elcograf S.p.A.

1

To the Beeby family near and far:

Mum

Duncan, Jana & Emma

Chris, Katka & Elena

Chapter One

Orkney, July 1943

The first thing Sally Hartley saw when she stepped onto the stony path outside Kyeness signal station was the glint of copper in a puddle. 'Oh look – a penny!' She stooped to check it was lying head-side up before seizing it. She waved it in the face of her friend and sister Wren, Mary Griffiths. 'See a penny, pick it up and all day long you'll have good luck.'

Mary raised her eyes heavenwards as though praying for help. 'Don't tell me you actually believe that.' Before Sally could draw breath to reply, Mary went on, 'No, don't bother to answer. After two years, I know how seriously you take your superstitions.'

'You can scoff all you like,' Sally said, tucking the penny into her pocket, 'but thanks to this, it's going to be a good day.' And despite her weariness from a whole night spent on watch, she set off to Stromness with an extra spring in her step. She had the rest of the day and the whole of tomorrow free. The sun was shining, and a skylark soared and dived overhead, filling the air with its joyful song. It promised to be a perfect summer's day, and who knew – with the help of her lucky penny, perhaps it would turn out to be even better than she had thought?

She couldn't resist a glance across the water to the island of Hoy. With its towering cliffs and hills, Hoy could be seen from just about anywhere in Orkney's West Mainland, and in the eighteen months she had been in Orkney, Sally had become accustomed to orienting herself by it – on the days it wasn't shrouded in mist, at any rate. However, in the past seven months, it had become something more. For Adam Clark, the man she had been in love with ever since she had first seen him in Whitby before the war, had arrived in Orkney just before Christmas and was serving in Lyness on Hoy – the main naval base in Orkney. Although he had promised to keep in touch now they were based so close to each other, his letters had been few and far between, and she had only seen him in Stromness twice since bumping into him last Christmas. It was a painful reminder that although she knew in her heart they were perfect for each other, the message hadn't got through to Adam yet. As far as he was concerned, Sally was just a girl he knew from home.

Sally stuck her hand into her pocket and closed it around her lucky penny. Maybe today was the day that all changed. She had to believe Adam would return her feelings soon. She didn't know how much longer her heart could bear the constant weight of longing.

'What are your plans for the day?' she asked Mary in an attempt to banish her suddenly gloomy thoughts.

'Breakfast, sleep and then write a letter to Joe,' Mary replied. A shadow seemed to pass over her face. 'I haven't heard from him in over a month. I hope he's all right. Iris hasn't heard from Rob either.'

'I'm sure it's just the post acting up,' Sally said. 'With all that's going on in Sicily, I expect the mail from the Mediterranean must be in chaos.' Mary's sweetheart, Joe, had sailed for the Mediterranean after Christmas. Their friend, Iris Tredwick, also had a sweetheart on the same ship. Sally felt for them both as they lived from one rare letter to the next. It was important to remember that her heartache couldn't compare with Mary and Iris's, who constantly dreaded news of their loved ones' injury, capture or death. She especially felt for Mary whose fiancé had been killed at the start of the war. She had only dared to acknowledge her feelings for Joe at Christmas, then had been forced to say goodbye to him the very next day. Sometimes life seemed unbearably cruel.

Mary gave her a wan smile. 'I'm sure you're right. No news is good news, after all.' She drew a deep breath. 'Anyway, it's a lovely day, too good to waste. Perhaps I'll walk up to the Heddles' later. I'd like to send a sketch of Curlew Croft to Joe, remind him of the good times we've spent there.'

'I'm sure he'll love that.' Then as they continued their walk, the conversation turned to what film was showing at the Garrison theatre that evening. The temporary gloom lifted from Sally's heart, and she looked forward to the luck the coming day would bring.

–

Three hours later, after breakfast and a refreshing nap, Sally changed into the pretty frock Iris had made for her last year and headed out into Stromness. After all, her penny's luck only lasted for a day, and it wouldn't have much chance to bring her good fortune if she remained indoors. Mary was too involved in writing to Joe to want to come out, and Iris was nowhere to be found, meaning Sally was forced to go alone. She didn't mind, though. She tucked the penny into her cardigan pocket and set out. Once she had got a few errands out of the way, she felt the need for some refreshment after being out in the sunshine. Accordingly, she made her way to the Beehive, hoping there was some cake on the menu.

The Beehive was popular with service women who preferred to eat and drink in a quieter and less smoky atmosphere than the NAAFI, and today the cafe was even more crowded than usual. Sally couldn't help but notice that women on more than one table were studying newspapers with an air of excitement. Seeing a blonde head bent over a newspaper at the corner table she usually occupied with her friends, Sally took a seat opposite the young woman, thinking it was Iris.

3

'What's happened?' she asked, glancing at the chalked menu above the counter. 'Why is everyone glued to the newspaper?' She decided on carrot cake and, with her mouth watering in anticipation, she turned her attention to Iris.

Only it wasn't Iris. Although the hair was the same colour, there the resemblance ended. This girl's face was pretty in its own way, rounder than Iris's and with lips painted a vivid shade of scarlet. Pale brows were drawn together in a frown above a pair of hazel eyes that regarded Sally with a wary expression.

'Gosh, I'm so sorry.' Sally rose hastily, knocking over the salt cellar with her elbow as she did so. 'I thought you were someone else.' She replaced the cellar then, seeing a pile of spilled salt on the tablecloth, threw a pinch over her left shoulder.

'Oh, don't worry,' the girl said. 'You're welcome to join me. I'm new here, and I don't know anyone. I could use the company.' From her accent, she came from southern England. It wasn't as refined as Iris's, though, reminding Sally a little of Joe's accent.

'Thank you. If you're sure.'

The girl nodded, and Sally sat back down. 'I'm Sally. Sally Hartley. I'm one of the visual signaller Wrens working up at Kyeness.'

The girl's guarded expression faded. 'That's wonderful. Me too! I arrived this morning. I'm Tessa Bligh. It's a bit of luck running into you here.'

'Is this your first posting?'

Tessa shook her head. 'I spent a year at Harwich. It's a very busy port, and it was a huge responsibility. I gather Kyeness is quite small. I suppose they wanted a Wren up here with wider experience. I'm not sure how I feel about being sent to the back of beyond, though.'

'It might be a small signal station but it's in a vital location.' It was on the tip of Sally's tongue to point out that she, Iris and Mary had stopped a U-boat the previous Christmas until she remembered that was a secret. 'Scapa Flow is where the Home Fleet is based, after all.'

'Of course.' If Tessa had patted Sally on the head, she couldn't have been more patronising. 'Still, I'm sure I'll be able to suggest some improvements.'

So much for the lucky penny, Sally thought, glancing around the cafe, desperate to see a friendly face. If there had been anyone she knew, she would have exclaimed something about needing to speak to them urgently, extricating herself from Tessa and her condescending ways. Sadly, there was no one.

The bell above the door jingled, giving her a surge of fresh hope; Sally slipped her hand into her pocket and clutched the coin. Surely now its luck would kick in and bring her one of her friends.

It wasn't one of her friends but someone whose presence brought fresh faith in her penny. For the person who stepped through the door, looking smart in his naval uniform, was the man she had been longing to see for weeks: Adam. Her heart gave a lurch as he looked around the tables as though seeking someone. *Please don't let him be meeting another girl*. If he was, she would use her penny to pay for her tea and never believe they could be lucky ever again.

After an agonising few seconds, Adam's gaze turned to the corner table, and his face lit with recognition as their eyes met. Sally released the coin with a silent prayer of gratitude when he approached.

'Adam, how lovely to see you. Won't you join us?'

She knew a moment's dismay when he chose the seat beside Tessa, then decided sitting opposite was preferable so she could study his face. She was aware of the other women regarding him with interest and felt a flutter of enjoyment knowing that the handsome petty officer was with her. Of course, it would be better if Tessa weren't present, especially considering the way Tessa sat a little straighter and batted her lashes at Adam.

'What are you doing in Stromness?' Sally asked Adam after reluctantly introducing him to Tessa.

The bell jingled again; Adam's gaze switched from Sally's face to a point over her shoulder for a moment before his focus returned to her and he replied. 'I got forty-eight hours leave and thought I'd use the time to explore Mainland.'

Sally tried not to mind that he hadn't said he'd made the trip across from Hoy to see her. Knowing that they were meant to be together, it was both frustrating and heartbreaking that Adam remained silent about his feelings. She couldn't help remembering what her mother had told her about the first time she had met Sally's father. 'I knew we belonged together the first time I laid eyes on him,' she always said. 'You'll know too, when you meet the man you're destined to marry.' And she had. Shortly before the outbreak of war, she had attended a dance and had walked up to the only person she recognised – the girl from the fishmongers where she worked. Only when she reached Pauline's side did she realise she was standing with a handsome young man. 'This is my brother, Adam,' Pauline had said. Sally had looked into his face as she shook his offered hand and had felt a jolt in her chest when their eyes met. From that moment, she had known she was in love. It was hard to believe Adam had failed to feel the same electricity, yet he had never said anything. When Adam had joined the navy without declaring his feelings for her, it must have been because he'd thought it unfair to tie her down when his future was so uncertain. At least, that was the conclusion she'd clung to for comfort in the tearful days that had followed his departure. However, now they were based so close together, she lived in hope that he would finally ask her out.

'Do you plan to go anywhere besides Stromness?' *Please let him be staying in Stromness.* Then they would be bound to see each other again.

'I've heard great things about the Ring of Brodgar. I thought I'd hitch a lift there.'

'Oh, it's magical. I went just before Christmas.' Sally summoned her courage. 'It was freezing cold. I'd love to see it on a sunny day like today.' Surely he would take the hint. She wasn't bold enough to invite herself along, but a walk in a romantic spot couldn't fail to loosen his tongue. She slipped her hand in her pocket to touch the penny again.

Adam toyed with the sugar tongs, not meeting her eyes. 'I would enjoy that.'

Sally's heart soared. But before she could dream of walking hand in hand around the mysterious stones, Adam added, 'I arranged this trip with a friend from Lyness, though. We're going together. Maybe another time.'

'Oh, that's fine. I understand.' Sally beamed at him to hide the disappointment. She thought Adam looked disappointed too, and she hugged the knowledge to her heart that he had wanted to go with her.

But if he had wanted to see her, an annoying voice in the back of her mind said, why hadn't he written to let her know he had leave? Oddly, the voice sounded a little like Mary's. Sally couldn't deny that although he had promised to keep in touch, he only occasionally replied to her weekly letters and even then his notes were little more than excuses why he couldn't meet up.

'Anyway, what would you lovely ladies like to drink?'

While Adam gave the order to the waitress, Sally couldn't tear her eyes from him, drinking in his handsome features. His fair hair was cropped shorter than she remembered, although it seemed only to emphasise his sculpted cheekbones and deep blue eyes. If anything, he was even more handsome than he had been on the day they'd met. Sally wished Tessa would catch on and leave so she and Adam could be alone. Much to her annoyance, however, once the waitress left, Adam didn't return his attention to her but addressed Tessa, asking how long she had been in Orkney and how she was finding it. Sally did her best to ignore the stab of jealousy. After all, he was only being polite; he could hardly ignore Tessa, even if he did prefer Sally's company. Anyway, it gave Sally more time to study him without him noticing.

When she did glance aside, seeing the newspapers that seemed to be the focus of several excited conversations, she was reminded that she still hadn't heard that day's news. 'Has something happened?' she asked. 'What's everyone taking about?'

Now Adam turned his gaze to her, his eyes opened wide in astonishment. 'Haven't you heard?'

'Heard what? I've been on watch all night.'

'Mussolini has been overthrown.'

The words sent a thrill through her veins. 'Who's taking over? What does it mean for us?' She thought briefly of Rob and Joe before remembering the Italian prisoner of war she had met in hospital. She remembered Aldo Vanni from time to time, wondering how he was coping with life as a prisoner on the tiny island of Lamb Holm. How would the news affect him?

'Marshal Badoglio. It's not clear what it means for us yet.' Adam didn't look too concerned. Maybe he, unlike her, didn't know anyone based in the Mediterranean. Then another thought occurred.

'Some friends here have a son who's a prisoner in Italy. What does it mean for him?' It would be wonderful if Elspeth and Archie's son would be freed soon.

Adam shrugged before turning to smile at the waitress who brought their tea and cakes. 'I don't suppose it will make any difference to them. I can't see them being freed. We're still at war with Italy, remember.'

He sounded unconcerned, but it was unreasonable of her to expect him to show compassion for a man he had never met. He glanced at his watch. 'Goodness. I'm meeting my friend in fifteen minutes. I'd better hurry.'

'I'll pour the tea.' Keeping her head lowered in case her despondency showed in her face, Sally poured a dash of milk into each cup then picked up the tea strainer.

'How do you two know each other?' Tessa asked.

Sally drew a breath to reply, but Adam got there first. 'Sally knows my sister. We've met a few times in Whitby. Pauline made me promise to look out for Sally when I moved up here.'

That stung. Would Adam have ignored her if not for his promise to Pauline? He made it sound as though Sally was nothing more to him than a passing acquaintance. Sally swallowed, not trusting herself to speak.

Meanwhile, Tessa chattered on. 'Oh, is that where you're from? I've never been to Yorkshire but I'd love to go. It sounds so wild and romantic.'

'You'd love it. The best place in the world.' Adam's attention was wholly on Tessa now. He went on to describe the various locations he thought Tessa would enjoy.

Sally made one more attempt to assert herself once she was certain her voice wouldn't wobble. 'My favourite place is Whitby Abbey. It's so—'

But before Sally could explain how the abbey had entranced her romantic soul, Tessa spoke over her. Her whole body was angled towards Adam, effectively blocking Sally from the conversation. She touched Adam's arm as she spoke, and Sally could only watch with a growing lump in her throat as Tessa dominated the conversation.

'I'd never been farther north than Norwich until I joined the WRNS,' Tessa said. 'Perhaps I should visit Yorkshire on my next leave. Wouldn't it be fun if you got leave at the same time? You could show me around.'

'You never know,' Adam replied.

The bubble of happiness that had formed around Sally upon Adam's arrival burst, leaving her with the same wretched heaviness of heart she always felt after each meeting with him. She drank her tea, more to ease the tightness in her throat than because she wanted it. One day, Adam would look at her and realise that they would be perfect together. Unhappily, that day was not today.

A few minutes later, Adam rose and pulled some change from his pocket. Then he hesitated. 'This is embarrassing,' he said. 'I seem to have left most of my money behind, and I don't know how much I'll need today.'

'Oh, don't worry.' Only too happy to do something for Adam, Sally pulled out her purse. 'I'll pay.'

And Adam was gone with nothing more than a brief word of thanks. No promise to meet another day.

She and Tessa didn't linger over their drinks but left soon after. Much to Sally's relief, Tessa said she wanted to explore Stromness, leaving Sally to return to the Wrennery alone with her thoughts; she didn't think she could bear Tessa's company a moment longer.

On her way, she happened to glance down one of the side lanes that led to the water. Acting on a sudden impulse, she darted down the lane and flung the lucky penny into the sea. The noise from the harbour was so loud she couldn't hear the tiny splash as it struck the water. The harbour might not be a wishing well, but she screwed her eyes tightly shut and made a wish anyway. 'I wish Adam would notice me at last,' she whispered, picturing the penny sinking into the depths. She contemplated the oily water for a while, listening to the gulls wheeling overhead and the incessant hum of activity from the docks. Then she turned and made her way to the Wrennery.

Chapter Two

No matter how much Sally tried to persuade herself that Adam couldn't possibly be interested in Tessa, she couldn't dispel the persistent ache in her chest. How many more lonely days would pass before Adam returned her feelings? How long would she have to endure his seeming indifference? She was sure they were meant to be together, so why hadn't the message got through to him? It was getting ever more difficult to remain cheerful in his company when her heart was slowly breaking. How could an emotion that was supposed to lift one to the highest heights have brought her so low?

By the time she reached the Wrennery, she had played out the encounter in the Beehive over and over in her mind until she couldn't separate the facts from her fears. If only Adam had given some indication that he preferred her to Tessa, she wouldn't now be picturing Tessa and Adam, hand in hand, announcing their engagement. It was all too much for Sally, and as she pushed open the door, her eyes brimmed with tears. She tore through the entrance hall, hoping to reach the cabin she shared with Iris and Mary before anyone saw her; she didn't think she could mask her distress for much longer. As luck would have it – the bad luck that had dogged her heels all morning – she met Mary at the foot of the stairs.

'Hi, Sally. I wondered where you had got to,' Mary said. 'Coming to dinner?'

'In a moment.' Sally clamped her mouth tight to stifle a convulsive sob and made a gesture she hoped Mary would interpret as her needing to put her bag away. Before Mary could say anything more, Sally pushed past and bolted upstairs.

'Sally?' Mary's voice echoed up the stairwell.

Gripping the banister, Sally paused, drew a deep breath and looked down at Mary's upturned face. 'You go on. I'll be down in a minute.'

For a moment, Sally was afraid Mary would follow her. She gazed up at Sally, concern etched upon her face. Then she shrugged. 'I'll save you a seat.'

By the time she had climbed the two flights of stairs to the attic, tears were pouring down her face. She burst through the door and flung herself onto her bed, relieved to be able to give vent to her feelings at last.

'Sally, whatever is the matter?'

Sally sat up with a start, dashing the tears from her eyes. Her vision cleared to see Iris perched upon her bed, her fountain pen poised above her writing case which lay open upon her knees. 'Shouldn't you be on your way to Kyeness by now?' she asked, unable to prevent an accusatory tone creeping into her voice. That was the trouble with being a Wren – no privacy to have a good cry when you really needed it.

'One of the officers is coming to check the log,' Iris replied. 'I just had a message offering to give me and Sue a lift to the signal station.' Sue was another of the Wrens based at Kyeness. Iris pulled a face. 'Obviously it's too much to expect an officer to walk all that way, even if it's all right for us mere Wrens to do it several times a day in all weather. Anyway, it gives me time to finish my letter to Rob before I have to leave.'

By this time, Sally had managed to get her tears under control and blown her nose. Feeling more able to string together a coherent sentence she said, 'Have you heard from Rob yet?'

'No, but don't change the subject. What's wrong?' Iris put aside her letter and scooted to the edge of her bed, regarding Sally intently.

There was no avoiding the subject. Anyway, now Sally could speak without bursting into tears, she found she longed to confide in a friend. 'It's Adam,' she said. 'I met him today.' Out poured the whole story – the hope that this time he would declare his feelings for her, followed by the crushing sense of being small and insignificant when Tessa Bligh had taken over.

At the mention of Tessa, Iris's face twisted in dislike. 'So you've met Miss High and Mighty. I had the pleasure of showing her around this morning, and I was not impressed.'

Feeling somewhat cheered that she wasn't alone in her dislike, Sally said, 'I wish I hadn't met her. She ruined my morning. It all started so perfectly. The weather was wonderful and I found—' Sally bit off mention of her lucky penny; Iris had hardly any more patience than Mary with her superstitions. 'I found out about Mussolini being overthrown. But I mistook Tessa for you in the cafe and ended up sharing a table with her.'

'You thought Tessa was me?' Iris pulled a face.

'I could only see her hair at first. As soon as she looked up I realised my mistake, but it was too late by then. But the worst thing happened when Adam arrived, and instead of a cosy chat just the two of us, Tessa took over.' A fresh wave of desolation struck Sally at the memory. 'She blocked me out of the conversation altogether.'

'How rude,' Iris said. 'I hope he made an effort to include you.'

'Well, no… she didn't really give him the chance.' Sally wouldn't let herself reflect on Adam's lack of consideration. He would have been perfectly attentive if Tessa hadn't been present. 'Honestly, if she'd moved her chair any closer to him, she'd have been sitting in his lap.'

Iris scowled. 'You mean he ignored you too? Honestly, Sally, you deserve better than that. If you ask me, he's not worth your time.'

'How can you say that? You don't know him. You can't judge him on that one incident.' Unable to meet Iris's gaze,

Sally glanced at the 'bluey' — the aerogramme upon which Iris had been writing her latest letter to Rob. Not a scrap of space had been left unused, and Iris had written in extra-small handwriting, obviously to fit in as much as possible. Curiously, that cramped letter was a symbol of the extravagant love Iris and Rob felt for one another. A fresh surge of longing swept through Sally. If she could have one wish, it would be to experience the same relationship with Adam.

'I don't know how much longer I can wait.' The words burst out of her before it had fully registered that she had spoken them aloud. 'Why won't he see that we're meant to be together?'

She looked at Iris then and saw her friend regarding her with sympathy. After a long pause, in which Iris seemed to be carefully weighing her words, she asked, 'What makes you so sure he's the one for you?'

'I knew the first time I saw him.'

'Knew what?'

'I felt...' Sally thought of the thrill fizzing through her veins at the sight of Adam's handsome face and struggled to put it into words. 'Electricity,' she said. 'It was just how my mother said it would be,' she added, feeling on firmer ground. 'She always used to tell me how her skin had tingled all over the first time she met my father, and that was how she knew they were meant to be together. She said that's how I would know when I found the one for me.'

'I didn't feel like that the first time I met Rob.'

'You were seasick! But you knew you liked him the next time you met.'

A soft smile played on Iris's lips, and Sally knew Iris was remembering their first outing in Stromness when they had gone to the Women's Voluntary Society Christmas party and met Rob again. 'Well, I admit I liked him, but I didn't think he was going to be a significant person in my life.' Iris's smile faded. 'I just wish he wasn't so far away. It was bad enough when we had that U-boat attacking our ships, and we had to watch the whole thing from Kyeness. It's so much worse not knowing how he is. Even when I get a letter, all that tells me is that he was fine at the time of writing.'

Sally looked at her in sympathy, knowing there was nothing she could say or do to make Iris feel better. While Adam remained frustratingly silent about his feelings – and he *must* have feelings for her, she had to believe that – she did at least have the comfort of knowing he was safe in Lyness.

After a silence heavy with dread, Iris gave her head a little shake as though trying to throw off her fears. 'Anyway, we're supposed to be talking of you. You need to make the most of your time with Adam while he's here. I can't believe I haven't even met him yet. What's he like?'

'He's lovely.' Sally felt her melancholy lifting as she thought of him. 'He's so good-looking. He's got these wonderful blue eyes that I could drown in, and when he smiles, he gets the most gorgeous dimples. No man with a smile like his could be anything other than perfect.'

She looked at Iris, expecting her to appear pleased. Instead, she was frowning. 'I didn't ask what he looked like. I want to know if he's kind, if he makes you laugh, what his interests are.'

'Well… he… of course he's kind. He…' But try as she might, she couldn't think of a single conversation where he had told her what he liked to read or his interests. Now she thought about it, their conversations had never got past small talk. She couldn't even be certain what he had done for a living before the war. She had a feeling he had worked in one of the boatyards, but she wasn't sure. She felt the heat of a blush stealing into her cheeks. 'We never really spoke about that sort of thing,' she said.

Iris leaned her elbows on her knees. 'Then I suggest the next time you see him, you try and find out a little more about him.' She gave a wry smile. 'It's probably best you find out if he likes pulling the wings off butterflies *before* you find yourself married to him.'

'Oh, he'd never do that. I'm sure he's—' Sally stopped, realising Iris was teasing her. 'I suppose you're right. I should learn more about him.' She sighed. 'Assuming that Tessa Bligh gives me a chance.'

The door opened as she was speaking and Mary marched in. 'I thought you were coming to dinner. Where have you been?' Then Mary gave Sally a sharp look, and Sally became all too conscious that her eyes must be reddened and swollen. 'What's happened?'

'Not what, who,' Iris said. 'Tessa Bligh.'

Mary snorted. 'Tessa Blight, more like. I take it you've already met that baggage, then. I've just had the pleasure of her company in the mess, thanks to your absence. I had to put up with her telling me how wonderful she is and how she's sure she's been posted to Kyeness to set us mere mortals a good example.'

Iris rolled her eyes then sprang up from her bed. 'I pity the poor Wren who has her for oppo on her first watch. Anyway, I'd better shake a leg or I'll miss my lift. See you all later.' So saying, she swept from the room.

When the door had slammed behind her, Mary gave Sally a rueful smile. 'Actually, that was another reason I came to find you. Evelyn's gone down with shingles, so they've had to switch our watches around. Guess which lucky Wren is now on morning watch tomorrow with our lovely new arrival?'

'You're joking. Not me?'

'Fraid so.'

Sally slumped back on her bed with a groan. 'I almost envy Evelyn. I think that penny must have been cursed.'

—

Aldo heaved a sigh as he helped lower the block of stone into the truck. His friend, Enrico Donati, clapped his shoulder, raising clouds of fine stone dust. 'Good work. That's our quota for the day. Coming to the blockships later? Luigi and I are going to try to catch a lobster.'

'Maybe.' Aldo rotated his shoulders to work out the kinks from heaving heavy weights all morning.

He considered the offer as he followed the men out of the quarry. On the one hand, lobster would make a welcome change from the usual fare they got at Camp 60. On the other hand, it was a rare day of sunshine, too good to waste picking his way over the rotting hulks that had been scuttled to block the channel between Lamb Holm and Orkney's mainland. He ached all over from his shift at the quarry, and an afternoon lying outside, letting the sunshine soothe away the soreness, was appealing.

Accordingly, once they made the short crossing to Lamb Holm by boat, he declined to accompany Enrico. Instead, he collected the roughly shaped piece of driftwood he was working on and the box of tools that Captain Lawler, one of the British officers, had loaned him when Aldo had discovered a talent for wood carving. Settling himself outside the hut in a patch of sunlight, he selected the carving knife from the box and began whittling the wood. Soon a pile of chippings lay on the grass and the rough shape of a cat emerged. As well as scrounging driftwood, he was also able to salvage good quality wood from the blockships, and he had built up a reasonable trade, exchanging carvings for camp tokens, cigarettes or chocolate. Several British guards had even commissioned pieces to be sent home to family members.

As often happened when alone, his thoughts drifted to Sally. Sally, the girl with the bright eyes and romantic soul he had met while in hospital. Was she still in Orkney? He wondered if their paths would ever cross again. That was the thing about the war: it brought you into contact with people you would never have met had you stayed at home, but then it tore you apart with no knowing if you would ever meet again. He hoped he would run into her again, though. He sensed in her a kindred spirit. When he was with her, he felt as though miracles were possible. Meeting Sally Hartley had been the one bright spot in his life here at what felt like the end of the world. That time he had first seen her, he had not only been in pain following his appendectomy but also suffering the agony of losing his brother. Sally's kindness to him – despite the fact that he was an enemy prisoner – had been a balm to his broken heart, and he had been eager to do something for her in return, which was why he had given her his precious St Christopher medallion.

Sally's kindness had extended beyond their time in hospital. Before Christmas, she had sent him a parcel, full of practical items like soap, pyjamas and razor blades and also treats like chocolate bars and fruitcake. Moved to tears, in return he had persuaded one of the British officers to deliver a carved crib scene to her. He had made the nativity pieces intending to trade them with the guards, but the knowledge that she still remembered him more than made up for the loss.

He was jolted back to the present when the sun was blotted out by a tall, broad figure looming above him. 'Have you heard the news?'

Aldo scrambled to his feet and took a step to his left so the wall of his hut was no longer at his back. He knew to allow an escape route when Gianni Bernardi was around. 'What news?'

'Mussolini has been deposed.'

Aldo was careful not to let his delight and relief show. He hated everything about the man who had led Italy into this disastrous war, but Gianni venerated him. One of Aldo's teeth was still loose from the last time he had insulted Mussolini without first checking Gianni was out of earshot. 'What does that mean for us?'

'No one knows yet. They say Badoglio has taken over.'

'But what about the war? Is he going to surrender?'

Gianni spat, aiming at a spot close to Aldo's feet. 'Even if he does, we will remain true to Il Duce. The British are our enemies, and we must never forget. They sent us to this desolate hole, and when we get the chance, we will make them sorry. And you, baker's boy, will help or I'll disfigure your smile permanently.'

Aldo kept silent, not taking his eyes from Gianni's face, not wanting to provoke another fight yet unwilling to profess loyalty to a man he despised. Gianni evidently took his silence as acquiescence, for his mouth twisted in a satisfied smile. 'We will make them pay,' he said. He spat again, then marched away.

Aldo released a shaky breath then went to find a clean patch of grass to resume his rest. He lay back, flinging his arm over his eyes to shield them from the bright sun. He hated himself for not speaking out. The trouble was, there was no avoiding the likes of Gianni while stuck on this tiny island. For a moment he found himself wishing he hadn't given away his St Christopher, because he had the feeling he was going to need all the protection he could get. Still, he took comfort in knowing Sally had it. She would take care of it, he knew, and he liked to think it kept him in her thoughts. The St Christopher was the only thing he had from his mother, who had died when he was just five years old. It had kept him safe through fierce fighting in North Africa, and he was convinced it was the only reason he was alive and safe in Orkney and not dead like his brother. He had hidden the silver pendant in the hem of his tunic when he had been captured, dreading losing it to a light-fingered guard. He kept it safe throughout the long journey to Orkney, only daring to liberate it once he was satisfied that the British soldiers guarding Camp 60 were a decent lot. However, not long after, he had caught Gianni looking at it with a covetous gleam in his eyes, probably working out how many cigarettes he could trade it for. No, it was safer with Sally. He hoped it was bringing her good fortune.

His mother had been convinced of its luck and had pressed it into his hand on her deathbed, telling him how it had kept his father safe through the Great War. If only he had been wearing it when the earthquake had struck, maybe he wouldn't have been killed. As it was, there had been no one to look after him and his brother after their mother had died two years later, so they were sent to an orphanage. His last words to his mother had been a promise to look after his younger brother. Aldo swallowed, feeling the hopeless ache of loss that always assailed him when he thought of Carlo. He closed his eyes yet couldn't escape the images flooding his mind. Of Carlo grinning, saying, 'See! Told you we'd make it.' Then his smile freezing as a dark stain blossomed across his chest and his knees buckling. Aldo had caught him, but the light had faded from his eyes before Aldo could lower him to the ground. Aldo had wanted to stay with him but had been swept away as the British troops closed in.

He had known from the start that this war was a terrible mistake. He was glad Mussolini was gone, and he prayed the deposed dictator would die for forcing his countrymen to fight and be killed for a cause many of them didn't believe in. There were a few fascists like Gianni, of course, but Aldo did his best to avoid their company. He certainly wasn't going to join in with whatever disruption Gianni had in mind, and he would do his best to persuade his friends to stay out of it too.

Chapter Three

It wasn't just the loss of her long-awaited day off causing her low mood, nor was it even the prospect of spending five hours alone with Tessa, Sally reflected as she bolted down her porridge early the next morning. It was also that Adam would be in Stromness on leave, and she had hoped to run into him again. At least she wouldn't be on watch with Tessa that evening – she had the afternoon and evening off before returning to her usual watch rotation the next day. Of course, she would have to endure the forty-five-minute walk back from Kyeness in Tessa's company before she could be rid of her. Sally sank further into gloom.

'There you are. I've been waiting for you.' Tessa, already wearing her gaberdine raincoat, had entered the mess without Sally noticing and now stood at her elbow, tapping her watch.

'What?' Sally glanced at the clock. 'But we don't have to leave for another ten minutes.'

'I want to arrive in good time on my first day. I'll need to accustom myself to the way things are done in Kyeness. Although,' Tessa gave a tinkling laugh that made Sally shudder, 'I'm sure I'll have plenty of ideas for improvements. The signallers at Harwich were most appreciative of all the little suggestions I made.'

'I bet they were,' Sally muttered to herself as she carried her dish and half-finished tea to the serving hatch. 'So thrilled they sent her to Orkney.'

She gave herself a mental talking to as she hurried to fetch her gear. Tessa might have been tired yesterday after her long journey. Crossing the Pentland Firth was enough to bring the worst out in anyone, especially after the interminable train journey. She should give Tessa another chance. And it was surely a sign of her dedication to her job that she wanted to arrive in good time for her first watch. Sally should encourage her.

Accordingly, she smiled brightly at Tessa when she met her by the front door. 'Let's go, then. It's quite a walk, but lovely at this time of year.'

Fifteen minutes later, however, Sally's resolution was being tested. 'I thought you said the walk was lovely.' Tessa pulled her raincoat more tightly around her with a scowl as squally drizzle hit them in the face. By this time they were out of Stromness, through the makeshift wire gate and climbing the hill they had to cross to reach the headland of Kyeness, where the signal station was situated.

'I love it.' Sally tipped back her head and drew a deep breath. 'The air's so clean, and just wait until this mist lifts – the view's amazing.'

'I'll take your word for it.'

Seeing Tessa's grumpy expression, Sally forbore to mention that the walk wasn't so pleasant in the winter when it was dark and icy. Winter was still months away, and she was sure Tessa would have settled in by then.

A few steps later, Tessa paused, clutching her side. 'How much farther?'

'About another thirty minutes.' Growing up in the North York Moors, Sally always found it more helpful to give distances in units of time, since half a mile could mean anything from a brisk ten-minute stroll along level ground to puffing and panting for half an hour or more if the path was steep or icy.

She glanced at Tessa, glad they'd left earlier than usual. After eighteen months of walking this path up to four times a day in all weather, Sally was fitter than she had ever been, even though she was used to the hills and moors around Whitby. If Tessa had led a more sedentary life before joining the WRNS, she would be bound to struggle at first. 'Where are you from?' she asked.

'Felixstowe,' Tessa replied. 'And did I tell you my first posting was near Harwich? A very busy port.'

'Yes,' Sally replied through gritted teeth. Then in a lower voice, she muttered, 'Several times.'

There was another pause in the conversation while Tessa started walking again and the only sound that could be heard above the blustery wind and the distant waves was Tessa's laboured breathing. Sally racked her brains for something intelligent to say about Felixstowe or Harwich, but knowing little about them, all she could say was, 'Mary's sweetheart comes from Ipswich. That's near Felixstowe, isn't it?' To which Tessa only responded with a curt nod, seemingly too out of breath to speak.

In one of the sudden changes of weather that Sally had grown used to, the clouds lifted as they walked on, and by the time they had reached the highest point on the path, the view had cleared enough for the sea to be visible. The Hoy hills slowly resolved from the mist until they had no more than the lightest veil of cloud skimming their tops.

'See,' Sally said, pointing across Hoy Sound. 'Is that not the most beautiful sight you've ever seen? I'll never tire of this view.'

'I'm already tired of this walk,' Tessa said. 'I can't believe the navy makes us walk all this way. When I was in Harwich we were given bikes. Why hasn't anyone requested them?'

'Can you imagine cycling up that path?'

'Well, no, but there must be a road or track. How did they get the trucks out to build the signal station in the first place?'

'There is, but it's a much longer way round. It's a steep climb up the road out of Stromness, so we'd have to push our bikes most of the way to the top. Then it's a really rough, stony track. It'd be tough going even on the rare times you weren't peddling into a headwind.'

'It can't be as bad as you make out.' Tessa increased her pace now they were on the last stretch descending the gentle slope to the clifftop where the signal station stood. 'I can't believe none of the Wrens have complained about it. I'll be sure to mention it to one of the officers.'

'Be careful you don't get a reputation as a complainer,' Sally said.

'How come when a man makes a suggestion it's taken seriously, whereas a woman is accused of making a fuss? If the navy posts us to the back of beyond, it's their responsibility to make sure we can get to and from work safely.'

Much as Sally hated to admit it, Tessa had a point. She said no more until they reached the signal station, running over in her mind the things she needed to show Tessa.

They were greeted by Iris and her oppo, both of whom were looking impatient to leave after a whole night on watch. Iris, looking down at them through the open hatch of the signal room on the upper floor, caught Sally's eye and raised her brows, which Sally took as an enquiry into how her walk with Tessa had gone. Sally gave a tiny side-to-side waggle of the head, attempting to convey that it hadn't been too bad.

'I'll stay on in the signal room for a few minutes if you want to show Tessa around,' Iris called.

'That's very kind. Thank you,' Tessa replied. 'I'm sorry we're a bit late. My fault – I wasn't expecting such a strenuous walk.'

'You'll get used to it,' Sally told her, determined to give Tessa the benefit of the doubt. After all, she hadn't got on very well with Iris when they had first met and now she counted her as one of her best friends. If Tessa had had the manners to apologise for making Iris have to stay at her post past the end of her watch then she couldn't be all bad.

Still, Sally didn't waste time showing Tessa around, first taking her outside to show her the privy, coal bunker, flag locker and flag mast. Not that anyone could have missed this last feature. Not only was it tall enough to be seen from some distance, but the wind was knocking the halyard against the pole with an insistent chime. 'We'll have to raise the ensign at 0900. But, of course, you'll have done that at your last post, too.'

'Oh, yes, this is all very similar, although it was much more modern, of course. I expect we were kept more up to date there, which is why they sent me to Orkney. They'll want someone here with more experience to show the Wrens what's new.'

Something about the way Tessa said 'more experience' threw Sally's mind back to the way Tessa had inveigled herself upon Adam the day before. She swallowed, feeling a fresh wash of misery. If only it had fallen on Iris or Mary to show Tessa the ropes. They wouldn't have put up with any nonsense. Iris would have frozen Tessa with a look that had been honed by generations of Tredwicks when faced with an impertinent upstart. Mary would have cut her down with a comment so caustic it would have melted the flesh from her bones. All Sally could do was mutter, 'I'm sure we'll all be very grateful.' Even then, she couldn't inject her words with the desired level of sarcasm.

Tessa seemed to take them at face value and gave her grating laugh. 'Oh, I'm sure I'll have as much to learn from you.'

Once Sally had given her a quick tour of the signal station's ground floor − galley, sitting room and bunk room − they climbed the metal ladder that led through the hatch and into the signal room.

'I'll leave you to it, then,' Iris said, turning away from the window. 'It's all quiet out there for now.'

Tessa took Iris's place straight away, standing beside the telescope. Just before Iris descended the ladder she took Sally's arm, pulling her close so she could murmur in Sally's ear, 'I'm going to Curlew Croft this afternoon. I want to hear how the Heddles are taking the news about Mussolini. Why don't you come along?'

The Heddles lived in a cottage close to Kyeness. They had opened their home to Sally, Iris and Mary soon after the three girls had arrived on the island, and Sally had taken an instant liking to Elspeth and Archie, who the girls had come to regard as substitute parents. Their warm kitchen had become a place of refuge to the girls whenever they had needed advice or a shoulder to cry on – or simply an escape from the pressures of the war for a few hours. Shortly before Christmas, the Heddles' son, Don, had been captured, and was now in a prisoner-of-war camp in Italy. Consequently, they scoured the newspapers for any news regarding the war in Italy. Sally knew they would be wondering if the latest developments there would have any effect on Don's situation.

She nodded. 'I'll come straight over if Tessa doesn't mind.'

Iris glanced at Tessa before replying, 'Have fun. I'll tell the Heddles to expect you.'

Once Iris had gone, Sally said to Tessa, 'I don't know if you heard that, but do you think you can find your way back to the Wrennery on your own at the end of the watch? I'd like to visit some friends who live nearby.'

For a fleeting moment, a wistful expression crossed Tessa's face, and Sally felt mean for not inviting her. However, before she could explain, Tessa replied in over-bright tones, 'Oh, I'll be fine. Don't worry about me.'

Sally felt like a complete heel. Although Tessa hadn't impressed her at their first meeting, the poor girl was new to Orkney and must be feeling lonely. She shouldn't allow herself to be prejudiced against Tessa simply because Tessa obviously admired Adam. 'You could come and meet the Heddles if you like. I should warn you, though, that their son is a prisoner of war in Italy, and they're bound to be worried with all that's happened.'

'I wouldn't want to intrude on your friends. I can manage on my own. Now,' she went on before Sally could repeat her invitation, 'why don't you show me the main points of interest?'

Tessa walked out onto the balcony, her stiff body language making it clear the conversation was over. Feeling as though she had failed in her last chance to befriend Tessa, Sally joined her and explained where Kyeness lay in relation to the geography of Orkney. Still a little needled by Tessa's evident belief that Kyeness was a backwater, she stressed the strategic importance

of Hoy Sound, and how the narrow channel between Mainland and Hoy was one of only two entrances into Scapa Flow,
the anchorage for Britain's Home Fleet. She was gratified to
discover that there hadn't been an anti-submarine indicator loop
near Tessa's last station, so Tessa did, at least, have one thing she
needed to learn. When Sally explained how it played a vital
role in detecting U-boats attempting to make their way into
Scapa Flow, she took satisfaction in seeing grudging interest
in Tessa's expression. It was clear she had realised that maybe
Orkney wasn't the backward outpost she had thought.

Just when Sally was starting to think she had been unfair in
her early judgement of Tessa, her first barbs began to show.

'The friend you were with yesterday – Adam. Where is he
based?'

'On Hoy.'

Tessa pointed to the hills across Hoy Sound. 'Just there? It
must be nice to have him so close.'

'No, he's in Lyness, down in the south-east of the island. He
doesn't often make it to Mainland.'

Tessa fiddled with the telescope, swinging it on its stand.
'How long have you known him?'

'About four years.'

'So he's an old friend?'

'You could say that.' While Sally hadn't hesitated to share her
hopes and dreams with Iris and Mary, she didn't feel comfortable letting Tessa know of her longing to be much more than
friends with Adam.

'It must be nice being comfortable enough with a man to be
just friends,' Tessa said. 'I suppose he sees you as quite one of
the boys.' She fluffed her hair and gave the tinkling laugh that
Sally was coming to dislike. 'You know, it's such a relief to hear
you say that. I can say it now, but I thought Adam was rather
taken with me.'

Sally felt as though she'd swallowed a lump of lead. The
worst thing was, she couldn't make any claim on Adam, no

matter how convinced she was that he would one day return her feelings. 'I doubt you'll see him for a while. As I said, he doesn't often get the chance to visit Mainland.' And when he did, Sally would never tell Tessa.

'Where there's a will, there's a way,' Tessa said. 'Why wait for him to come here? I hear there's a cinema at Lyness. I know where I'm going the first time I get the chance.'

Sally stared at her. It had never occurred to her to visit Lyness, although now there were Wrens posted there, she had heard it had a good social scene.

'Of course,' Tessa went on, 'I wouldn't dream of making a move on Adam if you and he were together. Now I know you're just friends, though...' She gave Sally a sweeping look that took in her appearance from top to toe. 'Well, he'd have asked you out by now if he was interested, wouldn't he?'

Would he? Sally felt crushed. Together with Tessa's look, which had seemed to assess and then dismiss her, she had never felt so small. But Tessa couldn't be right. She had to believe it would all work out in the end. That's what her mother had said. If she and Adam were meant to be together, and she was sure they were, then nothing could keep them apart. Not even Tessa Bligh. Tessa could scheme all she liked; she couldn't stop destiny running its course.

–

'Tell me how your first watch with Tessa Blight went.' This was Iris's greeting when Sally arrived at Curlew Croft at the end of her watch.

'You shouldn't call her that,' Sally said. 'Give her a chance.' She hung up her raincoat and then turned to Elspeth Heddle, who was sitting at the kitchen table, chopping cabbage. 'Anything I can do to help?' She was half hopeful the chickens would need feeding. It had been her favourite task as a girl when she and her mother had lived on her uncle's farm.

'The kettle's on, and I would love some tea if you'll be kind enough to make a pot, but other than that, you can sit here and talk. You lasses work so hard, you shouldn't have to do all our work too.'

'Oh, but I enjoy it.' When her uncle had been injured and unable to keep the farm, the family had moved to Whitby, and Sally had mourned the loss of the farm almost as much as she lamented her uncle's accident. Helping out around the Heddles' croft reconnected her with the happiest time of her childhood. She was about to explain that when the battered cast iron kettle whistled shrilly. Sally hastened to pick up a dishcloth and lift it off the stove.

Elspeth's husband, Archie, stomped in from the fields just as Sally carried a tray bearing the teapot and milk jug to the table. He was carrying a folded copy of *The Times*, which he dropped on the table before going to the sink to wash his hands. 'Malcolm Spence dropped this off for me. He knows we're anxious about the news from Italy.' With a clank, he poured water from a bucket into the sink and started to lather his hands.

'Has anything else happened?' Elspeth looked anxious.

'I don't know yet.'

Elspeth opened the paper while Sally poured the tea. 'Nothing new,' she said after scanning the first page. 'I just wish I knew what this meant for Don. They're saying Italy might surrender. Doesn't that mean Don might be coming home?'

Archie finished drying his hands, seeming to draw out the action before finally taking his seat at the table. 'I wish that were true,' he said at last. 'It might only make matters worse.'

'How so?'

'I dinnae think the Germans will sit back and allow our men to go free, do you?'

There was an uneasy silence. Sally sipped her tea, grimacing at the bitter taste. The Heddles' sugar supplies were so low, she hadn't wanted to take any for herself, and Iris had also declared that she preferred her tea without sugar, even though Sally knew she usually liked two teaspoons.

After a while, Elspeth straightened up and gave a smile at the two girls that seemed a little forced. 'Anyway, tell us what's going on in your lives. Any news from Rob or Joe recently? I do miss seeing them at this table.'

Iris's face brightened. 'I got a letter from Rob today.' She pulled a bluey from her pocket. It was very creased, looking as though Iris had already read and reread it many times.

'Well, that's good news.' Elspeth's face creased into a genuine smile. 'What does he say?' Her eyes twinkled. 'That won't embarrass us all.'

A faint blush tinged Iris's cheeks. 'There's nothing like that. Letters are censored, you know.' She unfolded the letter. 'He can't say anything about the war or where he is, of course, but he's well and enjoying life on board the *Kelpie*. Oh, and he sends greetings from Joe in case his letter has gone astray.'

'Mary will be pleased,' Sally put in.

Iris nodded. 'Apart from that he just writes about some of the funny things happening on board. He says Joe drew an unflattering sketch of one of the petty officers when he was asleep in the mess, and now the petty officer has sworn revenge.'

'Better not tell Mary that or she'll be even more worried than she already is,' Elspeth said. Sally was glad to see the news about Rob had eased some of her worry lines.

'Tell us about Tessa,' Iris said after a pause. 'How did her first watch go?' For Elspeth and Archie's benefit, she added, 'We've got a new signaller – Tessa Bligh. She hasn't made a very good first impression.' Her blush returned. 'But as I'm very fortunate to have friends who didn't give up on me after the first impression I made, I'm prepared to give her a second chance.'

'It wasn't too bad.' Sally wondered whether to mention that she felt Tessa had been very dismissive towards her but decided against it. It had only been an impression and it sounded feeble when she tried to form the experience into words. *I felt as though she took one look at me and judged me incapable of holding Adam's heart. Or anyone's heart, come to that.* No, it was silly. And she agreed with Iris that she needed to give Tessa a chance. Instead, she told them how Tessa had seemed a perfectly competent signaller. Even so, she couldn't resist adding, 'She seems to have plenty of ideas on improving the place, though. She wasn't happy with the long walk and thought we should demand better transport.'

'She's not wrong,' Elspeth said. 'I think it's a scandal you young lasses are expected to do that walk alone day and night and in all weather. The WRNS should take better care of you.'

'Imagine if we could be driven there,' Iris said. 'Think of all the extra free time we would get. It was a real treat to get a lift yesterday and have more of a break between watches.' Then the gleam died from her eyes. 'They'd never do that, though. It feels like we've been forgotten, which is so unfair, considering how hard we work.'

'Tessa said she'd suggest we get bicycles.'

Iris snorted. 'I wish her luck with that. Imagine cycling up that stony track into the wind. I'd rather walk, thank you very much.'

Chapter Four

Despite everyone but Tessa's objection to the idea, the Wrens of Kyeness were given bicycles. Three weeks after Tessa spoke to their supervisor, a truck arrived at the Wrennery and deposited four ancient bicycles.

'I think Noah must have used these to get around his ark,' Mary said, heaving one onto its wheels and scratching at a patch of rust on the handlebars.

Sally glanced at her watch. 'Tessa and I are due on watch at 1300, so we should leave in half an hour if we're walking.'

'Better leave now if you're using this rust bucket.'

Sally had to agree with Mary's opinion. Although the tyres were fully inflated – she checked them all to make sure – the treads were so worn that they would be unsafe for cornering at speed. They also hadn't been supplied with any tools or puncture repair kits. 'I can see half our wages will be spent on keeping these on the road.'

She was about to announce that she would walk to Kyeness today and insist on trying out the bikes on Stromness's more forgiving roads before cycling to Kyeness. However, Tessa chose that moment to make an appearance. She gave an exclamation of delight when she saw the bikes. 'How wonderful!' She turned to Sally. 'That means you and I will be the first to ride them.'

'You don't mean to take them all the way up to Kyeness before we give them a proper test?'

'Of course I do. The navy would never have provided us with faulty gear.'

No, they hadn't bothered to give them anything at all until Tessa had complained. Sally couldn't help feeling a twinge of irritation that she and the others had accepted bad treatment. She had to admire Tessa for speaking out, even if it did mean she would now have to wrestle an unwieldy bicycle all the way to the signal station. She made one last objection. 'We don't have any puncture repair kits, and we don't know whether these bikes will cope with the rocky track. It would be awful if they made us late for the watch. Remember, we'll have to take the longer route if we cycle, so it would take ages to walk if anything happened.' Iris was currently on duty and Sally would hate to be late relieving her.

'No problem. I brought my repair kit with me. We'll leave now. Even if anything happens, we'll have plenty of leeway to get to Kyeness on time.'

Great. So now the bicycles meant she had to leave even earlier than usual. Tessa wouldn't take no for an answer, though, and insisted Sally fetch her gear and leave right away.

Sally made one last attempt to reason with her. 'Would it not make sense to wait until we're positive the bikes are safe?'

An expression of concern spread across Tessa's face. Fake concern, Sally was sure. 'I'm sorry. I'm being tactless. Perhaps you never learned to ride a bike?'

A couple of the watching Wrens giggled, although Sally was grateful to see Mary didn't join in. Heat flooded her cheeks, and she was reminded painfully of the teasing she had endured as the new girl in school when her family had first arrived in Whitby.

Mary intervened. 'I think Sally's right. You don't want to find out the brakes are faulty when you're approaching the bottom of Hellihole Road at high speed.' Hellihole Road rose steeply from the main street running parallel to Stromness's waterfront. Anyone cycling to Kyeness would have to use this route rather than the more direct footpath, and Sally was pain-fully aware that, as Mary said, cycling back from Kyeness to

Stromness involved descending the steep, cobbled lane on a bike with untested brakes and worn tyres.

Tessa's faintly mocking tone had nettled her, though, and she felt the need to prove herself. She'd show Tessa she wasn't someone who would meekly step aside when faced with a challenge. Mary had given her a way out, but she knew if she took it, she might as well paint 'Welcome' across her face and allow Tessa to use her as a doormat. 'Of course I can ride a bike.' Then, to Mary: 'I'm sure we'll be fine.' She selected the sturdiest-looking machine, wheeled it a few paces and then pressed the brake levers. The brakes held firm, and a quick inspection showed her that the brake pads were nice and thick and still had plenty of wear left in them. 'Here,' she said, wheeling the bike to Mary, 'hold this for me while I fetch my things.' Now she'd inspected this bike, she wasn't going to let Tessa take it. Mary gave her an encouraging smile and a tiny nod to show she understood.

Sally didn't waste time fetching her gear and even though her cabin was on the floor above Tessa's, she was back outside at the same time.

'I know why you're doing this,' Mary said in an undertone, once Sally and Tessa had stowed their goods into their bicycle baskets and tucked the voluminous hems of their bellbottoms into their socks to avoid getting them tangled in the chains. 'But try not to break your neck.'

Sally gave Mary a rueful smile and swung her leg over the crossbar. Then, ringing her bell to give an impression of cheeriness that she didn't feel, she rode off, forcing Tessa to follow. It wasn't long before she came to her first test – the steep uphill section of Hellihole Road. Bracing herself, she changed down to the lowest gear and stood on her pedals as she tackled the slope. She was pleasantly surprised to find the gear transition smooth; clearly whoever had issued the bikes had ensured the chains had been oiled. Growing up in Yorkshire meant she was used to cycling up and down hills, and thanks to the amount of walking she had done in Orkney, her legs and lungs were stronger than ever. Nevertheless, her muscles were soon burning and her lungs bursting as she struggled to reach the top of the ascent. On this type of hill, she would usually get off and push. However, hearing Tessa puffing behind her like a steam train made her all the more determined to pedal the whole way up.

Feeling as though her lungs were about to explode from her chest, she gave a strangled croak of relief when the road levelled and the houses lining the road gave way to fields. Looking left, she caught a glimpse of silvery blue: the narrow strip of sea between Mainland and Hoy.

Tessa drew level; Sally couldn't deny a feeling of satisfaction upon seeing her red, shiny face and hearing how she still gasped for breath.

'That was... steeper... than I'm used to,' Tessa said between breaths. 'Still,' she went on when she could breathe more freely, 'I dare say it will get easier with practice.' She shot Sally a triumphant look. 'That's the hardest part out of the way, and we should be there much sooner than if we'd walked.'

'Assuming we don't pick up a puncture on the track,' Sally muttered, immediately hating herself for her negativity. After all, if they could cycle easily to Kyeness, it would make a huge improvement to their lives.

In the event, they managed the track without too much difficulty. The first section was uphill and they had to cycle into a brisk headwind. Nevertheless, the going was not as tough as climbing Hellihole Road had been. Although they had to manoeuvre around the lumps of rock protruding from the track's surface, the obstacles weren't as bad as Sally had feared. How easy it would be at night she couldn't say, but she had to admit the bicycles had considerably reduced their journey time. She shot a longing glance at Curlew Croft as they sailed past, waving at Archie who was emptying a bucket of water into a trough. He straightened and raised his hat, looking startled.

They were very early for their watch. Seeing Iris out on the balcony as they approached the signal station, Sally rang her bell and waved, laughing at her friend's exclamation of surprise. Iris, leaving her oppo in the signal room, came out to inspect the bikes. 'How long did that take you?'

Sally glanced at her watch. 'About twenty minutes.'

'Much better than walking,' announced a smug Tessa.

Sally chided herself for her resentment. Tessa had used her initiative to suggest something that would make the Wrens' lives a little easier, and all Sally could do was begrudge her success. 'I can't deny I look forward to getting back to the Wrennery in good time after our watch,' she said. She should focus on the benefits and not worry that Adam would hear about Tessa's enterprise. She had always believed that the success of one member of the team was of benefit to them all. She wouldn't stop believing that just because it was a rival for Adam's affections who had managed to procure the bikes.

—

Iris came outside to meet them when they returned to the Wrennery that evening. She was accompanied by two of the other off-duty Wrens, curious, Sally was sure, to discover how she and Tessa had fared with the bikes.

'You've made good time coming back,' Iris said.

Evelyn, one of the other Wrens, addressed Tessa. 'I can't believe no one else thought to request bikes before. This is a big improvement.'

Iris caught Sally's eye, her mouth set in a wry twist. 'True, although I wouldn't fancy cycling in strong winds. I'd feel safer on my own two feet.'

While Sally was grateful for her friend's sympathy, she had to be fair to Tessa, much as her triumph rankled. 'They will be useful at other times, though. It *is* nice not to spend so much of the day walking to and from Kyeness.'

Iris squeezed Sally's arm in silent support then said, 'What do you think it'll be like in the dark?'

'We'll find out when Mary and Pat get back from the evening watch.' When they had arrived to relieve Sally and Tessa, Sally had been surprised to see they had ridden the other two bikes.

'I wanted to wait until we found out how you and Tessa got on,' Mary had murmured to her in an undertone when Sally had gone out to meet them, 'but Pat wouldn't hear of it. She thinks the sun shines out of Miss Blight's—' She cleared her throat. 'She thinks Tessa can do no wrong,' Mary had scowled. 'She didn't even give me a chance to test the lamps, so if we're not back by midnight, send out a search party. We'll have turned the wrong way in the dark and plunged over the cliffs at Birsay.' This being a point at the northern end of the island, Sally doubted she was being serious.

Even Mary, though, had been unable to deny the bicycles would save time in good weather and had grudgingly admitted that it would make a nice change to get back from the evening watch before midnight.

Sally was grateful for her two friends' support, however. Seeing how the other Wrens flocked around Tessa, praising her for her bravery in daring to approach their superiors and suggest an improvement, she would have felt very alone if it hadn't been for Iris and Mary. It was clear Tessa was already popular with the others. It seemed Tessa only showed her claws with Sally; when anyone else was around she was positively angelic. It was a mercy she had two good friends in Iris and Mary who believed her without question. Sally was starting to doubt herself, though. What if she was imagining Tessa's hostility? What if she was letting her feelings for Adam, and Tessa's obvious admiration for him, cloud her judgement?

This uneasiness that she was doing Tessa an injustice persuaded Sally to refrain from any further complaints about her to Iris and Mary. The shielded lamps on the bikes had proved to provide just enough light to steer by, and Tessa had basked in the glory of being the most popular Wren at Kyeness. For now it was enough for Sally to know she had the support and trust of her friends, and she didn't want to create any ill feeling among the other Wrens, which she was sure would happen if she dared to utter any criticism of everyone's new favourite Wren. The watch rotation meant she had to work with everyone eventually, and she didn't want to lose anyone's trust. There was also the growing conviction that Tessa had been nothing but pleasant to everyone else, making Sally wonder if she had been over-sensitive to Tessa's remarks.

September arrived, bringing with it that sense of fresh energy and new starts that she always associated with that time of year. Even though it was years since the month had marked the start of a new school year for her, she had never shaken off the feeling. Sally had been disappointed not to see Adam at all since their interrupted tête-à-tête in the Beehive. However, that changed on the first Saturday in the month, when Sally strolled into Stromness the day after standing the night watch with Tessa. Tessa had been all smiles and friendliness with Sally for some time, leading Sally to the conclusion that she had imagined her barbs. Therefore, when Tessa had asked if she would like to meet her later for tea in the Beehive, Sally had agreed without hesitation. Iris and Mary were on watch, and it was always nicer to have company. Tessa had gone into Stromness earlier, saying she had some errands to run, so Sally had arranged to meet her in the Beehive at eleven.

When she pushed open the door, her heart sank at the sight that met her eyes. Adam was there. And while she had to admit this was an answer to her prayers, those prayers had never included a request to see Tessa beside him, her face only inches from his, laughing at something he had said. A sound like a swarm of bees filled Sally's ears and her nose started to itch, something that always happened when she was fighting tears. The door was right behind her, tempting her to flee, to escape to a secluded corner of Stromness until she'd overcome the desire to cry. Unfortunately, Tessa chose that moment to glance up. Her eyes met Sally's and she waved, beckoning her to join them. Sally had no choice but to take a seat at their table.

'Look who I ran into,' Tessa said, patting Adam's arm in a proprietorial manner that set Sally's teeth on edge. 'Of course, he was the perfect gentleman and absolutely insisted on buying me a drink. I told him I was meeting you, but he said you wouldn't mind.'

Sally had been so preoccupied with looking at Tessa together with Adam, wailing inwardly at the signs of their closeness, that she hadn't noticed the pot of tea on the table in front of them until now. Judging from the half-empty cups and the plates holding nothing but crumbs, they had been there, together, for some time.

Don't cry in front of them. She'd never live it down. Taking her time hanging her raincoat on the back of her chair, she fought to regain her composure.

'Why don't I order you some tea?' Adam said, catching the waitress's eye. He ordered a pot of tea, not giving Sally the chance to say she'd prefer a cold drink. Not that Sally thought she'd be able to force any words through her tight, aching throat. However, when Adam tried to order her a slice of carrot cake, Sally shook her head.

She cleared her throat. 'No, thank you.' Her voice rasped and she cleared her throat again. 'Really,' she added when Adam's eyebrows shot up. 'I'm not hungry.' Thankfully, her voice sounded stronger, and Adam sat back without pressing her further. She might have recovered enough to speak, but there was no way she'd be able to swallow lumps of cake.

'How are you getting on, Sally?' Adam asked when the waitress had gone.

'I—'

Adam carried on without waiting for her answer. 'Tessa was telling me all about the bicycles she persuaded the navy to get for you all. Sounds like a jolly good idea. I bet you're all glad to have her on the team.'

'The bicycles have certainly made our lives a little easier,' Sally said, avoiding having to say how glad – or not – she was to have Tessa around. It was cruel that the only time she got to see Adam, Tessa had to be there as well. Part of her wished she could run away. She would if it weren't for the fact that she would be leaving the two of them alone.

Tessa leaned forward. 'Are you feeling all right, Sally? You sound a little hoarse.'

'I'm fine, thanks.'

'Are you sure? You might have a cold coming on. Perhaps you should get some rest in the Wrennery.'

'What? No! I had a frog in my throat, that's all. I'm fine now.' And her indignation achieved what clearing her throat had failed to do – her voice came out loud and strong. The cheek of the girl! It was clear Tessa was trying to get rid of her so she could have Adam all to herself. Well, it would take more than Tessa Blight's feeble plotting to make her leave.

The waitress returned with her tea at that point, giving Sally a moment to gather her thoughts. The matronly waitress gave her a smile that looked sympathetic, making Sally painfully aware of the times she had sat in the Beehive with Iris and Mary, telling them about Adam and how she knew they were meant to be together. Mrs Spence, the waitress, knew all the servicewomen and men who flocked to the little cafe, and had undoubtedly overheard their conversations. Sally could only hope she didn't realise the man Tessa was fawning over was the same man Sally had raved about.

Sally poured her tea, too desperate to have something to occupy herself with to wait for it to brew. Her hand shook, making her miss the tea strainer, depositing more tea leaves than usual into the cup. Although she was trying to get used to taking her tea without sugar, she allowed herself the luxury of a single lump. She stirred the pale, milky drink, watching the tea leaves swirl in the mixture while she racked her brains for a conversation starter. 'Have you heard from Pauline recently?' She turned to Tessa. 'I think we mentioned Pauline before – Adam's sister.' In other circumstances she would have felt ashamed for flaunting her prior claim to Adam and his family, but she wasn't going to sit back and let Tessa hog the conversation again.

'I got a letter from her last week. She's going out with an RAF pilot. Sounds serious. I wish I could meet him and satisfy myself he's suitable.'

Much to Sally's annoyance, before she could comment, Tessa said, 'It must be hard, being so far away.' She squeezed his arm and moved closer.

Sally looked away, not wanting the others to see the pain in her eyes. Was Tessa deliberately trying to make her feel like a gooseberry?

After an uncomfortable ten minutes, Adam glanced at his watch. 'I'm sorry, ladies, but I must dash. Promised to meet a friend.' He left a handful of change on the table to cover the payment and left. No smile at Sally. No mention of meeting her for a proper chat. Sally watched his retreating back, feeling as though a cold hand was squeezing her heart. How many more times would they meet and their relationship remain unresolved? She didn't know how much longer she could bear it.

Once Adam had left, she turned back to Tessa to find her not gazing after Adam but watching Sally with a speculative gleam in her eyes and a self-satisfied smile that sent a chill through her veins. Sally had a horrible feeling her longing had been all too visible while she had been watching Adam and that, while he had seemed irritatingly blind to it, Tessa certainly hadn't. While Sally had had no fears about sharing her feelings with

Iris and Mary, with Tessa she felt as though she had handed over a weapon to be used against her.

'Are you sure you won't have anything to eat?' Tessa asked. 'You do look rather peaky.'

Sally shook her head. 'I'm not hungry.' She swallowed some of the tea, grimacing at the grittiness. At least her cup would have a substantial amount of tea leaves to read when she had finished. Maybe she would see something encouraging, like an angel, foretelling good news. Or Tessa sailing away south.

Tessa picked up her own cup and eyed Sally over the rim as she took a sip. She had long, elegant fingers with perfectly trimmed nails. It made Sally want to hide her own hands with their rough, bitten nails and ragged cuticles. She couldn't help seeing them both through Adam's eyes. Tessa was so much more polished than Sally and clearly spent much more time on her appearance. Although Sally, with Iris's encouragement, had started to wear lipstick and a little powder when going out in the evenings, she hadn't bothered to make up her face for a trip into Stromness. Now she wished she had at least put on her new Yardley 'Natural Rose' lipstick. Iris had talked her into buying it when they had seen it in the NAAFI. If it hadn't been selling out fast, and Iris hadn't convinced her that the colour suited her perfectly, Sally might have hesitated to splash out three shillings on something as frivolous as make-up. However, seeing the queue of servicewomen, all frantic to get their hands on a new lipstick, Sally had known it might be weeks or even months before she got the chance again, so she had treated herself. At nearly a third of a week's pay, though, it was strictly reserved for special occasions; today, Sally had done nothing more than brush her hair before leaving the Wrennery.

Tessa, on the other hand, had clearly spent some time in front of a mirror. Her eyebrows were pencilled into symmetrical arches; her complexion was so even it could only be with the help of powder, yet there was no tell-tale smudge around the jaw or hairline, and how she managed to keep on her bold red lipstick without leaving half of it on her cup, Sally would never know. It was the hair that made Sally feel their differences most keenly. Tessa wore her hair up while in uniform of course but now it fell in glossy golden waves to her shoulders, not a strand out of place. Sally's hair was mousy – there was no other word for it – and she was sure it must be messy from her walk.

Adam wouldn't mind, though. He would look at more important things than appearance. Surely he would be more interested in a genuine and loving heart than glossy hair and manicured nails? She had to believe that.

'Of course,' Tessa said, putting down her cup, 'I keep forgetting that you and Adam know each other from home.'

'As I said, I've known him for a few years now.' Sally was grateful for the chance to assert her better knowledge of Adam.

'It's just that I would never have guessed you came from the same place. Adam seems so... sophisticated.'

'I hadn't noticed.' Sally hoped her dismay didn't show. Was Tessa implying that Sally was plain and unstylish? She curled her hands into loose fists to hide her nails.

'Oh, he's ever so good-looking. Haven't you noticed? And his accent...' Tessa gave an exaggerated shiver. 'It's so northern and masculine.'

Sally felt her face burn. Her accent was the same as Adam's; did Tessa think *she* sounded masculine? Unsure how to respond, she drained her cup and then gazed at the leaves speckling the white china. Nothing showing Tessa with a dagger through her chest, worse luck. She instantly hated herself for that thought and bit her lip as she turned the cup.

'Ooh, a ring,' she said, forgetting herself in her excitement.

'What?'

'The tea leaves.' Sally's face burned hotter. Why couldn't she have kept quiet? Now she would have to explain herself and face who knew what ridicule. 'A ring means love and marriage in my future.'

'Well, of course there is. I'm sure there's someone out there for you.' The implication being that Sally hadn't met him yet.

43

Sally gave up. It was clear she and Tessa were never going to get along so she might as well stop trying. 'I hope you're right.' She pushed away her cup. 'Actually, I've just remembered an errand I need to run.' She rose, waving a vague hand in the direction of the town. 'I must dash.' Without waiting for Tessa's reply, she hurried to the counter to pay, then left without looking back.

Chapter Five

'She said what?' Mary looked up from her sketchbook, pencil poised in mid-air.

'She said she was sure there was someone out there for me. But the way she said it, it sounded like she meant, *even* for me. As though it was hard to believe someone might actually fall in love with me.' Sally clenched her fists in the grass at her knees and tore a clump from the roots.

'The cow.' Mary put aside her pencil and paper and wrapped her arms around her knees, regarding Sally with a scowl. It was the following day and the first time Sally had had a chance to speak to her friends since that awful conversation in the Beehive. Iris, Mary and Sally all had a free afternoon and as it was warm and sunny, they had walked to the cliff top near Curlew Croft and were making the most of the sunshine. No doubt the autumn gales would soon arrive, so none of them wanted to miss what could be the last of the fine weather. Mary had produced the sketch book Joe had given her and had started to draw, although she hadn't let either of the other two see what she was working on. Iris had lain back on the springy turf and gazed up at the clouds, shading her eyes with one hand. Unable to relax, Sally had poured out her tale as soon as she sat down.

'I hope you gave her what for,' Mary said now.

'Not exactly.' Sally couldn't meet Mary's gaze.

'What *did* you say?'

'I just said I hoped she was right.'

'What? You should have told her you were fighting off suitors but if she asked nicely you'd put in a good word for her with the unsuccessful ones. That would have wiped the smug expression from her face.'

'I couldn't say that.' Sally gazed at Mary, caught between shock and admiration. 'I'm not like you. I wish I was more daring but I could never say something like that.'

Iris stirred and sat up, brushing grass from her back. 'That's probably for the best. You've got to work with her, after all.'

Mary snorted. 'Doesn't seem to stop her being rude to Sally.'

'I know but are you sure you didn't take it the wrong way, Sally? She's always been nice to me.'

This was what Sally had been afraid of. It was true – Tessa seemed to have reserved her digs for Sally, and only showed her claws when there were no witnesses. 'You should have seen her, Iris. She knew she was hurting me and she enjoyed it. I could see it in her eyes.'

'Then why is she always fine with the rest of us?' Iris, Sally could tell, wasn't convinced. She couldn't blame her – if the situation was reversed, she would find it hard to believe that a person who acted all sweetness and light around her was being nasty to someone else. It hurt, though. She hoped she would believe Iris without question if the same thing happened to her.

Sally's dismay must have shown, for Iris looked contrite. 'I'm sorry, Sally. Of course I believe you. I only wondered if Tessa was like me. You know how I'm always blurting the first thing that pops into my mind without thinking it through. But if you say Tessa said what she did with the intention to hurt, then I believe you and I'll agree with Mary that she's a complete cow.'

The heavy weight that had seemed to be crushing Sally's chest now lifted. She smiled at Iris. 'I did wonder if I was being over-sensitive at first. After yesterday, though...' She thought back to the look on Tessa's face and shook her head. 'No. She meant it. And for the record, although you can be a bit unthinking at times, you're never nasty. I know you always have the best intentions. I don't feel that way about Tessa.'

'Fine. In that case, what can Mary and I do? Do you want us to talk to her? Give her a piece of our minds?'

It was tempting, oh, so tempting to hand the problem over to her friends and hope they would make everything better. After a moment's hesitation, she shook her head. 'Thank you but no. You can't be around all the time I'm with her. I have to deal with Tessa myself or it might make her worse.'

'You're probably right,' Iris said. 'I'll be keeping an eye on her, though.'

'Me too,' said Mary. 'And if you change your mind, I'll be only too happy to teach her a lesson.'

'I know. Thanks. Just one thing, though – what should I do?'

Mary, who had resumed her drawing, paused again. 'I take it you don't want to resort to insults?'

'Much as I wish I could, no. As Iris said, I have to carry on working with her.'

'Why do you think she's picking on you?' Iris asked.

'Easy,' Mary said before Sally could answer. 'She's set her sights on Adam and is warning Sally off.'

Sally had to agree. 'It's the only reason I can come up with. She definitely likes him.'

'Don't hate me for saying this.' Mary sounded unusually hesitant. 'But is Adam really worth it? I thought he was very off-hand with you when I met him at Christmas. You should be with someone who cares for you and cherishes you, not someone who can't even be bothered to reply to your letters and only invites you to have tea when he's at a loose end.'

'Oh, you've got him all wrong. I think you met him on a bad day. He's lovely, really. Anyway, I got a ring in my tea leaves yesterday. That means love and marriage and there's no one else I like so it must be with him.' She decided not to reveal that the ring had been towards the bottom of the cup, which meant she might have to wait for the love to happen.

'Really? You're going to eat your heart out over this man because of a clump of tea leaves? Honestly, Sally, use your common sense. Don't look for signs, look at him! What has he ever said or done that proves he has any feelings for you?'

At times like this, Sally wished Mary didn't have to be quite so brutal with her opinions. 'Lots of things. You've only met him the once. But he's a perfect gentleman. Most of the time.' She didn't want to think too hard about what Mary had said. Didn't want to admit that her feelings were all based on the jolt of electricity she'd felt when they'd first met all that time ago.

'You're right of course,' Iris said. 'We don't know him, and I think we should change that. He's on Hoy, isn't he?' When Sally nodded, Iris went on, 'We should go there. They sometimes invite Wrens from elsewhere to their concerts and dances. Next time they have one we'll do whatever it takes to wangle a free day so we can go. Then we can see Adam for ourselves.'

'Good idea,' Mary said. 'You never know, seeing you in Hoy might give Adam the boost he needs to ask you out.'

Another event, however, thrust the thought of meeting Adam on Hoy out of Sally's mind for a while. Only a few days after their lazy afternoon in the sunshine, Sally and Mary went to visit the Heddles after standing the morning watch together. Iris, who had been back to the Wrennery for a nap after night watch, walked up to meet them, and they strolled together to Curlew Croft.

Elspeth greeted them in the kitchen, all of a flutter. 'Oh my goodness, have you heard? The Italians have surrendered.'

Sally gaped at her. There had been rumours and speculation ever since Mussolini had been deposed but now it had happened she found it hard to grasp. 'What does that mean?'

Elspeth shook her head. Her eyes were bright and she pressed her lips together tightly as though trying to control tears. 'No one knows yet. What it means for the prisoners of war there, I mean. But everyone says the Germans are going to send in their troops. I can't bear to think of Don a prisoner of the Nazis.'

Sally took Elspeth's hand and squeezed it, pouring all her love and support into that gesture, unable to find adequate words. For most of the country, the Italians' surrender would be celebrated. In homes like this, however, where people worried for loved ones in prisoner-of-war camps, there would be no celebration. The thought of these prisoners now coming under Nazi authority must be very frightening indeed.

Mary swept up to the range and tied an apron around her waist. 'Well, your Don won't thank us if we allow you to go hungry. Sally, you make us all some tea and I'll see what I can rustle up for dinner. Iris can set the table.'

It was immediately apparent no preparations had been made for a meal. Once Sally had set the kettle on the range, she went with Mary to investigate the contents of the larder. Out of the corner of her eye, she saw Iris put an arm around Elspeth's shoulders and lead her to a chair. Elspeth looked as frail and careworn as she had the day she had heard her son was missing, presumed dead. Sally hoped for her sake that they would soon hear more definite news about the fate of their men who were prisoners of war in Italy.

—

Aldo was in the mess hall, toying with the watery vegetables on his plate, when he heard the announcement. He and his fellow prisoners had been braced for it ever since they had heard of the Allied invasion of Italy five days earlier. They had a radio in the mess hall, and when the news came on, a hush fell, allowing the newsreader's voice to ring out.

'Italy has signed an unconditional armistice with the Allies, General Dwight D. Eisenhower has announced.'

A ripple went around the room. Here and there, a faint hiss could be heard as men translated the words into Italian for their friends whose command of English was not so good. Aldo himself needed no translation, having taken advantage of English lessons at the camp during his free hours.

Finally the message got around everyone.

'We can go home!' one man cried. An instant later, everyone was speaking at once, talking of their homes and families, and whatever the newsreader said next was drowned under a hubbub of voices.

Enrico slapped Aldo on the back. 'Did you hear that? We're going home!'

Home. It meant nothing to Aldo. Not now that Carlo was gone. There was no family waiting for him. No home town or village where he was known and missed by all. He and Carlo had grown up in an orphanage. If it hadn't been for the kind baker who had given him a job when Aldo was old enough to leave the orphanage, they would have been forced to beg. What did he have to go back to? Around him the noise level had risen to a roar. Here and there, men thumped the tables; others hugged, tears pouring down their cheeks. Aldo felt dissociated from the celebrations. Personally, he was glad Italy had finally surrendered, yet all he could think of was Carlo, who hadn't lived long enough to benefit from it.

Eventually, Enrico grabbed his shoulders and shook him. 'Why the long face? This is good news.'

'Good?' a voice spat in Aldo's ear. With a sinking heart, Aldo saw Gianni beside him. His face was twisted in a snarl. 'What is good about it? We have been betrayed by our own government.'

Aldo could only suppose Gianni had mistaken his gloomy expression for dismay at Italy's capitulation and was expecting Aldo's agreement. Thankfully, he was spared having to respond, for at that moment one of Gianni's cronies took Gianni by the arm and led him to a quiet corner.

Aldo turned back to Enrico. 'Of course it's good news.'

'It's better than good. We're not enemies with the British any more. They can't keep us prisoner. Don't you understand? We can go home!' Enrico's face was lit up with joy, and Aldo knew he needed to bring him down to earth.

'I don't think it's going to be as simple as that. If we've surrendered to the Allies, then the Germans are now our enemies. Do you think they're going to stand back and let the Allies march all the way to Austria through Italy?'

Enrico's face fell; he crossed himself. 'Heaven help us. They're going to try and take over, aren't they?'

Aldo nodded. 'Even if the British could spare the ships to send us home, they can hardly send us into the middle of a battlefield.' He jerked his head to where Gianni and his friend were talking in low tones, scowling. 'Especially not when plenty of Italians have made it clear they wouldn't hesitate to take up arms against the Allies, surrender or no.'

—

Aldo's prediction proved to be true. In the days that followed, the news was full of German troops storming Italy and the fierce fighting that had broken out as these troops met the Allies advancing from the south. It was clear that the war in Italy was a long way from being over.

A few days after the capitulation, Aldo bumped into Captain Lawler, the friendly officer who had loaned Aldo his wood-carving tools. Knowing that Enrico was desperate to find out what was going to happen to the Italian prisoners, he asked the captain if there was any news.

Lawler shook his head. 'We're awaiting confirmation of your status from the British government but until then, life in Camp 60 will continue as before. As soon as we hear more we will let you know.'

Aldo thanked him and went to look for Enrico. However, he was dragged to a standstill when someone grabbed his arm. It was Gianni. 'How can they keep us prisoners?' Gianni's face was mottled with anger. 'They have no right – we are no longer their enemy.' Clearly he had overheard Aldo's brief conversation with Captain Lawler.

'Use your brain. Northern Italy is under German occupation. Even if the British could get us home, we'd be in danger of ending up prisoners of the Germans.'

'I wouldn't be taken prisoner. I'd join them.'

'Well, in that case you should tell the British, and I'm sure they'd release you at once.'

Unfortunately Aldo's sarcasm seemed to go right over Gianni's head. 'Maybe I should. They can't keep us here.'

He marched off, although thankfully not towards the camp commandant's office. He was probably going to speak to the other prisoners to see how many felt the same way. A few did, Aldo knew, and they persisted in their loyalty to Mussolini even though he was no longer in charge. Aldo could only hope that for the sake of the peace of the camp, most were happy, as he was, to wait out the war in Orkney.

'There you are.' A hand tapped Aldo's shoulder and he turned to see Enrico grinning at him. 'I saw you talking to Lawler. What did he say? Will we be given more freedom? It would be nice to meet some of the girls on the island.'

Aldo laughed and made a gesture that took in the limits of Lamb Holm. 'Take a look – no girls here. Nothing but grass.'

'I don't mean *here*. But I've seen pretty girls on Mainland. Imagine if we were allowed to visit Kirkwall. We could take them to dinner.'

'How would we pay? They won't accept camp tokens.' The prisoners weren't paid for their labour in money. Instead, there was a system in place that meant they were rewarded in tokens which they could exchange in the camp for items such as cigarettes, soap and writing paper. 'Even if we are allowed out, we'll be dependent on the islanders' hospitality. Hardly something any girls will find attractive.'

Enrico's face fell. 'I suppose you're right.' Then he brightened. 'We'd still see them though. Girls, I mean.'

Aldo couldn't help laughing at his friend's naive optimism. 'It would make a change from your ugly face.'

'Of course, you might see your friend again.'

'What friend?' Despite his feigned innocence, Aldo knew exactly who Enrico meant. He didn't want him to know how often his thoughts focused on Sally.

'You know, the girl you met in hospital. You liked her, didn't you?'

'Of course. Anyone would.'

'She must have thought a lot of you to send you that Christmas parcel.'

'Maybe.' Aldo tried to appear nonchalant. He would have been embarrassed to reveal the number of times he had caressed each item in the parcel, knowing that she had chosen them for him. Even now, the joy of knowing she had thought of him hadn't worn off. 'Perhaps she just wanted to do a good deed for Christmas.'

'It might have been more. Imagine if you could meet her again and find out.'

Aldo was trying not to. He kept telling himself he mustn't build dreams of a great romance upon the shaky foundations of a few snatched conversations. She had been kind to him at a time he had needed kindness and the warmth of human friendship. That didn't mean they were fated to be together. 'I doubt I'll see her again even if we are allowed out. She wasn't local. She was a Wren. She could have been posted elsewhere by now.'

'She was still here at Christmas, so you never know. Is she based nearby?'

'I don't think so. She said she was in Stromness. That's in the west of the island, I think.'

'Oh well, forget it. There are plenty of lovely young women on this side of the island, and with luck we'll get to meet them.'

But Aldo couldn't forget her. That was the problem. He was dreaming of a woman who might as well be on the moon for all the chance he had of seeing her again. Even if a miracle happened and they were given permission to leave the camp, he had no way of getting as far as Stromness.

Chapter Six

Sally awoke to the sound of rain battering the windowpanes and groaned. Then she remembered Tessa was her oppo that day and groaned again. Thanks to the vagaries of the watch rotation, she hadn't been on duty with Tessa much, and had managed to avoid her the rest of the time. As a result, the remainder of September had passed by with no further trouble. She had even managed to agree with the others about the success of the bicycles without needing to grit her teeth too hard.

The first week in October, however, marked a change, and Sally had seen to her dismay that she and Tessa would be spending a lot of time together. Starting today.

Although she was usually a morning person, she didn't greet the day with her accustomed smile. It didn't help that she was getting up in the dark – the days were getting rapidly shorter, and the sun had not yet risen. She was approaching her third winter in Orkney, and instead of looking forward to the crisp, frosty days and starry nights she had enjoyed last time, she now dreaded all the long, dark and dreary hours in Tessa's company.

She glanced at Mary's and Iris's beds, but they were empty, both of her friends having been on watch that night. It was a reminder that in addition to more time with Tessa, she also had less time with her friends. Wonderful.

The day got worse from there. Fearing the strong winds around the headland might make cycling dangerous, Sally suggested that they leave early and walk to Kyeness. To her dismay, Tessa wouldn't hear of it. 'This is precisely the reason I asked for bicycles, so we wouldn't have to do the walk in the dark. Nothing stopping you from walking alone if you want.'

But the Wrens weren't supposed to go alone beyond the bounds of Stromness in the dark. Anyway, however tempting it was to get away from Tessa and let the fresh air blow away her gloom, she couldn't bring herself to let Tessa go all that way alone.

Accordingly, they left together by bike. As ever, it was a strenuous ride up the hill out of Stromness, although Sally was sure her muscles were getting stronger. When they turned onto the track that led past Curlew Croft to the cliffs, however, the full force of the wind blowing in from the sea hit Sally in the face. This was another uphill section, and while the gradient was less steep than Hellihole Road, the effect of the wind made it seem steeper. Soon Sally was standing on her pedals, calf muscles burning, her pulse pounding in her ears. At least the sun was rising by this time, so they weren't forced to endure the struggle in the dark. She also derived some satisfaction from the sight of Tessa's struggles. Perhaps she would think twice about insisting they cycle when the weather was bad.

Sally gasped with relief when they reached the top of the rise. It was still heavy going, but now she only had to fight the wind and not gravity as well. She had relaxed too soon, though, for a moment later it struck her that the ground seemed far more rutted and bumpy than usual. She soldiered on for a few more yards but she found herself needing to pedal ever harder. Soon Tessa was some distance ahead and getting farther away with every passing second. Only then did it occur to Sally that one of her tyres might be flat. Glancing down, she saw the front tyre was fine. The rear tyre was more difficult to inspect. She twisted in her saddle and managed to get a fleeting glimpse, enough to see it was, indeed, flat. Before she could right herself in the saddle, a strong gust caught her off balance. The next moment, the bike was toppling sideways, and when she tried to stick her foot out to steady herself, her shoelaces caught on the pedal.

Dry-mouthed, all she could do was fling out her hands to break the fall and brace herself for the inevitable impact.

She hit the ground with a force that drove the air from her lungs. Sharp stones and gravel tore through her gloves and pierced her skin. The weight of the bike crashed down on top of her, driving her knee against a jagged lump of stone sending shooting pains up and down her leg. Then she was lying on the cold ground, all alone apart from the wailing gulls circling overhead.

She lay on the hard, rocky ground for a moment, immobile from shock. Then her various scrapes and bruises made themselves known and she started to test her arms and legs to check her injuries. Once she was satisfied she had suffered nothing worse than bruises, she extricated herself from the bike and staggered upright. She looked for Tessa, expecting to see her speeding back to help, only to spot her far ahead, apparently oblivious to Sally's accident. She cupped her hands around her mouth and yelled, but the wind whipped her voice away. With a sense of helplessness, she watched as Tessa swooped around a bend in the track and disappeared from view.

Even if the rear tyre hadn't been flat, she felt too stiff and sore to ride. Instead, she hauled the bicycle onto its wheels and grasped the handlebars, drawing a hissing breath as her raw palms protested. Walking was painful but she found she could let the bike take her weight. In this manner she hobbled slowly along the track.

She had just drawn level with the Heddles' croft when she saw Archie striding towards her. She sobbed in relief when he took the bike with one hand and gripped her elbow with his other to lend her support.

'I was in the field when I saw you take a tumble. Are you badly hurt?'

'Just a few cuts and bruises, I think.'

'Come into the kitchen and let Elspeth take a look.'

'I can't. I'll be late.'

'I'm sure your friend will cope alone for a while. You can't go to work in this state. Come along.'

Feeling too shaken to put up any further argument, she let Archie lead her to the cottage.

'Oh my stars, what happened to you?' Elspeth was in the yard, feeding the chickens when they arrived. She glanced from Sally's dirty, torn coat to the bike and pursed her lips. 'I saw another Wren cycle past a few minutes ago and wondered why she was alone. Don't tell me she didn't even stop to help?'

Sally shook her head, too close to tears to trust her voice.

'Take her into the kitchen, Archie, and set the kettle to boil. I'll be in as soon as I've finished here.'

Sally let Archie help her into the kitchen without a word. He stood the bike outside the door then ushered Sally through, relieving her of her coat and gas mask as soon as he'd shut the door behind them. While he filled the kettle from the water jug and set it on the range, Sally inspected her hands and knees. She peeled off her gloves, mourning the holes in the palms. They were her only pair and now she was going to have to spend her free time that day darning them if there was any chance of them being fit to wear when she returned for the evening watch. Her hands were scraped raw, with grit embedded in the palms. Her right stocking, which she always wore over the legs of her trousers to prevent the wide hems from getting caught, was also ripped, and there was a hole on the right knee of her trousers. She didn't like to inspect her other injuries with Archie present but from the throbbing of her knee, she guessed she had a hefty bruise.

She looked up when Archie set down a basin of water on the table, together with soap and a flannel. 'Elspeth will be along soon,' he said. 'Why don't you wash the gravel from your hands. I'll go and start work on your bike.'

She was dabbing at her hands with the wet flannel when Elspeth hurried in and went to wash her own hands. 'You poor lass,' she said, looking over her shoulder at Sally while she rinsed off the soap and groped for a towel. 'At least it happened close enough for us to help. What was your friend thinking, leaving you all alone?'

'She's not my friend.'

Elspeth shot her a sharp glance but said nothing. She replaced the towel and then rummaged in a cupboard near the door. 'Now, where did I put it? Ah, here we are.' She pulled out a battered white box marked with a red cross and came to sit beside Sally. 'Let's take a look at you.'

Wincing, Sally rolled her torn trouser leg above the knee. It was badly grazed and throbbed in time with her pulse.

'That'll be a lovely colour tomorrow.' Elspeth produced a bottle of TCP from the first aid box and unscrewed the cap. The disinfectant smell filled the kitchen, taking Sally back to her childhood days. 'I'm afraid this is going to sting.'

Elspeth carried on her chatter as she helped Sally wash her cuts and grazes, possibly to take her mind off the pain. Sally was thankful for this, not wanting to have to answer the question about why Tessa hadn't stopped. She wouldn't have left her worst enemy alone after falling off their bike. Even if Tessa had failed to see her fall, she would surely have noticed Sally's absence before she had gone far. Did she really feel so much dislike for her that she wouldn't come back to help?

Finally, once she had dabbed iodine and arnica on Sally's cuts and bruises and covered the worst cuts with sticking plaster, Elspeth looked up. 'Not as bad as it could have been, considering. I think you'll live.'

Sally managed a watery smile. 'Thank you. I'm just grateful you and Archie were nearby.'

Sally was straightening her clothes and brushing off the worst of the dirt when there came a knock at the door. Elspeth went to open it.

'I don't suppose you've seen Sally, have you?' It was Iris, her voice ringing with concern.

'I'm in here,' Sally called.

Iris swept inside, taking in Sally's dishevelled appearance with a single glance. 'What happened?'

By the time Sally had finished explaining, Iris's expression of concern had faded, and her mouth was pulled into a tight scowl. 'That Tessa Bligh has some explaining to do. Mary and I were worried sick when she turned up alone and couldn't say where you were. Did she see you fall?'

'I don't know. By the time I'd picked myself up, she was too far ahead to hear when I called.'

'How are you feeling?'

'A bit shaken up, not to mention sore, but I'll be fine. I'd better get to the signal station. Is Tessa there alone?'

Iris shook her head. 'Mary stayed on while I came to find you. Are you sure you feel up to standing watch? We can send someone to cover for you if you'd rather stay here.' She gave a grim smile. 'I quite understand if you don't feel like facing Tessa just yet.'

Sally rose, feeling every bruise and aching joint. There was no real harm, though, so she said, 'It's fine. I feel much better now, and it wouldn't be fair to drag anyone else out here.' She gathered her belongings, helped by Iris. 'Elspeth, do you mind if I leave my bike here? I don't feel like riding at the moment. I'll fetch it when I come off duty.'

'Of course. Why not stay for lunch? You'd be very welcome to stay until your next shift, if you're back on this evening. You might be feeling better now but riding back and forth between here and Stromness won't be easy when your bruises develop.'

'Thank you. If you're sure, I'd like that.'

'Iris, you and Mary would also be welcome, of course.'

'Thanks. I'll tell Mary. I'm sure she'd like to come.' Iris took Sally's arm. 'I'll walk to the signal station with you.' From her grim expression, Sally feared she was planning to tear into Tessa for leaving her alone.

She pulled her arm from Iris's grasp. 'Promise me you won't say anything to Tessa.'

'Why? She should have been looking out for you.'

'I know. But I need to deal with her myself. If you get involved on my behalf, it will only make matters worse.' Part of Sally longed to let Iris or Mary to tackle Tessa and put everything right, but she knew deep down that if she didn't solve the problem herself, it would never go away.

Iris didn't reply straight away but chewed her lip while Sally pulled on her coat. Only when Sally was ready to leave did she finally say, 'Fine. I won't say anything. But I expect a full account of her abject apology when I see you this afternoon.'

—

Iris accompanied Sally up into the signal room, ostensibly to collect Mary but, Sally guessed, it was more likely that she wanted to see Tessa's reaction for herself.

Tessa was gushing in her apology. 'Oh my goodness, Sally, I only noticed you weren't with me when I got here. What happened?'

Once Sally had told her tale, Tessa fell over herself to apologise. 'I'm so sorry. I was in a world of my own but I should have paid more attention. Are you sure you're all right? I can stay here alone if you don't feel up to it.'

'I'm fine, really. Just a bit bruised.'

'I feel awful. I did wonder if I should go back to look for you when I got here and noticed you weren't with me, but I thought I should let Iris and Mary know first. Honestly, I couldn't hear a thing above the wind whistling in my ears.'

Mary had been regarding Tessa with pursed lips and now had her say. 'Maybe you'll admit that using bikes isn't always the best way to get here.'

Tessa looked contrite. 'I suppose you're right. I'll have to resign myself to walking when the weather's bad. What happened to your bike?'

'It got a puncture. Archie Heddle is mending it for me so I'm going there for lunch.'

'Good idea.' Mary folded her arms and glared at Tessa. 'I'm sure Tessa won't mind returning alone.'

'Oh, but that would mean she'd have to come back here alone for the evening watch.' Sally hadn't thought of that when she'd accepted Elspeth's invitation. Perhaps she ought to ask Tessa to join them. As if the day wasn't bad enough already. Sally immediately hated herself for the unkind thought even while she longed for a few hours away from her tormentor.

Tessa gave a negligent wave. 'I'll be fine. It'll still be light.'

'That's settled,' said Mary before Sally could object. 'Come on, Iris. I don't know about you, but I'm overdue for breakfast. My stomach feels as though my throat's been cut.'

With that, Sally watched her two friends depart down the ladder, leaving her alone with Tessa. She walked to the window and gazed out across the sea while listening to Iris and Mary's chatter as they gathered their belongings and put on their coats. Then she heard the door slam and she was alone with Tessa.

Tessa joined Sally at the window. 'I am sorry,' she said. 'I should have realised you're not as strong as me. I should have looked out for you.'

—

'What a cheek. She really said that?' Mary looked as though she was going to storm straight back to the Wrennery and throttle Tessa.

'Yes. She said I wasn't as strong as her.' Sally, sitting at the kitchen table with the Heddles and Mary and Iris, toyed with the generous helping of corned beef hash that Elspeth had piled on her plate. Although it was usually one of her favourite meals, her throat felt too tight to force anything down. 'Honestly, she seemed to imply I was some kind of delicate invalid.'

'The cheek!' Mary repeated, shaking her head. 'You're just as strong as anyone here. You grew up on a Yorkshire farm, for goodness' sake. It's not like you're an upper-class society girl who won't stir out of doors until the servants have swept all the puddles from the path. No offence, Iris.'

'None taken.' Iris, eyes twinkling, piled her fork with a healthy amount of food. 'I can even eat sandwiches without asking for the crusts to be cut off these days.'

'Anyway,' Mary went on, 'Tessa won't be sneering at you when the weather starts getting really bad. I'd like to see her match you when we have to walk to Kyeness through deep snow.'

Elspeth put down her knife and fork, looking thoughtful. 'I don't think I've met this Tessa.'

'She's one of the new visual signaller Wrens,' Iris told her. 'She's all sweetness and light with everyone else but she's set her cap at a young man Sally likes and doesn't seem to be above petty jealousy. Probably realises no sane man would look twice at her with Sally around, so she's doing all she can to dent Sally's confidence.'

'Sounds like she's lacking in confidence herself,' Elspeth said. 'Trying to make herself feel better by making Sally feel small. I hope you're not taking it too much to heart, Sally. She wouldn't treat you like that if she didn't feel threatened by you.'

Sally hadn't looked at it that way before and felt a little happier. She took a mouthful of the stew, suddenly realising how hungry she had become.

'Did you say you'd had a letter from your mother?' Elspeth asked Iris, and Sally was glad of the change of subject. It was also a reminder that she wasn't alone in having troubles, for Iris's relations with her mother were still strained. Letitia Tredwick had cruelly blamed Iris for her father's death and had cut off her allowance. However, she had written her a brief note at Christmas, and Iris had been hopeful that they would be able to mend matters next time they met.

Iris nodded. 'It was as short and formal as ever, but she did have some news.'

'She's having a passionate affair with the gardener?' Mary said.

Iris choked, and Elspeth hastened to slap her on the back. 'You'll be the death of me,' Iris said, wiping her eyes once she could speak again. 'Imagine how much easier my life would be if it was true, though. She could hardly complain about Rob being "beneath me". No,' she went on, 'she's written to say a cousin in the navy has offered her use of his house in Yorkshire while it's standing empty, and she's decided to take him up on his offer.'

Sally pricked up her ears at mention of her home county. 'Whereabouts in Yorkshire?'

'I can't remember the name of the village but she said it was near Helmsley.'

'That's not far from where I grew up. It's a lovely town. I wonder why she's leaving Buckinghamshire?'

'She doesn't say, but reading between the lines, I think she wanted to be somewhere where she didn't run into memories of Daddy around every corner.'

'Sounds sensible to me,' Elspeth said. 'I hope she finds some peace there.'

'Me too.' Iris picked up her fork. 'Anyway, she says she hopes I'll be able to visit soon, so I think she's serious about wanting to make up with me.'

And as the conversation turned to the likelihood of Iris's mother accepting Rob as a potential son-in-law, Sally forgot her bruises and the question of why Tessa was so set against her.

—

Aldo left his sleeping hut and scowled at the swirling mist that meant he could barely see the next hut. Working in these conditions was never pleasant. The work gang was assembling by the gates and he went to join them. Much to his surprise, the British major in charge of Camp 60 was there, with an officer Aldo didn't recognise. The major held a clipboard; the two men spoke in low tones, their heads bent over the clipboard.

'We are going to be moving sixty of you to Stromness,' the major began, once all the prisoners were gathered.

Aldo's head jerked up. Stromness? He was sure that was where Sally had said she was based. Was she still there? The major was still speaking, and Aldo strained to hear what he was saying above the growing murmur of the Italians. 'The men going to Stromness will be working in the docks and will be housed with the Pioneer Corps at Bruna Camp. As for your status—' Here the major was required to raise a hand for silence as the mutterings turned into demands for payment and the freedom to leave the camp. 'As for your status,' he repeated once the noise had died down, 'we are still awaiting confirmation. I am sure we will get news soon but in the meantime please be patient.'

But what did 'soon' mean? Aldo wondered. Days? Weeks? Months? And even if they were given more freedom, those in Camp 60 would continue to be limited to this tiny, bare island. There was nowhere to go and nowhere to spend any money even if they were finally paid in British money.

In Stromness, on the other hand, there would be shops and people. And Sally. His nerves tingling, he pushed his way towards the front of the crowd, his hand going to the neck of his tunic. As ever, he was momentarily surprised when his fingers failed to find his St Christopher, only this time the action brought back stronger memories than ever of Sally. He flung up a prayer to the heavens. *Please let my name be on the list. Please send me to Stromness so I can see her again.*

By now he was near the front of the crowd, and his muscles tensed when he saw the major glance at his clipboard again. It must surely hold the list of men who were going to Stromness. Quivering with hope, he waited for the major to speak again.

The major cleared his throat then indicated the man beside him. 'This is Captain Briars from the Pioneer Corps. If I call your name, you are to line up at the gate. The following men are to accompany him to the trucks waiting on the mainland.'

He raised the clipboard to eye level and started to read names. Aldo clenched his hands, desperate to hear his own name called. The third name was, 'Bernardi, Gianni.' Aldo cursed under his breath as he watched the bull-like figure of Gianni detach itself from the crowd and line up by the gate. Now if Aldo got his heart's desire and was sent to Stromness, he would have his old enemy to contend with. The sixth name called was his friend, Enrico Donati. Aldo crossed his fingers and prayed. He didn't want to stay in Camp 60 without his best friend, even if it did mean putting up with Gianni's unpleasantness. Aldo counted the men adding to the line. Fifty-six, fifty-seven, fifty-eight... His heart sank. Only two places remained. Then the major called: 'Vanni, Aldo.'

Heart pounding in relief, he went to join the line. Once the remaining place had been allocated, the major told them to return to their huts to gather up their belongings and be ready to leave in ten minutes.

Enrico thumped him on the back as they jogged towards their hut. 'Things are looking up, Aldo. We might get to see some girls at last!'

But there was only one girl in Aldo's mind as he made a bundle of his meagre possessions.

Chapter Seven

Shouldering his possessions, Aldo was lining up with the other Italians destined for Stromness when Captain Lawler called him back. Much to his surprise, he saw the captain was holding a toolbox, which he presented to Aldo. With it was the half-finished carving of an angel he had started. The Italians had recently been given permission to build a chapel in Camp 60, and Aldo had offered to make an angel for it. Captain Briars now thrust it, together with the tools, into Aldo's arms. 'Here. You've put these to much better use than I ever could.'

'I can't take these.' Aldo stroked the lid of the box then offered it back to Lawler.

Lawler shook his head and made no move to take it. 'All I ask in return is that you finish the angel and ask Captain Briars to send it here for the chapel. Now go on, before you get left behind.'

Captain Briars was already leading the men through the gates, and Enrico was beckoning, shouting to him to hurry up.

All Aldo could do was stammer his thanks and promise to send the angel when it was ready, then he ran to catch up with the group, hardly able to believe his luck.

Once they reached the mainland, walking across on the stone-filled wire baskets that now rose above the water, they found several trucks awaiting them. He clambered into the same one as Enrico, glad to see Gianni was in a different one. He preferred to avoid Gianni as much as possible, although he feared that now they were in a group of just sixty, that might prove more difficult. The truck jolted forward with a grinding

66

of gears, and soon Lamb Holm and Scapa Flow were out of sight and they were travelling inland. The mist lifted as they went.

'How far is Stromness, do you know?' Enrico asked.

Aldo shook his head, trying to remember the little Sally had told him about the town where she was based. 'I know it's on the western side of the island, but I don't know how big the Orkney mainland is,' he confessed.

To Aldo, eager to see his new home, the place where he hoped Sally still lived, the trucks seemed to lumber along at barely more than walking pace. The road they followed climbed a slight rise, and Aldo looked about with interest. Glimpses of the sea could be seen to the left of the road, and the landscape was dotted with farms and looked almost as bleak and bare as Lamb Holm. After twenty minutes, they crested a hill, and Aldo saw a large cluster of buildings, sandwiched between the foot of the hill and the sea.

'Is that Stromness?' Enrico asked, half rising and leaning over the side of the truck.

Fearing he might tumble out, Aldo grabbed his collar. 'Idiot.' He pulled Enrico back down onto the floor. 'Anyway, this isn't Stromness. It's Kirkwall. Look, there's the hospital where I had my appendix out.' He pointed at the place as their truck trundled past. 'We've reached the north coast.'

He looked about with as much interest as Enrico as they drove through the town. From this point on, everything he saw was new; it was the farthest he had travelled since they had arrived at Camp 60. Even though the north coast was only minutes from the south coast, Mainland still felt like a vast unexplored expanse to someone who had spent nearly two years on Lamb Holm. Above all, there were real people out on the streets. By 'real' he meant anyone who wasn't a prisoner, soldier or construction worker, for those were the only people he'd mixed with for a long time. It was strange to see a crocodile of schoolchildren and remember that life continued as normal. Then he saw that the children and the two middle-aged women accompanying them all carried gas masks, and hated the reminder that even the innocent weren't untouched by the war.

Soon the truck left Kirkwall. Aldo didn't know whether his vision was tinted by the excitement of being somewhere new after so long, but the land seemed greener and lusher here, and the glimpses of sea looked bluer. It was definitely more hilly. He soon got a sense that Mainland must be longer than it was wide, for it took about an hour, travelling at the same snail's pace, to reach Stromness. After following the north coast for some time, they turned south. For a while he thought his next sight of water must be the harbour at Stromness until he realised he was seeing a large loch. Two lochs, he realised, seeing the narrow strip of land separating them.

After what felt like an eternity, the truck descended a hill, bringing Stromness and its harbour into view. The town was smaller than Kirkwall, clustered around the waterside and rising steeply behind. Now it was Aldo's turn to lean out of the truck, drinking in the sight, wondering where Sally might be. Perhaps she was strolling through the town at this very moment. Much to his disappointment, the truck turned into the Pioneer Corps' camp before reaching the main town.

The huts of Bruna Camp sprawled at the foot of a hill, and Aldo wondered which one would be his new home as the convoy of trucks bounced over rough ground, heading for a group of Nissen huts near the perimeter. Once his truck had lurched to a halt, the men scrambled out and joined the other Italians who milled around beside their trucks. A British corporal approached, holding yet another clipboard, and ordered them to line up in alphabetical order. Aldo took his place at the other end of the line from Enrico.

Captain Briars addressed them once they were quiet. 'In a moment, Corporal Thomas will assign you to a hut. You will leave your belongings there, then Corporal Thomas will take you to the mess for a meal. Until we have confirmation of your status from the government, you are required to remain in the camp when you are not working at the docks, but you are free to move where you like within its boundaries.'

This was an improvement. There seemed to be much more going on in this camp. It was larger for a start, not to mention that they had a completely new view. The only downside was that he was housed in a separate hut from Enrico.

When he went to go inside his hut and bag his bunk, someone grabbed his arm. It was Gianni. 'Keep your eyes open around the camp,' he hissed in Aldo's ear. 'We must never forget they are our enemies. Look for any way of disrupting them.'

Aldo sighed. 'This has gone on long enough, Gianni. I am not a fascist. I have no desire to hurt anyone here.'

'But you fought bravely in North Africa.'

'Because I wanted to stay alive. We have no need to fight now. Besides, the British are no longer our enemies. We surrendered, remember.'

A flash of hatred twisted Gianni's face. 'We should never have done that. It was a disgrace. Humiliation. I don't care if we surrendered. The British will always be our enemies. And if you refuse to accept that then you are my enemy also.'

Gianni spat at Aldo's feet then stalked off to his own hut.

Shaken, Aldo turned to go into the hut, only to stop when he heard a faint meow. A small black cat peered up at him from behind an upturned crate.

'Hello there.' Aldo dropped into a crouch and held out his hand, allowing the cat to sniff his fingers. 'You were wise not to come out when Gianni was here. I wish *I* could have avoided him.' A moment later, a tiny pink tongue darted out of its mouth, and Aldo grinned as the cat licked his fingers and started to purr. 'I want to make it clear that I could have beaten him in a fight. I just don't want the British to mark me out as a troublemaker.' Aldo gave a self-conscious chuckle. It was a good thing no one was watching him; they would think him mad, talking to a cat. On the other hand, it helped ease the sick tension that he always felt after an encounter with Gianni. He scratched the cat's head, smiling as its eyes became contented slits. 'Are you hungry? You look quite thin. Perhaps I can save you some scraps from the mess hall.'

Despite finding the cat soothing, he must have still looked upset when he followed the others to the mess, for Enrico cocked an enquiring eyebrow at him. Aldo gave a quick shake of the head, not wanting to be overheard. 'I'll tell you later,' he said in an undertone.

The mess was set up as the type of canteen that could be found in any military camp anywhere in the world. There was a counter at one end where cooks presided over pots of indeterminate stews and vegetables, and the rest of the room was filled with ranks of long tables and benches. Many of the tables were already occupied when the Italians filed in; men looked up from their food and regarded them with expressions varying from curiosity to outright hostility. Aldo was discouraged by the hostility but not surprised. It wasn't so very long ago that they had been enemies. Some of the men present might very well have lost friends or family at the hands of the Italians, just as Aldo himself had lost friends to the British. Not to mention his brother. While he himself didn't feel hostility to anyone here, he could understand how loss might make someone regard him that way. Personally, he blamed Mussolini for bringing Italy into the war. He had not wanted to fight but had had no choice in the matter. He guessed there must be many men on both sides who felt the same way.

At the counter, Aldo was presented with a plate heaped with a greyish stew and vegetables boiled to a pulp. It was much the same fare he had eaten throughout his time in Orkney, and it was something of a comfort to see the British were presented with exactly the same food. It was not, as some men had complained back in Camp 60, a way of demoralising the prisoners.

None of the British men gave any sign of making room for the Italians at their tables. Still, there were enough free tables closest to the draughty entrance for all the Italians to find seats. Aldo and Enrico squeezed onto the end of a bench. Their companions entered into a noisy conversation about their new location and the possibility of catching the eyes of any of the local girls. Aldo, still shaken from Gianni's words, was in no mood to join in.

'Are you going to tell me what's bothering you?' Enrico asked once they had both cleared their plates. He picked up his mug and peered into it with a dubious expression.

Aldo glanced around to see where Gianni and his cronies were sitting. They were two tables away, too far for them to overhear him over the racket of voices and the rattle of eating irons upon plates. Nevertheless, he kept his voice low as he told Enrico about his encounter with Gianni.

Enrico pulled a face. 'Gianni's in my hut, worse luck.' He took a tentative sip from his mug and gagged. 'Uurgh. This is disgusting.'

Aldo sniffed at his own mug. It was very stewed tea. His tongue seemed to curl up on contact with it. 'Tastes like they used the water from a truck radiator,' he said. 'Anyway, what do you think I should do about Gianni?'

'Just try and avoid him. He's trying to stir up trouble with the men in my hut, telling them it's their duty to disrupt the British as much as possible. Apart from his two friends, no one else wanted anything to do with him.'

'Good. I just want a quiet life. Pity it won't be so easy to avoid him here.'

He would do his best, though. He had the feeling Gianni was going to bring down a lot of trouble on himself, and Aldo wanted to be far away from him when that happened.

—

'Did you hear we've got some Italians working at the docks?'

71

Sally, who had been sitting with Mary and Iris in the common room, knitting another pair of socks, dropped a stitch when she heard the comment from one of the Wrens sitting behind them. The Wren who had spoken was Evelyn, another of the signaller Wrens, and she had addressed the remark to her friend. Sally pricked up her ears.

'Really?' Evelyn's companion said. 'Where from?'

'One of the POW camps on Lamb Holm, I think.'

'What – they're driving them all the way across the island each day?'

'No. They've been moved to a camp outside Stromness.'

Sally bent her head over her knitting, easing her knitting needle through the dropped stitch before it unravelled. For some reason the news made her heart beat a little faster. She was being foolish. There were lots of Italian prisoners; it was unlikely Aldo would be among the group moved to Stromness. Even if he was here, what did it matter? She wasn't interested in him. She was in love with Adam, and nothing would change that.

'Any ideas what to do today?'

Sally jumped, hearing Iris's voice. She had been so engrossed listening to Evelyn and her friend, she had lost track of her conversation with Iris and Mary. 'Oh, I thought I'd go for a wander in Stromness.'

'Stromness. Really?' Iris nudged Sally in the ribs. 'Not planning to go for a walk around the docks to ogle the handsome Italians, are you?'

Sally felt her cheeks burn. 'What do you mean?'

'Oh, come on, Sally. I saw how you reacted when Evelyn mentioned the Italian prisoners. You can't tell me you're not a little bit curious to find out if your handsome POW is among them.'

'I need to send a postal order to my mother,' Sally protested. But when Iris lowered her own knitting and regarded Sally with raised eyebrows, Sally folded. 'Oh, all right. I admit I'm curious. But it's not what you think.'

'Why – what am I thinking?'

If Sally's cheeks burned any hotter, she would be able to fry an egg on them. 'You think I'm sweet on him. But I'm not. You know I love Adam.'

Iris raised her hands in mock surrender. 'All right. I'm sorry. If you say you have nothing but platonic feelings for him, then I believe you. But you do want to know if he's here.'

There was no point in denying it. 'So what if I do? He was kind to me in hospital and he was good company. And I never got the chance to thank him for sending me that lovely crib scene.' She managed to recover her composure and add, 'Anyway, I have to go to the post office. Are either of you coming with me?'

Iris glanced out of the window. 'I'd rather stay in. It's raining.'

'I'm sure it'll clear up. You know the saying – rain before seven, sun by eleven.'

Mary snorted. 'More like rain before seven, rain by eleven, and every hour in between.'

Sally shook her head. 'You have no soul. Come on, one of you has to come with me. I don't want to go on my own.' She had just seen Tessa leave, announcing that she was going into the town. Sally couldn't bear the thought of bumping into her without the protection of one of her friends. Tessa always restrained herself when Sally was with Iris or Mary and reserved the worst of her barbs for when they were alone.

'I'll come,' Mary said. 'I could do with some more yarn. What do you say, Iris? A little rain won't hurt you, and we could grab a cup of tea at the Beehive afterwards.'

'I suppose you won't take no for an answer.' Iris folded away her knitting. 'Come on then, if we're going.'

Fortunately there wasn't much of a queue at the post office, so Sally dealt with the postal order very quickly. After a trip to the drapers for Mary to purchase more yarn for knitting sailors' socks, it seemed too soon after breakfast for going to the Beehive.

'I feel like a bit of a walk,' Sally said, 'to stretch my legs.'

'Because we don't get nearly enough exercise walking back and forth between here and Kyeness,' Mary said.

'Oh, don't tease her,' Iris said. 'Anyway, I need to warm up, so a walk is a good idea. Where do you fancy going – out onto the cliffs? Or a stroll towards the docks perhaps?' The sparkle in Iris's eyes brought the blush back to Sally's cheeks.

Mary saved her from answering. 'The cliffs will be too muddy. Better head for the docks.' She and Iris grinned at each other, and Sally knew it would be some time before they tired of teasing her.

Even knowing she was the subject of her friends' amused regard, Sally couldn't resist craning her neck to watch the dock workers when they reached the waterfront. There was a group of men clustered around one of the cargo ships and although they were too far away to see clearly, she thought she could see the red 'target' patches on their backs and hips. Aldo had told her that all the prisoners had been forced to sew the red circles onto their uniforms to make them visible should they attempt to escape. 'How they expect us to escape from an island, I don't know,' he had concluded. Privately, Sally had thought it was more to humiliate them. An exercise in control. Considering the Italians were no longer officially prisoners, it seemed harsh to make them continue wearing the patches.

When they got closer to the water's edge, they were able to pick out more details. 'It *is* the Italians,' Sally said when she could make out the red circles on their uniforms more clearly. She could hear them now, calling out in an unfamiliar language. It was a rapid, musical sound. She couldn't discern any words but it made her smile, the accent reminding her of Aldo and his persistence in seeking her out at the hospital. The sound seemed to match his good humour, somehow.

Of course, it was foolish to hope he would be here. He was probably still miles away on Lamb Holm, and it was unlikely they would ever meet again. The thought made her sad. Although they hadn't spent much time together, her heart had gone out to him, knowing how lonely he must be feeling so far from his home. He had put a brave face on his capture and had done his best to entertain and cheer her after the incident that had put her in hospital with concussion. She would have liked to see him again and assure herself he was well.

She was on the point of turning away when a figure walking down the gangway caught her eye. He was tall and, despite the bundle he was supporting on his shoulders, walked with the same jaunty gait she associated with Aldo. It couldn't be him. It was too much of a coincidence. Her feet seemed rooted to the spot, however, and she couldn't tear away her gaze as he drew closer. He carried his burden to a truck on the dockside and heaved it inside. He paused for a moment, wiping his brow on his sleeve, and then looked up. Their eyes met, and Sally felt a jolt of recognition. There was no mistaking the dark, almost black hair and the broad smile.

'Sally?' Aldo said.

Sally moved forward until only the width of the truck separated them. 'Aldo, it is you.' Now they were closer she could see his face, hands and clothes were smeared with grey dirt.

'When I was told I was coming to Stromness, I hoped I would see you,' Aldo said in his accented English. It had improved since she had last seen him, no doubt picked up from the British labourers and engineers at the causeway construction site. 'I didn't think it would be so soon.'

'When did you get here?'

'Yesterday. Your St Christopher must have guided you to this spot.'

Sally laughed. 'I was just out for a walk. How are you?' She pointed at the smudges on his uniform. 'How did you get so dusty?'

Aldo pointed back to the ship. 'The hold is full of dust.' When Sally pulled a face, he dismissed her concern with a wry smile. 'It is dirty work but much better than the quarry.'

'But they are still making you work. I thought that might stop after Italy surrendered.'

Aldo shrugged. 'We cannot go home. I think the British do not quite know what to do with us. We are still waiting to hear what will happen. In the meantime, we work. I do not mind. It is better than doing nothing.'

A British corporal walked towards Aldo. 'Back to work with you.'

On the point of turning away, Aldo said, 'We will see one another again, yes?'

'I hope so.' Then, before Aldo was out of earshot Sally called after him, 'Thank you for the crib scene. It's beautiful.'

He turned, ignoring the corporal for a moment and his shining eyes locked with Sally's. 'Thank you for your gift,' he called back. 'And for giving me hope.'

Then he turned and disappeared back into the ship.

Sally allowed Iris and Mary to tug her away from the docks and back into the town. 'I can't believe I actually saw him,' she told them. 'I never seriously thought he'd be here. I thought he'd still be on Lamb Holm.'

Iris glanced at her, eyes dancing. 'If our positions were reversed, you do know what you'd be saying to me right now, don't you?'

'No. What?' Sally's head was spinning too much to think straight.

'You'd tell me it was fate. That Aldo and I were destined to be together.'

'Then it's a good thing you don't believe in destiny,' Sally retorted. 'You're always telling me it's nonsense.'

'I don't know. You were right about me and Rob.'

'And me and Joe,' Mary put in. 'I think you've got a point, Iris. Maybe there is something to Sally's beliefs after all.'

Sally looked from one to the other of her friends, hardly able to believe her ears. They had never ceased to tease her about her little superstitions, the way she always had to wait to see a second magpie should she see only one at first. Sally had never been offended by this, coming as it did from a place of affection rather than sneering or looking down on her. Sally had accepted her friends didn't share her beliefs, especially her belief in destiny, that there were particular people in life they were fated to be with. Sally herself had been forced to amend her beliefs a little when Mary had fallen in love with Joe, despite having lost the love of her life three years earlier.

Iris nodded. 'There's no doubt about it, Sally. You and Aldo must be destined to be together. Why else would he have been sent here, and why else would we have arrived at the docks at just the right time to see him?'

It took Sally a moment to realise Iris was joking. She forced a laugh. 'You almost had me fooled then. How many times do I have to tell you I'm going to end up with Adam?' No matter what obstacles the fates seemed to be strewing in her path to love.

They were on the point of turning up a lane that led to John Street when Mary said, 'Don't look now, but Tessa Blight is behind us, and she's giving you a very odd stare, Sally.'

Of course nothing could stop Sally looking back. Letting her gas mask case slip from her shoulder, she gave a pretend exclamation of annoyance when it hit the cobbles behind her and turned to pick it up. As she did so, she shot a glance back towards the docks and saw that Tessa was, indeed, about ten yards behind. For a brief instant Sally thought her expression was one of speculation. Then their eyes met. At that distance it was pointless to pretend she hadn't noticed her, so Sally gave her a quick wave before running to catch up with the others. Halfway up the lane, she couldn't stop herself from looking back again. Tessa hadn't followed. Instead, she had turned to face the ship the Italians were unloading.

'Do you think she saw me with Aldo?' Sally asked.

'No idea.' Mary tugged Sally's arm. 'Come on, I'm gasping for a cup of tea. What does it matter if Tessa saw you, anyway? You weren't doing anything wrong.'

'I suppose not.' But Sally felt uneasy, as though she had handed Tessa a weapon. While she and her friends enjoyed tea and carrot cake at the Beehive, she couldn't shake off the feeling, no matter that she tried to persuade herself she had done nothing wrong.

–

The question of whether Tessa had seen her speak to Aldo was answered the next morning. She was back on watch with Tessa, and they hadn't been at their post long before Tessa asked, 'Who were you talking to at the docks yesterday – it wasn't an Italian prisoner of war, was it?'

'They're not prisoners any more,' Sally replied, trying to evade the question. 'We're not at war with them now.'

'Then you *were* speaking with one of them?'

Sally could see Tessa wasn't going to give up. 'Yes. I had an accident last year and ended up in hospital.' In fact, it had turned out not to be an accident at all but it had been some months before her memory of the event had fully returned, at which point she realised that she must have been attacked by a man who was later revealed to be an enemy agent. After the man had finally been captured, the authorities had warned her, Mary and Iris not to mention it to anyone else, stating it would be demoralising for people to learn there had been a spy on the island. 'Aldo – the Italian you saw me with – was in hospital at the same time, and we made friends.' Sally couldn't suppress a smile as she remembered how Aldo had managed to escape from his ward to sit with her.

Tessa's eyes went wide. 'You weren't scared? He could have used you as a hostage to make his escape.'

Sally laughed. 'He would never have done that. He's the kindest soul you could ever imagine. Besides, where would he have run to? He'd have had no way of escaping from the island, even if he did manage to make it to the coast.'

'I suppose not, but I wouldn't have dared mix with a prisoner, however friendly he might appear.' Tessa seemed to have recovered from her surprise at Sally's story and a faint sneer had returned to her tone. 'I wouldn't want to fall for a foreigner. It strikes me as being very unpatriotic.'

Sally, who had gone to great lengths not to argue with Tessa before now, couldn't let this comment pass. 'Unpatriotic? Since when did being kind to someone who was far from home make you unpatriotic?'

'Imagine how our men would feel if they knew British girls were mixing with the soldiers they had been fighting. It's our duty to support our men, not consort with prisoners.'

Sally stared at her, mystified. 'It's our duty to stand watch here. That's how we help our men. How we spend our free time is nothing to do with them.'

'And how would Adam feel if he knew who you had been speaking with?' A sly look crossed Tessa's face.

'I would hope he'd approve of me being kind to a fellow human being.' Even as she said it, Sally wondered if it was true. What did she really know of Adam's feelings and beliefs? Despite her conviction that he would eventually notice her, their conversations had never strayed beyond surface matters.

'Perhaps you should tell him, see what he says.'

'Maybe I will.' Although suddenly she was less sure that Adam would respond in the way she wanted. It was as though a closed door in her mind suddenly stood ajar, revealing a sliver of light. Part of her wanted to push it open; another part of her was afraid of what might lie beyond.

Chapter Eight

Sally had still been unable to shake off that uncomfortable feeling some days later. It was, she decided, like waking up from a nightmare which evoked powerful feelings of fear and dread that lingered for the rest of the day. How well did she really know Adam? But whenever she tried to address the thought, her mind veered away from it. Maybe it was because Adam was now in Orkney. When he had been with his ship or, later, in Whitby recovering from his broken leg, it had been comforting to think of him, to know that one day they would be together. But now he was in nearby Lyness and suddenly the distant, hazy future was here. Only nothing had changed – Adam still hadn't confessed his feelings about her. She was starting to wonder if the truth behind the door in her mind was that he didn't love her and never would. She said nothing about this to Iris or Mary. After declaring to them so confidently that she and Adam were supposed to be together, how could she confess that she might have been mistaken?

But she couldn't have been mistaken. She had been right about Iris and Rob and right about Mary and Joe. Surely she knew herself better than she knew the others. She couldn't be wrong about something so close to her heart.

Even so, she couldn't entirely rid herself of the feeling of unease. It gripped her now as she strolled through Stromness, wondering how to spend the time before she was due to go on watch that afternoon. She had tried to while away the time in the common room, knitting, but she had been unable to concentrate. She had ended up casting on so many accidental stitches that the sock she was knitting would only have been useful if the Royal Navy had started recruiting elephants. She had packed her wool away and walked into the town hoping the fresh air would clear her head.

It was only now, a quarter of an hour into her walk, that she noticed her feet had led her down to the water. Shouts of men unloading a ship caught her attention and she found herself studying them, looking for a glimpse of Aldo's tall figure. She couldn't see him, though. Anyway, what would she have done if he was there? She didn't think it was unpatriotic to be friends with an Italian, but interrupting him at work certainly wouldn't go down well with the British guards.

A cold raindrop fell on her nose, swiftly followed by more. She couldn't afford a soaking when there would be no time to dry her clothes before going on duty, so she set off at a brisk trot for the Beehive. Hopefully the rain would have stopped before it was time to leave.

Two young women she didn't recognise were sitting at her favourite table in the corner. As she hesitated between a table close to the fire, which might get too warm, and the draughty table beside the door, one of the women gave her a cheery wave. 'Do join us,' she said. 'This is our first time in Stromness, and we could do with someone to tell us about the best shops.'

Only too glad for company to distract her from her thoughts, Sally took a seat at their table. 'You've already found the best cafe. That's a good start. Are you in the WRNS, then?' Neither of them were in uniform, although they wouldn't be if they were off duty. Sally was wearing her uniform but only because she was going back on watch later.

Both the girls nodded then one of the girls, who had a good-humoured face said, 'We're based in Lyness, at the communications centre. We only arrived two weeks ago, so everything feels very new and strange. I'm Alice, by the way, and this is Sarah.' The freckle-faced redhead beside her grinned.

Sally introduced herself and explained where she worked then said, 'I remember how strange everything felt when I first arrived. Everything suddenly seemed so much more serious, standing watch for real rather than practising sending messages during training. Don't worry though – you'll get used to it in no time. What's Hoy like? I've never been there.' She couldn't help feeling a pang of jealousy that these two young women were living on the same base as Adam. She wondered if they had met him.

'The base is fine,' Alice replied. 'There's lots to do and so many people, it feels like a proper town. We haven't seen much of the island, though. With the nights drawing in, we don't get enough daylight to explore. Today's our first full day off, but we needed to run some errands in Stromness.'

'It felt quite adventurous having to take a drifter to the nearest town,' Sarah said. 'Stromness feels like a huge city after a fortnight on Hoy.'

'Probably how I feel visiting Kirkwall,' Sally told her with a laugh. 'You're lucky living on a big base, though. We feel quite isolated up at Kyeness.'

'Oh, you should visit. There's going to be a big dance in a couple of weeks. Why don't you come?'

A voice came from behind Sally. One that made her tense. 'A dance at Lyness? What fun!' Uninvited, Tessa Bligh sat in the unoccupied chair next to Sally. 'Do introduce me to your new friends, Sally.'

Sally could have wept. She had no choice but to make the introductions and then watch Tessa turn on the charm and dominate the conversation. Tessa managed it expertly, deflecting any questions aimed at Sally, and by the end of ten minutes, Tessa, Alice and Sarah were chatting as though they had been best friends all their life, leaving Sally nothing to do but watch, like a spectator at a tennis match. If she could have done so, she would have left. No one would have noticed. The trouble was, she had already ordered tea, so she had no choice but to pin a smile on her face and pretend she would be happy to go to the dance with Tessa. The date was mentioned, and

Tessa announced that as they both came off watch at 1800 that evening and weren't back on duty until the following afternoon, there would be no difficulty in getting late passes. Sally's brief dream of meeting Adam at the dance and spending an evening in his company crumbled to dust. Tessa, she was sure, would do all in her power to ensure Sally didn't get so much as a minute alone with him.

She was half tempted to declare that she couldn't make it to the dance after all. If she did that, though, it wouldn't stop Tessa going. Then she would be faced with a whole evening spent imagining Tessa dancing the night away in Adam's arms. No, it was better to go. That way she still had a chance to catch Adam's eye. Maybe she could devise a way to distract Tessa for long enough to get Adam to herself for a while. It was even possible that Tessa would spot another man she preferred and abandon her pursuit of Adam. She wouldn't give up hope.

Even so, she finished her tea as quickly as possible and, muttering something about needing to run more errands before going back on watch, she made her escape. Once again, her feet led her to the piers, or as close as she could get without getting in the way of the men swarming around the ships. She didn't know why she wanted to catch another glimpse of Aldo. Maybe it was because he had been there for her when she had been recovering from her head injury, entertaining and cheering her up. She certainly could use some cheering now. She couldn't see Aldo, though, and eventually she made her way back to the Wrennery, bracing herself for another endless watch in Tessa's company.

—

Aldo heaved another crate into the waiting truck and paused to wipe his brow. He still found it hard to get used to the bustling port after so long spent going between Lamb Holm and the nearby quarry with no one for company but the men he worked with. Not that he was allowed to mix with the people of

Stromness, but it was a refreshing change to be able to observe people going about their lives. He would have loved to explore the town but for now they were escorted to the docks and back to the depot without being allowed to stray. Maybe when the British government finally finished their deliberations on the status of the Italians, he would be allowed further afield. For now, he was grateful for the change of scene.

He held his face to the sky, allowing the light rain to refresh his hot cheeks and rinse away the worst of the dust. Although the work here was not as strenuous as the quarries, it was still heavy work.

A movement caught his eye. A girl with light brown hair standing some distance away. Was it Sally? She wasn't looking in his direction, gazing instead at a different ship. It *was* her, he was sure. The only reason he hadn't immediately recognised her was because her expression made her look so unlike herself. Instead of the sunny smile and unfailingly optimistic expression that had drawn him to her from the first, her shoulders drooped and her lips were pressed tight together as though she was trying to prevent them from turning down. What had happened?

He took two steps in her direction, acting on instinct, wanting to comfort her. But a tap on his shoulder made him look round, and he saw one of the British guards. 'You know the rules,' he said. 'No mixing with the locals.'

Aldo nodded and returned to his work. When he looked again, Sally had gone.

As the day stretched on in a blur of hauling heavy loads interspersed with brief spells of rest, he couldn't get Sally's sad face out of his head. What had happened to her? Someone must have done or said something to crush her. He knew her well enough to know her disposition was unfailingly optimistic. It was what had drawn him to her when they had met at the hospital – her smile and kindness to him, even though he was an enemy. Others might have ignored him but she had made time for him despite her injury.

Finally, the order was given for the Italians to line up and begin the march back to camp. Footsore and weary from their labours, they formed a straggling line. Aldo walked beside Enrico. While he was never usually short of things to talk about, he didn't speak, too busy wondering about Sally.

'What's up with you?'

It took a painful prod to his upper arm to jerk him out of his reverie and realise that Enrico had spoken. 'What?'

Enrico rolled his eyes. 'I asked what was the matter. Honestly, if I'd wanted bad company, I'd have stood next to Gianni.'

'Sorry. I was thinking of Sally.'

'Your English friend?'

Aldo nodded. 'I saw her again today.'

'Here? I didn't see her.' Enrico had teased him relentlessly after he had met Sally at the docks the other day. Now he nudged Aldo with his elbow. 'She obviously can't keep away from you.' A pause, then, 'Unless she saw me and was drawn back here by my animal magnetism. Am I in with a chance, do you think?'

'No!' Aldo was shocked at the sharpness of his own voice.

Enrico laughed and held up his hands in surrender. 'I get the message. Don't worry – I'll stay away from your lovely English girl. There are plenty more pretty girls in Stromness.' So saying, he waved at a couple of young women in khaki uniforms who had stood aside to let the column go past. They giggled and waved back.

'You have an English girlfriend?'

Aldo jumped and glanced over his shoulder to see Gianni standing right behind him. He hadn't noticed him there until he spoke. How much had he heard?

Before he could answer, Enrico spoke. 'Haven't you heard? He met an English girl when he was in hospital and now his heart is bursting with love.' He clapped a hand over his heart, drawing out the word *amore* with an exaggerated sigh.

Trying to hide the alarm he felt at Gianni finding out about Sally, he buffeted Enrico on the side of his head. 'Idiot. I hardly know the girl.'

'But you—' Enrico stopped when Aldo gave him a swift kick on the ankle. 'Oh, yes, don't mind me, Gianni. I was only teasing.'

'That better be true. We should be spending our time working out how to get back to Italy, not consorting with the enemy.'

—

'You and your big mouth,' Aldo said to Enrico once they were back in their hut. Much to their delight, Enrico had managed to swap huts so he now occupied the same one as Aldo. Aldo was lying on his bunk, frowning up at the curved ceiling. 'Gianni's a troublemaker. You know that. Why did you have to tell him about Sally?' In his heart, he was berating himself for not checking to see if they were being overheard before speaking of her. He couldn't really blame Enrico for being his usual self.

'I'm sorry. I didn't think she was a secret.'

'She's not. Not really. But I'd rather Gianni not find out about her. You know what he's like.'

'Why does it matter?' Enrico leaned against Aldo's bunk, making it shake. He counted off his points on his fingers. 'Firstly, as you already said, there's nothing to know. I know I like to tease you about her but you've only met once since you left hospital. It's not as if you're actually having a relationship with a British girl. Secondly, what can Gianni do about it? He doesn't know who Sally is – I don't think I would recognise her if I saw her again – and even if he did, what could he do apart from tease you?'

'I don't know. I've got a bad feeling, though.' And although he would never admit it, it stung to know that what he and Sally had couldn't count as a relationship. Despite the fact that they had only met briefly, the memory of her was something he clung to, a talisman just as real as his St Christopher had once been. He didn't know why he felt uncomfortable about Gianni finding out about her. As Enrico said, there was nothing he could do about it. But a nagging sense that Gianni would use it against him gnawed at his nerves.

Chapter Nine

'Please say you'll come, Iris. Mary can't because she's on duty that night, but I can't bear the thought of going with just Tessa.' Sally turned pleading eyes on her friend. Her walk to the dockside and back through Stromness had done nothing to relieve her dismay at Tessa worming an invitation to the dance. By the time she had returned to the Wrennery, she was wishing Tessa might pick up a chill or dose of food poisoning that would put her out of action on the day of the dance. The thought had hardly crossed her mind when she was berating herself for being so mean-spirited. She had found Iris in the common room and instantly begged her to accompany them to Lyness. 'You did promise to come to Hoy to meet Adam, remember,' she finished.

Iris put down her knitting. 'I suppose it would be rather fun to see Lyness, and I haven't been to a dance for ages.' She looked wistful, and Sally knew she must be thinking of Rob, wishing he was still based nearby so he could have gone with her. Iris bit her lip. 'You don't think Rob would mind, do you?'

Sally looked at her in surprise. 'He trusts you. He would never expect you to shut yourself away from the world just because he can't be with you.'

'Oh, I didn't mean that.' A soft smile lit Iris's face. 'He made a point of telling me to go out and describe it all to him in my letters, to give him a glimpse of life beyond the *Kelpie*.' Iris's expression clouded. 'It's just… he's been away so long. I can't bear to think of him cooped up on that ship, unable to go out.

And he loves Orkney so much, it feels mean to tell him all about a trip to Lyness when he can't go himself.'

Sally studied her hands in her lap while she wondered how to reply. She wanted Iris to come with her and needed to examine her conscience to be sure she was persuading Iris to do the best for herself and not for Sally. She tried to put herself in Rob's shoes and imagine how it must feel to be miles from home and his loved ones. 'I don't think he would look at it that way,' she said finally. 'I mean, you know Rob best, so you might disagree. But I think your letters must be a window to the life he's fighting for. I think he'd be relying on you to live the life he wants to be part of.'

'Oh!' Iris sat bolt upright and groped in her pocket. A moment later she pulled out a crumpled letter. She unfolded it and smoothed the thin blue paper on her lap. 'That's just what he said in his last letter.' She ran her index finger down the page. Like Iris's letters to him, it was filled with cramped handwriting, not a bit of space wasted. 'Here. Listen.' She read from the letter. '*Getting your letters is always a treat. Last week the post brought me three letters from you – all dated before the one that reached me last month*.' Iris glanced up at Sally. 'We're getting each other's letters completely out of order. It makes it quite a challenge to piece all the events together.'

Sally nodded. Mary had said something similar, complaining that she often didn't understand what Joe was referring to until she received another letter some weeks later that had been posted a week or two before the one she'd received.

Iris resumed reading. '*I love hearing all about the places you're visiting and the people you meet. It brings home closer, and for a moment makes me feel as though I could step through the letter to the places you describe*.' Iris stopped reading and refolded the paper, giving it a loving stroke before tucking it away in her pocket.

'There you go,' Sally told her. 'I'm sure he doesn't want to hear about the socks you're knitting or the lumpy porridge you ate for breakfast. Come to the dance and write him a really entertaining letter all about it afterwards.'

'Oh, very well. But pray it's a calm night. I don't want to fall overboard again.'

Sally laughed, more from relief than from Iris's comment. As far as she was concerned, Iris's accident when she had been knocked out of the drifter returning her from a shipboard dance was nothing to joke about, knowing how close Iris had come to drowning. 'I promise to hold on to you all the way. Although if Tessa strays too close to the side I won't be in a hurry to stop her from falling.'

—

Sally counted down the days to the dance, her excitement rising as the day approached. Now that Iris was coming, she could ignore the fact that Tessa would be there too. She even dared to write to Adam, letting him know she would be at the dance and asking if he would be going. She didn't hold out much hope for a reply – he hadn't been good at replying to her earlier letters, saying that work kept him so busy he didn't have time for writing. However, the day before the dance she received a brief note thanking her for the letter and saying that he hoped to be at the dance.

'Is that all?' Mary said, looking at the letter that a delighted Sally had shown her. 'Waste of precious paper, if you ask me. He could have given you some news or said he was looking forward to seeing you.'

True, Sally couldn't help comparing it with the letter from Rob to Iris, but it was still a letter from Adam. A sign he knew she existed. 'He's very busy,' she said. 'It must be difficult for him to find time to write.'

Mary snorted. 'He's got an office job. You work all hours of the day and night but you still manage to write to your family and friends. And Joe's on active duty, for goodness' sake, yet he still finds time to write regularly. Even if the post isn't so regular.'

While this couldn't be denied, Sally tried not to think of it. When Adam finally got round to declaring his feelings for her, maybe he could be persuaded to write more often. A letter was a letter, and Sally would treasure this one. And anyway, she couldn't help hoping that tomorrow she would dance with Adam and he would finally realise that he was in love with her.

—

As promised, Sally kept a steadying grip on Iris's arm throughout the crossing to Hoy. Iris was understandably nervous, so they placed themselves well away from the side and Sally kept up a stream of chatter while the drifter chugged through the water, which was mercifully calm.

'Thank goodness for that,' Iris replied when Sally commented on the weather. 'I know Rob said he enjoyed reading all my news, but I'm sure he doesn't want a detailed account of the number of times I was sick over the side.'

The sun had already set by the time the boat was approaching Lyness, but the lingering golden light was enough to illuminate the naval base. Unlike Stromness, where the military and civilians existed cheek by jowl, most of Lyness seemed to have been constructed recently and was a purely military base. The drifter sailed up an inlet, and most of the buildings occupied a flat area beside the water. Behind this cluster of buildings, high hills rose which were mostly wild, although Sally could see a few flat-topped observation posts. She was more interested in the living areas, though, and eyed them curiously, wondering where Adam lived. Despite wishing she could see him more often, she decided that she was glad she was based in Stromness, where she felt part of the town. Apart from the activities organised in the base, she doubted there was much to do in and around Lyness.

She breathed a sigh of relief when the drifter bumped gently against the pier. Often passengers were required to use other boats as a kind of floating bridge to reach the shore, and she hadn't looked forward to the scramble from one boat to the next while wearing her best dress.

'At last,' Iris said, releasing a shaky breath. 'I'd persuaded myself a huge wave was going to hurl us upside-down at the last moment.'

Tessa stepped past them, head up and shoulders back as though modelling for a fashion house. 'Now this is more like it. I wish I'd been posted here instead of Kyeness.'

Sally rolled her eyes and took Iris's arm as they followed the group away from the pier and towards the buildings. Tessa seemed to have already asked around about the layout of Lyness, for she held forth in a clear confident voice. 'It's hard to believe all this was built in such a short time. Anyway, the dance is being held in the recreation centre, which I don't think is too far.'

Sally didn't need a guide, though. She could see men and women flocking from all corners of the base to a large building. As they drew closer, the sounds of clarinet, horns and drums drifted out to greet them. Once inside, she couldn't fail to be impressed. A live band was set up on stage playing swing music, and tables occupied about a third of the auditorium closest to the main entrance. However, most of the room was devoted to dancing, and there was already a crowd of couples swaying and twirling to the music. With a flutter of anxiety, Sally looked for Adam among the couples but couldn't see him.

'Now, where's that handsome friend of yours?' Tessa raised herself onto tiptoes and scanned the room with the intensity Sally usually reserved for observing the ships from the signal station. They had shed their coats, and Sally could see Tessa wore an elegant frock in a pale shade of lilac that suited her colouring. Sally wore the smartest dress she owned, which was the one Iris had made for her from a lovely Liberty print. It was clearly a daytime dress, though, and she felt underdressed compared to some of the women present.

Iris squeezed her arm. 'You look lovely.' She lowered her voice. 'Far prettier than Tessa.'

Sally stared at her. Had she spoken her thoughts out loud?

Iris laughed. 'Honestly, you're going to have to learn not to display every thought in your face. You were looking at all the dresses with such an expression of horror, I could see exactly what you were thinking.'

'I feel so out of place.' Then Sally felt the heat of a blush creep across her face. 'I mean, I love this dress, and if you hadn't made it for me, I don't know what I'd have worn, but I feel like a country mouse in the big city for the first time.'

'You don't look like it. Anyway, I made your dress using exactly the same pattern as I used for mine, so that makes two of us.' Iris indicated her own dress, made from a pretty daisy print.

Sally managed a smile, grateful for what Iris was trying to do. Nevertheless, she couldn't help feeling that Iris would look classy dressed in overalls. Sally, on the other hand, felt overshadowed by Iris and Tessa.

'Ah, there he is!' Tessa's voice broke into Sally's thoughts. Sally glanced at her to see she was waving at someone in a corner near to the door. Looking that way, her heart skipped to see Adam.

'Over here, Adam,' Tessa called.

Whether Adam could hear her over the music and happy voices was debatable. However, Tessa's frantic waves must have captured his attention for he glanced up, gave a little wave and moved in their direction.

'I'm glad you could make it,' he said when he was close enough to be heard. 'The three of you look lovely. Always good to see some new faces at one of our dances.'

Tessa swatted his arm lightly. 'You are terrible, not inviting us. We had to wait for an invite from a friendly Lyness Wren.'

'Oh.' Adam shifted from foot to foot. 'I didn't think you'd want to come so far.' He shot a glance back at his table before adding as though in afterthought, 'I'm jolly glad you did, though.'

'Well, there's an easy way for you to make it up to us.' Tessa nodded towards the dance floor then gazed up at him through her eyelashes in a coy invitation that made Sally seethe inwardly.

Adam shot another glance back at his table. Following his gaze, Sally saw a tall, fashionably dressed young woman rising and accepting the arm of a young chief petty officer. He turned back to Tessa with a slight scowl before he seemed to recollect himself, and his expression cleared. 'Of course.' He offered Tessa his arm. 'Would you like to dance?'

Tessa made a show of hesitating, then took his arm. 'If you insist,' she said. As they headed towards the dance floor, the lively song the band was playing came to an end, and they struck up a slow, dreamy number. Tessa glanced over her shoulder and shot Sally a triumphant grin.

'Come on, let's find a table,' she said to Iris, determined not to let Tessa ruin her evening.

Iris cast a thoughtful look at the couple before following Sally to a table near the edge of the dance floor. 'So that's Adam,' she said, reminding Sally that Iris hadn't been with her at any of the times she had bumped into Adam.

'Isn't he wonderful?' Sally asked, pulling out a chair.

'Well, I—'

But Iris was interrupted by a cry of joy from the next table. 'Sally! It is Sally, isn't it?' It was Alice, one of the Wrens Sally had met at the Beehive, who had invited them to the dance. Sarah was also with her.

'Yes. How lovely to see you again.'

'Oh, I'm so glad you could make it. Come and join us.'

Sally, all too pleased for a distraction from the sight of Tessa in Adam's arms, took a seat next to Alice. She introduced Iris and in turn was introduced to Alice and Sarah's friends. She couldn't help letting her gaze drift over the dancers, though, and soon let Iris carry the conversation while she watched Tessa and Adam. If Tessa pressed herself any closer to Adam, she'd be wearing his uniform. She gazed up at him, fluttering her lashes and looked as though she would never let him go. Sally's only comfort was that Adam didn't appear to be equally enraptured. She shouldn't have doubted him, she knew. It was another sign that, deep down, Adam had feelings for Sally even if he hadn't admitted them to himself. Sally drifted into a daydream where it was she and Adam on the dance floor, swaying in time to a slow, seductive number, with Adam gazing lovingly at her, whispering the words she had longed to hear for so long.

'That's right, isn't it, Sally?'

'What?' Sally turned to Iris with a start.

Iris gave a sympathetic smile, as though she knew exactly where Sally's thoughts had been. 'I was telling Alice about the Heddles, and how welcoming the locals have been.'

'Oh, yes.' And Sally launched into an account of how the Heddles had made them feel at home when they were new to Orkney, gabbling a little in her embarrassment at being caught in a daydream. She could only hope that she hadn't been drooling when she'd looked at Adam.

Even so, when the song drew to a close, she felt her pulse speed up as she looked for Adam so she could attract his attention and let him know where she was sitting. He would ask her next, she was sure of it. Seeing Adam and Tessa not far away, she managed to catch Adam's eye and beckon them over to the table. Much to her annoyance, however, Tessa clapped her hands when the next number started.

'Oh, this is one of my favourite songs.' She caught Adam's hand and tugged him back towards the dancing. Of course, Adam had no choice but to comply and lead her back to the dance floor.

As it turned out, neither Iris nor Sally were obliged to sit this dance out. Three ratings who Alice evidently knew approached the table. 'Are you going to introduce us to your friends?' One of them asked.

Alice obliged, and the one she introduced as Sam turned to Sally. 'Would you like to dance?'

Sally was tempted to say no; she had no desire to dance with anyone other than Adam. The object of her affections, however, was at that moment twirling Tessa, who spun so fast that her dress fanned out, revealing her stocking tops. Raising her chin, Sally plastered a smile onto her face. 'I'd love to dance,' she replied. She would show Tessa she refused to be upset by her exhibition.

As it turned out, Sam was good company, and he chatted as they danced, telling Sally about his sweetheart who worked in the Land Army. Sally, relieved that Sam was already spoken for and making it clear he wanted nothing more from her than a dance, enjoyed the music and did her best to ignore Tessa's exultant eyes whenever they drew close. Sam was a good dancer, and Sally had fun whirling about the floor, her hair whipping in her face and her skirt swishing around her knees. By the time the song ended in a long, drawn-out chord, she was out of breath and ready to return to the table.

Iris, too, was pink in the cheeks and her face was lit with a beaming smile. 'And I thought cycling up Hellihole Road was good exercise,' she said, laughing as she downed a glass of lemonade. Sally was glad she was enjoying herself and putting her worries for Rob aside for the evening.

She sat straighter when Adam approached the table, leading Tessa, and smoothed her hair from her face. Surely now it was her turn to dance with Adam.

'That was fun,' Tessa said, sinking into the seat Adam pulled out for her, fanning her face. 'It was lovely to see you dancing, too,' she said to Iris and Sally. Then she addressed the others at the table. 'From all accounts, Iris is practically engaged to a chap serving in the Med, so it's wonderful she can join in here and have fun.'

Sally, glancing at Iris, saw her frown, and couldn't blame her. What business of Tessa's was it that allowed her to shout about Iris's personal life to a group of people they barely knew? She could only conclude that Tessa was letting Adam know Iris was unavailable.

'And you, too, Sally,' Tessa gave Sally a saccharine smile.

'I don't have a sweetheart,' Sally said.

'Oh, don't be shy. I saw you with that Italian the other day.' Tessa addressed the others at the table. 'A group of Italian POWs have arrived at Stromness, and Sally here is friends with one of them. Well, I say friends. They both looked completely smitten with each other.'

If Tessa's intention had been to create a stir, she got what she wanted. There was a ripple of interest around the table, and Sally was bombarded by comments and questions from all the Wrens.

'Ooh, how romantic,' Alice said, her eyes wide.

'How did you meet?' Sarah asked.

'Is he handsome? I always think Italian men are so good-looking, with their dark hair and eyes.'

'A prisoner, though. How daring.'

Sally couldn't let this last remark go unchallenged. 'He's not really a prisoner any more.' She shot a glare at Tessa. After all, she had corrected Tessa on the matter before.

It wasn't Tessa's referral to Aldo as a prisoner that upset her, though. It was the conviction that she was trying to convince Adam that Sally's affections were given elsewhere. She fielded the flurry of questions as best as she could then hastened to add: 'We're only friends, though. There's nothing more to it than that.'

She looked for Adam among the faces surrounding her, willing him to believe her instead of Tessa, trying to convey that her heart would always beat for him. When she finally saw him, she faltered. There was nothing in his expression beyond vague interest. No hurt, no jealousy. It was not the face of someone who had just heard that the woman of his dreams was involved with another man.

He trusts me, she tried to tell herself. *He's not jealous because he knows in his heart that I'm in love with him.* Even so, it would have been nice to see some concern in his eyes, some fear that his love might not be returned. While that level of trust might be reassuring in an established relationship, it came across as somewhat arrogant from a man who had never even asked her to walk out with him.

A pretty young woman approached the table then. Her glossy blonde hair was piled on each side of her head in fashionable victory rolls, and her make-up was flawless. Dressed in a scarlet frock that wouldn't look out of place on the cover of *Vogue*, she moved with the grace of a dancer.

Alice looked up and smiled. 'Hello, Nancy. Come to reclaim your fiancé? Sorry we've hogged him for so long.'

It took a long moment for Sally to comprehend the awful truth. She smiled at the other men at the table, expecting one of them to jump to his feet and apologise to Nancy. Even when Adam put his arm around her shoulders, she expected him to lead her to her fiancé. It was only when he kissed her cheek and said, 'How about a dance to make up for my neglect?' that the full weight of comprehension crashed down on her head.

Watching Nancy smile into Adam's eyes, her face aglow, Sally didn't know how she managed to keep her composure. She turned to Adam and arranged her features into a smile. 'I didn't know you were engaged. Congratulations!' While Nancy might belong on the cover of *Vogue*, Sally deserved an Oscar for that performance.

Adam looked self-conscious. 'I didn't want to say anything until I knew my parents had got my letter. I didn't want them to hear it from anyone else.'

Nancy smiled up at him. 'It's been a bit of a whirlwind. But when you know you've met the right person, you just know, don't you think?'

'Yes. You do.' Sally wanted to hate Nancy, but she couldn't. She didn't know her from Eve, and she seemed perfectly nice. She couldn't blame her for loving Adam. Nancy hadn't set out to hurt Sally, and had no idea she had crushed her hopes and dreams.

Chapter Ten

Watching Adam lead Nancy onto the dance floor, Sally wished she could leave; she didn't think she could hide her heartbreak for much longer. On the other hand, she didn't want to draw attention to herself. Anyway, where would she go? It wasn't as if she could make her escape back to the Wrennery – the drifter to Stromness wouldn't leave for another three hours.

A tap on her shoulder made her glance up and she saw Iris leaning over her. 'Fancy coming to get some fresh air?' Iris asked. 'All this smoke is making my eyes sting.'

Her throat too tight to speak, Sally nodded and rose, blessing Iris for her quick thinking. She held onto her friend's arm to prevent them from getting separated in the crush and made a beeline for the door. The moment they were through the blackout curtains and outside, she allowed her face to crumple and let the tears flow.

Iris's arm wrapped around her shoulders, and she was vaguely aware of being guided away from the door and down a more secluded side road. The music faded until she could hear nothing but the drum beat and the thrum of the double bass.

'I'm so sorry, Sally,' Iris said. 'Did you get no hint at all that Adam was attached?'

'No.' Her voice sounded croaky, as though she hadn't used it in weeks. She cleared her throat and tried again. 'I was so sure we were meant to be together.'

'I know.' Iris gave her a squeeze.

Sally fumbled in her pocket for a handkerchief and dabbed her eyes. 'I feel like such an idiot. I'm sure everyone must be laughing at me.'

'Of course they're not.'

'But everyone knows how I felt. Tessa's going to have a field day.'

'I wouldn't be so sure about that. Did you see her face?'

Sally shook her head. She had been too busy trying to hide her own reaction to spare a thought for Tessa.

'Well, let's just say she didn't react as graciously as you. She looked as though she'd been sucking lemons.'

Despite her heavy heart, Sally couldn't hold back a chuckle. 'Poor Tessa.'

'Poor Tessa indeed. It was obvious she was trying to make you look bad in front of Adam, so she got what she deserved. I'm just sorry you had to get hurt at the same time.'

'I don't understand, though. He hardly knows Nancy, and we were so right together. Why couldn't he choose me?' Although Sally tried to control the wobble in her voice, she couldn't stop her last words from ending on a wail.

'I know. It seems so unfair. I do understand how it feels, though. Just count yourself lucky you didn't mistakenly think he'd proposed to you. I had shown off my engagement ring to my mother before I found out what I thought was a proposal had been a mistake.'

Sally sniffed and blotted the last of her tears. 'I forgot about that.' Poor Iris had committed this blunder before Sally had met her, but Iris had shared the humiliating episode with her and Mary once they became friends. 'How long did it take you to get over it?'

'A while. It helped that I joined the WRNS and left home. It would have been worse if I'd been forced to watch George and Felicity billing and cooing at each other, not to mention having to explain to everyone that no, I wasn't engaged after all, but George had accidentally dropped Felicity's ring in front of me.'

Sally chuckled again. 'I'm sorry. But it does sound quite funny.'

'Oh, I don't mind now. I did meet Rob, after all, and he's wonderful. I can't imagine life without him.' She sighed, and now it was Sally's turn to be the comforter.

'He'll be fine, I'm sure of it. It won't be long before you're together again.'

'I hope so.'

They were silent for a while, and Sally tried to imagine letting go of her dreams of a life with Adam. The distant pounding of the music echoed down the street, and somewhere there was the drone of a generator. Then a thought struck that made her groan. 'Oh no.'

'What?'

'I've got leave coming up. My mum is bound to ask me if I've seen Adam. What am I supposed to tell her? She's just as invested in the relationship as I was.'

'You'll have to tell her the truth. Anyway, she might already have heard about Adam's engagement from his mother. I thought you said they know each other.'

'That's true. She'll be so disappointed. She'll want to know all about it, and I can't bear the thought of having to go through it all again.'

'I've got a suggestion.'

Sally gazed at Iris, whose pale face was clearly visible in the moonlight. There was such an air of confidence about her, it gave Sally hope. 'I'm all ears.'

'I think we're on leave at the same time, aren't we? The last two weeks in November?'

'That's right.'

'Well, my mother is staying near Helmsley, remember. Why don't we stick together and visit our mothers in turn? I could really use your support when I see my mother, and I can help you face yours. What do you say?'

Relief blossomed in Sally's chest. 'I think that's an excellent idea. It would be wonderful to have some moral support, and

I promise to do all I can to help you with your mother.' Then Sally remembered that Iris's home must be very different from hers. 'You won't mind sharing a room with me, will you? There isn't much space at home.'

'Don't be a chump. Of course I don't. Just promise we'll still be friends after you've met my mother.'

- -

The prospect of spending her leave with Iris was the bright spot that helped Sally through the next two weeks. No matter how much she told herself that her relationship with Adam had been all in her head, it was not easy to let go of her feelings.

'I wish I had been out with him and then broken up,' she said miserably to Iris as they watched the sun rise on one of their shared morning watches. 'At least I would have had some real memories to look back on. I just feel so foolish.'

'It will get easier, I promise. And there's nothing foolish in giving your heart to someone, even if your feelings weren't returned. Don't be too hard on yourself.'

Sally was more grateful than ever for Iris's friendship during this time. Iris understood how she felt, which helped enormously. Mary, too, was supportive. Sally had braced herself for Mary to tell her that this proved her romantic notions and belief in fate was all nonsense and had been surprised and grateful when Mary had said, 'I'm sorry, Sally. It's his loss. He'd have been far better off with you.' Even so, she hadn't liked talking about her suffering too much with Mary, mindful that Mary's own brush with heartbreak had been over a far more tragic reason, having lost her fiancé when the *Royal Oak* had been torpedoed.

Thankfully, she didn't share many watches with Tessa before the start of her leave. She dreaded the first watch, expecting more needling than usual in the light of Adam's news. She needn't have worried, though. Tessa was uncharacteristically quiet and they got through their watches by not speaking unless their duties required it.

'She'll be feeling a complete idiot,' Mary told her when she raised the subject with her two friends the day after her first watch with Tessa. 'She knows she made a fool of herself over Adam, with you watching. I expect she wants to forget about the whole experience.'

'You don't think I made a fool of myself too?' When Mary didn't answer immediately, Sally hung her head. 'Don't bother. You've given me my answer.'

'No – you've misunderstood. You didn't make a fool of yourself like Tessa did.'

'But I did in my own special way.'

'Now you're putting words in my mouth.' The corners of Mary's mouth twitched. 'I only hesitated because I was trying to work out how to answer. For the record, though, no, you didn't make a fool of yourself. You've known Adam for ages. More than enough time to work out if you had things in common and thought the two of you were suited. Tessa just decided to go for Adam to spite you, as far as I can tell.'

'If anything, Adam is to blame,' Iris said. 'He must have known how you felt and can't have failed to notice Tessa flinging herself at him at every given opportunity. He had plenty of opportunities to mention that he already had a sweetheart. But no, he enjoyed the attention of two pretty young women so didn't bother.'

It was this sage observation more than her friends' sympathy that helped Sally see that, given time, she would get over Adam. Iris was right. Even if he hadn't wanted word to get out about his engagement, he could have let her and Tessa know his affections were already promised elsewhere. It helped her see Adam in a new light and realise how selfish he was. Mary's comments also made her admit to herself that she didn't really know Adam. Over time, she had constructed a fantasy around him without really considering if they were suited. Still, even a fantasy was hard to let go, and she shed tears more than once when she thought no one was looking. She also hated the thought of disappointing her mother, who had suffered so much loss in her life. When Sally had first had her leave dates confirmed, she had been full of hope that she would finally have good news to share. Now she would only be the bearer of more bad news.

Accordingly, when Iris wanted to know where they would stay first, Sally voted for the Tredwicks' house. 'It's far more important for you to mend matters with your mother,' she said. 'Besides, with a few more days, maybe my mum will find out about Adam from his family.'

Therefore, when they arranged their travel documents, they both asked for tickets to Helmsley, and Iris wrote to her mother letting her know when they were due to arrive.

–

Iris grew quieter once their train crossed into England. The closer they drew to Yorkshire, the more pensive she became.

'Are you sure it's a good idea for me to stay?' Sally asked. 'I can easily get a train on to Whitby if you'd prefer to see your mother alone.'

'I'd really like you to come if you won't be too uncomfortable,' Iris said. 'I could use your support. But if you really can't face it, go on to Whitby, and I'll meet you in a few days.'

'Oh no, I'll come. I want to see how the other half lives.'

When they got out at Helmsley, carrying their bags, Iris looked around with a frown. 'The house is outside the town. I suppose we might have to hitch a lift or catch a bus.'

Unlike Stromness, however, there was a dearth of traffic. In Orkney, it was nearly always possible to hitch a ride from one of the many army trucks that made frequent trips between the various military bases. Here, the only wheeled vehicle Sally could see was a horse and cart pulled up outside the station, with an elderly man dressed in tatty tweeds leaning against it, reading a newspaper.

When Sally and Iris walked by, the man lowered his newspaper. 'Might one of you young lasses be Iris Tredwick?'

Sally's heart gave a lurch of happiness to hear a familiar accent. It suddenly hit her that here in Helmsley she wasn't so very far from the farm of her childhood.

'Oh, yes, that's me,' Iris said, sounding more upper class than ever in comparison. 'Did my mother send you?'

'Aye. I'm Jeremiah Parkin, the gardener. Hop aboard.'

They slung their bags into the cart, then climbed up to sit on the seat behind the driver. 'No wonder my mother didn't come to meet us,' Iris muttered to Sally as they arranged themselves to balance the cart. 'I can't see her being happy to be seen in anything apart from Daddy's Rolls.'

However low Iris had tried to keep her voice, Parkin had evidently heard. 'Oh, Mrs Tredwick uses the cart when needed. She's even learned to drive it.'

'She has?' Iris's surprise made Sally giggle. 'First she moves to the back of beyond, and now she's riding about in a horse and cart. I wonder if I should take her to a doctor.'

There was a green tartan rug on the seat beside Sally, and she unfolded it and spread it across their knees as Parkin urged the horse to a walk. Although the day was sunny, there was a decided chill to the air, and she was glad of the extra warmth. Once they left the town, they travelled for a couple of miles up a long slope, past fields and hedgerows. Something about the hypnotic beat of the horse's hoofs, combined with the low rumble of the wheels on the road, made Sally sleepy, and she found herself nodding off. She only woke fully when the cart turned down a narrow lane that descended into a wooded valley.

'So this is where my mother moved to,' Iris said, gazing around. 'It looks like the perfect place for her to get away from it all.'

It was certainly peaceful. The sun shone on trees at the peak of their autumnal glory, picking out shades of gold, copper and bronze. The leaves rustled in the gentle breeze, falling upon the cart like confetti. One curled beech leaf struck Sally on the nose, and she caught it with a cry of triumph. 'Yes! Now I'll have good luck.' Then she remembered the penny she had found. That hadn't brought her good luck but had heralded Tessa's arrival. She could only hope catching the leaf would be more effective than the penny.

Iris gave a small shake of the head, smiling. She refrained from comment, for which Sally was grateful.

After a while, Sally thought the area looked familiar. 'Hang on, I think I've been here before. This looks like Rievaulx,' she said.

'That's right,' Parkin said. He pointed ahead. 'The abbey's a little farther on.' He guided the horse into a driveway. 'We're stopping right here.'

'How wonderful. We used to come here for days out, sometimes. The ruins are so romantic.' She gazed around, entranced, as the cart rattled up a cobbled driveway and into a wide courtyard. At the far end stood a stone house which framed two sides of the yard. A stable block stood on the third side. Looking back down the drive, Sally could see a tantalising glimpse of crumbling walls nestling farther down the valley.

Grabbing her bag, she scrambled out of the cart and turned to Iris. 'Why did you never tell me your mother was in Rievaulx? I have so many happy memories of this place.'

Iris's cheeks, already pink from the ride atop the open cart, turned a deeper shade of red. 'I'd never heard of the place and didn't know how to pronounce it. How do you say it again?'

'Reevo.' Sally giggled. 'It is a funny name. French, I think.'

'What's so special about the place?'

'There's a ruined abbey in the bottom of the valley. We used to come for picnics before the war. I hope we'll be able to visit while we're here. It's stunning. Even more beautiful than Fountains Abbey, I think.'

Iris raised her eyebrows. 'Then I'll make a point of visiting. I have heard of Fountains Abbey, and always wanted to see it'

She hefted her bag. 'A shame Mary couldn't come. I expect she would have loved to draw the remains of an abbey.'

Sally nodded. 'She'd love it.' Then she turned to study the house. Now she came to look at it properly, it struck her how huge it was. 'You could fit my mum's house into this ten times at least. Is Tredwick Place as big as this?'

'Oh, it's much bigger.'

Sally stared at her in amazement. Only now did it hit her that Iris would consider the house in Whitby little more than a hovel compared to the large residences she was used to. She hoped Iris wouldn't look down on her when she saw how her family lived. She had never kept her humble background a secret, although she had never fully grasped just how wealthy Iris's family was. But if her family home was even bigger than this, it must be palatial indeed.

When the front door opened, and a tall, elegant woman who was an older version of Iris emerged, Sally knew a moment of trepidation. While Iris came from a wealthy background, she had spent the last two years enduring the discomforts of the Wrennery in Stromness without complaint. Yet she had often spoken of her mother as being highly conscious of her station in life. How would Mrs Tredwick react when faced with a visitor who had more in common with the gardener than her daughter?

'Wish me luck,' Iris muttered, then hurried to greet her mother.

Sally hung back, forgetting her own unease in her concern for Iris. She knew her friend had dreaded this moment, and she fervently hoped the two Tredwick women would be able to use this visit to make peace with one another. She waited until Iris had kissed her mother's cheek, then approached, praying Mrs Tredwick wouldn't sneer or banish her to the servants' quarters.

Iris placed a hand on Sally's shoulder. 'This is Sally Hartley, Mother. One of my best friends in Orkney. Sally, this is my mother, Letitia Tredwick.'

'It's lovely to meet one of Iris's friends.' Letitia held out a hand.

Startled, Sally shot Iris a glance then shook Letitia's hand, barely quelling the impulse to curtsy. From the tales Iris told, Sally hadn't expected Letitia to treat her with warmth and courtesy. 'Pleased to meet you. Thank you for letting me stay.'

'It's a pleasure. Iris has told me how hard you all work, so I do hope you make yourself at home and enjoy your visit.'

Sally followed Letitia and Iris over the threshold and into a spacious hallway. A plump, middle-aged woman stepped forward to take their coats.

Iris gave a cry of joy. 'Mrs Webb! I didn't know you were here as well.' She turned to Sally. 'Mrs Webb is our housekeeper from Tredwick Place.'

Mrs Webb gave Iris an indulgent smile. 'I couldn't leave your mother to fend for herself in this land of northern heathens.' She turned to Sally. 'Shall I take your coat, miss?'

Iris chuckled. 'Let me introduce you to my friend. This is Sally Hartley, a northern heathen.'

'Nice to meet you, Mrs Webb.' Although Sally had learned to imitate Iris's more southern manner of speaking, she couldn't resist emphasising her native accent.

Mrs Webb clapped a hand to her mouth. 'Lord bless me. I do beg your pardon, miss. No offence intended.'

'None taken,' Sally said with a laugh.

'Let me show you to your rooms,' Letitia said, once the girls had been relieved of their coats, and led them upstairs.

'This is a lovely house,' Iris observed as they crossed the thickly carpeted upstairs landing. 'How are you finding life up here?'

'I must say, I've enjoyed it more than I thought I would.' Letitia opened a heavy wooden door and ushered the girls inside. 'It's done me good to get away from Tredwick Place for a time. Until I came here, I hadn't realised how oppressive I was finding it, living in a house with painful reminders of your father around every corner. Staying somewhere new has given me a chance to think and decide what I'm going to do with my life now I'm all alone.'

'Not all alone. You've got me.'

'I know. But you can't call your time your own now you're a Wren.' Letitia drew a deep breath, and Sally was surprised to see she looked nervous. 'Anyway, even when the war's over, you'll have your own life to live. You and... and Rob.'

Iris's eyes widened; she opened and closed her mouth twice before finally saying, 'I suppose that's true. Well, I'm glad you've found the change of scene helpful.' Then she changed the subject, seeming to grasp at the first comment that popped into her head. 'This is a lovely room.' She pointed at the huge bed that was draped in a luxurious eiderdown that Sally, exhausted from hours of sitting on uncomfortable train seats, longed to sink upon. 'That bed looks so comfortable, you'll have to drag me out of it tomorrow.'

'Oh, this is Sally's room. Yours is next door. It's a little smaller than this, but I thought Sally should have the bigger room, being the visitor.'

'Oh my goodness.' Sally gazed around in awe, scarcely able to believe her eyes. She turned her back on the bed, fighting the urge to fling herself into its cloud-like comfort, and took in the large bay window with a cosy armchair arranged to make the most of the view, an oak dressing table with silver-backed brushes and a jar of cotton wool arranged upon it, and the stack of novels set upon the bedside table. 'This is too much. Iris, you have this room.'

'Absolutely not. Mother's right – you're our guest.' Iris took Sally's bag from her hand and placed it on the trunk at the foot of the bed. 'There. I'll go and put my bag in my room.' She dashed out before Sally could stop her.

'I'll leave you girls to freshen up.' Letitia paused, her hand on the doorknob. 'Dinner's at seven. No need to dress – it's just the three of us.' Then she was gone, leaving a cloud of expensive-smelling perfume in her wake.

Sally waited for a moment until she was sure Letitia wasn't going to return and tell her she'd made a huge mistake, and bundle her up to a distant attic room. Only when she heard Letitia speaking to Mrs Webb downstairs did she give in to her longing, kick off her shoes and fall onto the bed. She sank deep into the eiderdown, feeling it cradle her aching muscles, and groaned in bliss.

The sound of a soft step at the doorway made her sit bolt upright, but she flopped back down when she saw it was Iris. 'You're too late. Now I've tested the bed, you're going to have to fight me for this room.'

'Don't worry. I'm perfectly happy with mine. Got space for another?'

'Only if I don't have to move.'

Sally felt the bed dip as Iris sat beside her.

When Iris spoke, Sally wasn't sure if she was speaking to her or talking to herself. 'Do you think Mother's acting strange?'

'How would I know? I've never met her before.' Then, treading carefully, Sally added, 'I was surprised by her welcome, though. From what you've always told me, I half expected to be treated like a servant.'

'Exactly! Mother would never let me mix with your sort before.'

'My sort?' Sally was used to Iris's habit of blurting the first thing that popped into her head, but she wasn't prepared to let her get away with a comment as insulting as that. Or maybe it was seeing Iris so at home in this huge house that made her extra sensitive and suddenly wary of her friend, wondering how she would react when she saw her mother's tiny house in Whitby.

The mattress bounced as Iris shifted beside her, and her face appeared in Sally's field of vision, scarlet cheeks contrasting violently with the white ceiling. 'I'm so sorry, Sally. That was shockingly rude. You're one of my best friends, and you've got to believe I never think of you as different or... or beneath me. I just trotted out the line my mother always used to come out with when I was little and wanted to play with the local children.'

She looked so contrite, Sally's heart melted. 'It's all right. I know you didn't mean it.'

'I know, but there's no excuse. Please say you forgive me.'

'I forgive you.' Sally dragged herself into a sitting position and leaned against the headboard. 'Now tell me what's bothering you about your mother.'

Iris settled herself to sit cross-legged at the foot of the bed, looking relieved. 'I've never known her so accepting before. I'm not just talking about you. Did you notice how she mentioned Rob by name?'

'Well, yes. He is your sweetheart, after all.'

'I know. But the way she said it, she seemed to accept we would be together. And she called him Rob, not "that mechanic". Do you think she's ill?'

'She didn't look ill. I think you need to speak to her. Isn't it possible she's had a change of heart?'

Iris snorted. 'My mother?'

'Yes. What's so outrageous about that? You've changed a good deal since I first met you. Isn't your mother allowed to change too?'

Iris picked at the fringe on the blanket folded at the end of the bed. 'You're right, of course. I suppose I'm so used to the way she always dominated my life – passing judgement on anything or anyone she deemed unsuitable. I never thought she might change. Daddy was always the voice of moderation in our family, so after he died... well, I thought she would just get worse. She certainly seemed to, at first.'

Sally thought back to her own experience of loss. 'Your father's death must have turned your mother's life upside-down. I mean, I know it was terrible for you, too, but you had your work and friends to see you through. Your mother, though... if she's anything like my mother, her whole world would have revolved around her family. With you away, she's had to face being alone for the first time in her life.' She certainly knew that for her own mother, her father had been everything. That was why she had never considered marrying again, even though she had been a widow for many years now.

'I never looked at it that way before.' Iris pulled the blanket onto her lap and started to braid the fringe, seemingly unaware she was doing so. 'When she as good as threw me out of the house after the memorial service, I decided that was the way she would be from now on. Maybe I was wrong, maybe that was just how she reacted to her grief.'

Sally nodded. 'As she said, she's had time to take stock of her life now. You should take her at her word and try to mend your relationship with her.'

'I'll try. Things can't get any worse between us, after all.'

'Good.' Sally lay back down and let her head sink into the pillows. 'Now, I'm going to rest for half an hour before I have to get ready for dinner. I swear my body thinks I haven't left that wretched train. I can still feel it jolting.'

'Me too. Well, I'll leave you to it, then. I'm going to take a bath.'

'Just one question,' Sally called after Iris before she could leave the room. 'When your mother said not to dress for dinner, please tell me she doesn't expect us to eat in our birthday suits.'

Chapter Eleven

Despite her good intentions, it was nearly an hour before Sally found the wherewithal to drag herself from the most comfortable bed she had ever known. With only a few minutes to get ready before dinner, she made her way to the bathroom for a quick wash and then dashed back to the bedroom to dress. Having been reassured that 'not dressing' simply meant not donning evening wear – for which she was profoundly grateful, not possessing anything that could pass as an evening gown – she dressed in the tweed skirt Iris had made her for Christmas and her smartest blouse and cardigan. Although she tried to be quick, by the time she had powdered her face, applied her precious Yardley lipstick and brushed her hair into smooth waves, a glance at her watch before she left the room told her she was ten minutes late.

She could hear Iris's voice downstairs, so she hurried down, prepared to make her apologies. Following the voices, she approached an open doorway to the right of the front door, through which she could hear the crackle of a fire and see the glow of flames reflected in a glass cabinet. Drawing breath to announce herself, she stopped when she heard what Iris's mother was saying.

'I'm afraid I've been an awful fool, Iris. I do hope you can forgive me for what I said after the memorial service.'

Sally froze, not wanting to interrupt the conversation she knew was long overdue between mother and daughter. She tried to withdraw discreetly, only to step on a loose floorboard which creaked underfoot. Knowing she must have been heard, she strode into the room – a pretty parlour with large chintz armchairs arranged around an inglenook fireplace, watercolours on the walls showing views of Rievaulx Abbey in different seasons, a gramophone in one corner and display cabinets full of china figurines. In fact, she rather suspected Iris would call it a drawing room rather than a parlour. 'I'm sorry I'm late,' she said. 'My room is so lovely I didn't want to leave. I hope I'm not interrupting.'

'Not at all,' Letitia said with a gracious smile. 'I expect you must be hungry. Shall we go through to the dining room?'

Sally nodded, and Letitia led the way through a set of double doors and into a room dominated by a long, highly polished table with matching chairs. Three places were set at one end, and a vase filled with a bunch of dried lavender lent a splash of colour and a sweet fragrance to the room. There were French windows along the outer wall; Sally supposed they must lead to the garden although they were covered with thick blackout curtains.

'Do sit down,' Letitia said. 'I'll let Mrs Webb know we're ready to eat.'

Sally took her seat, and said to Iris in a low voice, 'I'm sorry I interrupted.'

Iris was smiling. 'It's all right. We had a good talk before you arrived. I think everything's going to be fine. I'll tell you all about it later.'

The meal was a happy affair. It was only now, seeing Iris looking so relaxed, that Sally realised just how tense she had been on the journey. It was good to see her talking to her mother with far more ease than she had done earlier. The lines of anxiety on Letitia's brow had cleared, and she spoke of her activities in Helmsley and the friends she had made in the Women's Institute. It seemed that Letitia had made herself a life in Yorkshire and was finding contentment in contributing to the war effort by things like fruit picking, making pickles and organising events for evacuees. In many ways, it reminded Sally of the work of the women in Stromness, who organised the weekly fourpenny bash for servicemen and women, ran knitting drives to make socks for sailors and collected newspapers and silver paper. Sally was overjoyed for Iris that her mother was getting on so well.

'I have to say,' Iris said, scraping up the last of the stewed damsons with her spoon, 'When I heard you were moving into cousin Peter's house, I thought you might be lonely away from your life at home. I'm glad to hear you've been so active.'

'Actually, I've got my sister to thank for that.'

Iris dropped her spoon with a clatter. 'Aunt Sybil?' Sally couldn't blame her for being surprised. Iris had met Letitia's sister for the first time only the previous year. Sybil had been estranged from her family since the Great War, when she had married a man from a lower class in defiance of her father. She had been widowed soon after, and Iris had always assumed she lived in poverty. It had taken a chance remark from her father to suggest that there was more to the story, and she had gone to visit Sybil in York, finding a woman who had carved out a respectable life for herself as a teacher. It was that visit that had influenced Iris to believe she could have a happy life with Rob even if she had to disobey her own father.

Letitia nodded. 'I must admit, when Peter told me this house was available, a big attraction of coming to Yorkshire was the thought that I would be within easy reach of Sybil. I was very lonely when I first came here but eventually I swallowed my pride and went to see her. She helped me see that although the pain of losing your father would never leave me, it would get easier. And she told me it was up to me how the rest of my life would turn out. I could mourn for ever or make an effort to involve myself in life and do some good. She spoke a lot of sense.'

Iris gave a reminiscent smile. 'I'm glad you've seen her. She really helped me put my life in perspective.'

'She did the same for me. The visit gave me pause for thought. Above all, she helped me recognise that times are changing. That I should be more accepting of people who come from different backgrounds. She suffered – we all suffered – when she was forced to choose between the man she loved and the father who told her he was unsuitable. I lost a sister thanks to that. But I won't lose a daughter.'

Letitia blinked, and Sally was embarrassed to see she was crying. She got the feeling that both Letitia and Iris had forgotten she was there – Iris was frozen in her place, her own eyes suspiciously bright. Sally would have left if there was a way of excusing herself unobtrusively. As it was, all she could do was examine the willow pattern on her plate as though she was utterly fascinated by it and deaf to everything being spoken around her.

'You won't lose me,' Iris said, her voice husky.

Letitia reached across the table and grasped Iris's hand. 'I can't tell you how sorry I am that I tried to make you stop seeing Rob. I hope you can both forgive me.'

'Of course I forgive you. I'm sure I speak for Rob, too.'

'I do hope I'll be able to meet him soon. He sounds wonderful.'

'He is.'

Sally chose that moment to sneeze, and fumbled in her pocket for her handkerchief, cheeks burning.

'What must you think of us?' Letitia told her. 'I am sorry for excluding you.'

'I don't mind.'

'Tell me a little about yourself. Are there any young men you have your eye on?'

Sally's heart dropped. In the excitement of going on leave, while she hadn't managed to forget about Adam and his unexpected engagement, she had at least been able to push him to the back of her mind. 'No, not any more. There was someone but I just found out he is engaged to someone else.'

'Oh dear. I'm sorry to hear that. But a bright, pretty girl like you shouldn't have a problem sweeping any man off his feet.'

'I think I'm going to concentrate on my work for a while.' At the moment, she couldn't bear to think of being in love with anyone other than Adam. She had spent years thinking of him as her future partner in life; she couldn't shift her affections to another man simply because Adam was spoken for.

'That's very sensible. No need to rush into anything.'

Letitia rose and collected the dishes. 'Well, I'm sure you girls are tired after your long journey. You probably want to turn in.'

'Oh no.' Sally picked up the glasses. 'We'll help with the dishes. Many hands make light work, that's what my mum always says.'

Iris nodded and reached for the jug of custard. 'Anyway, it won't be good for the digestion to go to bed straight after a meal like that.'

'That's very kind of you,' Letitia said. 'I must say, I've had to get used to many disagreeable chores since the start of the war, but doing the dishes is my least favourite.'

In the event, they discovered that Mrs Webb had already cleaned the saucepans and tidied the kitchen before retiring to her own room, so there was not much left for the three women to do once they had washed up their own plates and dishes. It was therefore not long before Sally and Iris were able to retire.

Sally wasn't surprised when Iris followed her into her room and shut the door behind her. 'I can't believe the change in my mother,' she said, sitting upon the dressing table stool and regarding Sally with shining eyes. 'I've been dreading this meeting for so long, and now she's nothing but accepting of me and Rob.'

'What did she say before I interrupted?'

Iris gave a little laugh. 'You should have seen me. I was all ready to go into battle and tell her nothing she could say would ever persuade me to leave Rob. But as soon as I entered the drawing room, she was full of apologies, telling me she never wanted to see me estranged from the family in the same way as Sybil. That she was sorry I hadn't fallen for a richer man, because she knew money would make our lives easier, but she respected my choice. And when I told her how wonderful Rob was and about his plans for starting up a boatyard after the war, she said she trusted my judgement and that I wouldn't have fallen in love with a man who was unworthy of me.' Iris laughed. 'Unworthy. Such an old-fashioned sentiment. But I know what she means.'

'I'm so happy for you,' Sally said. She was conscious of a twinge of jealousy, too. Iris had met Rob on the boat to Orkney and it hadn't taken long for them to become a couple. Why was it that love had come so easily to Iris, yet it seemed impossible for Sally? She hated herself for feeling that way, though, and was genuinely happy that Iris's mother had accepted the relationship.

'Mother even offered to reinstate my allowance,' Iris said.

'That's good news.'

Iris shook her head. 'I told her to keep it for now. I don't want it to come between me and Rob. Or make it awkward with you and Mary, come to that. I was terribly spoilt when I joined the WRNS and having so much money meant I wasn't really aware of the true value of things. This is going to sound silly, but I felt so proud of myself last Christmas that I was able to plan my spending enough to stretch to making you all presents and being able to help with the prisoner-of-war parcels. I wouldn't have thought twice about it with access to my allowance. I'm not saying I'll never ask Mother for help with big things, but I am enjoying planning my finances.'

Sally was impressed. 'I suppose I should stop wishing for a diamond necklace from you on my birthday then,' she said.

Iris laughed. 'I'll get you one when Rob makes his first million.'

'It's good to see you so happy with Rob. If only the war would end so we could get on with our lives.'

Iris's face clouded. 'I know. There's no sign of it being over any time soon. I'm making plans for a life with Rob when—' She bit her lip. She didn't need to say any more. Sally knew she was thinking of all the lives lost so far and how there was no guarantee any of them would still be around when the war ended. She wished she could assure Iris that all would be well but her unswerving belief in destiny had been shaken by Adam's news. If she had been wrong about him, who could say what else she was wrong about?

Iris straightened her shoulders and gave a smile that looked a little strained. 'Still, I'm going to count my blessings. We are all alive right now, and I've made peace with my mother. I should be happy about that and try not to worry too much about the future.'

'Good plan.'

'Anyway, now I've sorted out my problems far quicker than expected, we can spend more time solving yours. Tomorrow we decide how to tell your mother about Adam's terrible taste in women.'

—

Sally enjoyed her time with Iris's mother far more than she'd anticipated. Letitia was busy with the Women's Institute in Helmsley, meaning she regularly took the horse and cart to the town, leaving the girls to their own devices. Sally and Iris took long walks to explore the area, including one around the ruined abbey. The sun shone, and after the treeless expanse of Orkney, Sally enjoyed being in the tranquil woodland. With Iris not needing Sally's help to make peace with her mother, Sally had tentatively suggested leaving and going to Whitby alone. Iris wouldn't hear of it.

'You're obviously worried about what to say to your mother, and I want to support you. I hope she won't be as disappointed as you fear, but if she is, I'll be there. I won't leave you to sort out your troubles alone. Besides, you've earned a holiday. Let's make the most of these few days of peace so that you're fully rested and able to face your mother with a clear mind.'

Sally saw the sense in that and so didn't repeat her suggestion. It didn't stop her fretting about it, though. Another worry, although not one she could voice to Iris, was how Iris would view the tiny house in Whitby. Even had they not lost the farm, the much larger farmhouse was cramped and basic in comparison with the huge, comfortable house in Rievaulx. She had no fear of Iris mocking her or looking down on her, but it was hard not to look at the comfort Iris clearly considered normal and hope her friend wouldn't be miserable staying with her in Whitby. No matter how much she told herself Iris would take it in her stride, just as she had the basic conditions in the Wrennery, this would be the first time her friend saw the house Sally had grown up in since the family had lost their farm. While Sally had never tried to hide her background from Iris, it was one thing for Iris to have heard of her hard childhood; it would be quite another for her to see the Hartleys' tiny house.

Therefore, by the time the day arrived for Sally and Iris to take the train to Whitby, Sally was more nervous about Iris being there than she was about telling her mother about Adam. During the journey, Iris's obvious enjoyment of the scenery helped Sally push her worries to the back of her mind. After all, it was the first time in ages Sally had been there herself, and she enjoyed pointing out the places they passed and telling Iris about them. Yet when the train puffed into the station at Whitby, her fears returned, clouding her mind as surely as the smoke that obscured the platform.

Chapter Twelve

The wail of the gulls swooping and diving overhead greeted them as they stepped out onto the platform. 'Funny,' said Iris, gazing up, 'I know we have gulls in Stromness, but I don't notice them as much there. They're so loud, I can hardly hear myself think.'

'I think they come after the fishing boats when they're unloading,' Sally told her. 'It's the sound of home.'

'Will anyone come to meet us?' Iris asked.

Sally shook her head. 'Mum will still be at work, and Uncle Ted has trouble walking. It's not far, though. Only about a ten-minute walk.'

It was a surprise, therefore, that when they had surrendered their tickets to the ticket inspector and left the platform, Sally saw a tall, thin man with greying sandy hair grinning at them from beside the main entrance. 'Uncle Ted! I didn't expect you to come and meet us.'

Uncle Ted, who was leaning heavily on a walking stick, shifted his grip so he could greet Sally with a one-armed hug. 'You don't think I was going to miss a moment of your leave, do you?'

'But did you walk all this way?'

Ted grinned, looking pleased with himself. 'Now your mother's been earning more in her new job, she encouraged me to see a different doctor. He's given me some exercises to strengthen my back, and it's been slow, but I'm making a steady improvement.'

'But why didn't you tell me? None of your letters mention it.'

'I wanted to surprise you.'

'You certainly did that.' Then, recollecting herself, Sally turned to Iris who had been hovering behind her. 'Uncle, this is my friend Iris.'

Ted held out his hand. 'Pleased to meet you. Any friend of Sally's is welcome here, and she's told us so much about you and Mary that it already feels like we're good friends.'

As they walked off, Sally watched her uncle with keen eyes. While he was still evidently in pain – he wasn't able to hide the slight wince when he stumbled a little over an uneven paving slab – he was moving with much greater ease than Sally had seen since his accident. She took his free arm, her heart welling with hope and happiness. Compared to Ted's health, her own problems faded into insignificance. Whatever happened with her mother, she knew this would be a good holiday.

Uncle Ted was still unable to walk fast, so the journey that would usually take Sally ten minutes took nearly twice the time. Once they turned off the main road and into the dingy street leading to her home, Sally took a few sidelong glances at Iris. Iris, however, seemed happy to be out of the train and was looking about her with an open, interested expression. There was no sign of dismay at the prospect of spending the next few days in a narrow, terraced house.

When they turned into Gray Street, Sally saw it looked much the same as ever. It being now about four in the afternoon, children in school uniform were playing in the street, making the most of the last of the daylight before being called inside for their tea. When they came to the house with the red door about halfway down the road, Sally was pleased to note that the steps were freshly whitewashed with a pot of pansies beside them. She had feared her mother would be unable to keep the house clean and tidy without her help, but all looked in order from the outside.

'Here we are,' Ted said, leaning heavily on his cane to help him up the steps. He was looking tired now, so Sally said, 'I'll show Iris my room, then I'll put on some tea. Why don't you go and sit down, Uncle?'

'I won't say no to a nice spot of tea. I'll check on the fire.' So saying, Ted shuffled down the dark, narrow hall to the back room.

'This way,' Sally said to Iris, leading her up the steep staircase. 'I hope you don't mind sharing a room. I'm in the back bedroom. My mum has the front bedroom, and Ted sleeps downstairs in the front room. We'll be a bit cramped after the lovely house in Rievaulx, I'm afraid.'

'It'll be fine.' To her credit, Iris sounded perfectly happy to be there. 'I've been looking forward to meeting your family. Ted seems nice.' Then, as Sally opened her bedroom door and ushered her inside, she exclaimed, 'Oh, this is so pretty.'

Her mother must have taken a lot of time to make Sally's room look welcoming. There was the narrow bed under the window where it had always stood. The floor was covered with the same worn brown lino she remembered, with a new brightly coloured rag-weave rug on the floor beside the bed that would be much warmer underfoot. There was also a small bedside cabinet that Sally had never seen before. It was obviously second-hand, as it was scratched in places, however the golden wood was polished to a high shine, as were the neat brass handles on each drawer. In pride of place on top of the cabinet stood a little cut-glass vase holding a dainty bunch of heather. Squeezed between the foot of her bed and the wall stood a low truckle bed. Both beds were covered with pretty patchwork quilts – a vast improvement from the faded and threadbare candlewick bedspread that had previously covered Sally's bed.

Sally squeezed through the door, which couldn't open fully with the truckle bed in the way. After a pause, she dropped her bag upon the spare bed. 'You take the bed by the window,' she said to Iris. 'I did have the best room at your mother's house, after all.' She sat on the truckle bed and admired the quilt. It was made from squares of green and white fabric, sprigged with roses and daisies. 'Mum's certainly been busy. I never thought my room could look this nice.'

Iris was examining a little picture frame on the windowsill that Sally hadn't noticed until now. 'Did you find this four-leaf clover?' she asked.

'Yes, but we always kept it pressed in the family bible.' Sally knelt on the bed beside Iris to inspect the frame. It looked like a photo frame, made of a simple pine wood. A piece of cardboard had been mounted behind the glass – Sally was sure if she turned it over she would see it was cut from a cereal box. Stuck in the centre was her four-leaf clover. 'I found it when I was fourteen, the summer I left school. I had no idea Mum framed it.'

'Did it bring you luck?'

'I thought so. The day after I found it, I got my job at the fishmongers, meaning at least I didn't have to work gutting fish at the dockside.'

Iris wrinkled her nose. 'Definitely good luck, then.'

'And, of course, I wouldn't have met Adam if I hadn't got that job, because his sister worked there. I thought it was the luckiest thing that ever happened to me.'

Iris squeezed her arm. 'Just because Adam didn't turn out to be the right one for you, it doesn't mean you won't find someone else.'

'Maybe.' She sighed and turned away from the little frame and started to take clothes out of her bag. 'I thought I was getting over him, but returning here brings the feelings back. I spent so much time in this room, dreaming of the life Adam and I would have, and now it's all turned to ashes.' She crossed to the rickety wardrobe that stood opposite the window. Even the creaky hinge seemed to be a reminder of her girlhood dreams. She hung her clothes on the hangers, setting some aside for Iris's use. 'Anyway,' she said, making an effort to be more cheerful,

'I said I was going to concentrate on my work, and I meant it. I'm going to enjoy being home for a few days, then it's back to duty. Our work is far more important than having sweethearts.'

Iris nodded. 'I can't believe I wanted to marry to avoid doing war work,' she said. 'Being a Wren has taught me so much. If I'd married George, I'd have gone from being a spoilt daughter to being a spoilt wife and I'd never have learned to stand on my own two feet. Don't get me wrong – I've never felt so humiliated as by the mistake I made with George, and I felt awful for ages afterwards. It was the best thing that could have happened to me in the long run, though. Assuming we both make it through the war unscathed, I'm really looking forward to building a life with Rob in Orkney.'

'You definitely want to stay there, then?'

'Oh yes. Of course, it will seem much emptier once all the troops move out, but I love the community there, the way everyone pitches in to help each other out. I've decided to set up as a dressmaker. I've already got a long list of Elspeth's friends who have said they can't wait to order new clothes when rationing is over. It's a far cry from my dreams of being lady of the manor, but I think I'll get far more satisfaction out of making clothes and feeling I'm contributing to the household finances.'

'It sounds like a wonderful life.' Sally couldn't help but feel envious that Iris seemed to have her future worked out when Sally didn't even know what she could do for a living after the war.

Her stomach rumbled – a sharp reminder that she was supposed to be making the tea. 'Anyway, I'll leave you to unpack. I nearly forgot I promised Uncle Ted I'd make us tea.'

'I'll help.'

The girls went down to the kitchen, and Sally filled the kettle and put it on the stove while Iris hunted through the cupboards for cups and saucers and placed them on a tray. While they waited for the kettle to boil, Sally showed Iris the tiny bathroom that was built onto the back of the house. 'It gets pretty cold in the winter,' she said, 'although it's better than a tub in front of the living room fire. At least we have a decent landlord who was prepared to go to the expense of building it. This house is much better than some of the others hereabouts.'

'It's fine,' Iris said, obviously picking up on Sally's unspoken apology. 'It looks nicer than the bathroom at the Wrennery.'

Some of the tension in Sally's stomach uncoiled. She had let her awe at the obvious wealth of Iris's family get the better of her and had done her friend an injustice. She should have trusted Iris to accept Sally's home and not look down on her. After all, with Iris's tendency to blurt what was uppermost in her mind, she would have said if she wasn't happy to stay here.

Now the only obstacle to an enjoyable visit was breaking the news about Adam's engagement to her mother.

As if summoned by Sally's thoughts, her mother chose that moment to arrive. Sally was just carrying the tea tray through to the back room when the front door opened, and her mother stepped inside. Sally hurried to put the tray down upon the dining table before going back into the hall to greet her mother with a hug.

'How wonderful to see you,' her mother said, before releasing Sally and removing her coat and scarf. 'It feels like an age since you were last here.' Then it was Sally's turn to answer questions about the journey while Iris hovered in the background.

Finally, her mother looked up and smiled at Iris. 'Aren't you going to introduce me to your friend?'

Sally beckoned Iris forward. 'This is Iris Tredwick.'

'It's lovely to meet you, Iris. I've heard so much about you.'

'Not all bad, I hope,' Iris said, laughing. 'I'm pleased to meet you, Mrs Hartley. Thank you for letting me stay.'

'Call me Annie.' Sally's mum then enveloped Iris in a hug; Sally had to turn away to hide her smile at Iris's startled look. Evidently she was unused to being hugged by strangers.

When her mother released Iris, she turned to Sally. 'Was that a fresh pot of tea you were carrying? Be a dear and pour me a cup while I have a quick wash.'

A few minutes later, they were all sitting around the fire, drinking tea and nibbling Garibaldi biscuits. They had closed the blackout curtains and switched on the lights, and soon the room was warm and cosy. While Uncle Ted dozed in his armchair, the women chatted about the journey and how Iris and Sally had enjoyed their stay in Rievaulx.

Eventually, Annie put down her cup with a sigh and stretched her slippered feet closer to the hearth. 'There's nowt like a cup of strong tea to perk you up after a long day.' She addressed Iris. 'I'm right glad to meet you, Iris. Sally told me all about you in her letters and how you helped her when she had her accident in that storm. I'm glad I can finally thank you in person for all you did.'

Iris's cheeks turned pink. 'It's nothing she wouldn't have done for me had our positions been reversed.'

'Well, I'm very glad you were there for her.' After a brief pause, Annie added, 'Sally tells me you've met a nice young man in Orkney.'

'That's right. He's in the navy and works on a minesweeper.' Iris's face clouded. 'They've been sent overseas now. It's such a worry.'

Annie's face creased in sympathy. 'Sally told me that, too. I'm sorry you and so many families around the world are going through this.' Then she smiled at Sally. 'Maybe it was a blessing in disguise that Adam broke his leg not long after joining the navy. It looks like he's going to be based on land for the duration of the war. Fate must be smiling on the two of you.'

Sally tensed and caught Iris's grimace. She had hoped her mother would already have heard of Adam's engagement from Mrs Clark, and now it was clear she hadn't. Still, putting it off would only make the tale harder in the long run. Putting down her teacup, she smoothed her skirt over her knees then said,

'Actually, Mum, I've got some news that might surprise you.' She fought to keep her tone light.

'Oh? Something about Adam?'

Sally nodded, needing to swallow to relieve the tightness in her throat. Before she could get the words out, Annie gave a beaming smile and said, 'Has he asked you out at last? I knew it must be a sign when he was posted to Orkney.'

Sally had to stop this now. 'No, Mum. In fact, he's engaged. To another Wren. I met her a couple of weeks ago,' she added before Annie could interrupt. 'She's very nice. I'm sure they'll both be happy together.'

Annie gazed at Sally, and couldn't have looked more taken aback had Sally spoken in fluent Norwegian. 'What is he thinking? The two of you are perfect together.'

'Apparently *he* never thought that.' Sally couldn't keep the bitterness from her voice.

'But you were. He would have realised it sooner or later.'

Iris leaned forward and held Annie's gaze. 'It's Adam's loss, but it's this awful war, I'm afraid. It tears people apart who should be together and makes couples rush into marriage when if they waited they would see they weren't suited. Not that I know Adam or his fiancée well enough to know if they're suited or not.'

Sally gave her a grateful smile. 'I'm sure they'll be fine, and I wish them well.'

Her mother clearly wasn't mollified. 'I've heard nothing about it from Mrs Clark. Are you certain you aren't mistaken, dear?'

'He told me himself.'

Annie's shoulders slumped. 'I don't know what the world is coming to. If there was one thing I thought we could be sure about it was that you and Adam Clark were meant to be together. It was fate.'

'There now, Annie.' At some point Uncle Ted must have woken up, for he was sitting upright and looking at Sally's mother with an expression that seemed to contain a warning. 'What did I say about filling the girl's head full of romantic nonsense?'

Sally grinned at Ted. 'Just because you don't believe in true love, it doesn't mean I can't. I'm holding out for a love like Mum had with my dad.'

Ted seemed to be on the point of saying something else, but Sally knew all too well how he objected to her mother's romantic notions and didn't want to get into an argument now. Not when she was only with her family for a short while. 'I'm not in any hurry to fall in love again,' she said before Ted could get a word in. 'It hurt too much the first time around.'

Besides, the fact that Mrs Clark hadn't already told her mum about Adam's engagement intrigued Sally. It made her wonder if the engagement was very recent. If Mrs Clark hadn't heard about Nancy, perhaps the relationship was one of the hasty wartime ones Iris had spoken of. Although Sally wouldn't breathe a word of her thoughts to Iris or her family, she couldn't deny the faint flicker of hope that Adam's engagement might come to nothing.

Ted looked satisfied. 'That's very sensible.'

Sally gave him a smile then decided it was time to turn the conversation away from Adam and romance. 'Tell me about your new job, Mum. Are you enjoying it?'

Annie's face brightened. 'I love it. I thank my lucky stars that Mrs Brownlow was able to put in a good word for me at the hospital.' And she chatted happily about her work in the kitchens at the memorial hospital. 'The pay's so much better than I was getting before,' she finished. 'Now,' she said, turning to Ted, 'Have you told Sally your news?'

'Not yet.'

Ted was looking very pleased with himself, and Sally looked at him curiously. 'You told me how much better your back was. Do you mean you've got something else to tell me?'

'I was waiting until we were all together,' he said. Judging from the way he seemed to be trying to bite back a smile, he had an exciting announcement. 'I got a job.'

'Oh, that's wonderful. Where?'

'Entwhistle's Ironmongers, as a clerical assistant. I think Mr Entwhistle was hoping for a young person but as all the young folk hereabouts are doing war work, he was finding it impossible to fill the vacancy. He was a bit dubious when I asked if he would take me on, but he gave me a chance.'

'And now he says he doesn't know what he would have done without Ted,' Annie finished, with a fond look at her brother. 'Go on, tell Sally the best bit.'

'There's more?' Sally was thrilled to see how proud of himself her uncle looked. Having run a farm before his accident, it had been awful to see him struggle to come to terms with being dependent on her mother's wages for so long.

'Well, he only needs me for half the week, which gives me time to do a course on book-keeping. Once I finish that, he says he'll give me a promotion and put me in charge of the books as well.'

'I'm so pleased for you.' Sally gave her uncle a hug. 'Well, that calls for a celebration. How about I get us all a fish supper? My treat.'

Sally's days in Whitby passed by in a happy blur. She was soon able to see how much pride Ted took in his work, and how delighted he was to be able to contribute towards the household expenses. Her mother, too, looked less careworn, and Sally could see how she enjoyed having a little extra money to make their home look pretty. While it would never be as nice as the farmhouse they had shared with Ted, it was now a welcoming place to come home to each day. It lifted Sally's spirits to hear her mother singing as she made the tea or swept the floors. It struck her that she hadn't seen Annie so happy in a long time.

Iris, too, seemed to be enjoying her time in Whitby. While Annie and Ted were out working, the girls would wander along the river to watch the boats, climb the steps up to the abbey or explore the winding lanes through the old part of the town.

'I'm so glad I've seen your home,' Iris said on their last day. They were strolling back to the house on Gray Street, carrying the groceries they had spent much of the morning queuing for. With both Annie and Ted in work, it was getting harder for them to do the food shopping so Sally and Iris had volunteered to take the ration books and help them stock up before they left. 'Now, when you talk about your home and family, I can picture all the places and people you mention.'

There was one person Sally had not met so far, and as though summoned by her thoughts, she appeared around the corner before Sally and Iris could turn onto Gray Street. 'Sally Hartley! I heard you were home on leave.' It was Mrs Clark, a tall thin woman wearing a raincoat and a sky-blue headscarf scattered with gold and white polka dots.

'Oh, hello Mrs Clark. It's lovely to see you,' Sally said, and introduced her to Iris, adding, 'Mrs Clark is Adam's mother.'

Mrs Clark's smile broadened. 'Oh, you've met Adam too? I suppose you've heard the exciting news.'

Sally's heart sank. Thankfully, she wasn't required to speak at that point, for Mrs Clark ran on without leaving either girl the chance to talk. 'He's got himself engaged to a lovely young woman.'

'Yes, we've met her,' Iris said with a glance at Sally. 'She seems very nice. Congratulations.'

Sally recovered her voice enough to say, 'Yes, congratulations.' She cleared her throat then added, 'We met her at a dance a couple of weeks ago. I liked her.'

'That's good to hear. I won't be able to meet her until after the wedding, so I'm pleased to hear good things about her.'

'I'm sure she would be able to visit before the wedding, even if Adam can't get leave at the same time. Wrens going on leave can request a travel warrant to any train station they want.'

'I know that. But they've managed to organise the wedding for next month, and they'll be spending what honeymoon they can get in Scotland.'

'They... next month?' Any hope that the engagement was a moment of madness that Adam would recover from died in Sally's heart. If they had gone so far as to plan the wedding, then neither Adam nor Nancy were going to change their minds.

'Yes, a Christmas wedding.' Mrs Clark dabbed at her eyes. 'So romantic. Adam said now he'd met the woman he wanted to marry, what was the point of waiting?'

'Why indeed?' Realising she sounded more like she was offering sympathies at a funeral, Sally hastily said, 'Well, do pass on our best regards to the bride and groom-to-be.' She indicated her shopping. 'I must get this home for my mother.'

She hurried away without checking to see if Iris was following. Only when she rounded the corner did she relax her face muscles to let her bright smile fade.

A hand clutched her arm. 'Are you all right, Sally?'

Sally slowed her pace and gave Iris a rueful smile. 'I will be.'

'It must have been a shock.'

'I didn't know what to say.' Sally gave an angry laugh. 'The Clark family seem set on springing unwelcome news upon me at all times. Thanks for helping me out, though. If I'd have been on my own, I'd have just stood there, opening and closing my mouth like a fish.'

'Any time. What are friends for? If it's any comfort, you looked quite calm and collected.'

'Really? That's good. I felt like she'd just socked me in the stomach with her handbag, and I'm glad it didn't show. She's a terrible gossip, and I know she'd love to tell all her friends how broken-hearted I looked to hear of her son's wedding.'

'Do you still feel broken-hearted, then?' Iris gave her an anxious look.

Sally thought about it. 'It still hurts, I can't deny it. I'm glad I know, though. About the wedding, I mean. It must be like ripping off a sticking plaster. It stings like fury, but it's better to get all the pain over with in one fell swoop.'

'That's the spirit. Now you know, you can get on with your life. There are plenty of men who would love to go out with you. You should consider it. Show Adam — and Tessa — you're not eating your heart out over him.'

'Maybe. I'll think about it.' Although Sally thought it would be a long time before she could face going out with anyone who wasn't Adam. 'Come on. Mum'll be home soon, and I want to cook supper before she gets in and does it for me.'

As soon as Sally and Iris got back to the house, they put the shopping away and prepared a corned beef hash. Sally's mum was still at work, and with Ted being at his book-keeping class, it meant they had the house to themselves to make a nice farewell meal for Annie and Ted. Once the stew was simmering on the stove, Iris went to start packing while Sally remained in the kitchen to keep an eye on the pot. Now she didn't have to put on a brave face for Iris's sake, she couldn't prevent the tears from falling.

Hearing her mother's voice outside, she wiped her eyes and went to open the door for her. She stopped in surprise when she saw her mother was not talking to a neighbour, as Sally had supposed, but to a middle-aged man whose bull-like build and grizzled hair reminded her a lot of Archie Heddle. Annie had her hand on his arm as though they had been walking like that, and the man was gazing down at her with a slightly dazed look, as though he couldn't quite believe he was there. He held a large umbrella which he angled to protect Annie's head, meaning that the light rain was pattering on his hat and shoulders, although he didn't seem to notice. Annie's face was rather pink, and Sally thought she looked years younger as she gazed at the man with an openly adoring expression.

Conscious that she was intruding upon their privacy, Sally ducked back inside and pulled the door closed, careful not to make a noise. She went into the kitchen and stirred the corned beef hash while awaiting her mother. Was she in love with another man? While Annie had every right to see anyone she wanted, she had always told Sally she could never love another man after her father. Sally had loved listening to her mother tell her the story of how she had met her husband, who had died when Sally was still a baby. Growing up without a father, Sally had always been aware of an ache of something missing when she watched her friends with their dads. She had swallowed her mum's tales of her dad with the eagerness of a starving child. Although she couldn't deny her mother a second chance at happiness, Sally wondered at the change in her.

It was also impossible not to feel sorry for herself, when everyone around her was in love and she had just learned that the only man she had ever loved was about to marry another woman. Try as she might to stop them, more tears escaped; Sally blotted them with her hanky, trying desperately to erase all traces of her tears before her mum came in.

It was only a minute or two later when she heard Annie's step in the hall and the front door closing. When she came into the kitchen, Sally turned, giving what she hoped looked like a sunny smile. However, Annie took one look at her face, and her own soft smile faded. 'Oh, love, what's happened?' She pulled Sally into a hug.

Faced with such sympathy, Sally couldn't stop fresh tears from falling, and although she hadn't wanted her mum to see her upset, it was a relief not to have to pretend any more. Pressing her hot face against her mum's shoulder, breathing in the comforting scent of lavender, she poured out the news of Adam's wedding, letting go of her questions about the man outside for now.

'I was so sure I was going to end up with him,' she said finally, pulling away to wipe her face. 'I remember what you said about meeting Dad, how your hands tingled when your fingers touched his. That's exactly how I felt when I first met Adam.'

'Oh, love. Maybe Ted's right. Maybe I have been filling your head with romantic ideas.'

'But it was love at first sight with you and Dad, wasn't it?' What with seeing her dreams of Adam being well and truly shattered, she couldn't bear to lose another of the pillars her life had been built upon. If there was no such thing as love at first sight, then the world would be a very dark and bleak place indeed.

'Of course it was. It was just how I've always told you.'

'That's good. I always love hearing about Dad.' Sally dabbed away the last of the tears, then folded her handkerchief. 'I wish I'd known him. One day I hope I'll marry a man every bit as wonderful as him.'

At this, Annie seemed to wince, and Sally frowned. 'Is something wrong?'

'Of course not. My feet are aching after standing up all day, that's all.'

Sally gave Annie a long look. 'It's not anything to do with the man I saw you with just now, is it?'

Pink colour stained her mum's cheeks. 'You saw me with Harry?'

Sally nodded and explained what she had seen from the doorway. 'Not that you shouldn't see another man, if that's what you want,' she hastened to assure her. 'I was just surprised, considering you've always told me you could never love anyone else after Dad.'

'Oh dear, I'm sorry you had to find out this way. The truth is, it's early days and I wanted to wait until I was sure.'

'You don't have to tell me anything if you're not ready.' Although Sally was burning to hear more.

Annie must have sensed the questions Sally was holding back, for she smiled and nudged her daughter with her elbow. 'And you would be happy to return to Orkney knowing nothing about the new man in my life?' She shook her head. 'Never fear, Sally. I wouldn't do that to you.' Annie leaned against the counter and her face grew pensive. 'Well, as I said, his name's Harry. Harry Rowbotham. He's an ambulance driver, and I met him at the hospital. He's always had a kind word for me from the first time we met. I turned him down the first few times he asked me out and, to be honest, I thought he wouldn't ask again. That was when I knew I *did* want to see him. I'd got myself in such a knot, because I'd meant what I always said to you about not wanting to get involved with another man after your father.'

'Because you didn't think you could ever love again,' Sally finished for her, like a child who knew a favourite story word for word.

Annie was putting on an apron, and didn't acknowledge Sally's remark. She tied the strings in an even bow before continuing. 'Anyway, to cut a long story short, he did ask me again, and we've gone for walks together a few times.'

'And do you like him?'

Annie's cheeks were turning a deeper shade of pink. 'As I said, it's early days, but yes, I do. You don't mind, do you?'

'Why should I mind? I want you to be happy. I was surprised, that's all.' Sally hoped her expression didn't reveal her reservations. While she wanted her mother to be happy, it was hard to let go of her notion that her mother and father had shared a once-in-a-lifetime love.

'Harry is a widower. His wife died five years ago. He told me he loved her very much and thought he had no room in his heart for anyone new. But when he met me he said he found a new space in his heart that he hadn't known was there before.' Annie looked down for a moment and then said, 'I know it must be strange seeing me with Harry. All I ask is for you to give me time to see if there's a place in my heart for him. And if there is, I hope you'll be able to accept him.'

Sally's tears were no longer ones of self-pity but of happiness. 'Of course I will. I'm glad you've met someone. My friend Mary thought she would never love again after losing her fiancé but she's met a lovely young man. I hope you can be as happy as her.'

Annie pulled Sally into another hug. 'I hope so too. And you'll find someone new, just mark my words.'

The sound of Iris's feet descending the stairs reminded Sally that she and Annie weren't alone in the house. She pulled away and blotted the last of her tears. 'I must look a fright.' Then she gave her mother a gentle push towards the door. 'Anyway, I was supposed to be making the tea while you rested. Go and sit down.'

And as she poured boiling water into the teapot, she did her best not to dwell on her mother's slight hesitation when Sally had reminded Annie of her frequent declarations that she would never love again.

Chapter Thirteen

'You know, as lovely as it was to be on leave, I'm excited to be back in Orkney,' Sally said. After the interminable train journey, she and Iris had caught the boat from Scrabster, just outside Thurso. Thankfully, the crossing was relatively smooth, and now they were safely back in Stromness. Sally shut the wardrobe door, having unpacked the last of her clothes, and paced to the window. It was a sunny day and unseasonably warm for the end of November, and Sally longed to revisit her favourite haunts in Stromness and reacquaint herself with Orkney life. 'Shall we go for a walk? It's too lovely to stay indoors and I want to stretch my legs after the journey.'

'I don't.' Iris sounded strained. Now Sally came to look at her properly, she saw her face was very pale.

'Do you still feel seasick?'

Iris nodded then lay back on her bed with a groan. 'I'm going to stay here. Hope the room stops moving soon.'

'Do you want me to get you anything?'

'Besides a causeway to Scotland so I never have to cross the Pentland Firth again? No thanks. Have fun.'

Mention of the causeway reminded Sally of the Italian prisoners of war and the work they were doing building causeways on the eastern side of Scapa Flow. Those thoughts inevitably led to Aldo. Maybe that was why Sally allowed her feet to carry her to the docks. She wouldn't see him, of course, but it was interesting to watch the heavy loads being hoisted from ship to shore.

Sure enough, when she was close enough to see that there was a ship being unloaded, she saw a hoist lift an army truck and swing it high into the air. She watched, marvelling at how such a thin-looking crane could manage to lift that heavy truck. She was so engrossed in the sight, she didn't immediately notice a group of men sitting on a wall about ten yards away. Once she had assured herself that the truck would make it safely to dry land and not be dropped into the water, she spotted them, noticing the red circles on their uniform that revealed them to be Italians. At that moment one of them turned, and their eyes met. It was Aldo.

'Sally!' He dropped from the wall and closed the distance between them. 'I haven't seen you for so long I was afraid you had left Orkney.'

'I went home on leave but I'm back now.' Then she felt bad, mentioning a trip home so casually. 'I'm sorry. That was thoughtless of me when you don't know when you'll ever be able to leave here.'

Aldo shrugged. 'It's not your fault. Anyway, I never really had a home. I was orphaned when I was young and now—' he looked at his feet, his dark brows drawn together '—now I have no one. Orkney's as good a home as any.'

'I'm so sorry.' Now Sally felt bad she hadn't known. She had spoken a few times with Aldo when she had been at the hospital, yet she had never thought to ask about his family. 'My father died when I was a baby,' she said, 'But I always had my mum and uncle. It must be awful to be alone in the world.'

Idiot. Why had he brought his lack of family into the conversation? When he'd seen Sally, his heart had given a joyful swoop, and he'd spoken without thinking.

He grinned in an effort to make light of his careless comment. 'You can't really miss what you never had,' he said. 'I prefer to look forward, not back.'

'Oh? And what do you look forward to?' Sally's holiday had obviously done her good: there was a sparkle to her eyes that had been missing the last time he had seen her, and she smiled at him in clear delight. That was one of the things he liked about Sally: she never hid her feelings, and her unerring optimism always made him feel better.

Aldo leaned closer. 'I look forward to a time when I can take you for dinner or dancing without being chased down by armed guards.' So saying, he glanced over his shoulder at the guards who accompanied the Italians to the docks. Fortunately, they were watching a second vehicle being winched into the air, and they hadn't noticed that Aldo had strayed from the group who were taking their permitted fifteen-minute rest.

Sally's face coloured, and she stepped back. Aldo immediately worried that he had come on too strong. 'That was stupid of me,' he said. 'Forget I said it.'

Sally gave a little shake of the head. 'It wasn't stupid. I just didn't have a very good time at the last dance I went to.'

Then you went with the wrong man. He resisted the urge to say that, though, and simply said, 'I am sorry to hear that.'

They stood in silence for a while, and Aldo could have kicked himself for reminding Sally of an unhappy time. He groped for another subject of conversation but before he could say anything, Sally spoke. 'I can't believe they still make you wear those awful target patches. How can they do that? You're not prisoners any more.'

'Not officially. They cannot decide what to do with us, I think.'

'Well, I hope they work it out soon. You're doing work for the British, after all. They should give you something in return.'

'The officer in charge said he would let us know as soon as your government has reached a decision.' He grinned. 'They have other, more important things on their mind, no?'

'Equally important maybe.' Sally gave a small smile.

'In a way, I am glad we have been forgotten. What if they move us somewhere else?'

Sally's expression of dismay made warmth bloom in his chest. 'I hope not. I would miss you.'

Aldo opened his mouth to reply, then saw the guards striding in his direction. 'I must go. But when I am free to visit the town, we will meet again, yes?'

'I would like that.'

'Come on, mate. Back to work.' One of the guards took his arm and tugged him towards the waiting ship. Aldo gave no resistance but looked over his shoulder and blew Sally a kiss. 'I will see you again!'

She smiled and waved, and Aldo whistled a cheery tune as he resumed his work.

Later, back at the camp, Aldo sat on a crate outside his hut, whittling a toy soldier from a piece of wood one of the guards had brought him. He had promised to make the man a present for his nephew in return for a bar of chocolate. Already his mouth watered, as he imagined the sweet treat melting on his tongue.

Movement on the ground caught his eye; a moment later, the black cat was winding itself around his legs, purring. Having seen the tiny creature a few times now, he had saved a few scraps of corned beef in his handkerchief on the chance he might bump into the cat again. Now, he unfolded the hanky and held out his hand to the cat. The feline hesitated for a moment, then darted forward, took a lump of meat in its mouth and returned a short distance away where it crouched over its treat and gobbled it up. It repeated the action until all the meat was gone. Finally, it licked Aldo's hand clean of every last fragment.

'You liked that, didn't you, Cat? I'll have to remember to share more food with you.' Aldo scratched the cat's head, grinning at the way its whiskers tickled his palm while the rough tongue cleaned his hand.

He pondered the cat for a moment. 'I can't keep calling you Cat. You need a name.' Aldo stroked it absently while he thought. 'I'll call you Nero. You're a black cat, after all. I know some people say black cats are unlucky, but I think you're lucky because I saw Sally not long after I met you for the first time.'

Nero purred and rubbed his head against Aldo's knee. After a few seconds, apparently realising there was no more food forthcoming, Nero trotted away across the grass, his tail high in the air.

Aldo watched him for a while then returned to his work. Once satisfied that the soldier's face was as smooth and round as he could make it, he rummaged in the toolbox and pulled out the awl, using the sharp point to work tiny holes for eyes. The handle was a little loose, and he made a mental note to see if he could fix it when he had a spare moment.

A shadow fell over his work, and a meaty hand pulled the stick from his hand. 'What do you think you're doing, working for that scum?'

Aldo rose and snatched the soldier back. He glared at Gianni. 'What I do in my free time is my own business.'

'Not when it involves doing a favour for the enemy.'

Aldo sighed. It seemed Gianni was never going to change. 'You do know the British are no longer our enemies?'

'They are Mussolini's enemies.'

'Mussolini is finished, and I hate what he has done to Italy.'

The words had hardly left Aldo's mouth when Gianni leaned towards him, his face twisted in a murderous scowl. Although Aldo didn't shift his gaze from Gianni's, from the corner of his eye he saw Gianni's fist swing towards his jaw. He had been too slow to evade a punch from him once before and he wasn't about to let it happen again. Using one of the tricks he had learned against the bullies at the orphanage, he twisted sideways at the last moment, leaving Gianni lunging forward, his fist meeting empty air. Now his assailant was off balance, it was a simple matter to catch his swinging arm and throw him to the ground. Gianni landed on his back with a thud, the air leaving his lungs with an audible whoosh. He floundered on the ground for several seconds while he fought for breath.

By this time, a group of Italians had gathered and several of them laughed at the sight of Gianni on the ground looking like a stranded fish.

Finally, Gianni managed to drag air into his lungs and stagger to his feet. Aldo took a few steps back, glad to see a couple of British guards approaching.

'You'll pay for that,' Gianni snarled. 'Tread carefully, or you might find a dagger in your back one of these days.' He took a few paces away only to pause and look back, giving a nasty chuckle. 'Wait. I've got a better idea. What about that British girl you're friendly with? You wouldn't want any harm to come to her, would you?'

Aldo's blood froze. 'You wouldn't dare.'

'What's the trouble here?' The guards had reached them.

Aldo, breathing heavily and with fists clenched, couldn't organise his thoughts to give a coherent answer in English. Gianni, however, gave the guard a charming smile. 'Just a little disagreement. We've sorted it now.'

'That better be right. Back to your huts, both of you.'

Glad to get away from Gianni, Aldo went into his hut and slumped on his bunk. Threats to himself he could brush off. He could look after himself. But Sally? Had Gianni seen them together? It was perfectly possible. Both times he had spoken to Sally at the dockside, he hadn't felt the need for concealment. Gianni could easily have seen them. And Enrico had teased him enough times for Gianni to overhear. For the first time, Aldo wasn't sorry that they were still confined to the camp because that did at least mean Gianni could do nothing to harm Sally. When they were finally given more freedom, however, he would have to keep a close eye on him.

–

Seeing Aldo had given Sally the perfect end to her break. She had befriended him at first because she felt sorry for him, being forced to do hard labour far from home. Now, she couldn't deny that she liked knowing he was based nearby. If Aldo, who had every right to be miserable, could put such a cheerful face on life, then she could face her own troubles with no complaint. Even when she discovered that her first watch would be with Tessa, she refused to let it get her down.

One of the advantages of cycling to the signal station was that there wasn't the same opportunity for long chats during the journey. The steep hill out of Stromness always left them too out of breath for speaking, and once they had turned off the tarred road, they needed to concentrate on avoiding potholes and large stones. Sally was glad of this as she cycled with Tessa the next morning, for it occurred to her that this was their first time on watch together since the dance at Lyness. Until now, Sally had been too full of her own woe to wonder overmuch about Tessa's reaction to Adam's news, and her heart was still feeling too bruised to want to discuss it, as Tessa surely would.

The discussion couldn't be put off for ever, though. Once they had taken over from the Wrens on night watch, refilled the coal bucket and hoisted the ensign, Sally found herself alone with Tessa with not a ship in sight to require their attention.

It didn't take Tessa long to introduce the subject. 'Why didn't you tell me Adam was seeing another woman?' she asked.

Sally stared at her. 'I didn't know.'

'Oh come on. I thought you were supposed to be friends from way back. You can't expect me to believe he would have kept something that important from you.'

Sally did another visual sweep of Hoy Sound before replying. The trouble was, she was having to face up to the fact that much of her so-called relationship with Adam had been in her head. She had allowed her romantic notions to blot out reality and refused to accept that she and Adam were little more than passing acquaintances. As a result, she had mistaken polite interest on his side for a serious attachment, ignoring any evidence that contradicted her belief and pouncing on anything that she could take as a sign they were destined to be together.

'I gather it was a whirlwind romance,' she said finally.

'Was?'

Even though Sally was no fan of Tessa, she couldn't ignore the eager hope that rang from that single word. She wouldn't let her worst enemy cling to a futile hope. 'I only meant that they're about to get married. Adam's mother told me when I was home. She hadn't known for long either.'

'I don't believe you.'

'Why would I lie?'

'I think you were jealous. You didn't like that a newcomer had the gumption to organise bikes when you'd had to slog here on foot for months. And you especially didn't like the praise I was given.'

Sally shook her head, stunned into silence. She hadn't been keen on the bikes, especially after her fall, but she was prepared to admit that they were handy when the weather was good enough to cycle. Where had all this bile come from? She didn't understand why it seemed to be directed at her alone and not towards any other Wrens.

'So,' Tessa went on, taking advantage of Sally's momentary silence, 'when you saw I fancied Adam, you thought you would get one over on me by making me look a fool in front of him. What do you say to that?'

'You're wrong. I mean, I saw you liked him but I promise I didn't know about Nancy. It was as much of a shock to me as it was to you.' Sally could have gone on to explain how upset she had been when Adam's announcement had dashed her dreams so brutally. But if Tessa hadn't seen that for herself, she wasn't going to make herself vulnerable by revealing her deep hurt.

'Well, I don't believe you, and if I can think of a way to get back at you, I will.' So saying, Tessa flounced over to the window and gazed out to sea, her arms folded across her chest. Sally watched her for a moment then took up a station on the opposite side of the room and stared in the other direction.

It was going to be a long, boring watch.

Chapter Fourteen

November passed into December, and despite Tessa's threat, nothing terrible happened. Gradually Sally lowered her guard and turned her mind to other matters. What with her trip to Yorkshire and her problems with Tessa, Sally hadn't given any thought to Christmas, so most of her free time was now spent in a mad scramble to make gifts for her friends and family. Iris's stock of fabrics, purchased before the war, proved a godsend, for she now had several remnants left over that were too large to discard yet not big enough for garments. Iris told Sally and Mary they were welcome to anything they could make use of, and Sally gratefully seized upon a length of sky-blue cotton with yellow polka dots that was just large enough to make a headscarf for her mother. She also found several smaller pieces of plain blue cotton that she could cut into squares and hem into handkerchiefs for Uncle Ted, Archie and Aldo. She selected three of the largest pieces for Aldo so he could tie them around his face to protect his mouth and nose from the dust when working in ships' holds. She took pleasure embroidering his initials into them, picturing his delight upon receiving a gift. Now she knew Aldo had no family, she wanted him to know she was thinking of him, and maybe he would feel less alone.

Of course, having a gift for him also meant she had a valid excuse to seek him out at the docks, and so on her first free afternoon once the handkerchiefs were finished and wrapped in newspaper, she made her way to the waterside with them in her coat pocket. As luck would have it, she found him perched on a wall enjoying a brief break.

His face lit up beneath its coating of grime when he saw her. He fished in his pocket and pulled out a small lumpy bundle wrapped in newspaper. 'I have been keeping this, hoping I would see you before Christmas.'

Sally laughed and held out her own parcel. However, they only had time to exchange gifts before one of the British guards chased Aldo back to the ship. 'I will open it at Christmas and think of you,' he called as he departed, blowing her a kiss.

Despite urging from Iris and Mary, who were almost as eager as Sally to learn what Aldo had given her, Sally waited until Christmas morning to open his gift. The three friends had arranged to wait until they were together in the evening before opening their gifts from each other. However, Sally couldn't resist unwrapping Aldo's present the moment she woke up. She eased back the folds of paper to reveal a delicate brooch in the shape of a tree with spreading branches, formed from twisted wire. It was so beautiful she couldn't bear to be parted from it while on duty, so she pinned it beneath her lapel and went on watch feeling as though she was wearing some kind of talisman. And, indeed, it did seem to bring her protection of a sort, for a few days later, Sally received a letter from her mother, telling her she had met Mrs Clark, who had insisted on showing her the wedding photograph Adam had sent. It was only then that Sally realised she hadn't thought of Adam for days.

A more welcome letter arrived for the Heddles. Four days after Christmas, Sally, Iris and Mary made their way to Curlew Croft, clutching their Christmas gifts, and were greeted by an ecstatic Elspeth. 'We've had the most wonderful news,' she told them with tears in her eyes. 'A letter from Don arrived this morning. He escaped from his camp when the Italian guards surrendered, and he's made it to Switzerland. He's interned there now, of course, but at least we know he's safe and well.' Elspeth and Archie's relief and joy brought an extra sparkle to their delayed Christmas celebrations.

The arrival of 1944 was accompanied by a blast of Arctic weather. Tessa, who had been on leave over Christmas, returned, and the respite Sally had known from her snide digs came to an end.

'It doesn't matter what I say, she refuses to believe I didn't know of Adam's engagement,' Sally confided to Iris and Mary when they were huddled in front of the common room fire one stormy evening. She had been on watch with Tessa twice that day and was relieved to be back in the company of her friends.

'Stay on your guard around her,' Mary said. 'She's got something up her sleeve, you mark my words. I've caught her glaring at you a few times when she thought no one was watching, and yesterday, she gave you a look as if to say she knew something you didn't.'

'I don't like the sound of that.'

Iris was tapping her chin, looking thoughtful. 'I hope she's not trying to turn the other Wrens against you.'

'What do you mean?'

'Well, I overheard her talking to some of the others yesterday. She said something like, "She needs to be taken down a peg or two." I didn't really register it at the time, but now I wonder if she was talking about you.'

'I hope not.' A horrible thought struck. 'She hasn't approached either of you, has she?'

Iris shook her head.

'And if she did, we'd tell her where to go,' Mary said.

'Anyway, the others didn't look like they agreed with whatever she was saying,' Iris added. 'I'm sure she won't turn anyone else against you. Everyone with sense likes you and knows you'd never do anything to hurt Tessa.'

'Even if she is Orkney's worst blight,' Mary put in.

Sally smiled and tried to feel comforted. 'I hope you're right,' she said. 'I can't think what I've done to turn Tessa against me, but I can cope if it's just her. I'd hate for the other Wrens to get involved.'

Iris patted her arm. 'They won't. Everyone else likes you.'

'And if anyone does anything to hurt you, we'll give them what for,' Mary said. Then she picked up the newspaper and opened it at the crossword. 'Now who can help me with five down?' With that, the matter was closed.

But Sally got a cruel reminder a week later. She and Iris, who were on the morning watch together, awoke to find the ground covered in two inches of snow, making cycling impossible. On discussing their options over breakfast, they decided to wear wellington boots and carry their shoes to put on once they reached Kyeness. Accordingly, once they'd collected their gear from their cabin, they raced down to the hallway where they kept their boots and pulled them on. Sally's boots were a tight fit around the ankle, and by the time she had wrenched them on and tucked in her wide trouser legs, time was getting on.

They set off at a brisk pace – almost jogging – to make up for lost time, and Sally was concentrating so hard on her breathing that she only noticed an uncomfortable prickle around her feet and ankles once they had left the lane and were striding up the path towards the headland. The itching grew more intense until she was forced to stop and try scratching her feet through the rubber boots.

Iris didn't notice Sally had stopped at first. It was only when she turned to speak that she paused and looked back. 'What's the matter?'

'It must be my new stockings. They're itching like fury.' In desperation, Sally tried to stick her gloved hands inside her boots but she couldn't reach past her calves.

Iris trudged back down the snowy path to Sally. 'Is there anything I can do?'

Grimacing, Sally shook her head. She straightened up and resumed her walk. 'Nothing, short of swapping stockings with me, and I wouldn't wish these even on Tessa. Goodness only knows what they're made of. It feels like nettles. Tell me something to take my mind off it.'

By the time they reached the signal station, the itching had driven Sally to a frenzy. Leaving Iris to go up to the signal room to relieve the night watch, she tore off her boots and stockings, scattering them on the floor, and stared with dismay at the raised red welts speckling both feet.

'Oh that looks nasty.' Sally had been so absorbed scratching her feet that she hadn't noticed the two Wrens who were about to leave descending the ladder. Now Sue Walker was regarding her with sympathy.

'New socks,' Sally explained. 'I won't be buying any more of these.'

'I should think not. Funny. My hands looked like that after my little brother put itching powder in my gloves. Where are they from? I must remember not to shop there when I need new stockings.'

'They were a Christmas present from my mother, so you're probably safe.'

'That's a relief. I've got some calamine lotion back at the Wrennery. Let me know if you want to borrow any.'

'Thanks, I might take you up on that.'

A gust of icy wind tore through the room when Sue opened the door. Then, with a cheery farewell, the two Wrens slammed the door behind them, leaving Sally regarding her stockings with disfavour. They didn't look itchy. In fact, they had felt soft and comfortable when she had put them on that morning. She had, after all, sat through breakfast without feeling any discomfort, so why had they caused her such a problem once she had gone outside?

Then Sue's comment filtered into her consciousness. Itching powder. Surely not?

Seizing one of her boots, she tipped it up and drew a sharp breath when a fine powder drifted onto the floor. It was a light beige colour, and when Sally looked at it closely she saw it was made of tiny fibres. She frowned as memories returned of an incident from her school days, of the havoc a group of boys had created after a weekend spent picking rosehips. A moment later she was storming barefoot up the ladder, holding the rungs with one hand while clutching the offending boot in the other.

'Itching powder.' Sally flung the boot onto the floor beside Iris.

Iris jumped and looked at Sally with wide eyes. 'What?'

'In my boots. Someone put itching powder in them.'

'That's horrible. Who would do that?'

'I'll give you one guess.'

Iris's expression hardened. 'Tessa.'

Sally nodded. 'Not that I can prove it, but I'm sure it's her. She's just got back from holiday. What's the betting she's got a kid brother and got the powder from him?'

'Just say the word, and I'll collect all the powder from your boots and sprinkle it in her underwear drawer.'

'Much as I'd love to see her squirm, I don't think that's a good idea.'

'It'd be funny.'

'I know, but then what? She retaliates by putting itching powder in our beds, and then we don't sleep and make a stupid mistake when we're on duty. I refuse to stoop to her level.'

'I hate to let her win, though.' Iris gave a deep sigh and turned back to the window. 'Oh, wait. There's a ship approaching.'

There was a pause in the conversation while Iris signalled the standard challenge and received the reply. Sally noted the name of the ship and entered the exchange in the log and also telephoned through to the station monitoring the anti-submarine loop to let them know HMS *Newgale* was about to cross. Once the flurry of activity was over, she became aware that her bare feet were freezing on the polished concrete floor. At least the chill had soothed the itching, and the welts had faded.

'Do you mind if I go and wash out my stockings and boots? I can't bear the thought of the walk back with itchy feet.'

Iris glanced round and then down at Sally's feet, which were turning a delicate shade of blue. 'At least they match your uniform. Go on – I'll manage on my own for a while. It's not exactly busy. I've actually brought a pair of stockings with me to darn the heels, and you're welcome to borrow them. Your feet must be like blocks of ice. You'll find them in my coat pocket. I doubt you'll get yours dry before we have to leave.'

'Thanks, that would be marvellous.'

Feeling much warmer wearing the borrowed stockings and her shoes, Sally emptied out all the powder from her boots. She was reluctant to rinse them out, knowing they would never dry before the return walk. However, she used a cloth to reach right to the toes and was satisfied that she had managed to get most, if not all, of the powder out. Then she went to the sink in the galley. Using the laundry soap the Wrens shared, she scrubbed and rinsed the stockings until her hands were red. Finally, she brushed her trouser hems, to remove any of the itching powder that might be clinging to them.

'Feel better?' Iris asked when Sally returned to the signal room carrying the wet stockings, which she hung beside the stove to dry.

'Much. I've decided what to say to Tessa as well.'

'Oh, what?' Iris's eyes sparkled.

'Absolutely nothing.'

'Are you mad? You can't let her get away with this.'

'I'm not. Think about it. Tessa's been hugging herself all morning, imagining my suffering. When she comes to relieve us this afternoon, she'll be expecting me to be complaining about my itchy feet or even accusing her. So she's all prepared to defend herself.'

Enlightenment dawned on Iris's face. 'And when you smile and say nothing, she'll wonder if she put powder in the wrong boots.'

'Exactly!'

'You're a genius! I'd never have thought of that. Tessa's going to be watching all the Wrens, wondering if any of them are going to start complaining of itchy feet.' Iris glanced at the socks draped on the stove's guard rail. 'Make sure you clear those away before she gets here or they'll give the game away.'

When Tessa and Mary arrived a few minutes before one in the afternoon, Sally was ready. Her feet, encased in Iris's warm, if worn at the heel, stockings, were feeling much better, and her washed stockings were safely folded away in her coat pocket. They were still wet and would need to be hung up as soon as she got up to her cabin, but she thought getting her pocket damp was a small price to pay for the confusion Tessa would suffer.

'Anything to report?' Tessa asked as she and Mary walked into the signal station, stamping their feet to shake the snow off their boots.

'Nothing. It's been very quiet.' Sally pulled on her boots, praying she had got rid of all the itching powder. If she hadn't, she would have to suffer in silence because there was no way she was going to give Tessa the satisfaction of knowing how much discomfort her trick had caused. She had to hide a smile at Tessa's narrowed eyes as she looked from Sally's feet to her face and back again. Straightening up, she gave Mary and Tessa a smile. 'Good job the sky seems to be clearing. It should be a lovely walk. I might even take a longer route back to enjoy the view.' Then raising her voice, she called, 'Are you ready, Iris?'

'Coming.' Iris emerged from the galley, already bundled in her outdoor gear. 'See you later, then, you two. Hope you have as quiet a watch as we did.'

With that, Sally and Iris left the signal station.

Sally managed to hold back her giggles until they had put enough distance between them and the signal station to ensure they wouldn't be overheard. 'Did you see Tessa's face? She couldn't believe it when I put on my boots without any mention of being itchy.'

'I bet she'll be in a right panic now, wondering whose boots she messed with.'

'I wish we could have found a way to tell Mary. It might have made her afternoon more bearable.'

And they strode back to Stromness, laughing at Tessa's inevitable loss of peace of mind. It was only when they were strolling along the lane with the Wrennery in sight that it occurred to Sally that she had been able to enjoy the walk without any regretful thoughts about Adam. Perhaps he hadn't been the love of her life after all.

—

The weeks passed at Bruna Camp, and Aldo managed to avoid Gianni. Gianni made no further attempt to single him out, making Aldo wonder if he had forgotten his threat. Aldo couldn't forget it, though, and continued to keep a wary eye on him.

Something else that appeared to have been forgotten was the Italians' status since the capitulation. As the first signs of spring appeared, and daisies and dandelions pushed their way through the grass, there was still no news, and the Italians were growing impatient. While the seemingly endless dark of winter had made them want to huddle in their huts when they weren't working at the docks, the arrival of longer days made them long to escape the confines of the camp and explore. While their guards told them to be patient, that they were still awaiting the results of discussions between the British, American and Italian governments, the outbreak of arguments and even fights was the inevitable result of fraying tempers.

'It's all very well them telling us to be patient,' Enrico said to Aldo one day as they sat outside their hut, 'but they aren't stuck here with no sign of ever being let out.' He picked at the grass by his feet, his mouth turned down in a scowl. 'I bet they're pleased we can't go out, because they're scared all the girls will ignore them and flock around us if we were allowed anywhere near them.'

Aldo, despite his own frustration, couldn't help laughing. 'There is more to life than girls, you know.' He pulled his handkerchief from his pocket and unwrapped the scraps of fried chicken he had lifted from the canteen earlier and held a piece out to Nero, who was curled up beside his feet. 'Here you are, little fellow. I remembered you.'

Enrico wrinkled his nose. 'This is why we need to get out and meet girls. If you've been reduced to stealing food for a stray cat, then you're in a bad way.'

Aldo was saved from answering by a summons to the parade ground. 'Maybe this is the news we've been waiting for,' he said as he tipped the rest of the meat on the ground for Nero and followed the group converging on the parade ground. He took his place beside Enrico and stood to attention, only noticing that Gianni was just in front of him when it was too late to move away.

After the roll call, Captain Briars stepped forward and addressed the group. 'I have news which should be welcome to you all. It has been agreed that you are to be given the chance to work as volunteer cooperatives. If you agree, your group will become an Italian labour battalion, and you will continue to work at the docks, although with changes to your conditions. First, instead of receiving camp tokens, you will be paid in local currency, at seven shillings a week.'

'Real money!' Enrico hissed in Aldo's ear. 'We'll be able to buy girls drinks.'

Aldo rolled his eyes and concentrated on the rest of the announcement.

'For those who wish it,' Captain Briars continued, 'you can arrange for some of your pay to be sent to your families in Italy.'

There were murmurs of approval through the group at this. Aldo knew that for many of his fellow prisoners, worries about their families had preyed on their minds and he knew many of his friends would be happier facing the rest of their enforced stay in Britain knowing they were once again able to contribute to their loved ones.

'You will also be glad to hear you will be given new uniforms.'

This was greeted with a cheer. Having to wear the hated red target patches was a humiliation they all found hard to bear.

Aldo listened to the remainder of their new conditions with a lighter heart. They would no longer be marched to and from the docks by armed guards but their own NCOs would take over responsibility for the group. When they weren't working, they would be free to exercise outside the camp provided they did not go more than five miles away and returned by ten o'clock in the evening. Much to Enrico's disappointment, though, they were forbidden from going to bars or forming relationships with the local women. This got the loudest groan. 'But they'll never be able to enforce it,' Enrico said, and Aldo privately agreed.

Thinking the announcement was over, Aldo expected Captain Briars to send them away. Instead, he put his hands behind his back and raised his chin. 'One last thing.' His tone was deadly serious, and Aldo felt a prickle of unease. His countrymen evidently felt the same way, for the mutterings gradually died away. Briars waited until everyone had fallen silent and was facing front once more. 'You each have a decision to make. If you are willing to abide by these rules, then you will remain here voluntarily, and we will trust you to continue to work to the best of your ability, stay out of trouble and not attempt to escape. Any of you who cannot accept this offer will be moved to another camp where you will continue to be treated as prisoners. You have one hour to decide. At the end of this time, Sergeant Bianchi will ask each of you for your decision.'

With this bombshell, Briars dismissed the group.

'Well, I'm accepting it,' Enrico said as they made their way back to their hut. 'Why wouldn't I? Anything to get out of camp.'

Aldo had to agree, and despite the warning not to mix with the local women, he felt a thrill at the prospect of being able to meet Sally. 'I'm accepting too.'

But a man ahead of them was saying, 'Anyone who accepts is selling out. I'll never change my mind.'

Aldo looked for Gianni, for surely he felt the same way. He would be removed with the other POWs, and Aldo needn't fear for Sally any more. He saw Gianni grab the arm of the man who had just spoken and mutter something in his ear. The man yanked his arm away. 'Never!' He shoved Gianni in the chest, sending him staggering backwards. Gianni hurried away, head down.

Enrico nudged him. 'What was all that about?'

Aldo could only shake his head.

It was not long before they found out. An hour later, Aldo and Enrico told their sergeant that they would be happy to accept the offer. All but two men in their hut said the same. A short while later, five men, including the two from their hut and the one who had declared he would never accept the offer, were driven away in a truck. Much to Aldo's dismay, Gianni was not among them.

'I don't understand,' Aldo said to Enrico. 'Gianni's Mussolini's man through and through. I wouldn't have thought he could accept the conditions.'

'Perhaps he doesn't mean to,' Enrico replied. 'He might think he can serve Mussolini better by pretending to go along with it.'

Aldo's heart sank. He had a nasty feeling Enrico was correct, and if so, he dreaded the outcome.

Chapter Fifteen

Just over a week later, the first real change in the Italians' conditions became apparent. Although Aldo had taken advantage of the freedom to wander outside the camp within certain limits, he hadn't yet gone into Stromness. To start with, he hadn't wanted to go until he had a little money, so he was waiting until their first Friday's pay arrived. Then, even when he did have his seven shillings rattling in his pocket, he felt self-conscious in the old uniform with the red patches.

However, on this day, the Italians returned to the camp to find their new uniforms awaiting them. They were marched into a tent where they were handed a stack of clothes including brown jackets and trousers. The jackets had 'Italy' on the shoulder. When Aldo got back to his hut, he immediately changed into his new clothes, feeling as though heavy shackles had been removed.

Wandering back outside, he noticed that the other Italians seemed to feel the same way. They all walked a little taller, their heads held high. Until now, the Italians had kept themselves separate from the British soldiers in the camp. Now, they strolled to where a group of British men were playing football.

When one red-haired private missed an open goal, Enrico cupped his hands around his mouth and shouted, 'My grandmother wouldn't have missed that!'

The private looked annoyed, but one of the other players clapped him on the back then called back, 'Want to show us what you can do? I bet you can't beat us.'

Before he knew what was happening, Aldo found himself on the field, representing his country against the British. What followed was possibly not the most elegant game of football that had ever been played. There were many more fouls than goals, and twice the British and Italian sergeants had to step in to prevent a fight. Aldo was grateful Gianni wasn't around, for he would surely have leapt at the chance to pick a fight with some of the British men. Apart from those two incidents, both teams seemed to take the fouls in their stride and as the match progressed, they were able to put aside their differences and concentrate on the game. Aldo hadn't played football since they had left Lamb Holm, and he couldn't remember the last time he had had so much fun. It felt good to chase the ball and let the worries and frustrations of the last few months roll away. The game ended in a narrow 2-1 victory for the Italians. The British took their defeat in good humour and shook hands with the Italians.

'You might have beaten us,' the British sergeant said, 'but you wouldn't stand a chance against the Royal Engineers.'

'Or the boys from the Ness Battery.'

'Nah,' said another. 'They couldn't even beat the Wrens.'

This led to much laughter until someone suggested, 'Why not hold a tournament?'

Enrico puffed out his chest. 'We will beat all of you.'

This was greeted by cheers from the other Italians and jeers from the British.

'You're on,' the sergeant said. Aldo seemed to remember hearing the other men calling him Sergeant Locke. 'I've got friends in the other camps. Give me a few days and I'll see what we can arrange.'

Aldo thought everyone would forget about the tournament and was therefore surprised three days later when Sergeant Locke paid a visit to the Italians. 'The tournament's on a week Saturday,' he told them. 'Put together two teams and prepare to be thrashed.'

'Do you think our watches have been quieter than usual recently?' Sally asked Iris as they left the signal station after a dull morning watch and went to fetch their bikes. It being an unusually balmy day in mid-April, they had elected to cycle that morning.

'It was certainly quiet today,' Iris said, fastening cycle clips around her ankles to keep the hems of her bellbottoms out of the bicycle chain. 'But activity around Scapa Flow always varies. You know that.'

'I suppose. Don't you get the feeling something is brewing, though?'

Iris wheeled her bike onto the track and swung her leg over the crossbar before answering. 'No. Why – did a black cat cross your path recently? No, wait. You saw a strange light in the stars.'

Sally laughed. 'Nothing like that, but I'll let you know if I see any fiery comets tonight.' Funny how she didn't mind Iris and Mary's teasing, yet Tessa's comments never failed to get under her skin. She supposed it was because Iris and Mary's ribbing came from a place of friendship. Sally knew there was true affection behind it, whereas Tessa, for whatever reason, wanted to make Sally miserable. Why else would she have pulled that trick with the itching powder? No friend would have done that to her.

'Come on,' Iris said. 'Last one to the Wrennery has to sweep the cabin floor.'

Sally jumped into the saddle and set off a fraction after Iris. 'Even if I lose,' she called, 'you still have to tidy the mess you left on the floor before I sweep it.'

They raced neck and neck for most of the way, although Sally suspected Iris was holding back, not wanting to pull ahead in case Sally had another accident and Iris didn't notice. However, Sally didn't have the nerve to swoop down Hellihole Road at the same breakneck speed as Iris, and even though she pedalled furiously once they turned onto Alfred Street for the last leg to the Wrennery, she had no real hope of catching up. They parked their bikes, panting and laughing, then hastily tidied their hair before going inside.

In the event, it didn't matter who had lost the race, for when they climbed the stairs to their cabin they found that Mary had already tidied and swept. Now she was sitting cross-legged on her bed, writing a letter.

'Give Joe my regards,' Sally said, slinging her gas mask over the back of a chair.

'Will do.' Mary put the letter aside, however, and jumped to her feet, looking at Sally with a faint smile. 'I have news that might interest you.'

'Oh? What's that?'

'There's going to be a football tournament on Saturday.'

'Why would that interest me?'

'Because of who's playing.'

Sally shook her head, puzzled. 'I don't understand.'

Mary's face lit up in a wicked grin. 'It's a tournament between the various camps around Stromness, and that includes the Italians. They're fielding two teams. Everyone was talking about it in the mess just now. We're all invited to watch.'

'Does that mean the Italians are allowed out of the camp at last?'

Mary shrugged. 'It must do.'

'When is it?'

'Saturday afternoon.'

'Perfect! I'll have just come off night watch, and you and Iris have the day off. We can all go.'

Mary gave her an arch smile. 'I thought you weren't interested in football.'

'I know, but I want to see Aldo if he's there. He's a friend, and I should support him.'

Iris, who had been hanging her jacket in the wardrobe, now closed the door and dropped onto her bed with a sigh. 'And I suppose that as friends, you expect us to go along to a tedious football tournament to support *you*?'

'Exactly.'

'Are you sure you and Aldo are still just friends?' Iris asked. 'I notice your walks seem to take you to the docks more often than not.'

'The docks are interesting. Besides, I don't see Aldo every time.'

'But you do look for him?'

Sally flung her pillow at Iris. 'I told you, we're just friends. I still haven't got over Adam.' Was that true, though? She thought about him less and less. Was it her love for Adam she clung to, or her belief that what she had felt for Adam had been true love and not some passing infatuation? She shook her head as though shaking away the thought. 'Anyway, please say you'll come. What if Tessa's there?' Although she hadn't tried any mean tricks since the itching powder incident, Tessa hadn't stopped her snide digs whenever she and Sally were alone.

Mary wrinkled her nose. 'I hate to say it, but I overheard her saying she wanted to go.'

'There you are, you have to come. Please don't make me spend an afternoon with her all alone.'

'Don't worry. We'll go.' Iris tossed the pillow back onto Sally's bed. 'Even if you do think it's a good idea to throw pillows at us.'

—

The day of the tournament arrived, and to Sally's delight it was a clear, sunny day and looked set to stay that way. She had been on night watch with Sue, and as soon as they were relieved, they raced back to the Wrennery on their bikes, determined to get a few hours of sleep to be fresh in the afternoon.

No sooner had her head hit the pillow than someone was shaking her shoulder.

'Come on, sleepy head. You have to eat now if you're going to have the energy to endure hours of football.'

Sally opened her eyes to find Iris staring down at her. 'Nice to see you so enthusiastic.' She swung her legs out of bed with a groan and went to wash and dress. Since she was off duty, she didn't have to wear her uniform, and as she opened the wardrobe to examine her clothes, she found herself wondering how Aldo would react to seeing her in a pretty dress. In the end, she reluctantly rejected the pretty Liberty print frock in favour of the tweed skirt that had been a present from Iris. Although it was sunny, there was a chill to the air, and she opted for warmth over appearance. Then her eyes lighted on a dark green ribbed jersey with a delicate lacy collar that she had bought in Helmsley. She had chosen it because it was a perfect match for one of the colours in her skirt. It had been an extravagance but now she was glad to have something both elegant and warm. She did her best not to think too hard about why she felt the need to look good today.

After the meal, she, Iris and Mary made their way to the other side of Stromness to the Royal Engineers camp where the tournament was to take place. They wore their light gaberdine mackintoshes, but these were more for something to sit on as there were still no clouds in the sky.

'Have either of you ever been to a football match before?' Mary asked.

Iris shook her head. 'My old school was not too far from Wycombe Wanderers' football ground, but my mother would never let me go near there on a match day.' Iris pulled a face. 'It was always very rowdy, though. I hope it won't be like that here.'

Mary snorted but said nothing.

'I used to watch the boys play football at school,' Sally said, 'but I've never been to a proper match.'

'Looks like this is going to be a fun day, then,' Mary remarked. 'I've never seen a match either, but if it's anything like rugby, it's going to be noisy.'

Sally wouldn't be put off, though. Spring was in the air, she and her friends had the day off and they were going to see Aldo. Or she hoped they would. It only occurred to her as they approached the playing field that he might not be on either of the teams. Would he still be there if he wasn't playing? She dreaded to think how she would ever face her friends again if she forced them to endure a tournament none of them was really interested in without seeing Aldo at all.

She needn't have worried. When they arrived, two teams were warming up on the pitch, and her gaze flew straight to Aldo who was jogging towards the centre.

There was quite a crowd gathered. News of the tournament seemed to have caused a lot of interest among the servicemen and women of the town. Sally recognised several young women from the WAAF and the ATS sitting in groups and, of course, the off-duty girls from the Wrennery. Seeing Tessa sitting in a group midway down one side of the pitch, Sally steered a path to the other side in the hope Tessa wouldn't notice her. Luckily, Tessa was too occupied in chatting to some men from the Royal Engineers and didn't so much as glance in their direction.

'Looks like Tessa isn't too heartbroken over Adam,' Mary said once they were out of earshot.

'It would be good if she fell in love with a nice man,' Sally said. 'She might stop picking on me.'

'Maybe, but I pity the poor man who ends up with her,' Mary said.

Finding a spot with a clear view of the pitch, they spread their macs on the ground and sat down. Sally propped her elbows on her knees and gazed at the players, enjoying the warmth of the sun on her back.

'Have they started yet?' Iris asked.

'I think they're just warming up.' Sally pointed at the players. 'Look, there's Aldo.' As she watched, Aldo and all the other players gathered around the centre of the pitch. She was glad to see the Italians were wearing football kits; possibly the men from the camp had managed to organise them as there was no way the Italians would be able to provide their own sports gear. It was good to see this evidence that they were being looked after and included in local events. 'I think they're about to start,' she said, when the players jogged to take up their positions on the field.

Sure enough, the referee blew his whistle, and one of the players in the centre kicked the ball down the field. There followed a lively match that none of the girls could follow, as none of them knew the rules. Not that Sally was trying to follow the match; she was more occupied in trying to see where Aldo was. However, the players dashed around the pitch so energetically, it made it difficult to pick out their features.

About ten minutes into the match, the British goalkeeper made a dramatic save then booted the ball back up the field to the cheers of the spectators. However, a gust of wind caught the ball and it rolled off the pitch, not far from where Sally and her friends sat. One of the Italian players ran to collect it and, with a pleasurable jolt of surprise, Sally saw it was Aldo. She waved at him, and Aldo, on the point of throwing it in, gave a start of surprise and fumbled his throw. The ball landed at the feet of a British player, causing several of the Italians to gesticulate wildly and shout at him. As they used Italian, Sally couldn't understand what they were saying but judging from the tone, it was not complimentary.

Aldo gave a little shrug, sent a beaming smile at Sally and then ran back onto the pitch. He redeemed himself a short while later when one of his teammates kicked the ball across the goal, and Aldo leapt into the air and headed it straight into the net.

Sally sprang to her feet, cheering like a mad thing. Aldo was too far away at this point to hear her, but she carried on all the same. She was pleased to see a ripple of applause from the spectators. Not as enthusiastic as it would have been had the British team scored, but it was nice to see the Italians being treated with respect by the spectators.

Even Iris and Mary seemed to take more interest in the game after that, cheering along with Sally when one of the players made a run towards goal. Fifteen minutes later, the referee blew his whistle, and the teams gathered beside each goal.

'Is that the end of the match?' Iris asked.

'I think it's half time,' Sally replied, dredging details of school matches from her memory. 'They'll change sides in a minute and start again.'

It was soon apparent she was correct, for after the players had had a drink, they took their places again and play resumed. Almost immediately one of the Royal Engineers made an exciting run for goal, skilfully dribbling the ball around two of the Italians and making a clever feint when approaching a third, fooling him into darting in the wrong direction. The Royal Engineer sailed past him and sent the ball flying into the net. Sally cheered along with everyone else, but from the lurch of disappointment she instinctively felt, she could no longer deny she was rooting for the Italians to win. She looked for Aldo among the players and saw him clap the shoulder of the player who had been fooled, obviously consoling him. The player had been walking away from the goal with a drooping head. Whatever Aldo had said must have worked, however, for he nodded at Aldo and ran to take his position with his head held high.

Only minutes after play resumed, this player intercepted the Royal Engineer who was in possession of the ball, cleverly took it and aimed a perfect pass forward that landed at the feet of another Italian. Seconds later, the ball was in the net, and the Italians were 2-1 up. Sally thought she might cheer herself hoarse. She had hardly stopped yelling when the referee blew his whistle again in three resounding blows, and the Italians leapt in the air, celebrating their victory.

Much to Sally's joy, once the players had moved off the field to make room for the next match, Aldo came jogging towards them.

'You played really well, Aldo. Well done,' Sally called as soon as he was close enough to hear.

Aldo grinned. 'We won. That is the important thing.'

'Come and sit down.' Sally shifted to the edge of her mac to make more room, although there was still not enough space for them to sit together without touching. When Aldo sat beside her, his knee nudged her thigh, and she was keenly aware of the heat radiating from his body. Sally felt an odd flutter in her stomach, and every inch of her skin prickled, making her acutely aware of his nearness.

She groped for something to say – anything to take her mind off these unaccustomed sensations. 'Are you allowed out of your camp every day or have they made an exception for today?'

'Every day. And we have new uniforms. You should see them. Much better than the old ones.'

'That's wonderful. I might see you in Stromness sometimes, then.'

'You will see me for sure if we arrange to meet. You said we would when I was allowed out, remember?'

Heat spread up her throat and across her face. 'I... yes, I did.'

'Good. Then I can buy you a drink, now I have money.'

Although Sally was looking at Aldo, she was sure Iris and Mary were watching them with ears flapping. There was no escaping it – she would be in for an interrogation when they got back to the Wrennery. Deciding she shouldn't appear too eager to meet him alone, she pointed to where a van stood with a queue of people. 'You could buy me a drink from there, if you like. It looks like they're selling refreshments.'

Aldo's face fell. 'I have no money with me today.'

Now she felt awful. Of course he wouldn't have brought money to play football. He looked so disappointed, she rose and held out her hand. 'It's your lucky day. I have money, and I'll treat you to a drink to celebrate your victory.'

He grinned and took her hand, and Sally gasped at the touch. His hand was strong, and as he pulled himself to his feet, she felt his fingers tense around hers. Once he was on his feet, they stood, gazing at each other, hands clasped until Aldo suddenly seemed to recollect himself and released her. 'It is not our victory yet. We must win the final.'

'I'd still like to get you a drink. At least walk with me to the van, because I'm thirsty even if you aren't.'

'Then thank you. I would like that.'

They joined the queue, and Sally suddenly felt at a loss for words. Odd, considering she had never had trouble talking to him before. Then she remembered she had just watched him play, and so congratulated him on his goal.

'It was a lucky shot,' Aldo said. Then he looked thoughtful. 'I have made friends with a black cat. I think he brought me luck.'

'Oh, I love cats. What is he called?'

'Nero.' He grinned. 'It is Italian for black.'

'Maybe he's your lucky charm.' Sally hesitated, then pulled out her St Christopher from the neck of her jumper. 'This is mine.'

'Then I am happy I gave it to you.' He smiled into her eyes, and Sally felt as though she suddenly couldn't get enough oxygen. His eyes were dark brown – she had always known that – but until now she had never noticed the amber flecks sparkling in their depths.

'Next. *Next!*'

Sally looked up with a start and saw they were at the front of the queue. The woman behind the counter was glaring at them.

'I'm sorry. I—' She glanced at the list chalked on a little blackboard. 'I'll have a ginger beer. Better make that three – one for Iris and Mary as well.' She paused, aware she was gabbling in her embarrassment, and took a breath to collect her wits. 'What will you have, Aldo?' She couldn't bring herself to meet his gaze, terrified of forgetting herself again.

'Whatever you're having, please.'

Sally held up three fingers. 'Four binger geers, please.' Her mind replayed what she had just said. 'I mean, ginger beers.'

The woman didn't look impressed. 'Make up your mind. Is that three or four?'

'Oh.' Sally glanced at her hand and felt her face burn. She raised a fourth finger. 'Four, please.'

She couldn't escape from the van quickly enough once she'd paid, handing Aldo his drink, then clutching the three other bottles to her chest as she scurried away.

Still flustered after giving Iris and Mary their drinks, she suggested to Aldo that they take a stroll around the field.

'I would like that,' Aldo replied. 'But I must return to the team soon.' He pointed at the pitch, where a second team of Italians were playing the Pioneer Corps. 'We play the winners of this match in the final.'

'Oh.' Sally hadn't even realised she had been surrounded by a bubble of happiness until it burst at Aldo's words. 'How long do we have?'

'About fifteen minutes. I must join my team before the end of the match.'

'I'll be cheering you on.'

'Even if we are playing the British?'

'Of course. I don't know anyone in the Pioneer Corps, but I know you.'

Aldo levered the top off his bottle and took a drink. He raised his eyebrows. 'This is good. What do you call it?'

She made a supreme effort not to muddle her words this time. 'Ginger beer.'

'I must remember to look out for it when I go to Stromness.' He suddenly laughed. 'I am free to go to Stromness! I cannot tell you how wonderful that feels.'

Sally raised her bottle to him in a toast. 'To freedom.'

Aldo clinked his bottle against hers. 'And to money in your pocket. That is another kind of freedom.'

'I suppose you're right. I hadn't thought of it that way before.'

'I know I'm right.' He grimaced and took another drink as though rinsing away a bad taste. 'I grew up in an orphanage, you know, and I never had any money of my own.'

'Do you remember your parents?'

'My father was killed in an earthquake when I was too young to remember, and my mother died when I was five. That St Christopher,' he pointed at the medallion that was now glinting in the sunshine at Sally's throat, 'was the only thing I had from her.'

Sally, aghast, put her drink on the ground then reached behind her neck for the clasp. 'Then you must have it back. It's far too precious for me to keep.'

'No.' Aldo dropped his bottle, took her hands and gently pulled them away from the necklace. He didn't release her hands, though, and Sally made no move to free them.

She shivered, although she wasn't cold. His hands enveloped hers, warm and strong, and she couldn't drag her gaze away from his. His eyes were fringed with long black lashes, and his black brows were drawn together, not in a frown but as though what he was trying to convey was the most serious thing he had ever said.

'I gave it to you as a gift because you were kind to me when I had gone without kindness for a very long time. It felt right for you to keep it, and it still does. Please don't turn it down.'

'I... of course, if it means that much to you. It's special to me. I wear it all the time.'

Aldo smiled, and his eyes creased at the corners. 'I'm glad.'

A faint glug drew Sally's attention to Aldo's ginger beer lying on its side in the grass. She gave a cry. 'Your drink!' Freeing her hands, she picked it up before all the liquid could pour out and handed it back to him. She needed him to be holding the bottle, not her hands, because she couldn't think straight when he was touching her.

She struggled to remember what they had been speaking of. 'What did you mean by saying money in your pocket was another kind of freedom?'

'Well, it was a hard life in the orphanage. The staff did their best but there were too many children for them to care for properly, and some of the children were...' he tailed off as though grasping for a word. 'What do you call it when someone picks a fight with other children for no reason?'

'A bully?'

'Yes. Some children were bullies and were cruel to those who were younger or weaker or just different in some way.'

'You don't have to explain what bullying is like.'

Chapter Sixteen

Sally's voice was hard, and Aldo gazed at her in concern. From her troubled expression, he could tell that she knew exactly what bullying was like. 'I'm sorry,' he said. 'You were bullied too, yes?'

She nodded, biting her lip. Her distress seemed too acute for someone who was remembering a past hurt.

'Is someone bullying you now?'

'Perhaps. I don't know what it is, really. I can't think what I've done to deserve it.'

'Nothing. You must believe that. It is not your fault. Who is it? What has she done?'

Sally shook her head. 'Maybe later. Tell me about the orphanage.'

Aldo hesitated then decided that he couldn't force her to tell him something she was clearly uncomfortable about. Privately, though, he hoped she would confide in him so he could give the bully a piece of his mind. 'I wasn't bullied myself. It was my younger brother, Carlo.' Aldo swallowed. It hurt to talk about Carlo. He could no longer think of his brother without remembering his last glimpse of him, of those sightless eyes, the face smeared in blood. Sally was waiting for his tale, though, so he cleared his throat and soldiered on. 'Carlo was two years younger than me. He was a daydreamer. He would wander about in a world of his own and told me stories about friends who weren't real.'

Sally's eyes lit up. 'Oh, I had an imaginary friend. I was very lonely when we first moved to Whitby, so I made up a friend called Lizzie.'

Aldo smiled. 'You and Carlo would have understood one another, I think.' Maybe it was Sally's dreamy, romantic nature, so like Carlo's, that had called to him when he had first met her at the hospital. He had felt very alone there – ill and frightened and still grieving for Carlo. Maybe that was why meeting her had felt like a kind of homecoming. 'Sadly, an orphanage is no place for a dreamer. He was an obvious target for those who wanted to lash out at the world for the cruel hand they had been dealt. I protected him as best I could. I wasn't afraid to fight when I had to. But I couldn't be with him every minute of the day.' Aldo took another swig of ginger beer, wishing he could forget those dark days. 'So I used to tell him that we would run away together. We made all sorts of plans, and I think they were what kept him going.' It was certainly what had kept Aldo going. 'But I had no money and I could do nothing without it.'

Sally's eyes widened. 'So that's what you meant by money making you free.'

'Exactly. When I was fourteen, I overheard a man in church say he was looking for a helper in his bakery. I didn't wait but went straight up to him and begged for the job.' Aldo smiled at the memory. He couldn't have been a prepossessing sight in his threadbare clothes, and Signor Lombardi had probably been afraid he would have been robbed of all his possessions if he let such a rascally looking child in his bakery. 'I shall be forever grateful that his wife was there. I swear Signor Lombardi was opening his mouth to tell me where to go, but she cuffed him round the ear and told him that of course he would take me on. And that's when my life changed. I earned just enough to allow me to rent a room, and I moved Carlo in with me. As soon as he was old enough, Signor Lombardi took him on as well.'

Sally's eyes glistened, and she blinked away tears. 'Carlo is lucky to have such a good brother.' Then she frowned. 'Wait. I thought you said you didn't have any family.'

Aldo opened his mouth, but his throat was suddenly too tight to speak. He didn't have to say a word, though, for he saw comprehension dawn in Sally's face.

'Oh, Aldo. I'm sorry. How tragic.' She placed a hand on his arm, and Aldo was surprised and moved to see tears glinting in her eyes.

Whether from speaking of Carlo's death for the first time or from the evidence of Sally's compassion, Aldo didn't know. But it was as though he had kept his grief locked in a box deep in his heart, and now the lid had sprung open. Afraid he might break down in front of her, he drew a deep, shuddering breath and waited until he had regained control. 'It was quick and I was with him at the end,' he said.

'That's good. That you were with him, I mean. He died knowing you were there, that you loved him.'

'That's true. I suppose it was a better end than was granted to many poor souls in this war.' He gave himself a mental shake. 'I am sorry. It is a sunny day, I am no longer a prisoner and I am in the company of a beautiful young woman. I should be celebrating the happiest day I have known in a long time, not making you cry.'

'I don't mind. I'm glad you told me. It must have been a heavy burden to carry alone.'

He nodded. He found Sally's matter-of-fact sympathy did help, and he felt lighter than he had since before this terrible war had started. He decided it was time for another toast. He raised his bottle and said, 'Here's to a new start.' And he drained his bottle.

Sally returned the toast then asked, 'How are you going to spend your free time now you can go out?'

'I can't go far – only within five miles of the camp.'

'That's still far enough to see all of Stromness and the hills around us.'

While Captain Briars had told the Italians they were not allowed in bars, he had made no mention of cafes, and Aldo was determined to test the limits of his restrictions. 'What about a cafe in Stromness, at the same table as the most beautiful girl in Orkney?' This met with such a long pause that Aldo felt obliged to add, 'I mean you.'

'Oh, I knew you meant me. Only—' Sally clapped a hand to her mouth. 'I just realised how big-headed that made me sound. I don't really think I'm the most beautiful girl in Orkney. Oh, and I'm not fishing for compliments, either.'

By this time her cheeks were bright scarlet, and Aldo feared she was about to turn him down. He held out his hands in a calming gesture. 'I did not mean to make you uncomfortable. You do not have to meet me again of course, but you are my only friend outside the camp, and I would be sorry to lose you.' He indicated the empty bottle in his hand. 'I did promise to buy you a drink, though, and since you bought me this it would be only fair to allow me to repay your kindness.'

Sally looked reassured. 'I suppose it couldn't do any harm. It would be nice to see you again.'

'Wonderful. Are you free next Saturday?'

'I'm on watch in the morning, but I could meet you around two.'

'Perfect. I look forward to it.'

At that point, another girl ran up to them. Aldo didn't think she was one of the young women Sally had been sitting with. She was dressed in a thin, pretty frock despite the chill in the air and her hairstyle and make-up made her look as though she paid a lot of attention to fashion magazines. 'Sally, is this one of the Italian team members?' She pointed at Aldo but didn't address him, which he thought was rude.

'I am. Why?' he asked.

She gave him a cool look, her gaze sweeping from his head to his toes as though judging him. 'Your team want you back,' she said. 'The final is starting soon.'

Aldo stared at the pitch and saw the match had ended. From the Italians' downcast expressions, he guessed they had lost, so his team would be facing the Pioneer Corps. 'Thank you,' he said to the girl. Then he turned to Sally. 'I will see you on Saturday. Where shall we meet?'

'Outside the church – the one with the spire,' she said. 'You can't miss it.'

'Until then.' He jogged away, raising a hand in acknowledgement when Sally called out, 'Good luck!'

He jogged on a little farther and glanced back over his shoulder to get one last glimpse of Sally when he heard the blonde girl say, 'I can't believe you're seeing that man again. Or is it because you can't get a proper British man to notice you?'

It wasn't just the words but the sneering expression that made Aldo see red. Remembering what she had said about bullying, he knew without doubt that this was the person who had been making Sally miserable. Without thinking, he turned and marched back towards the pair. Not wanting to hurt her, he quelled the temptation to seize the girl by the arm. Instead, he leaned over her, making her take an involuntary step back. When he spoke, he kept his voice low to avoid making a scene. 'You can insult me all you like,' he said. 'I don't care what you say about me. But don't you dare insult my friend again. She is worth a thousand of you. If you cannot hold your tongue around her, then I will have to teach you a lesson.'

The girl opened and shut her mouth a few times, her eyes wide. Aldo took one last look at her, taking satisfaction in the way she seemed to have lost her voice. He doubted anyone had dared speak to her like that before. Finally, she squeaked, 'Well, really!' and then hurried away.

He glanced at Sally, about to ask if she would be all right, when at that moment, one of his teammates dashed up. 'Come on, Aldo, you're holding up the match!'

All he could do was wave and call, 'See you on Saturday!' The beaming smile she gave as he dashed off was all the reassurance he needed.

Unfortunately, he was so busy looking back at Sally, he came within a whisker of barrelling into Gianni, who was regarding him with narrowed eyes. Aldo could only hope he hadn't seen him with Sally, remembering his earlier threat. Cursing himself for not taking more care over Gianni's whereabouts, he muttered a half-hearted apology before joining his team. He belatedly noticed that his hands were sticky from the ginger beer that had spilled from his bottle. Shoving his less messy hand in his pocket, he was disconcerted not to find his handkerchief. Strange. He had got into the habit of always keeping one with him so he could use it to collect scraps of food for Nero, and he was sure he remembered pocketing one of the initialled hankies Sally had given him. He hoped he hadn't dropped it; he didn't want to lose anything he'd had from Sally.

This, of course, led to more thoughts of Sally. He was going to see her again in a week! Now he would do his utmost to help his team to another victory to crown the perfect day.

'Are you still going to pretend you don't have feelings for Aldo?' Iris asked as the three friends made their way back to the Wrennery at the end of the tournament. 'I think your cheers must have been heard all the way in South Ronaldsay when his team won.'

'I was happy for him,' Sally said. 'He's had an awful time, you know. Not just being taken prisoner, but he watched his brother die. He deserves a victory at last.'

'Is that what you were talking about when you went to get the drinks – his brother?'

'That and other things.'

'Is that a blush on your cheeks, Sally?' Mary was laughing. 'Go on – what other things did you talk about? How your hair is like a cascade of silk and your eyes like stars?'

Sally drew herself up to her full height, which was all of two inches taller than Mary. 'Interesting. I take it that's how Joe talks

177

to you. Aldo, on the other hand, was telling me about his early life.'

Iris patted her on the shoulder. 'I'm sorry. We shouldn't tease you. We were just having fun but we won't do it again. Will we, Mary?' This last sentence was spoken in tones a strict schoolmistress would be proud of.

'Of course not. Sorry, Sally.'

Sally looked from one to the other. 'I don't understand. You weren't so keen on me befriending him when I first met him.'

'That was when he was a POW,' Iris explained. 'However friendly he was, he was an enemy, and you could have got into no end of trouble if anyone suspected you were in a relationship with him. But that's all changed now. He's working for us, and it's nobody's business if you want to be friends with him.'

'Tessa wouldn't agree.'

'Why? Has she said anything?'

Sally hadn't had a chance to tell Iris and Mary what Tessa had said, because the match had already started by the time she had re-joined her friends, and she had been too occupied in cheering Aldo on to get into a conversation. Now she explained what had happened.

Mary's face was grim by the time Sally had finished. 'What a cow,' she said. 'What in the world have we done to deserve her? Just wait 'til I give her a piece of my mind.'

'Don't,' Sally pleaded. 'Aldo already gave her an earful.'

'He did?' Mary looked pleased. 'What did he say?' Once Sally had related Aldo's words as well as she could remember, Mary hooted. 'About time someone told her what's what. I think I'm starting to like him. Sally, I know you don't need it, but for what it's worth, you have my blessing if you want to carry on seeing him.'

'That's lucky,' Sally couldn't resist saying with a grin.

Iris clapped her hands. 'I knew it. You've arranged to see him again, haven't you? When?'

'Next Saturday afternoon.'

'Dash it. That's when Mary and I are on watch so we can't keep an eye on you.'

'Honestly, there's nothing for you to keep an eye on. Can't Aldo and I enjoy a cup of tea together without the two of you spying on us? Did I follow you when you were seeing Rob? Or you, Mary, when you started seeing Joe?'

Iris patted her shoulder. 'I suppose you can look after yourself. Just promise to tell us all about it afterwards.'

'Fair's fair,' Mary put in. 'We told you all about Rob and Joe, remember.'

Sally shook her head. 'How many times have I got to say it – I'm not going on a date with him.'

'Ah,' said Mary, 'but when I started meeting Joe it was just as friends, and look at us now.'

No matter how much Sally protested, Iris and Mary refused to accept she and Aldo would remain just friends, and although Sally didn't mention it, she couldn't help remembering her reaction when Aldo had taken her hands in his. Did she feel more than friendship for him? Could she truly have got over Adam so quickly?

When they reached the Wrennery, Mary and Iris went straight inside, but Sally lingered outdoors and wandered up the lane to the water's edge. Standing on the grassy bank, she gazed across the harbour. A sprinkling of daisies covered the grass; she picked one and plucked the petals one by one. 'He loves me, he loves me not.' When she started it was Adam's face she pictured. But when she pulled off the last petal, to the words, 'He loves me,' she saw Aldo, smiling at her, saying she was the most beautiful girl in Orkney.

Chapter Seventeen

All through Sally's morning watch on Saturday, nothing could spoil the pleasant thrill she felt at the prospect of meeting Aldo later. Not even having Tessa as her oppo. It was just the anticipation of seeing a friend, she told herself, and tried to forget Iris and Mary's teasing. It was only natural that they would want her to find love when they were so happily in love themselves, but Sally didn't want to rush into anything considering she had been so wrong about Adam. After mistakenly believing the jolt she'd felt upon shaking hands with Adam to be a sign that they were fated to be together, she wasn't going to let her fancies lead her astray just because she had felt a thrill at Aldo's touch. She would take her time.

Tessa was unusually subdued all morning. Although Sally expected her to start making critical comments about her or Aldo, she said nothing beyond what was necessary to carry out their duties. Sally could only hope that Aldo's words had made her stop and think about her behaviour.

Her excitement rose to a crescendo when Iris and Mary arrived to relieve them. Tessa greeted them with a tight smile then said to Sally, 'I hope you don't mind me going on ahead. I have errands to run.' Sally could only give her a distracted nod before she was racing away on her bicycle.

Mary watched her go, frowning. 'What's up with her?'

'I don't know. She's been quiet all morning.'

'Probably terrified of getting another tongue-lashing from Aldo.' Mary grinned. 'I wish I could have seen it.'

'Speaking of Aldo,' Iris said, eyes twinkling, 'I'm surprised you aren't racing off yourself. I thought you were looking forward to today.'

'I am. I'm just a bit nervous now.'

Iris regarded her with sympathy. 'That's understandable, but you got on like a house on fire last week. You'll feel fine when you see him. Now go and enjoy yourself.'

'And tell us all about it later,' Mary called after her, when Sally was about to close the door behind her.

Although her nerves eased during the ride back to the Wrennery, her jitters returned in full force at her first glimpse of Aldo on top of the steps outside the church. He wore a new uniform in a smart shade of reddish-brown, and he seemed to stand a little taller than when he had worn the old uniform. He was looking in the other direction, giving her a moment to admire his dark, ruffled hair and broad shoulders. Then he turned, and their eyes met. Her breath caught in her throat, and she knew she could no longer deny the attraction she felt for him. At the same time, she could almost hear Iris's voice, lecturing her. *Your trouble is, your mind skips straight from attraction to marriage. Don't let your imagination run away with you. Just enjoy the afternoon and decide if you want to meet again at the end of it.*

Aldo waved and descended the steps two at a time. She was so flustered, she didn't protest when he stooped to kiss her on each cheek. 'You have been on duty, yes? Have you eaten?'

'Not yet.' Not wanting him to feel obliged to buy her lunch, she added, 'I'm not terribly hungry, though, so I don't mind if you've already eaten.'

'Nonsense. You must eat, and I am hungry too. Where shall we go?'

Sally directed him to the Beehive, and her heart skipped when he offered her his arm as though they were on a proper date. As they strolled down the street, Aldo confided in a low voice, 'I do not think we are supposed to take girls out, but I don't think anyone will stop us, do you?'

Sally looked around, half fearing to see soldiers converging on them, rifles raised. Thankfully, all she saw was people going about their business. There were several other men dressed in the same uniform as Aldo, with 'Italy' written clearly upon their shoulders, and although they attracted curious stares, no one challenged them. 'I think we've got away with it,' she said with a grin.

Aldo gallantly held the door open for her after climbing the steep steps up to the Beehive and Sally knew a brief moment of worry when they went to sit at the table in the far corner, fearing the waitress would tell them to leave. But no one challenged them, and her fears subsided.

Aldo picked up the menu. 'It is good I took English lessons in Camp 60 or I might need you to read it to me. What will you have?'

'Oh, I know you promised to buy me a drink, but you don't have to get my food as well.' It suddenly occurred to Sally that although Aldo was now being paid, he wouldn't be getting much.

'I know, but I want to treat you. I insist.'

She couldn't help comparing this meal with the time she had eaten here with Adam and ended up paying for it herself. She had to admit it made a pleasant change to be with someone who wanted to treat her. 'That's very kind.'

Aldo gave a dismissive wave of the hand. 'You are the kind one. I have looked forward to today all week.'

Sally felt the heat rushing to her cheeks as she studied the menu. Not that she needed to read it — she knew it by heart — but looking at him would make her even more flustered. 'I think I'll have the soup. It's very good.'

'Then so will I.'

Once they had given their order, Sally, who was still feeling a little tongue-tied, remembered that this was Aldo's first visit to the town. 'What do you think of Stromness?'

Aldo raised his eyes to the ceiling with a gesture that spoke of utter bemusement. 'I cannot understand the street names.

The same street has different names. Is it John Street, Victoria Street or Dundas Street? I don't know!'

Sally laughed. 'It becomes Alfred Street further on.'

Aldo shook his head. 'Then I am glad I didn't go that far. I think it is done to confuse foreigners.'

'You'll get used to it.'

'I suppose so. Other than that, I like Stromness.' He made a gesture as though closing a book. 'But anyway, I did not ask you out to discuss street names. I want to learn more about you. I told you about my childhood last week. What about yours? Where did you grow up?'

And so Sally told him all about the farm on the North York Moors, the move to Whitby and working at the fishmongers. As she talked, she forgot her nervousness and she felt as though she and Aldo had known one another for years.

'So you also worked in a shop – you in a fishmongers, I in a bakery,' Aldo said when she finished. 'We have much in common, no?'

'No, I mean yes, I suppose we do.'

'And you never knew your father, either, and then lost your home when your uncle had his accident. You must have had to grow up fast. You are strong to take on that responsibility at a young age.'

'I never looked at it that way before. I don't think I was as strong as you. From what you say, you were always looking forward to a future that would be better. I was always looking back to a past that was gone for ever.'

Aldo shrugged. 'We all have different ways of coping. I was forced to plan for the future for my brother's sake. From what you say, though, you had to help provide for your mother and uncle from a young age, and who can blame you if looking back helped you cope? It doesn't mean you aren't strong.'

Their soup and tea arrived at this point, and Sally was saved from answering. She buttered a roll with great concentration while she pondered what Aldo had said. It was true she had felt a greater need to obey superstition after Ted's accident, and her love of fairy tales and listening to her mother's stories about her father had also started then. Was Aldo right and it was just her way of handling her loss? If so, perhaps it was time she tried letting go of some of her superstitious habits.

The soup, as usual, was delicious – brimming with chunky vegetables and thickened with barley, it made a filling meal. Aldo ate with gusto, and Sally smiled to see his obvious delight at such simple fare.

'Ah, you are laughing at me,' he said as he mopped up every last drop of the soup with his bread. 'But you must understand how special this is for me.' He gestured around the cafe. 'Maybe this is normal for you, but I have been locked away for years. I feel like I must pinch myself to know I am not dreaming.'

'I'm sorry. I didn't think—'

'No, don't apologise. I was beginning to fear this day would never come but now it is here, I cannot contain my joy.'

Sally listened to him, mesmerised by the gestures he made as he spoke. It was almost like watching a dance that described the emotion behind his words. Every movement of his hands and tilt of his head conveyed his thoughts and feelings far better than words alone, until she could almost believe that she would understand even if he spoke in Italian. So entranced was she that only belatedly did she realise he was talking about her again.

'And best of all,' he was saying, 'I can celebrate my new freedom with you, the most beautiful woman in Orkney.' Then he stopped, looking stricken. 'I did not think to ask before. Perhaps you already have a young man in your life.'

Sally found she had to close her hand around her teacup to stop its trembling. She had tried to persuade Iris and Mary that she and Aldo were just friends, although she had known deep down that Aldo's feelings for her were more romantic. She could let him down gently now and say she was interested in another man and she needn't say that man was married to someone else. Alternatively, she could let go of her fear and admit that she was single.

She drew a deep breath. 'No, there isn't another man.' Too late did she realise that by saying *another* man, she was implying that Aldo was already a part of her life. Aldo clearly didn't miss her slip, and his eyes gleamed. She felt the need to explain about Adam so he would understand she needed time.

That's when it struck her that she was considering more than friendship with Aldo. It was a scary thought, and her shock made her blurt her next words without thinking. 'There was someone I liked, and I thought he liked me but I was wrong. I made a bit of a fool of myself.'

'If he didn't like you, then *he* was the fool.'

The absolute conviction in his voice set her pulse aflutter. After years of waiting for Adam to notice her, it was something of a revelation to be confronted with Aldo's obvious interest. She hadn't realised until now how small it had made her feel to be so thoroughly overlooked by the man she had set her heart on. She couldn't understand why she had clung to her belief that he was the one for her for all that time. Yet another nail in the coffin for her superstitious beliefs.

'That's a lovely thing to say.'

'It's true. I wouldn't say so if I didn't mean it.'

Even had she wanted to, she couldn't have dragged her gaze from his. Did he truly mean what he said or was it just flattery? She searched his eyes for any hint of insincerity, wishing Iris and Mary had come to watch over her after all, so she could ask for their opinion. Every instinct told her he *was* sincere, but her mistake over Adam had shaken her confidence. Still, they weren't here so all she could do was trust her judgement and pray it didn't let her down again.

Perhaps Aldo sensed her confusion, for he gave a little wave of the hand as if in apology and said, 'Tell me about that girl who was unkind to you last week. She is the bully you were talking about before, no?'

Relieved to be released from his intense gaze, she said, 'Yes, although she wasn't so bad this week. Perhaps your warning worked.'

'Let us hope so. But you will tell me if she bothers you again? As I said, I have some experience with bullies. I might be able to suggest ways to help.'

'Oh, but I could never get into a fight.'

Sally's horror at the thought of squaring up to Tessa like a boxer must have shown on her face for Aldo laughed. 'I would not recommend a fight – it would only get you into trouble. But there are other ways to deal with bullies.'

'Like what?' Sally leaned forward across the table.

'It is mostly how you act and how you hold yourself. A bully enjoys seeing your fear – it gives them a feeling of power to know they can make you feel that way. They will pick on someone who appears nervous or lacking in confidence, because they know they can easily frighten them. If you are not afraid of them, they will eventually give up.'

Was that why Tessa had picked on her – because she had thought Sally was nervous or lacked confidence? Sally didn't think she was nervous, although she supposed her superstitious actions might make her appear so. Maybe she did lack confidence when it came to men, though. It was impossible to remain confident when the man you loved never treated you as special. Perhaps she had been drawn to Aldo from the start because he had made his interest clear and had gone out of his way to be with her. It was certainly a boost to her confidence to know he had enjoyed her company that much. Anyway, she would remember Aldo's advice and make an effort to appear confident when Tessa was around.

'That does make sense,' she said. 'I'll remember that.'

'And let me know if you need more help?'

'I will.'

'Good.' Aldo grinned. 'That means you want to see me again.'

She smiled back. 'I suppose it does.' And before they said goodbye, she had promised to see him the following week when she had a free evening.

'You should bring him here.' Elspeth covered the teapot in a knitted tea cosy that Sally had made for her at Christmas and carried the tea tray to the table.

Sally stared at Elspeth across the remains of the Sunday lunch she, Iris and Mary had been enjoying with the Heddles. 'Bring who here?'

Elspeth gave a slow shake of the head. 'Your young man, Aldo, of course.'

'You know,' Mary put in. 'The one you've been talking about non-stop all through lunch.'

'Oh. Have I?' Heat spread across Sally's face. It was over a month since Sally's meal with Aldo at the Beehive, and she had met him three times since then. Each meeting had been more enjoyable than the last, and she was eagerly anticipating the next one. 'Well, I'm sure he'd like to meet you. He's not my young man, though.' She saw Iris and Mary exchange glances and grin. 'No, really. We're just friends.'

'Of course,' Mary said. 'Although if Joe saw me look at any of my male friends the way you looked at Aldo the other day, he wouldn't be happy.'

Elspeth gave Mary a light cuff on the side of her head. 'There now, don't tease the poor lass. If she says they're just friends, then that's what they are. Anyway,' she turned her back on Mary and addressed Sally, 'I'd be delighted to meet him. When are you seeing him again?'

'Not until June the fifteenth.' Nearly a fortnight away, and already Sally was missing him. She had tried to arrange an earlier date but she was having to work extra shifts to cover for two Wrens who were ill.

'Then it's settled. Bring him here for supper. I expect he'll need feeding up.' Elspeth turned to Iris and Mary. 'What about you two – will you be able to come?'

'Try and stop us,' Iris replied. 'We haven't spent much time with Aldo, and I for one want to see if he's good enough for her.'

'Mind yourself, lass, or you won't get any fruitcake.'

Iris held up her hands in mock surrender. 'All right, Elspeth. I'm sorry.' And she changed the subject, much to Sally's relief. Even so, Sally was glad Iris and Mary wanted to spend more time with Aldo. Despite their teasing, she valued their opinion and wanted to know what they thought of him, her experience with Adam having severely shaken her confidence in her own judgement.

At the end of the afternoon, Mary and Iris walked Sally to the signal station where she was due on watch for the evening. It was too much to hope that they would remain quiet on the subject of Aldo now they were no longer under Elspeth's eye.

Sure enough, Iris spoke up as soon as Sally had collected her bike. 'Come on, Sally. You talk about Aldo an awful lot for someone who's just a friend. How do you really feel about him?'

'He's lovely. I always used to get tongue-tied around Adam, but I have no problem chatting with Aldo.' The old Sally would have enthused about the thrill she felt whenever she saw him but now she held back, remembering her resolution not to let her imagination run away with her. 'I suppose it's because we're just friends.' Sally stressed the 'just friends' part to reassure Iris and Mary that there was no danger of her creating another fantasy romance.

It sounded lame, even to herself, and she wasn't surprised when Iris looked sceptical. 'Or maybe you find him easy to talk to because you're so well suited. What do you talk about?'

Iris thought they were well suited? A rush of pleasure seemed to warm Sally from the inside. 'Oh, everything. Sometimes he tells me funny stories about his friend Enrico or about goings-on in the camp. He's a really good listener, too. He likes to hear about my life.' In fact, Sally had found herself sharing things about the dark days following her uncle's accident that she hadn't even said to Iris or Mary, about her fears that Ted would die and her loneliness after moving to a new home where she had no friends. In return, he told her more of his brother – how he had protected him at the orphanage and of the happier times after he had been employed at the bakery. Realising she had gone quiet, she hastily said, 'I think I know him far better than I ever knew Adam.'

'I'm glad,' Iris said. 'He sounds like he has your best interests at heart and is truly interested in you. Not like Adam. I can say it now, but I never really liked him. Even before I met him, I hated how unhappy he seemed to make you. I could tell he never considered your feelings.'

Sally bit her lip and watched the wheel spokes gleam in the sunshine as she pushed her bike along the track. 'I suppose you're right, only I didn't like to admit it. It's why I always felt deflated after seeing him.'

'I know.' Iris sounded grim. 'And believe me, if he hadn't gone and got himself married to someone else I would have tried to warn you.'

'But Aldo, now, he's a different kettle of fish,' Mary said. 'He pays you proper attention.' Then Mary sighed. 'It's a shame he'll be going back to Italy after the war, otherwise I think you'd be perfect together.'

The icy chill that seized Sally at those words took her by surprise. 'Returning to Italy? I never thought of that.' She'd grown so used to the routine of life in Orkney that she'd forgotten it was only temporary. For a fleeting moment she found herself hoping the war would last for a long while so she and Aldo needn't be apart, then she hated herself for wishing something so terrible.

She glanced at her friends, half expecting them to have read her thoughts and be looking shocked. If anyone would want a speedy end to the war it would be Iris and Mary, who had lost loved ones and were now separated from their sweethearts.

Thankfully, they gave no sign of having detected her treacherous wish and were regarding her with sympathy.

'He must want to go back to see his family,' Iris said. 'But there's no need to think too far ahead. My advice is to enjoy his company while you can and don't make trouble for yourself ahead of its time.'

'I'll try. He doesn't have any family, though. He's an orphan.' And now another thought crept into her mind. What if he wanted to stay in Britain? Would he be able to?

Then she caught herself and laughed.

Mary raised her eyebrows. 'I didn't realise orphans were so funny.'

'It's not that. I just realised that I've been trying to make you all believe that I feel nothing more than friendship towards Aldo, then at the first mention of him going home, I realise saying goodbye to him would feel like the end of the world.'

'So you do have feelings for him,' Iris said. It was a statement, not a question.

'I suppose I must. Or, at least, I want to have time to decide if I do.' She walked a few more steps in silence then said, 'I've never met anyone like him before. He's always struck me as kind and gentle, if a little playful. But when he overheard Tessa make a catty remark, he didn't hesitate to give her a piece of his mind. He gave me some good advice about coping with her, too.'

'Did he tell you to tip her over a cliff?'

Sally glared at Mary and shook her head in exasperation. 'No, because he doesn't want me to be hanged for murder.'

'It wouldn't be murder. It would be a service to the world. They'd probably give you a medal. Ow.' Mary rubbed her arm, and stared daggers at Iris, who had just elbowed her. 'What did you do that for?'

'Because I want to hear what Sally has to say. Go on, Sally, what did Aldo tell you?'

'Well, he seems to have had a lot of experience with bullies in the orphanage where he grew up,' Sally said, then went on to repeat Aldo's advice.

'Sounds sensible,' Iris said, 'Although I've never thought of you as lacking confidence, so I still can't think why Tessa chose to pick on you. But you definitely need to show her that you're not bothered by her needling.'

Sally nodded. 'I know. After all, that's what I did in a way with the itching powder incident. She didn't try that again, did she?'

'I might have had something to do with that,' Mary said with a grin. 'Didn't I tell you what I said to her?' When the others shook their heads, she went on, 'I was on watch with her right after you told me about the itching powder. I told her I wondered if there was anything wrong with Second Officer Wendleton because I'd seen her stagger around in the snow, stamping her feet and looking most peculiar.'

Sally laughed. 'You didn't! I'd love to have seen Tessa's face when you told her that.'

'It was quite a sight. I swear she went several shades paler.'

'I almost feel sorry for her,' said Iris with a grin. 'If she had any itching powder left, I bet she raced back to her cabin to get rid of the incriminating evidence. She must have been living in dread of Wendleton going on the warpath.'

'I don't feel sorry for her. It was a mean trick to pull, and I hope my tale about Wendleton put the fear of God in her.'

'I think it must have done,' Sally said. 'She might have carried on making her snide remarks, but at least she hasn't tried anything like that again. Anyway, I'm going to try what Aldo suggested. I'm going to act like nothing she says bothers me and hopefully she'll get bored and give up.'

'I suppose it's good advice,' Mary said. 'And you can always tip her over a cliff afterwards if it doesn't work.'

They carried on to the signal station, laughing and inventing new and terrible punishments for Tessa, until it was time to part ways.

'Enjoy your watch,' Iris said as they paused beside the gate. 'At least it should be quiet. I don't know where all the ships have got to lately.'

'It's not just the ships,' Mary said. 'Haven't you noticed there are fewer troops around? I was in Stromness yesterday and it was positively deserted.'

'Now you come to mention it, it *is* quieter than usual. I wonder why.' Then Sally dismissed the thought and headed into the signal station.

It was probably a good thing her watch was uneventful that evening, for her head was full of what she had come to realise about Aldo. The thought of him leaving and returning to Italy for good had filled her with dread. Although he had made it clear he was interested in her, he hadn't put any pressure on her to say if she returned his feelings or not. But now, the thought that he planned to return to Italy as soon as he could made her wonder what he wanted from their friendship. Was she just a casual diversion for him, a way to forget his hardships for a while, or did he want more? And if he did want more, what future could they have? At the thought of the future, Sally's head went into a spin, for it was an unanswerable question. Iris was right; Sally needed to take things one step at a time and see where it led without thinking too far ahead. But she was now clear about one thing: she was coming to care for Aldo very much.

Chapter Eighteen

Only two days later, the reason for the troops' removal from Orkney became apparent when the whole island was abuzz with news of the Normandy landings. After years of hearing reports of the harrowing damage done to the Arctic convoys, it was wonderful to have good news at last. When the news first broke, rumour said that the Allies would be in Berlin within a few weeks, and the war would be over. Even when it became apparent that the Allied advance, although happening, would be slow, there was a sense that victory was now inevitable even if it didn't happen that year.

It soon became obvious that the Nazis hadn't given up the fight when a new horror fell on the south of Britain – flying bombs. Although Orkney was out of range, it was a strange and helpless feeling to hear reports of bombs dropping out of the sky onto the houses of London with little warning. Sally felt for Iris who had friends and relatives based in London, even though her mother had moved away from the south-east. The flying bombs did affect Orkney in one very obvious way: all the barrage balloons were removed from their locations around Scapa Flow and taken down to London and the south-east coast in a bid to provide more protection against the menace. It happened very quickly, and Sally, stepping out into a clear June morning at the end of a night watch, felt as though she were entering into a new and alien landscape. She had become so accustomed to seeing the silvery grey balloons in the air all around that she had forgotten they weren't part of the coastline.

Even so, despite the reason, she couldn't help rejoicing in the clear view and hoped it augured well for that evening, as it was the day she was taking Aldo to Curlew Croft.

As she was wheeling her bike onto the track, she froze. Perched on the top of the coal bunker was a magpie. A single magpie. One for sorrow.

She should wait for another. She hadn't waited that day on the farm when she'd been in a hurry to return home and read her book, and look what had happened later that very day – her uncle had fallen from his horse and life had never been the same again.

She glanced at her watch. Time was getting on, and she would miss breakfast if she didn't get back soon. She also wanted to have a good sleep so she would be fresh for the evening. A few minutes wouldn't hurt, though, and surely she would see a second magpie. She propped her bike against the fence and looked around.

Worryingly, the clifftop was devoid of magpies, except for the one still perched on the coal bunker, tilting its head this way and that. She held her breath and listened for the rapid machine-gun fire of a magpie's call but all she could hear was the twitter of dozens of unseen small birds and a curlew whistling its haunting song. Time was ticking by; she had to leave now if she was to have a hope of getting breakfast.

Hadn't Iris and Mary always teased her over her superstitions and tried to persuade her not to let them rule her life? Her uncle's accident, they argued, had been a horrible coincidence. To do them justice, they seemed to be able to ignore single magpies or spilt salt without terrible things happening to them. If she asked Iris and Mary, she knew what they would say. They would tell her to go and not let her life be ruled by superstition.

She returned to her bike, feet dragging. Then another thought struck – she might see a second magpie on her ride to Stromness, and that would count, wouldn't it? Her mind made up, she grabbed the bike and set off.

Although she failed to spot another magpie, her mind turned to Aldo and how much she looked forward to seeing him again. Therefore, once she had finished her breakfast and was settling down to sleep, she was able to dismiss her fears. She even looked forward to telling Iris and Mary and hearing them praise her for making a sensible decision.

–

As had become their habit, Sally met Aldo outside the church again later that evening. Her heart skipped when he kissed her on each cheek, and this time she didn't step back so quickly. Instead, she lingered in his hold, enjoying the feelings of warmth and security that came from being close to him. 'I hope you're not too tired,' she said when she eventually stepped back. 'We've been invited to tea with some friends, and they live a couple of miles away.'

'I will go wherever you like,' Aldo replied. 'Only I must be back at the camp by ten.'

'Don't worry. Mary and Iris will be there too, and none of us have late passes.'

They walked down the street, Sally pointing out where Dundas Street became Albert Street, and then on to the far end of town where the Wrennery stood.

'This is where you live?' Aldo peered up at the tall, stark, gabled building, wrinkling his nose. 'I think perhaps the hut where I stay is not so bad.'

'I'm used to it. I share a room with Iris and Mary, and it's quite cosy really, even though it does get freezing cold in the winter.'

They were about to walk on when the door opened and Tessa walked out. She hesitated when she saw Sally with Aldo, then she squared her shoulders and, much to Sally's surprise, marched up to them. Sally braced herself, expecting a snide remark. Instead, Tessa said in a low voice, 'I was hoping to speak with you. Do you have a moment?'

'Can it wait? We're expected up at Curlew Croft.'

'All right. How long will you be? I'll go for a walk but I'll be waiting in the common room when you get back.'

That wasn't Sally's idea of a pleasant end to the day. However, she doubted Tessa would be put off, so she might as well get it over with. She would be with Iris and Mary by then, of course, so at least they would be nearby for moral support. She agreed, saying she would be back before ten, and then carried on with Aldo up the path to Kyeness.

'Has she upset you at all since I spoke to her?' Aldo asked.

'No. She's been rather quiet, actually. Anyway, let's not spoil the evening by talking about her.' And they fell into an easy conversation, Sally pointing out all her favourite views as they climbed the hill and saw Hoy Sound and Stromness spread out below them.

'You love it here, yes?' Aldo said after Sally had made them stop to admire their first glimpse of the sea beyond Hoy Sound.

'I do. I wasn't so keen at first. We – Iris, Mary and I – first arrived here in the middle of winter.' Sally shuddered, remembering. 'It was so cold and bleak, I thought I'd never get used to it. I did, though, and I've made wonderful friends and have a job where I know I'm helping the war effort. It's been one of the happiest times of my life. What about you – do you like it?' Then she remembered that Aldo had come here as a prisoner and thought of the tiny, bleak island where he'd been held at first. 'Sorry. That was a silly question. You must have had an awful time here. I couldn't blame you if you wanted to leave and never see Orkney again.'

'It was awful at first, but then I met you.'

It was as though an unseen force had taken hold of her body, turning her head until her eyes locked with Aldo's, heart hammering against the cage of her chest. He was looking down at her with an expression of tenderness that made her catch her breath. 'I...' But she had no idea what to say. All she could do was carry on gazing at him, unable to look away.

'Whenever I feel lonely or sad, I think of you and I feel better. Meeting you was like meeting an angel.'

Sally laughed, breaking some of the tension. 'I am *not* an angel.'

'You were to me. You brought a ray of light into my life when all was dark. Then at Christmas, you sent me those wonderful gifts. You did not forget me.'

'How could I forget you? I was feeling ill and lonely in that hospital all by myself. I was so glad you escaped from your ward to see me.'

The tension was back. In an automatic gesture, Sally raised her hand to clutch the St Christopher. A moment later, Aldo's hand enclosed hers, and her heart thumped so hard she was sure he must feel it even through their joined hands. He was going to kiss her. If she'd asked herself five minutes earlier if that's what she wanted, she wouldn't have known the answer. But right now, all her doubts and worries faded away and she knew that if he didn't kiss her soon, she would expire from disappointment.

He didn't let her down. Stooping, he pressed his lips to hers in a gentle kiss that was more a question than an expression of passion or love. It lasted only a few seconds, and then he backed away a fraction, regarding her with raised brows. Fleeting as the kiss had been, her lips tingled as though touched by a live wire. She stood still, quivering in expectation, yet he didn't move to kiss her again. Then it dawned on her that he was waiting for her. She could kiss him back, or step away. If she stepped away she knew he wouldn't try again. She didn't even have to think. Lifting her face, she pressed her lips to his.

When she had imagined her first kiss, she had thought there would be violins playing like in romantic films, and that she would instinctively know what to do. This was nothing like the kisses she had seen at the cinema although it was still lovely. She didn't know what to do with her hands, and because she was standing on tiptoe, she gripped his arms to steady herself. For the first time she felt the firm muscle hidden beneath his sleeves, the result of many months of hard labour. Only moments ago she had thought that kissing him was the right thing to do. Now she was reminded of the gulf between them — not that he had been a prisoner but that he came from Italy and would probably return there as soon as he could.

She broke the kiss and dropped her hands, missing the contact immediately. 'I'm sorry,' she said. 'I shouldn't have done that.'

'Why — didn't you want to?'

'No, I did.'

'You didn't enjoy it?'

'No, I mean yes. I liked it.'

'Then what is wrong?'

'This is all too… complicated. I could be posted somewhere else any day. You might be sent back to Italy.'

'That is true. I know you can't help where you are sent, but I can tell you that if they try to send me back to Italy, I will fight to stay as long as you want me here.'

'Oh.' As far as romantic declarations went, it wouldn't have made it into a Hollywood film, but Sally thought it the most romantic thing she had ever heard. She remembered Iris's advice not to think too far ahead but to enjoy Aldo's company while she could. Now she saw what Iris meant. She couldn't control what happened tomorrow, but for now she wanted to be with Aldo. 'Iris gave me some advice the other day, and she's right. I'll accept whatever happiness we can have today because we don't know what tomorrow will bring.'

Aldo had been watching her with anxious lines creasing his brow. Now he relaxed and held out his hand. 'That is very wise advice. I like your friends.'

'That's good, because they're going to be at Curlew Croft too.' Then she glanced at her watch. 'Oh my goodness! We'll be late if we don't hurry.'

Feeling somewhat dazed at the turn of events, although happy, she took his hand and tugged him along the track.

Chapter Nineteen

Aldo's heart sang as he walked with Sally, cradling her hand in his as though it was a fragile piece of china. Although he had dreamed of kissing her ever since they had first met, reality outstripped imagination. When he had planted that first kiss upon her lips, he had feared she might run away or tell him she could never feel that way about him. Instead, she had welcomed the caress and returned it with a kiss of her own. While neither had spoken of their feelings, let alone love, he knew his heart was irrevocably given.

He couldn't ignore Sally's worries, though. Neither of them knew what would happen in days to come and until he knew what lay ahead, he couldn't ask her for any form of commitment. Not when he was powerless to keep any promise he might make to her. But today they were together, and the sun was shining. He would enjoy this moment and try not to think about the inevitable separation to come.

The track led downhill to a headland, and now he could hear the waves pounding against the cliffs. A squat, square concrete building stood on the headland, and the track ran past it along the clifftop.

'That's where I work,' Sally said, pointing to the building. 'Curlew Croft is a little way down the track.' Although her tone was conversational, it held a slight tremor, and he guessed she was still thinking about the kiss.

Aldo glanced at the signal station. 'You must feel very alone, working all the way out here.'

'No, I love it. And I'm never alone – we work in pairs.'

'I'm glad to hear it.' Deciding that Sally, like him, would prefer not to dwell on the implications of the kiss, he said, 'I still think it was brave of you to leave your life behind and come all the way up here.'

'I don't feel brave. And I didn't have much choice where I was sent.'

'If there wasn't a war on, what would you have liked to do?'

'Oh, that's easy.' Her face took on a dreamy expression, and Aldo knew she was picturing her vision of the life she had been denied. 'I wanted to be married and have a house near the sea, with hens and a garden where I can grow my own vegetables. What about you? Would you have stayed in the bakery?'

'Yes, but I wanted to run my own bakery one day. You might not believe it, but I was good. I made bread, of course, but also cakes and pastries. You should try my cannoli.'

'What are they?'

Aldo frowned, struggling to find the right words. 'They are rolls of fried pastry with a creamy filling.'

He described his other favourite pastries until she gave him a little push. 'Stop it – you're making me hungry!' Then Sally stopped and pointed at a building a couple of hundred metres farther along the track. 'There's Curlew Croft. Complete with hens, I might add.'

'A little house by the sea, like your ideal home.'

Sally regarded it with a tilted head. 'I suppose it is. I don't have big dreams.'

'It sounds like a good one to me.'

'I can't see it happening any time soon, if ever. I know I can't expect everything I want in real life.'

To Aldo, that was the saddest thing he had heard in a long time. If he was free, he would offer her everything she asked and more. However, he wasn't free, so he held his tongue. All he could say was, 'Don't give up on your dreams too easily. You deserve everything you wish for.'

Sally gave him a beaming smile and squeezed his hand. What she might have said in reply, he never found out, for they were approaching the cottage. Sally was on the point of speaking when the door opened and a tall, middle-aged woman with ashy blonde hair escaping from a bun dashed out. Her face was pink and harassed. 'Oh, there you are, Sally. Thank goodness. The hens have escaped from the yard and into the field. Would you be a dear and help us round them up? Iris and Mary are there already but they're nowhere near as good as you with poultry.'

Sally nodded, and Aldo said, 'I will come too. The baker I used to work for kept hens, and I helped with them sometimes.'

Sally glanced at him, eyes wide, then made a hurried introduction. Elspeth regarded him in silence for a moment as though assessing him, then smiled. 'A useful man to know. I'd be glad of any help you can give.'

So instead of the evening he had pictured spent sitting around a table, drinking tea, he found himself running through a field, dodging cows and cow pats, and chasing chickens that had clearly had their feed laced with something that gave them extra energy. The air rang with laughter, squawks and the occasional indignant moo. By the time he had cornered the last hen against a feeding trough and grabbed it before it could escape, he was sweaty, dishevelled and grinning like a schoolboy let loose in a sweet shop. Sally was laughing and breathless, her face glowing from the exercise. She linked arms with him as he carried his charge to the shed where the hens were to be shut until Archie could mend the wire fence.

Once Elspeth had secured the door, she turned to Aldo and looked him up and down. 'Well, that was quite the introduction. I'm glad Sally decided to bring you along today. Now, come in, the lot of you, and have a wash before tea. Although what we're going to have I don't know. I've been too busy chasing hens to make anything.'

Elspeth ushered them into the kitchen, where they were able to dust themselves down and wash their hands in the sink, using the buckets of water that Mary carried in from outside. Once

Aldo felt more presentable, he noticed Elspeth was reaching for a large jar on a high shelf, so he got it down for her.

'Oh, thank you,' she said. 'You're very kind.'

'Is there anything else I can do to help?'

'Not unless you can make a chicken pie for us in double-quick time.'

'I can do that if you show me where you keep your ingredients.' He grinned, knowing Elspeth hadn't meant him to cook, but he had taken one look at the kitchen with its huge range and long, wooden table and had longed to work in it. Without waiting for Elspeth to reply and, seeing the jar he had retrieved contained flour, he tipped a quantity into the bowl Elspeth had clearly got out for the purpose and set about mixing pastry.

'Well, I can see you know what you're about,' Elspeth said after regarding him with her hands on her hips for a while. 'Sally, you've found a good one. Make sure you hang onto him.' Then she went to the pantry and returned with the remains of a roast chicken.

Aldo glanced over his shoulder and winked at Sally, who was blushing a becoming shade of pink.

With Aldo making and rolling out the pastry and Elspeth preparing the filling, it wasn't long before the pie was in the oven. Elspeth then insisted he sit down while she made a pot of tea. 'You are a visitor, after all,' she told him as she stood the kettle on the stove. 'It isn't really the done thing to expect a guest to cook his own supper.'

'You didn't expect it, I offered.' Aldo sank into a chair at the table. 'Besides, Sally has told me so much about you, I don't feel like a stranger here.'

'There now, we've heard a good deal about you, too, so I suppose you're right. Well, you know where we are now, and you're welcome any time. We don't stand on ceremony here as I'm sure you've noticed.'

It was, to Aldo, a glimpse of the family life he'd been denied. He had never felt such a sense of belonging before. This was the scene he had imagined when growing up at the orphanage. He would make up stories in his head of a kind couple adopting him and Carlo, and he would imagine sitting in a kitchen not too different from this one, sharing a simple meal and talking about their day. Who would have thought he would have to come all the way to Orkney before realising that dream?

And as he sat around the table with the others, drinking tea while he let the conversation wash over him, breathing in the rich aroma of the cooking chicken pie, he let himself believe this was the first of many such evenings.

—

After one of the happiest evenings he had known, Sally glanced at the kitchen clock and said, 'I hate to say it, but it's half past eight. We ought to leave if Aldo's going to make it all the way across the town to Bruna Camp.'

They gathered their coats, and after a repeat of Elspeth's promise that Aldo would be welcome any time, they left. As they strolled along the track, they naturally split into two groups: Iris and Mary went ahead, snatches of their conversation about Mary's plans for her next sketch drifting back to Aldo on the breeze. He offered Sally his hand; warmth blossomed in his chest when she took it, shooting him a small smile. The same sense of belonging that he had felt in the kitchen stole around him again. He knew then that he had to speak up, tell Sally how much she meant to him even if he couldn't make her any promises. If there was any chance of his dream coming true with her in it, he needed to let her know.

Sally spoke before he could say anything. 'I'm sorry you ended up doing so much work this evening.'

'I'm not. It was fun. Truly,' he said, when Sally made an exclamation of disbelief. 'You know I never had a proper family. Tonight I felt part of one for the first time.' He went on in a rush, 'Sally, I know I said I have no future to make you any promises, but for as long as we are together here in Orkney, we will be together, yes?'

A sweet smile lit her face. 'Yes.' Then she tugged his hand. 'Come on, we'd better get a move on or we'll both be late and forbidden to go out again.'

Reluctantly admitting she was right, he denied himself the kiss he was longing to steal and quickened his pace until they had caught up with Iris and Mary. They climbed the path leading up the hill from the signal station together and as they went, he answered questions Iris and Mary had about his life in Italy and where he had learned to bake. When they reached the wire fence where the path led onto the road, they paused while Iris unhooked the loop of wire from the fencepost that made a rudimentary gate. Sally glanced along the side of the road and then frowned. 'That's funny. What's that on the side of the road? It looks almost like a—' She broke off with a cry of horror, clutching Aldo's arm. 'Oh my gosh, it is! There's someone lying there. They must be hurt or ill or—'

—

Sally clung to Aldo, hardly able to believe what she was seeing. She didn't like to finish her sentence by saying the person could be dead, but from the awkward angle of the limbs, whoever it was clearly lay where they had fallen.

The moment Iris got the gate open, Sally dashed onto the road and ran up to the body. No, not body. The person. She was aware of Aldo right beside her. She had hardly taken five steps before she saw her eyes were not deceiving her. It was a young woman, lying sprawled on the verge. She was wearing the navy blue skirt and jacket of a Wren. Sally heard someone give a moan; it took a moment to realise it was her. *Please don't let it be someone I know.*

Reaching the body, she knelt down beside it. The woman was lying on her face, her blonde hair in a tangle, stained with bright blood. Sally put a hand to the Wren's shoulder to turn her over, but Aldo caught her wrist.

'Wait. Maybe she was hit by a car. She might have broken bones. We must move her very carefully.'

Sally nodded, remembering the basic first aid training she had done on joining the WRNS. She glanced over her shoulder at Mary and Iris, who had caught up and were staring, aghast, at the crumpled figure. 'Can you support her head and neck while we turn her?'

Taking great care, they gently rolled the woman onto her back, then Mary rolled up her cardigan to support her head. 'Oh my God – it's Tessa!'

Chapter Twenty

Sally stared at the injured woman, scarcely able to believe what she was seeing. It was, indeed, Tessa. Her eyes were closed, her face streaked with blood from a wound on her scalp. A quick glance revealed many other bruises and scrapes, although it was the head wound that seemed the most serious. Tessa made no move or sound so it was with trembling fingers that Sally picked up one of Tessa's limp hands. They were icy cold, and for a horrible few seconds Sally feared the worst.

'I can't feel a pulse!' Her voice broke on a sob.

Beside her, she heard Iris give a low moan. Mary was whispering, 'This can't be happening,' over and over.

Aldo spoke, his voice calm and gentle. 'Try feeling her throat. Just to the side. It might be easier to find.'

Grimacing a little at the dried blood caking her throat, Sally complied. It took three tries but finally she felt a faint throb beneath her fingers. She let out a gasp of relief. 'She's alive.'

'Thank God.' Mary suddenly sounded brisk. 'We need an ambulance. I'll go for help. No, you stay here,' she said when Iris made a move to go with her. 'I'm a faster runner. I'll be quicker on my own.' So saying, she dashed away and was soon out of sight.

Sally turned back to Tessa, trying to force her frozen mind to remember more of her first aid training. By this time, Iris seemed to have recovered from her shock and she leaned over Tessa, saying, 'We need to check if she's still breathing.' There was a moment of agonising silence, broken only by the lapping of water a few yards away while Iris knelt with her ear close to

Tessa's mouth. All Sally could do was watch Iris's face, looking for a sign that she could feel a whisper of breath. Then Iris's frown of concentration eased. 'She's breathing.'

Sally sagged in relief. 'What else should we do?' She answered her own question as another memory from her early training returned. 'Check for bleeding.'

She did a rapid inspection, looking for signs of fresh blood. 'It looks like most of the bleeding has stopped,' she said at last, sitting back on her heels. 'Of course, she might be bleeding inside, but we can't do anything about that. Most of the blood is dry, which makes me think she's been here a while.' There was a patch of blood on the shoulder of Tessa's jacket and a small tear. This blood was also dry, so Sally decided against removing her jacket to examine the wound, as she thought moving her might make the injuries worse.

Aldo removed his tunic and draped it over Tessa. 'To keep her warm,' he said.

'I don't understand,' said Iris, who had been examining the spot where Tessa had lain before they had turned her. The grass was flattened and stained with blood. Most horrifying to Sally was the large sticky pool where her head had been. 'If she was hit by a car, why didn't the driver stop?'

'Why was she hit at all?' Sally said. 'I mean, it's nearly midsummer – the sun's still up. I can understand a driver not seeing her during the blackout, but she must have been clearly visible.'

'I wonder how long she's been here?' Iris said.

Sally shrugged. 'Long enough for most of the blood to dry. I suppose now that we all cycle to Kyeness, there aren't so many people walking along this lane in the evenings.'

There came the sound of rapid footsteps; Sally looked down the road to see Mary approaching at a run. When she reached them, she bent over, putting her hands on her knees as she fought for breath. 'Ran into Second Officer Wendleton,' she managed between gasps. 'She's sending for an ambulance and the police.'

'The police?'

Mary nodded. 'She didn't get like this on her own, did she? If she was hit by a car, the police need to track down the driver.'

'I suppose.' Sally hadn't considered that a crime had been committed, just that Tessa had had a terrible accident. But Mary was right. If she had been hit by a car and the driver had left her, the police had to be involved.

It wasn't long before the ambulance arrived, and it was a relief to know Tessa was in good hands. She was just being lifted onto a stretcher when another car rolled up and a middle-aged man in police uniform stepped out, together with Second Officer Wendleton.

'I'm Sergeant Frazer,' the policeman said, pulling out a note-book and pencil. 'Can someone tell me who found the young lady?'

'It was us,' Iris said, indicating the three friends plus Aldo.

Frazer held his pencil poised over the page. 'Names?'

'Iris Tredwick,' replied Iris, tapping her chest, 'and this is Sally Hartley, Mary Griffiths and Aldo Vanni.'

'Vanni?' Frazer regarded Aldo with narrowed eyes, seeming to notice him for the first time. 'You're one of the Italians from Bruna Camp?'

'I am.'

'And what are you doing on this side of town at half past nine in the evening?'

'I am allowed out until ten.' Aldo's tone of voice was respectful, although Sally could tell he was indignant. 'And I am well within the allowed five-mile radius.' He held eye contact with the sergeant until Frazer looked down at his book to scribble another note.

'I see,' Frazer said finally. 'Well, if you have nothing else to say to me, you should get back to camp before you're reported missing. I might have more questions for you tomorrow.'

He stood, evidently waiting for Aldo to leave, giving him no choice but to comply. Aldo shot Sally an apologetic look and collected his tunic from the ambulance driver, who had now covered Tessa in a blanket. Then he started to walk away.

But Sally couldn't bear to let him leave without saying goodbye properly. 'Wait,' she said, and caught him up, forcing him to stop.

Aldo took her hand. 'I am sorry the evening has ended this way.' Then he lowered his voice, meaning Sally had to strain to hear his next words. 'I was going to kiss you goodnight, but I do not think the policeman is the kind of man who likes seeing British girls being kissed by foreigners.'

'That's his problem.' And surprising even herself, Sally raised herself on tiptoes and planted a kiss on his lips, not caring that the others, her superior officer included, could see. Then she gave him a little push. 'Now go before you really are late.'

She watched for a moment as Aldo jogged away, wondering how an evening that could have begun with such promise could end so horribly. At the last moment before she turned away, Aldo spun round and jogged backwards for a few steps. He blew a kiss to Sally then faced front and sped away.

She returned to the others. Her heart sank when she saw the scowls directed at her from both Wendleton and Frazer. When Wendleton squared her shoulders and drew breath to speak, Sally braced herself for a reprimand, only to be spared when a member of the ambulance crew called Wendleton over.

Thankful for her reprieve, Sally joined Iris and Mary on the roadside while Wendleton and Frazer spoke to the ambulance crew in hushed tones. Mary, although she had retrieved her cardigan, had not put it on. She hugged it to her chest in the way a frightened child might cuddle a toy. She looked at Sally with haunted eyes. 'I told you to tip her over a cliff. I wish I'd never said that. I feel like I ill-wished her.'

'Don't be silly.' Sally put an arm around Mary's shoulders and found she was shivering. 'I thought you were supposed to be the sensible one and I was the one with her head full of silly notions.'

Then she remembered the magpie. She had seen a single magpie and hadn't waited for another. Was this some twisted trick of fate? She could dismiss Mary's fears, because she knew Mary hadn't really wished Tessa harm. But hadn't Sally wished she could be rid of Tessa? And she couldn't deny that when she had seen only one magpie all those years ago on the farm, Ted had had his accident later that day. And now Tessa had been hurt after Sally had not only seen a single magpie but had wished Tessa elsewhere.

Iris seemed to shake herself out of her daze. 'Sally's right,' she said to Mary. 'What happened to Tessa was a terrible accident. None of us liked her, but we mustn't forget she was pretty awful to Sally, so we wouldn't be human if we hadn't caught ourselves wishing she was out of our hair.'

Hair. Sally couldn't help wishing Iris hadn't said that. Now she was picturing the matted mass of Tessa's hair, caked in blood. She covered her mouth and gagged, taking a few steps away so her friends wouldn't notice. She walked out into the road then stopped, her nausea forgotten. There on the road were a few brownish splashes. Surely that was blood. She glanced back at the verge to see how far it was from where they had found Tessa. Too far for it to be Tessa's blood, surely. It didn't make sense. Unless Tessa had moved after being hit.

She approached the sergeant. 'Excuse me, but you might want to see—'

'I'll do the talking, thank you very much, miss.' Frazer scowled at her. 'I don't know what you think you're doing, cavorting with that Italian, but you should be more careful who you go out and about with. What do you really know about him?'

'A lot, as it happens.' Sally couldn't believe what she was hearing.

'Hartley, watch your tone.' Second Officer Wendleton had evidently finished her conversation with the ambulance driver and now stood at the sergeant's shoulder, her face wearing a matching scowl.

'But—'

'Do as I say.'

Sally subsided. 'Sorry, ma'am.'

'Now go and stand with Tredwick and Griffiths. I believe the sergeant has some questions for you all.'

'Indeed I do.' The sergeant produced his notebook again and went with Sally and Wendleton to the others. Behind them, the ambulance roared into life. There came the slam of doors followed by the sound of the ambulance driving away. Sally sent a prayer for Tessa's full recovery along with it.

'Now,' Frazer said when they were grouped together at the roadside, 'I gather you young ladies are the ones who found Tessa Bligh. Do any of you know what the time was?'

Sally exchanged glances with Iris and Mary. 'I know we left Curlew Croft at about half past eight,' she said.

Frazer made a note. 'I see. And how long does it take you to walk from there?'

'About three-quarters of an hour,' Iris offered.

The sergeant made another note. 'So that would mean you arrived here at around nine fifteen?'

Sally nodded. 'That sounds about right.'

'And she was unconscious the whole time?'

Sally nodded again.

'Did you move her?'

'She was lying face down, so we turned her over.' Sally hesitated. 'How is she? Did the ambulance driver say?'

Frazer looked grave. 'I don't know but she doesn't look good.'

'Where are they taking her?'

'Kirkwall.'

Second Officer Wendleton stepped in. 'Do you have any more questions for the girls, Sergeant? If not, I need to see them back to the Wrennery.'

'That's all for now, although I may have more questions later.'

Sally remembered the blood on the road. 'But what about—?'

Wendleton silenced her with a gesture. 'Enough, Hartley. It's bad enough that you're mixed up with that Italian. The least you can do is stay silent unless you're asked to speak. I've got enough to worry about with Bligh in the hospital, leaving me to reorganise the watch rota.' She turned to Iris. 'Tredwick, I believe Bligh was supposed to be your oppo on watch tomorrow morning?'

'Yes, ma'am.'

'Right, then Hartley, you'll have to stand in for her.'

Sally couldn't stay silent. 'But that leaves me on a double watch.'

'You can take that up with Bligh when she wakes up. If she wakes up. Not another word.' She marched down the road, summoning the girls to follow with an imperious gesture.

Sally didn't dare so much as exchange a glance with her friends but walked, head down, burning at the injustice. After a while, she felt a hand squeeze her arm, and sensed Iris beside her, lending her silent support. Sally couldn't bring herself to even smile at Iris, though, until Wendleton had seen them inside. Once they were dismissed, they ran straight up to their cabin.

'What a cow,' Mary said. 'Fancy making you do a double watch.'

'It's so unfair.' Iris dropped onto her bed, kicking off her shoes. 'Honestly, Sally, I don't mind standing watch alone tomorrow morning. It's so quiet at the moment, I know I can manage.'

'Better not. The mood she's in, I wouldn't put it past her dropping in on Kyeness to check up on me. She wasn't impressed by me being with Aldo. What did the sergeant call it – *cavorting*?'

Iris snorted. 'Cavorting? I ask you. If that tame peck was cavorting, I dread to think what she'd say if she'd caught me and Rob saying goodbye the day he left Orkney.'

'I think you're right, though, Sally,' Mary said. 'Best not to do anything that might get you in trouble with Wendleton.

If you're not careful she'll end up putting you on back-to-back watches for twenty-four hours.' Then she glanced down at the cardigan she still clutched and threw it to the floor with a shudder. Sally saw it was stained with blood.

Iris picked it up and placed it with the kit she had ready to take to the signal station the following morning. 'I'll put it to soak at Kyeness. You're on watch in the afternoon, aren't you? It'll be easier to wash out after a soak.'

'Thanks. You're a brick.' Mary pulled out her pyjamas from under her pillow and started to unbutton her blouse. 'Poor old Tessa, though. I wonder what she was doing out there on her own?'

This jogged Sally's memory. 'I nearly forgot. I was setting out this afternoon when we saw her. She asked if I could give her a moment but I told her to wait until tomorrow.'

There were a few seconds of silence marked only by the ticking of Iris's alarm clock. Sally wondered if Iris and Mary were thinking the same thing – would Tessa have a tomorrow?

'I just—' Sally's voice shook. She cleared her throat and tried again. 'I feel awful now.'

'Why?' Iris asked. 'She never had anything nice to say to you. If you were with Aldo, she probably wanted to tell you off for being unpatriotic.'

'I don't think so. She seemed… subdued. And don't talk about her in the past tense.'

'I'm sorry. I'm sure she'll be all right. When she wakes up you can ask her about it.'

Mary finished getting changed. She picked up her sponge bag and then paused at the door, the glint in her eye making her look like her old self. 'I think that's enough doom and gloom for one night. We'll face tomorrow when it arrives. I'm off to brush my teeth and when I get back, I want to hear exactly how much cavorting you and Aldo got up to. I was as stunned as Wendleton when you kissed him!'

Chapter Twenty-One

Aldo hardly knew how he got back to Bruna Camp. All he could see as he walked was Tessa's ghastly blood-smeared face. When he reached his hut, he declined the offer to join in with a game of cards, muttering some excuse about being too tired. Stumbling to his bunk, he quickly changed and climbed beneath the thin blankets.

Although he usually put Nero outside before turning in, this time he welcomed the cat when he jumped onto the bed, purring. Nero climbed onto his stomach, kneading the blankets with his paws before settling down for a nap. Aldo wished he could drop off that easily. Absently scratching Nero behind the ears, he squeezed his eyes shut. If only he could forget the harrowing end of their evening and dwell on the glorious walk earlier when Sally had kissed him.

Sally had kissed him, and it had been every bit as wonderful as he'd imagined. Better than wonderful. Not only that, he'd also gained the approval of her friends and had spent an evening feeling like he had a family. He should be happy. Instead, all he could see when he closed his eyes was blood smeared across an ashen face and a tangle of matted hair.

It was a long time before he drifted into a fitful sleep, and it felt like only minutes later when he awoke to the sound of the others getting up and grumbling about another day at the docks. Aldo washed and dressed mechanically and only went to the mess for breakfast because Enrico dragged him there. Finally, in halting words, he explained to his friend what had happened.

Enrico heard him out then clapped him on the shoulder. 'Everything will be all right, you'll see. It's a good thing you were passing, or the poor girl might have lain there until morning.' He grinned. 'Soon, all the girls will want to meet the hero who saved the Wren's life.'

It was impossible not to be cheered by Enrico's irrepressible humour, and after breakfast, Aldo prepared for the march to the docks in lighter spirits. The labour battalion was marching out of the gates when a British corporal dashed up to the group. 'Fall out, Vanni,' he said. 'You're wanted for questioning.'

'It must be about the attack,' he told Enrico. 'I'll see you later.'

Enrico waved him off. 'Anything to get out of a day's work!'

Aldo followed the corporal and was ushered into an office. Waiting for him were Captain Lawler and Sergeant Frazer.

'There you are, Vanni,' the captain said. 'I gather you found a young woman last night who had had an accident.' When Aldo nodded he continued, 'Sergeant Frazer here has a few more questions for you.'

'Of course,' Aldo said. 'I am happy to help. How is she, if I may ask?'

'I don't have any news about her at this stage,' Frazer replied. 'Now please tell me what you were doing between the hours of five and eight o'clock yesterday evening.'

Aldo stared at Frazer, nonplussed. He had expected the sergeant to ask for more details about the precise time they had found Tessa and where she had been lying. 'What does that have to do with anything?'

'Just answer the question.' The sergeant's tone was hard.

'I had been invited to spend the evening with a couple who live near Kyeness.'

'Names? Address?' Frazer had his notebook at the ready.

'Archie and Elspeth Heddle. They live at Curlew Croft. I don't know the full address, but it is along the coast from the signal station.'

'Was anyone else there?'

'The Wrens I was with when we found Tessa.'

Frazer leafed a few pages back in his book. 'That will be Sally Hartley, Iris Tredwick and Mary Griffiths.'

'Yes.'

'Were you there the whole time between five and eight?'

Aldo had to think. 'I can't remember exactly what time I arrived. If I wasn't at Curlew Croft, then I was on the way there.'

'Alone?'

'No.' Aldo didn't name Sally, having seen the sergeant's disapproval of Sally's goodbye kiss. While Aldo didn't mind so much for himself, he didn't want to give the sergeant any more reason to treat Sally with contempt.

'I need to know who you were with.'

'Why? We found Tessa at sunset and we did all we could to help. Who cares what I was doing over three hours before?'

'Because we have reason to believe Ordinary Wren Bligh was not struck by a car, as we at first suspected, but was attacked.'

'What? But that's awful. Who—?' Aldo stopped, dry-mouthed, when it hit him exactly who Frazer suspected. 'You think *I* did it?'

'All I am doing at this stage is making enquiries. I suggest you cooperate and provide me with the answers I'm looking for. If your friends support your statement then you have nothing to fear. Now, who were you with on your walk to Curlew Croft?'

Aldo had no choice. 'Sally Hartley.'

'I see.' And from his tone, Frazer saw a good deal more than had actually happened.

Aldo's patience was wearing thin; he drew breath but at that point the captain chose to intervene. 'Sergeant, although you can be sure I will be having words with Vanni about the terms he agreed to upon joining the labour battalion' – Aldo's stomach lurched, remembering that the Italians were not supposed to have relationships with the local women – 'he has done nothing illegal. In fact, as far as I can tell, he was of great assistance in providing first aid to the unfortunate Wren. Do you have any evidence to suggest he was involved in the attack?'

Aldo shot Captain Briars a grateful glance, despite the threat of the talk about meeting women.

'I was coming to that. It might interest you to learn that there are several witnesses to an altercation involving Vanni and Ordinary Wren Bligh at a football tournament held some weeks ago.' Frazer turned to Aldo. 'What do you say to that?'

'What is an altercation?' Aldo couldn't help it. He knew it would only antagonise Frazer further but it was clear the policeman had made up his mind about Aldo and was going to twist any evidence to fit his theory. Aldo wasn't going to give him any information unless he could help it.

'You were seen threatening Ordinary Wren Bligh. Do you deny it?'

'Yes, I deny it. I made no threats.'

Frazer consulted his notebook. 'Then tell me your version.'

Aldo bristled, objecting to the sceptical tone Frazer assigned to 'your version'. 'I will tell you the *truth*. I had never met Tessa until that moment but I had heard from Sally how she was a bully, making Sally's life miserable. At the match I overheard Tessa make a cruel comment about Sally – I don't remember exactly what. So I told Tessa to hold her tongue.'

Frazer read from his notebook. 'You were heard to say if she didn't hold her tongue, you would teach her a lesson. What exactly did you mean?'

'Not that I would hit her! I would never hit a woman. I don't know exactly what I would have done but I would have spoken to her, not hit her.'

'And that is the only time you saw Bligh until you found her at the roadside?'

'Yes. No, wait. There was one other time, but I didn't speak to her. When Sally and I were passing the Wrennery, Tessa came out and asked Sally if she could have a word. Sally said she would see her later.'

'Is that all, Sergeant?' Captain Briars asked. 'It doesn't seem to me that you have anything to go on beside an argument that happened in April. That seems very shaky evidence.'

Frazer didn't reply immediately but drew a handkerchief from his pocket. He unfolded it and held it out for Aldo to see. In one corner, plain to see, were the initials 'AV'. 'Do you recognise this?'

It was futile to deny it. He had a matching one in his pocket. 'Yes. It is mine. I lost one at the football tournament. Where did you find it?'

Frazer didn't answer. 'I hear you are a keen carpenter.'

'I wouldn't call myself a carpenter. I make toys from drift-wood.'

'Where did you get your tools?'

'One of the officers at Camp 60 loaned them to me and he let me bring them here.'

'List them.'

Aldo couldn't work out where this line of questioning was leading, but he didn't hesitate to answer. 'I have some chisels of various sizes, a hammer, an awl—'

He would have gone on, but Frazer interrupted. 'I need to see them.'

'They are in my hut.'

Frazer rose and gestured towards the door. 'Then take me to your hut.'

Aldo had no idea what his carpentry tools had to do with anything but if showing them to the sergeant would prove he had nothing to do with Tessa's attack, then he had no objection. Accompanied by Captain Briars, he led the way to his hut and dragged the toolbox from under his bed. He went to open it, but Frazer stopped him. 'I'll do that.'

Aldo stood aside while the sergeant lifted the lid and whistled when he saw the tools within. 'I'm surprised they allowed prisoners to have tools like these.'

'I am not a prisoner any more.'

'Of course.' Frazer didn't look convinced. He pulled out some chisels, examined them and tossed them on the floor. Aldo winced to see objects that were precious to him being treated with such disdain. The sergeant appeared to be looking for something. 'I thought you said you had an awl.'

'Yes, it belongs on the right.' Aldo always returned each tool to the same place in the box so he could lay his hands on them quickly.

'I can't see it. Show me.'

'Here.' Aldo stooped to pick it up only to freeze when he saw the empty space where the awl should be. 'I can't see it.' He looked at the tools on the floor to be sure Frazer hadn't tossed it there without noticing. It wasn't there. 'I don't understand. That is where I always keep it.' He knelt on the floor to peer under the bunk in case it had rolled underneath, although he knew it hadn't. Sure enough, there was nothing there apart from a rolled up sock. He rose, with a weight of dread pressing upon him. It was clear from the sergeant's expression of triumph that he had known all along that Aldo would be unable to produce the awl. What Aldo couldn't guess was why it was important. And what was he doing with Aldo's handkerchief?

Captain Briars was clearly thinking along the same lines. 'I think we should return to my office.'

They crossed the camp in silence. Once they were back in the office, the captain spoke first. 'Now please explain what this is all about.'

Frazer thrust his chest out, looping his thumbs in his pockets, obviously enjoying the moment. 'As I said, we now know that Ordinary Wren Bligh was not hit by a car but was attacked.'

'How do you know?' Aldo couldn't resist asking. 'She had a head wound. A car could have caused that.'

'Perhaps, although the doctor didn't consider the wound to be consistent with injuries caused by being hit by a car. In addition, the young lady had a stab wound to the shoulder. Caused, I might add, by an awl.'

Aldo couldn't believe his ears. 'That is a lie. The other Wrens, they examined her for bleeding. They would have noticed if she had been stabbed.'

'Not if the implement was left in the wound. Which, as a matter of fact, it was.'

Captain Briars shook his head, looking as confused as Aldo felt. 'I don't understand. Even if Bligh wasn't losing blood, why didn't the Wrens who examined her notice the awl's handle sticking out?'

With a crashing sense of doom, Aldo knew what had happened before Frazer could answer. He closed his eyes, remembering how he had noticed that the awl's handle had worked loose. He had kept meaning to fix it but had never got round to it.

Sure enough, Frazer replied, 'Because the handle had snapped off, leaving the awl virtually invisible in the wound. As a matter of fact, this saved her from severe blood loss. However, it is highly unlikely the Wrens who found her would have spotted it with a quick inspection.'

'What about the handle?' Aldo asked. 'You can check for fingerprints.'

'And you are sure yours won't be there?'

'Well, yes, but so would the attacker's.'

Frazer made an exclamation of disgust. 'Stop lying, Vanni. You will make things much easier for yourself if you admit what you've done.'

'Easier for you and the real attacker, you mean.'

Frazer threw up his hands. However, the captain spoke up before Frazer could say more. 'I can't deny that Vanni's awl was used in this terrible attack and we will, of course, do all in our power to help you bring the culprit to justice.'

'I believe we already have the culprit.'

'You have a suspect, but the evidence against him is circum-stantial.' Captain Briars turned to Aldo. 'How many men know where you keep the tools?'

Aldo shrugged. 'All the Italians, certainly, and many of the British. It is no secret. Lots of men ask me to carve toys for their children.'

'As I thought. Sergeant, it is clear that someone in the camp is involved. No one else could have accessed those tools. But just because they belong to Vanni, it doesn't mean his was the hand that struck that poor Wren. He has told you where he was yesterday evening and who he was with. I suggest you start by seeing if he was where he says he was. If so, he couldn't have done it.'

Frazer looked downcast. 'Very well. I urge you to keep him in confinement until we have sorted it out.'

'He will be confined to camp. I don't have the manpower to keep him locked up, nor do I see the need.'

It was a dejected Sergeant Frazer who left the office. When he had gone, Aldo said, 'Thank you, sir. I appreciate your help.'

'As it turns out, I happen to believe you.'

Aldo stammered his thanks again, but the captain interrupted. 'Nevertheless, I have stuck my neck out for you. Do not make me regret it.'

'I won't.'

'You may go. You are not to leave the camp. Do I make myself clear?'

Aldo nodded and left.

Chapter Twenty-Two

Sally endured her double watch without complaint. There was more activity than usual out in Hoy Sound to keep her busy, for which she was grateful. Whenever there was a quiet spell, she found herself picturing Tessa's bloodied face. Of course, she and Iris discussed Tessa's accident between signalling flurries, and when Mary replaced Iris for the afternoon watch, Sally covered the same ground with her. She wondered endlessly whether Tessa would recover, what she had been doing out on that road alone and why, if she had been hit by a car, the driver hadn't stopped. Mary said there had still been no news of Tessa by the time she had left the Wrennery, and Sally was determined to seek out Second Officer Wendleton the moment they returned.

Cycling back to the Wrennery at the end of her interminable double watch, the stresses of the day suddenly overtook Sally, and she found tears pouring down her cheeks. It was as though something had snapped inside her. She had no control over it and was obliged to stop until the storm had passed. It took a while for her to notice that Mary was beside her, rubbing her back and speaking in a soothing voice.

Finally, the tears eased and she wiped her face, giving Mary a shaky smile. 'Sorry. I didn't realise how knotted up I was inside.' She swallowed, then put into words the dread burdening her heart. 'What if she dies? I couldn't bear it. I'd never be free of the guilt, knowing I'd wished her elsewhere.'

'Away from Orkney maybe but you didn't wish this on her. Isn't that what you told me yesterday?'

'I suppose it's hard to apply my own advice to myself, especially when—' Sally stopped herself in time. She had been going to say something about seeing a single magpie but changed her mind. 'Especially when I so badly wanted to be rid of her,' she said instead.

'You weren't the only one.' Mary gazed into the distance for a moment, looking grim. Then she gave a tiny shake of the head as though trying to dispel her fears. 'Whatever happens, we'll face it together. Come on. Let's get back and see if there's any news.'

Taking comfort from the assurance that she wasn't alone, Sally wiped away the last of her tears. 'All right. I'm ready.' She climbed back into her saddle and followed Mary down the track.

When they came to a stop outside the Wrennery with a screech of brakes, Sally saw a dark-haired man hovering on the other side of the road. He wore the brown uniform of the Italian labour battalion, and for one glorious moment, Sally thought it was Aldo. Then her heart sank when she saw it wasn't him, although she recognised him as one of his teammates from the tournament. She flung down her bike and went to speak to him. 'Are you waiting for me?'

The man nodded. 'I am Aldo's friend, Enrico. He ask me to give you this.' He handed Sally a torn scrap of paper. It held only a few scrawled words but they sent a chill through her bones.

The police think I stabbed Tessa and are determined to find me guilty. I am not allowed to leave the camp. Do not worry. Captain Briars believes me and will try to find the truth. I miss you.

Aldo

It was too much to take in. Sally put a hand to her brow as she studied the words, trying to make sense of them. Two statements stood out: Tessa had been stabbed and the police thought Aldo had done it. Both things were impossible.

She flinched when she felt a hand on her shoulder. Mary spoke. 'What's happened?'

Sally handed her the note without a word and turned to Enrico. 'This doesn't add up. Why do the police think Aldo did it? He wouldn't hurt a fly. Besides, he couldn't possibly have attacked Tessa because he was with us the whole evening.'

Enrico looked unhappy. 'I know, and that is what he say to the police. They do not believe him. They find Aldo's—' Here Enrico mimed pulling something from his pocket and holding it to his nose.

Sally watched, bemused, until it suddenly dawned on her. 'Handkerchief! Is that what you mean?'

'Sì. They find Aldo's handkerchief, although they do not say where.'

'That's ridiculous. Aldo could have dropped it anywhere. It doesn't mean he stabbed Tessa.'

Mary handed Sally back the note. 'This is crazy. Tessa wasn't stabbed. We'd have noticed.'

'But she was.' Enrico held out his hands in a placatory gesture when Sally drew breath to argue. 'I know Aldo would never hurt her, but the police, they think he did. Tessa was stabbed in the shoulder with a tool Aldo had. An awl, I think he calls it.'

Sally winced. She had seen Ted use an awl. It was used to work holes in wood and came to a wicked point. It would be like being stabbed with a skewer.

'Impossible,' Mary said. 'We'd have seen the blood. We're not blind.'

'The handle snap off and the spike was still in the wound. It stopped the blood.' Enrico darted a furtive glance up and down the road and leaned closer, lowering his voice. 'Aldo's awl is missing – the police make him look. And Aldo doesn't tell him but the handle on his awl was loose.'

'You mean someone stabbed Tessa then tried to make it look like Aldo did it?'

'That is what I believe.'

'Who would do such a thing?'

Enrico shrugged. 'Someone from the camp. Someone who wants to make the Italians look bad.'

There was so much Sally wanted to ask, especially concerning Aldo's state of mind. But before she could say more, Enrico said, 'I must go. I promised Aldo to return as soon as I deliver his letter.'

'Tell him I know he's innocent and I miss him,' Sally called after his departing back.

It was fortunate Enrico left when he did, for he had only just gone out of sight when the Wrennery door opened, and Second Officer Wendleton walked out. 'There you are. I've been looking for you two.'

Sally, relieved she wouldn't have to explain why she had been speaking with another Italian, hastily approached Wendleton with Mary and saluted. She was aching to ask if there was any more news of Tessa but remembering her reprimand from the previous evening, she held her tongue. She had no wish to do another double shift.

'Sergeant Frazer has been in touch,' Wendleton said after returning their salute. 'He has more questions for you and Tredwick and wishes to see you tomorrow morning at 0900.'

And I've got some questions for him, Sally thought grimly, although she held her tongue. 'Of course, ma'am. Where?' she asked instead.

'In Kirkwall,' Wendleton replied. 'Sergeant Frazer has still not been allowed to speak with Bligh and he wants to be nearby in case she recovers enough to talk.' Wendleton's face was grave. 'In fact, I'm very much afraid I have some disturbing news.'

Sally felt sick. 'She's not... going to die, is she?'

'No. At least, we hope not. The doctors say her injuries are serious but they expect her to recover. However, they believe she wasn't struck by a car but was attacked.'

'Oh, we—' In her relief, Sally was about to say they already knew that. Then a light kick on the foot from Mary reminded her that they weren't supposed to know. 'We've been so worried about her. I'm glad she'll be all right. Who would attack her, though?'

'That's what the police are trying to discover. They're sending a car for you at 0800 tomorrow morning so don't be late.' Then Wendleton's face softened. 'I know this has been a shock to you and I am grateful to you, Hartley, for doing a double watch at short notice. I've reorganised the rota now, and I've managed to get all three of you girls a clear day tomorrow. My advice is, tell the police what you know then enjoy your day off in Kirkwall and try and forget this unpleasantness.'

'We will, ma'am, thank you.'

The moment they were dismissed, they ran inside. 'I wonder if Iris knows.' Mary raced up the stairs. 'Good of Wendleton to give us the day off tomorrow. I take back what I said about her.'

Iris was in the cabin, polishing her shoes. The moment they burst in, she dropped the cloth she was using. 'Where have you been? Have you heard the news?'

'That Tessa was attacked or we've got the day in Kirkwall?'

'Both.'

Sally grabbed Iris's arm and hauled her, protesting, from her seat on the bed. 'Come on, there's something we need to do.'

'Can't it wait?'

'No. We need to have another look at the place we found Tessa.'

'What on earth for?'

'Because the police think Aldo did it, and from what his friend Enrico has just told us, they're not interested in finding the real culprit. And I think I saw something suspicious last night. I tried telling Frazer but he kept shutting me up.' Sally told Iris what she had learned from Enrico and showed her the note from Aldo.

Iris made no more complaint but pulled on her shoes. 'Come on, then. Show us what you saw.'

They strode up the lane to the place where they had found Tessa. If the police had searched the area there was no sign of them now.

'I thought I saw spots of blood on the road,' Sally said. 'Give me a moment to look.' She paced the road between the place Tessa had lain and where they had stood to speak to Frazer. 'They must be near here somewhere. Yes, here!'

She pointed at the brownish splashes. The others joined her, careful not to step on them. Mary crouched down to get a closer look. 'It does look like blood,' she said a moment later. 'But how could it have got here if she was stabbed over there?' She pointed to the still flattened patch of grass about ten yards away.

'That's what I wondered. I thought she had been hit by a car last night, of course. Now, I wonder if the blood came from the attacker. Maybe Tessa fought back and managed to wound him.'

'Good thinking,' Mary said. 'If that's true, then we can prove Aldo didn't do it, because he hasn't a scratch on him.'

Sally felt a surge of optimism. 'Let's look around and see if we can spot any more blood.'

They split up and walked slowly around their allotted areas, heads down. To start with, Sally had high hopes they would find something. After all, in the films she watched, the criminal always left a handy matchbook with a name or number scribbled on it, or an envelope with his address. In this case, though, unless the attacker was in the habit of dropping tiny pebbles or ants, he didn't seem to have left any trace of his presence.

She was about to give up when Iris, who was searching the verge on the opposite side of the road from where Tessa had been, spoke up. 'This is strange.'

'What?' Sally ran across to her, heart pounding.

Iris was standing beside the wire gate leading to the Kyeness path. She pointed to a patch of grass on the other side. 'Does the grass look flattened there? To me it looks like someone has lain there.'

'The attacker, maybe, lying in wait.' Feeling a tingle of anti-cipation, Sally unhooked the wire and pulled aside the make-shift gate. She could see what Iris meant – there was a depres-sion in the grass a few yards from the path. Mindful that they would have to share any significant discovery with the police, she inched her way as close to the spot as possible without disturbing it. 'You're right, Iris. It does look like someone lay here.'

'A man?'

Sally frowned, trying to estimate the height of the person who would have formed the depression. 'It looks a bit small for that. Hang on.' She bent down. 'Oh my goodness, that looks like blood.'

'Where?' Iris had joined her and was leaning over her shoulder.

Sally pointed out the patch where a larger stain than the ones on the road smeared the grass.

'Hold on, you two,' Mary called from a few paces away. 'I've got something here.'

'What?' Sally followed Mary's gaze and let out a yelp of excitement. Maybe not a piece of paper with the attacker's name and address conveniently displayed but a vital clue all the same. All but hidden in the long grass was a polished piece of wood, roughly cylindrical in shape. 'You genius, Mary. This has to be the handle that fell off the awl.' She frowned. 'Should we pick it up? We have to show the police.'

'They would probably want to see exactly where we found it,' Iris said.

Mary frowned up at the sky. 'Looks like rain. Wouldn't that destroy any fingerprints?'

Sally followed her gaze and saw dark clouds gathering. That made up her mind. 'I think it might, and if we're to have any hope of finding the real attacker, we need to make sure any fingerprints are preserved. By the time Frazer gets here from Kirkwall, it could have been raining for hours and probably dark, too. The quickest thing would be to hand this to him tomorrow.' So saying, she pulled out her handkerchief, which was clean, thank goodness, and reached for the handle.

'Wait.'

At Mary's barked command, Sally jerked her hand back.

Mary produced a sketchbook from her pocket and a pencil. Being a keen artist, she always kept them to hand. 'Give me a few minutes and I'll make a quick drawing of the handle in situ and also that patch of grass.' She waved at the flattened area.

'Good idea.' Sally and Iris moved away to give Mary space to see everything and get it on paper.

'Who do you think lay here?' Iris asked.

Sally had been wondering the same thing, and it came to her in a flash. She gripped Iris's arm in her excitement. 'Of course! It wasn't the attacker lying in wait. It was Tessa.'

'But Tessa was on the other side of the road.'

'When we found her, yes. But this is where she was attacked, and where she fell at first. Remember when I got knocked out?'

'I'll never forget it.' It was Iris who had found her, lying outside the signal station after a spy had hit her over the head. Not that Sally remembered about the attack until some months later.

'Well, one of the doctors told me it wasn't unusual for someone with a concussion to wake up, go about their business and then collapse later.'

Iris's eyes blazed in comprehension. 'Meaning where Tessa was found wasn't where she was attacked.'

'Exactly. It all fits.' Sally pointed at the flattened grass. 'Tessa was attacked there – stabbed and struck over the head. She fell and the attacker made a bolt for it. Very inconsiderately failing to leave his identity card behind.'

'And being in the long grass, she wouldn't have been visible from the road, so passers-by wouldn't have noticed her.' Iris looked almost as excited as Sally about the way they were piecing together what had happened.

'Of course! I wondered why no one else had seen her. Anyway, I don't know how long she lay here, but at some point she woke and tried to get up.'

Struck by a blaze of revelation, Sally nearly pulled Iris's arm out of its socket. 'Yes – it all fits! The awl was still in her shoulder, remember. She must have tried to pull it out. Poor thing – she was probably so dazed she didn't really know what she was doing. And we know the handle was loose because Enrico said so. The handle came off in her hand, and she dropped it.'

'Brilliant!' Iris freed her arm from Sally's grip. 'You're right – it does all fit. It's obvious what happened next. She staggered across the road, leaving the bloodstains you found, then passed out again on the other side.'

Sally could scarcely believe they had worked it out. 'Sergeant Frazer will have to listen to us now. Pity there's no clue to the attacker, though.'

'I know.' Iris looked worried. 'Sally, you do realise that if the awl was Aldo's, it will be covered in his fingerprints. What if the attacker was wearing gloves? Then there would only be Aldo's prints, and possibly Tessa's, and we'd be giving Sergeant Frazer exactly what he needs to convict him.'

'But Aldo was either at Curlew Croft or with me when Tessa was attacked. We saw her when we went past the Wrennery, remember, so we know she was fine then. When Frazer interviews us, he's bound to see sense.' She had to believe it.

Mary closed her sketchbook and put it away in her pocket. 'Right. I'm all done here. Plus, I've drawn a plan that includes the road, where we found Tessa and the location of the blood spots. If you want the handle, you'd better get it now. Those clouds are coming in fast.'

Sally pulled out her hanky and gingerly used it to pick up the handle, taking great care only to touch it at the very top and bottom, not on the main part of the grip where she expected most of the fingerprints would be. Keeping it wrapped, she placed the bundle in her pocket. Then she looked at Iris and Mary. 'Let's get back before it starts raining. I can't wait to see Sergeant Frazer's face when he sees what we've found.'

Chapter Twenty-Three

The police car arrived to collect the girls at eight the next morning on the dot. They passed the journey in grim silence, aside from the occasional musing on how Tessa fared. Sally spent most of the time mentally rehearsing how to persuade Frazer of Aldo's innocence.

Sergeant Frazer was waiting for them in a tiny office at Kirkwall police station. Before he could do more than ask them to take a seat, Sally poured out what they had found the previous evening and produced the awl handle with a sense of triumph. At her prompting, Mary handed over her sketch.

'Hmph, well, this is most irregular. It's vital that all evidence is collected in the proper fashion.'

Mary leaned across the desk, scowling at the sergeant. 'At least we—'

Sally hastily cut in, before Mary could accuse the police of not bothering to look for evidence at all. 'We did consider that, and we took great care not to touch the handle with anything other than the handkerchief. But it was about to rain, and we were afraid any fingerprints would be washed away.' It had, indeed, poured with rain not ten minutes after they had left, and the streets of Stromness had been glistening with puddles the next morning. Sally was sure none of the evidence would have survived the downpour.

'Well, you certainly did a thorough job.' Frazer glanced at Mary's detailed sketch. 'We'll have to see if we can retrieve any prints, of course, and visit the site ourselves. Now...' He pushed the handle and sketch aside and regarded the friends above steepled fingers. 'I'm sure your officer has explained that we are now treating this as a crime. The fact that you know there was an awl involved means you now know Ordinary Wren Bligh was stabbed.'

They all nodded. At this point, the door opened and another policeman entered and sat beside Frazer, who introduced the newcomer as PC Hammond, who was there to make notes.

Once the introductions were made, Frazer continued. 'I've asked you here to answer questions concerning yesterday's events. I will need to speak to you separately, starting with you, Miss Hartley.'

Sally glanced at Iris and Mary and nodded unhappily. She had thought she would be with Iris and Mary at all times, and didn't like to think of being questioned without them for moral support.

'Miss Griffiths and Miss Tredwick, please wait outside.' Frazer crossed to the door and held it open for them. 'PC Hammond will come and fetch you when we're ready.'

Sally watched them leave, feeling as though she were losing a lifeline.

'Now, Sally. May I call you Sally?' Frazer settled back into his seat and opened a folder that was placed on the desk in front of him.

Sally nodded again, her mouth dry. She shot a surreptitious glance at the folder, but Frazer's hands obscured the contents.

Frazer appeared to study the folder for a moment before turning his gaze back upon Sally. 'I need to understand where everyone was at different times during the evening. First of all, please tell me at what time you met Aldo Vanni on Thursday the fifteenth of June.'

Sally thought back, forcing her mind past their discovery of Tessa and back to the happier parts of the evening. 'I think it must have been around 1700.'

'Where did you meet?'

'On the steps outside the church.' Sally heard the scribble of pen on paper and shot a glance at the constable; his head was bent over a notebook, writing furiously.

'Did you go straight from there to Curlew Croft?'

Sally gave up trying to see what the constable was writing and looked back at Frazer. 'Yes. Well, we stopped for a moment outside the Wrennery, because we saw Tessa. She wanted to ask me something.'

'Oh? And what time was that?'

'It must have been about ten minutes after Aldo and I met.'

'What did Tessa ask you?'

'Nothing much. She said she had something she wanted to say, and we arranged to meet when I got back. I told her I couldn't speak then because I was due at Curlew Croft.' Sally felt another twinge of guilt as she explained. She couldn't imagine what Tessa had wanted to ask, and she had to wonder whether, if she had stopped to hear her out, Tessa would have stayed in the Wrennery all evening and not been attacked. 'Oh!' The exclamation escaped as a horrible thought struck.

'What is it?'

'Nothing really. I just wondered if she had walked down the road hoping to meet me when I came back. Maybe if I'd had time to hear what she had to say, she wouldn't have been hurt.'

'And you've no idea what she wanted to talk about?'

'No.'

'Very well. Returning to your movements. What time did you reach Curlew Croft?'

'Erm.' Sally gazed at a spot above the sergeant's head while she tried to remember. Then she recalled that she had dashed into the Heddles' kitchen so she could take off her raincoat before going to catch the chickens. She had glanced at the clock on her way back outside. 'It was a quarter past six. By the Heddles' kitchen clock.'

'A quarter past six? That's rather a long time to walk to Curlew Croft.'

Sally felt her face burn, remembering how they had dawdled on the path and kissed. It seemed centuries ago now and yet it had been an earth-shattering event in Sally's life at the time. 'Well, we weren't walking very fast. We were talking. You know how it is.'

Sergeant Frazer's face said he suspected all too well how it was. And if he knew anything, the word *cavorting* was involved.

Sally's face burned all the hotter as she answered endless questions about how long they had spent at Curlew Croft, whether Aldo had been present at all times, how well she knew Aldo and whether she had ever witnessed him being violent.

Sally's answers grew more indignant as the questions went on. It was clear that despite the evidence they had presented, Frazer was clinging to the notion that Aldo was the attacker. All she could do was pray that once everyone, including Elspeth and Archie Heddle, had confirmed that Aldo couldn't possibly have committed the crime, Frazer would finally turn his attention to finding the real culprit.

'One last thing before I let you go,' Frazer said. He leaned across the desk, his eyes glued to her face, making her skin crawl. 'Can you swear you were with him the entire time between meeting him at the church and arriving at Curlew Croft?'

'Of course I can. Are you calling me a liar?'

'No, but it has been known for young girls to get their heads turned by a handsome face. Sadly, there are many cases where criminal men use impressionable women to provide false alibis for them.'

Sally stared at him in disbelief. It hit her with a crushing sense of despondency that he was determined to pin the attack on Aldo, and nothing she could say would change his mind. He clearly couldn't dispute the fact that Aldo had been at Curlew Croft that night, so if that meant accusing her of providing a false alibi, then so be it. 'I would never do that,' she said finally. 'I would never defend anyone who could do such a terrible thing. I found Tessa, remember. I saw what the attacker did to her.' Her voice was shaking but she wasn't going to stop until she had had her say. 'If you think I could make up lies to protect the person who inflicted those injuries then you've got me all wrong.'

She had to stop then because she became horribly afraid her combined fear for Aldo and anger at Frazer would overwhelm her and she would start crying. Hardly the best way to convince Frazer she wasn't a flighty, emotional airhead.

Frazer's expression didn't change. He shuffled the papers in front of him and said, 'Well, thank you for your time. We shall, of course, investigate all the evidence.'

All the evidence that points to Aldo, Sally thought as she rose. She recovered herself enough to turn at the door and say, 'You might want to ask yourself how you can trust me to do my duty and protect the coastline, yet not trust me to tell the truth about a crime that horrifies me.'

She closed the door behind her, resisting the urge to slam it, then went to find Iris and Mary. They were not far – just around the corner, sitting on wooden chairs that looked like they'd come straight from a schoolroom. She collapsed on a chair, wincing as it gave an ominous creak, and buried her head in her hands.

'What happened?' Iris asked.

Before Sally could answer, PC Hammond appeared and summoned Iris.

Once she had gone, Mary moved into the chair Iris had vacated to be next to Sally. She put a hand on Sally's shoulder. 'What did that oaf say?'

'Only that I'm an impressionable, feeble-minded girl who lets her head get turned by a handsome man. He's convinced I'm covering for Aldo.'

'What? Just wait 'til it's my turn, I'll give him what's what.'

Mary half rose, but Sally pulled her down. 'It won't do any good. It'll just confirm his conviction that we're too carried away by our emotions to be trusted.'

'Really? It's thanks to us they stopped that U-boat the other Christmas and discovered Stewart was a spy. Not bad for a bunch of hysterical women.'

'That's what I said. Only not in so many words.'

'Good for you. You've discovered your inner lioness.'

Iris returned then, and Mary was summoned a short while later, so Sally was saved from commenting on Mary's preposterous observation. The way she was feeling, she didn't think she even deserved to be called a mouse.

Beside her, Iris sat in silence for a few moments, chewing her lip. 'You know, I think Sergeant Frazer has the brains of a slug,' she announced with the air of someone who'd made a great discovery.

'It's taken you that long to decide?' Sally couldn't help smiling, despite her worries.

'It took me a while to work out what animal to compare him with,' Iris replied. 'I'm still not happy with slug. It seems such an insult to the poor creatures.'

'What did he say to you?'

'I thought he wanted to confirm when you and Aldo arrived at Curlew Croft, so I jumped straight in and told him what I remembered. But he didn't seem interested in that. All he wanted to know was what I thought of you, whether you could be easily influenced, what your relationship is with Aldo.' Iris wrinkled her nose as though she could detect a disgusting smell. 'Skunk. I should have gone with skunk. No, wait. What's that slimy stuff on the bottom of ponds?'

'Talking about the lovely sergeant?' Mary was back.

Sally looked up. 'You weren't long.'

'No, well, the moment he started asking my opinion of you, I told him it was far better than my opinion of him, so did he really want me to go on?'

'You never.'

'I did. The poor constable looked like he was having a real struggle not to laugh, poor man. Anyway, the main news is that someone came in at that point to tell the sergeant that Tessa's awake. Frazer said we could go but be sure to get in touch if we remember anything else.'

'Tessa's awake?' Sally sprang to her feet. 'That's wonderful news. We should go and see her. It's not far to the hospital.'

'Will they let us in?' Iris picked up her gas mask which she had slung over the back of her chair.

'I'm jolly well going to try. If she can tell the sergeant who attacked her, Aldo's in the clear, and I want to know.'

'Fine,' Iris said. 'Let's go, then. If we get a move on, we might get there before Frazer.'

–

When they arrived at the Balfour hospital, they held a whispered conversation before they approached the main desk, the result being that Iris agreed to do the talking. With her crisp BBC accent, she could give the impression that although she wore the uniform of a humble Ordinary Wren, she was actually an important person with a God-given right to go where she chose. The girl at the desk was certainly taken in and directed them to Tessa's side ward.

When they got to the right floor, they found Tessa's door ajar, so Sally peered inside to check there wasn't a doctor or nurse with her. She was still not sure if Tessa was allowed visitors, and having got this far, she didn't want to be thrown out now. The room was empty of medical staff, and she saw Tessa lying in a bare room with stark white walls and just a jug of water on the cabinet beside the bed. She hesitated in the doorway, shocked by Tessa's appearance. Her pale face had a greyish pallor that brought back painful memories of Uncle Ted in the days following his accident; the flesh around her eyes and mouth looked almost blue. Bandages swathed her head and were just visible beneath the shoulder of her hospital gown. She was so still that Sally thought she must be asleep. However at that moment, the door Sally was still holding creaked; Tessa looked up, and their eyes met.

'You came to see me?'

Sally nodded and stepped into the room, only to freeze when a heavy hand descended upon her shoulder. Twisting around, she found herself looking into the stern face of Sergeant Frazer. 'Not so fast, young lady. I need to speak to Miss Bligh first. You can wait in the corridor and come in afterwards if she still wants to see you.'

Sally had no option but to retreat into the corridor and watch Frazer enter the room, followed by Constable Hammond.

'Sorry,' Iris said. 'He swooped in before we could warn you.'

Mary's lips twitched. 'I don't think pond slime can swoop.'

There was nowhere to sit, so they leaned against the wall, doing their best to appear invisible to uniformed women and men who scurried past. Sally drew a breath and wrinkled her nose at the smell of disinfectant. 'I hope we don't have to wait long. I hate the smell of hospitals. Not just the smell – the whole feel of the place. We're in a place where people have suffered and died. That kind of atmosphere seeps into the walls.'

Iris stood straight, away from the wall, and wiped her hands on her skirt.

Mary, watching her, snorted. 'I'm sure most of the patients recover. You and Aldo did.'

'That's right,' Iris said, looking relieved. 'You should be happy to be back in a place where you met Aldo. If you're looking for a romantic story, what could be more romantic than a pretty Yorkshire lass meeting a handsome Italian man and finding solace from their pain in each other's arms? They'll probably make a Hollywood film about it.'

'That didn't happen here!'

'Maybe not, but it clearly happened elsewhere, considering the way you said goodbye to Aldo in front of the police and Wendleton. I've been burning to ask you about it, but it didn't seem appropriate in the circumstances.'

It was only then that Sally realised she hadn't told Iris or Mary about kissing Aldo on their walk to Curlew Croft. As Iris had said, it hadn't felt right to speak of something so happy in the shadow of the terrible attack. Now, however, knowing that Tessa was awake and confident that the fresh evidence they had found would exonerate Aldo, Sally allowed herself to remember their kisses and hope there would be more. 'Well,' she began, 'you did wonder what took us so long to walk to Curlew Croft that evening!'

Iris and Mary crowed with delight.

'I knew you were sweet on him really,' Iris said.

'Why didn't you tell us before?' Mary asked.

Sally made a gesture that took in Tessa's room. 'I couldn't find an appropriate moment. Anyway, there's not much to celebrate considering Sergeant Frazer is doing his best to get Aldo convicted of the crime.'

In her indignation, her voice had risen. She only noticed when Iris made a shushing gesture. 'Keep your voice down or you'll get us kicked out.'

Seeing a window a little way along the corridor, Sally went to look out. Iris and Mary followed. It wasn't the loveliest view, overlooking as it did the sprawling huts of the temporary hospital. Sally couldn't bring herself to look away, though, remembering how she and Aldo had met outside one of those huts, and how his friendship had helped her on her journey to recovery. She closed her hand around the St Christopher medallion. 'I should have given it back,' she muttered, more to herself than to her friends. 'He needs it more than me.'

'St Christophers are supposed to keep travellers safe,' Iris said, 'so it's a good thing you've got it, because Aldo isn't going anywhere at the moment.' Then Iris clapped a hand over her mouth. 'Sorry. That was so crass, wasn't it? Me and my big mouth. I really must try and think before I speak.'

But Iris's embarrassment had succeeded where her previous attempts at comfort had failed. Sally giggled at her horrified expression. 'Please don't change. I like you just as you are.'

The door to Tessa's room opened, and the sound of Sergeant Frazer's voice drifted out. 'Are you sure you can't remember anything else?' There was a pause in which Sally could sense Iris and Mary as tense as she was, straining to hear what was said. Tessa evidently answered, for the sergeant said, 'Very well. Let one of the nurses know if that changes. I'll leave instructions for them to call me right away.'

Sally exchanged glances with her friends and saw her disappointment echoed in their expressions. She whispered, 'Sounds like she wasn't able to identify her attacker.'

Iris squeezed her arm. 'It'll take time. Remember how it took you a while to remember about your attack.'

Sally felt as though a leaden weight had settled in her stomach. 'It was months before I remembered about Stewart. I can't leave Aldo shut up for months.'

Frazer emerged from the room and glanced in their direction. 'You can see her now.' He gave a grim smile. 'Not that you'll be happy with what she can remember. She says the man who stabbed her was an Italian with dark hair and dark eyes.'

Mary put her hands on her hips. 'Which proves nothing. That could describe most of the Italians.'

Frazer simply shrugged and walked away, his shoes squeaking on the linoleum, the constable scurrying after him.

'He obviously didn't pay for his shoes,' Sally said. 'Come on, let's go and see Tessa.'

In the brief moment when Tessa had noticed her earlier, Sally had thought she was pleased to see her. Now, however, she couldn't meet Sally's gaze.

'Oh, it's you.' Tessa's fingers picked at the corner of her blanket. 'Come to gloat?'

'Gloat? Of course not.' Sally took the vacant chair at the bedside while Iris and Mary hovered near the door. 'We wanted you to know how sorry we are that this has happened to you. How do you feel?'

A crease formed between Tessa's eyebrows. 'You're not even going to ask me if I remember who did it? I thought you were here to save your precious Aldo.'

'No.' Sally crossed her fingers behind her back. Now she saw Tessa looking so ill and uncomfortable, all she wanted to do was offer her comfort. 'I had a concussion a couple of years ago, and I remember how awful I felt. We had to come to Kirkwall to speak to Sergeant Frazer, and we thought we'd come and see how you were.'

'Oh.' Then, as though the words had been dragged out of her, 'That was kind. Thank you.'

'Is there anything we can get you?' Sally glanced around the bare room. What it needed was flowers and cards. Sadly, these were in short supply in war-torn Britain, where all available land was given over to food production and paper was in short supply. 'Some magazines, perhaps?'

'My head hurts too much to read.'

'Of course. That was silly of me.' Then something occurred to her. 'Hang on, did Sergeant Frazer tell you he suspected Aldo?' That seemed unprofessional, even for Frazer. If he hadn't, though, how had Tessa known Aldo was a suspect?

Two pink spots appeared on Tessa's cheeks. 'No. I overheard you talking outside.'

'Oh. Well, anyway, we'll send you something to cheer up your room. It can't be nice to be here all alone with only blank walls to look at.'

Sally was desperately trying to think of something cheerful to say when a nurse entered the room. 'Who let you in? The patient needs her rest. Off you go.'

Sally rose, relieved to be spared more of the awkward conversation. As she was following Iris and Mary out, Tessa called after her, 'Thank you for coming.'

She seemed so changed from the girl who had made her life a misery that Sally looked back with a genuine smile. 'I'll come again if I can, and we'll send you something to cheer up your room. Although I expect your friends and family will send you enough cards and letters before long that you won't notice what we manage.'

Tessa looked away. 'Thank you,' she mumbled, without meeting Sally's gaze.

'And from Tessa, that was a resounding offer of friendship,' Mary said. But only once they were well out of earshot.

—

'What shall we do?' Iris asked once they were out of the hospital and breathing air that was free from the smell of disinfectant. 'We could go to a cafe or the shops or even the pictures. I wonder what's on?'

'I'm sorry.' What with Frazer's low opinion of her and Tessa not being able to clear Aldo, Sally didn't feel like a day out in Kirkwall. 'You two enjoy your day. I think I'll go back to Stromness.'

'But we've got a whole day off. What are you going to do?'

'Go to the Heddles'. There are always a few odd jobs that need doing, and the peace and quiet will help me decide what else I can do for Aldo. It doesn't feel right to have fun in Kirkwall while he's got this hanging over his head.'

Iris's face was a picture of dismay. 'You're right. I'm the one who should be sorry. I'll come with you.'

'Me too,' Mary added. 'Anyone know what time the next bus leaves? I suppose it will be too much to expect a lift from the police after what I said to Sergeant Frazer.'

Sally giggled and linked arms with them both. 'I think we can safely assume that we need to make our own way back.'

Iris glanced at her watch. 'The next bus goes in three-quarters of an hour.'

'Just time to pop to the shops and see if we can buy something for Tessa.'

In the end, they found a pretty card with a picture of pink rosebuds and forget-me-nots printed on very flimsy paper. Sally

243

also bought a lavender bag with a delicate lace trim, hoping the calming scent would help Tessa sleep. They all signed the card before returning to the hospital to ask the lady at the front desk to see their gift was delivered. When Sally dropped into her seat on the bus to Stromness, she was satisfied that although she hadn't discovered anything to help Aldo, she had, at least, done what she could to put an end to the feud with Tessa.

After the long bus journey on winding roads, it was a relief to get out at Stromness and stretch their legs on the bracing walk to Curlew Croft.

'You lasses timed that well,' Elspeth said when she saw them at the door. 'I was just about to serve soup for lunch, and I put on extra thinking you might call.'

They weren't about to turn down one of Elspeth's delicious vegetable soups, so they washed their hands and helped lay the table. Sally, who had been unable to eat breakfast that morning, now realised how hungry she was when the delicious aroma rising from the pot awoke her taste buds.

'That Sergeant Frazer was here yesterday afternoon,' Elspeth said once they were all tucking into their soup and bannock bread. 'What's this I hear about one of the Wrens being hurt?'

Sally was grateful Elspeth had brought the subject up herself, having been reluctant to spoil the peace of Curlew Croft with the tale. Now, she plunged into the story. 'The worst of it is that Sergeant Frazer is convinced Aldo did it,' she concluded, 'and I'm covering for him because I'm head over heels in love with him.'

'And are you?' Elspeth regarded Sally across the brim of her teacup. 'Head over heels, I mean, not covering for him. I know you'd never do that.'

'I'll never get the chance to find out at this rate.' Sally sighed. 'I mean, I was starting to get used to the idea that I'd been wrong about Adam and me being meant for each other. It took a while, but I've finally been able to admit that I have feelings for Aldo, and maybe he's the one meant for me instead. Only now he's stuck in Bruna Camp and I can't see him.'

'Sergeant Frazer needs to have his head examined.' Mary cut her bread with unnecessary force as she spoke. 'Any sane person would see that Sally would never cover for a criminal.'

Archie looked thoughtful. 'There's something about Sergeant Frazer you should know. His son was serving on the same ship as our Don.' He nodded at the framed photograph showing a man who looked like a younger version of Archie, dressed in naval uniform.

'Oh no.' Sally remembered all too well the Heddles' shock and fear when Don had been reported missing. 'Was he taken prisoner too or...'

'He was killed, poor lad. Frazer's wife died some years back, and his son was all he had. Well, grief affects us all in different ways, as you know. With Frazer it made him lash out at anyone he thought was to blame. The teachers who encouraged him to join up; the medics who passed him fit; most of all, the Italians. It was an Italian ship that torpedoed Don's ship, by all accounts.'

Sally understood. 'Do you think he's taking his anger out on Aldo because he's an easy target?'

'It looks that way,' Elspeth said. 'And out on you, Sally, for befriending him.' She sighed. 'Aye, that makes sense of the questions he asked yesterday. First, he wanted to know what time you all arrived at Curlew Croft that evening. When I mentioned you and Aldo arrived a little later than the others, he pounced and kept asking about my opinion of you. I gave him a piece of my mind, but he wouldn't give up.'

'That's exactly what he was like with me and Iris,' Mary said. 'Wanted us to tell him Sally was unreliable and easily led when everyone knows she would never support Aldo if he had attacked someone.'

'So what do we do?' Sally asked. 'I've given Sergeant Frazer the evidence we found.' She briefly explained about the awl handle and the conclusion they had drawn about Tessa's movements after the attack. 'He didn't seem interested, though, because he thought he already knew the identity of the culprit.'

'I'm afraid to say there isn't much else you can do.' Elspeth patted her arm. 'I know it seems unfair but you have to trust that Frazer will come to his senses. He hasn't arrested Aldo, after all, which means he must know he doesn't have any real evidence. You have to give it time.'

'That's all very well, but there's one thing you've forgotten.' Iris looked grave. 'The real attacker is still out there. What if he strikes again?'

'Aye, I wasn't forgetting,' Elspeth said. 'We'll all be keeping our ears and eyes open, and I urge you lasses not to wander anywhere alone until the real culprit is locked away.'

'It could take ages.'

'Aye, I know. Promise me you won't take any chances until this is resolved.'

Chapter Twenty-Four

Aldo paced up and down in front of his hut. He had begged Captain Briars to give him work in the camp to stop him dying from boredom, and when he had explained that he had been a baker before the war, he had been assigned to the canteen. Not that there was much baking involved, but he found the routine helpful in keeping his mind off the potential charges hanging over his head. He had never realised before how much his labour at the docks had given him a sense of purpose until he was no longer able to do it. While cooking in the canteen might be tedious, it was better than doing nothing.

Right now, however, he was off duty and waiting with growing impatience for Enrico. In the days since Aldo had been confined to camp, Sally had twice written to him, using Enrico to deliver her letters. Now, every time Enrico went to work at the docks, Aldo would pray that he would return with another message from Sally. He lived for those precious bits of contact with her. As he paced, Nero trotted at his heels. The other members at the camp had started referring to the black cat as his shadow, for Nero was often to be seen trotting behind him, more like a dog than a cat. Nero's fur was now sleek and shiny, and he had filled out, thanks to the scraps Aldo saved for him.

He stopped when he saw the barrier at the entrance being raised, and the Italian work party marching in, returning from the docks. Aldo perched on a crate, his leg jiggling with impatience, as he waited for Enrico's return.

He sprang up when he saw Enrico approach at a jog. 'Did you see her?' Aldo called as soon as Enrico was within earshot.

In reply, Enrico reached into his pocket and pulled out a letter, waving it like a flag.

'Yes!' Aldo snatched it and ripped open the envelope.

> *Dear Aldo,*
>
> *I have a whole day free after being on night watch, so I am writing this in the common room and looking forward to a quiet day. It goes without saying I would prefer to be with you. Have you heard any more news from Sergeant Frazer? We have heard nothing, and Mary is threatening to storm Kirkwall police station and demand to speak with his superiors. I would have done that long ago, except I'm afraid that would only confirm his suspicion that I'm a hysterical female who doesn't deserve his attention. I can't do nothing for much longer, though, despite Elspeth's advice.*

Aldo's heart lurched when he read this. He couldn't bear the thought of Sally getting into trouble on his behalf. He read on.

> *Anyway, it is nearly midday, and I want to see if I can meet Enrico so he can deliver this to you. Take care of yourself and Nero. Last time I met Enrico he told me you were working in the kitchen. I hope that is not as awful as it sounds. Your name will soon be cleared, have faith!*
>
> *Sally x*

Aldo read and reread the letter, then darted a surreptitious glance at Enrico to be sure he wasn't watching before kissing his finger and placing it on Sally's signature. It heartened him that she always signed her letters with a kiss.

'Who's that from?' Gianni was standing at his shoulder, scowling. Aldo had been so intent upon his letter that he hadn't noticed.

Before Aldo could put it away, Gianni snatched it from his hands.

'Give it back!' Aldo tried to grab it, but didn't watch where he put his feet and ended up tripping over Nero. Nero yowled and shot away, his fur standing on end. By the time Aldo had scrambled to his feet, Gianni had moved a few paces away and was reading the letter.

'Give it back,' Aldo repeated, lurching towards Gianni.

Gianni sneered, crumpled the flimsy paper and flung it to the ground. While Aldo picked it up he said, 'I thought I told you not to mix with British women.'

'She is my friend, and I will write to her if I choose.'

'I'm surprised she can write with an injured arm.'

'What do you mean? She's not hurt.' He glanced over at Enrico who looked on, with the air of someone who wants to help but doesn't quite know how. 'Sally isn't hurt, is she?'

Enrico shook his head. 'She is fine.'

'I must have heard wrong,' Gianni said with an air of nonchalance. 'You should tell her to be careful, though. There are dangerous men around.' He spat at Aldo's feet then sauntered off.

'And you're one of them,' Aldo muttered, smoothing the precious letter. He jogged over to Enrico. 'Are you sure Sally wasn't injured? Gianni seemed so convinced.'

'Honestly, she was fine.'

'Funny he thought she was. And with an injury that would make it hard to write. Unless...' A horrible suspicion was dawning on him. 'Unless he thought she'd been stabbed in the shoulder. Does he think Sally was the one who was attacked? Why would he think that?' Word had got out that a Wren had been injured. As far as he knew, however, no one apart from Aldo, Captain Briars and Enrico knew the identity of the Wren in question or the nature of her injuries. Knowing the perpetrator must have access to Bruna Camp, Briars had warned Aldo not to tell anyone details of the attack, including the Wren's name, so that the investigation wouldn't be compromised. As Aldo had already poured out the story to Enrico, he had made Enrico promise not to breathe a word to anyone, knowing he could be trusted.

Enrico's face was locked in a scowl. 'You think he was the attacker?'

'I wouldn't put it past him.' Then Aldo remembered the tournament. 'Wait! Remember when I warned Tessa to stay away from Sally?'

'What of it?'

'When I turned around, Gianni was watching us. He was too far away to hear what I'd said, though. He knew I was friendly with a Wren, but he didn't know her by sight. What if he thought Tessa was Sally? He threatened me before. He might have attacked Tessa to get back at me. He certainly knows where I keep those tools, and he would have had every opportunity to steal my handkerchief. I bet he planted it on her to cast the suspicion on me. It all fits.' Aldo was shaking in his excitement.

Enrico placed a hand on his arm. 'I think you must be right. But we can't prove it.'

It was Aldo's turn to scowl. 'Not unless he left his finger-prints on the awl.'

'Even then, he could say he'd picked it up one time when you had the tools out.'

Aldo cursed. 'I'm right, though. I know it. And now Gianni knows that it wasn't Sally he hurt, she could be in danger.' He grasped Enrico's arm. 'Promise me you'll keep watch on Gianni.'

'I promise.'

'I'd better warn Sally as well. Maybe she can persuade the police to investigate Gianni.' Without waiting for a reply, he went to write Sally a hurried note, telling her what he suspected.

Sally arrived back at the Wrennery after a quiet watch to find a letter from her mother waiting for her. She liked to savour letters from home in peace, so instead of joining Mary and Iris in the common room, where she could see them chatting and reading the newspaper, she headed up to their cabin. She waited only to remove her shoes before borrowing Iris's letter knife and slitting open the envelope. Then she curled on her bed, looking forward to the luxury of a few minutes in her mother's company.

> *Dear Sally,*
>
> *I've got some very exciting news to tell you, which I hope you will be happy to hear. Harry has asked me to marry him and I said yes! Now Ted is so improved and doing well in his job, he is able to take on the rent of the Gray Street house himself, so I will be moving into Harry's house after we are married. We have decided not to wait but have set the wedding for the tenth of August. We would have loved for you to have been there, of course, but knowing how difficult it is for you to get leave, we decided to have a very quiet wedding and a celebration all together when you can join us.*
>
> *I know this must come as a surprise, but I do hope you can be happy for us.*

Sally read and reread this news and could almost hear her mother's nervousness coming through. It was clear Annie was worried that Sally might not be able to find it in her heart to accept Harry into the family. Sally knew she would have to write back straight away to assure her that she was delighted. Although she had only met Harry briefly, she had a good feeling about him and knew he would take care of her mother.

She was already working out how to phrase her response as she read on. However, all coherent thought flew from her mind when she saw what else her mother had to say.

I have more news, and this is hard to write. There is something I should have told you long ago but couldn't bring myself to say. I know you must have thought it strange that I was walking out with Harry when I've always told you that I would never love anyone else after your father. After talking it over with Ted, I've decided it's time you knew the truth. In fact, Ted has long thought you should be told the truth, as he is worried that you have picked up your romantic ideas from the stories I told you about your father.

For they were stories. I hope this does not come as too much of a shock. I also hope you will forgive me for being too cowardly to tell you in person, but I know my courage would fail me if I had to try telling you face to face. When you were very young and used to ask me about your father, I couldn't bear to tell you the truth. I know how keenly you missed the families your school friends were blessed with, and so I found myself making up a story about a wonderful man who had swept me off my feet and who I had fallen in love with and now grieved. The truth is, that the reality of living with Gordon soon shook the stars from my eyes.

Before I go on, I must tell you that I have never associated you with your father. I have always loved you completely and you are the reason I cannot regret my marriage to him. But after we were married, Gordon changed. Nothing I ever did was right, and he believed in punishing me for every mistake. Ted called round unexpectedly one day and saw a bruise on my face before I could conceal it. Ted tried to make me leave with him but I was frightened that Gordon might attack him so I refused. Then one day not long after you were born, he did everyone a favour and got blind drunk at the pub and fell in a ditch and drowned on his way home.

I'd always intended to tell you when you were old enough to understand — our neighbours knew how

Gordon had died, so the truth would have reached you sooner or later, and I didn't want you to learn it from someone else. But then Ted had his accident and we moved to Whitby, where none of our neighbours knew about Gordon. I was so ashamed for falling for his charm that I couldn't bear to tell anyone the truth, and the longer I left it, the more you loved hearing the stories I made up about him and the more difficult it became to confess.

Sally couldn't bring herself to read the closing lines. She stared at the letter in shock. This must be what Uncle Ted had urged her mother to tell her. She had thought it must be about Harry. Her father had been no romantic hero but a drunken bully. She didn't blame her mother for not telling her the truth about Gordon Hartley. How do you tell your daughter that the father she'd always believed to be the perfect man had been nothing more than a violent brute? She couldn't blame Ted, either. He had done his best to persuade Annie to tell the truth but would not take it on himself to reveal something that was his sister's secret to tell.

No, the only person Sally blamed was herself. She had eagerly accepted every lie and been so gullible that she'd believed that fate or destiny would bring her the perfect man just as it had brought her mother and father together. But if destiny had brought her mother a man who beat and abused her, then Sally didn't want to believe in it any more. She had wasted years eating her heart out over Adam because of her mistaken faith that they were meant to be together; now she was able to look back with clear eyes, she could see that Adam had never given any sign of being remotely interested in her.

She didn't know how long she gazed, unseeing, at the letter in her hand, lost in self-recrimination. She only became aware of her surroundings when she heard footsteps on the stairs and the sound of Iris and Mary's voices. She thrust the paper into her pocket and hitched a bright smile onto her face when the door burst open.

Iris stopped dead just inside the room. 'Are you all right, Sally? You look like you've seen a ghost.'

Clearly her smile hadn't been as convincing as she'd supposed. Sally let her features relax and said, 'I just had a letter from my mum.'

Iris's brows drew together in concern. 'Has anything happened? Is she ill?'

'No, she's fine. She—'

'Well something's clearly happened. You're as white as a sheet.'

Sally shrugged and pulled out the letter, now crumpled from being thrust away in a hurry. 'Everything's a lie,' she said, her voice shaking. 'Everything she told me about my father was untrue.' With plenty of pauses to wipe away tears, she repeated what she had just learned.

'What an awful way to find out,' Iris said, sitting beside Sally and giving her a hug.

Sally blinked down at her hands. 'Is there a good way to find out your father was a thug? I completely understand why Mum couldn't tell me before, though. I always used to imagine my father was like a prince from a fairy tale. I must have made it impossible for her to destroy my illusions.'

The bed dipped as Mary sat on her other side. 'Don't blame yourself. You were only a child.'

'I suppose you're right.'

'Of course I am.'

Sally sighed. 'I've always believed in destiny bringing people together. I was so sure it had brought my mum and dad together, and although I made a mistake with Adam, I was starting to think maybe Aldo and I are meant for one another. But it's all a lie. I can see it now. It's just coincidence when two people meet and fall in love. If we'd been posted to Portsmouth instead of Orkney, maybe you and Mary would have met and fallen in love with different men.'

'Maybe,' Mary said. 'I was never much of a believer in destiny. I think we just have to make the best of what life throws at us.'

'I don't know,' Iris said. 'Maybe it's a mixture of the two. Who knows — maybe we would have met Rob and Joe some other way. It's hard to imagine life without Rob now. But I don't really believe in destiny either. At least, it might be real, but as we can't possibly know what the future has in store, we simply have to do as Mary says and do our best in whatever situation we find ourselves. Don't believe in destiny bringing you together but believe in yourself and your own choices and convictions. If you find someone worth fighting for then don't let yourself down.'

–

Sally was still pondering Iris's words a few days later. She had come off watch at 1300 and had a few hours to kill before going back on duty at 1800. At least the summer had brought calmer weather so they could cycle to the signal station once more, freeing up more off-duty time. The first thing she had to do was put the reply she had written to her mother into the post. It had taken several attempts to get the letter right. Not only did it have to convey her joy, it also had to assure her mother that she was coming to terms with the truth about her father. She hoped it would put her mother's mind at rest and convince her she understood why Annie had withheld the truth for so long. The letter had closed with Sally's heartfelt congratulations and a promise to visit as soon as she could. She had also written to Aldo, so once she had handed in her mother's letter for censoring, she decided to head into Stromness to see if she could find Enrico. He would probably be at work at the docks, although if she was lucky, she would catch him when he took a break. Sure enough, when she reached the docks, she saw several men in their distinctive brown uniforms swarming around a truck, Enrico among them. She knew better than to interrupt him while he was clearly busy, so she perched on a low wall and hoped he would notice her. About ten minutes later, he returned from transferring a crate to a ship and stood, mopping his brow. When he looked up, he happened to glance her way. After a quick glance at his fellow workers, he hurried to meet her.

'I have a message from Aldo,' he said without preamble. 'He has been worried about you.' He handed her a note, written on the back of the envelope she had used for her letter. She was disappointed to see only a few words but when she saw what he had written she felt as though an Arctic wind had suddenly blasted through the docks.

> *Dear Sally,*
>
> *I write this in a hurry. I think Gianni attacked Tessa but I have no proof. Please take care and stay away from him.*
>
> *Aldo x*

'Gianni?' she said to Enrico. 'Which one is he?'

Enrico pointed to a burly man walking into a shed about fifty yards distant. Sally couldn't make out his features, but knew she would recognise him if she saw him again. 'You must go before he sees you,' Enrico said. 'I promised I would keep an eye on Gianni and make sure he doesn't come near you.'

'You think he is dangerous?'

'I know he is.' Enrico's lip curled. 'He is a fascist. We were surprised when he agreed to the terms of being in a work battalion, and now we think he did it so he could make trouble. Do not let him near you. If he finds out who you are, you will be in danger. You must go before he sees you speaking to me.'

'Wait, why is Aldo worried Gianni will hurt me?'

Enrico grimaced. 'He did not want me to tell you in case it frighten you.'

'Too late. At least tell me why I should be frightened.'

After a momentary hesitation, Enrico shrugged. 'Very well. We think Gianni hurt Tessa because he thought she was you.'

'Why? And why would Gianni want to hurt me?'

'He saw Aldo speak with Tessa at the football. He already knew Aldo like an English girl called Sally.'

Comprehension dawned. 'So when he saw Aldo speak to Tessa, he thought that was me. It still doesn't explain why he wanted to hurt me, though.'

'Because Aldo make Gianni look a fool, and Gianni wanted revenge.' Enrico shot another glance at the hut. 'Now go, quick, before he comes out and sees you. He already knows Tessa is not you.'

Sally nodded and after muttering a quick thank you, she dashed away, heart pounding.

–

'We have to do something, and fast,' Sally said to Iris and Mary later that evening when they were knitting yet more socks for sailors in the common room. As she cast a row of stitches on one needle in preparation for starting a new sock, she recounted what Enrico had told her.

'Maybe we should go back to Sergeant Frazer and ask if he found any fingerprints on the handle,' Mary said.

'I suppose that's the logical next step. I can't see him paying any attention to me, though. Can you?'

Mary and Iris both shook their heads.

'If only there was someone else we could go to. Frazer must have a superior.' Sally couldn't feel any enthusiasm for the idea, though. Now she knew about Frazer's son, she was reluctant to cause him any trouble by going to his inspector behind his back. Then she remembered something. She dropped her knitting on her lap and groped in her pocket, pulling out the notes Aldo had sent her. She shuffled through them until she found the first – the one that told her he was confined to the camp. 'Wait, what about the captain at Bruna Camp? Aldo says he is sympathetic. Maybe he could chivvy the police along?'

Mary was gazing at her with raised eyebrows. 'You've kept all his notes?'

'So what?' Despite her bravado, Sally could feel the heat of a blush warming her cheeks. 'You can't tell me you haven't kept all Joe's letters.'

'Yes, but not on my person. And they are proper letters, not two-line scrawls.'

'Well, this is all I have of Aldo, apart from my St Christopher. Anyway,' Sally rushed on, not wishing to attract any more teasing, 'what if I go to Bruna Camp and talk to this captain? Maybe he can put some pressure on the police.'

'I suppose it's better than doing nothing,' Iris said. 'We could try talking to Tessa again, as well. Maybe she's remembered something.'

'That's a good idea.'

Iris looked regretful. 'It'll be a few days before I'm free to go to Kirkwall again, though.'

'That doesn't matter. I'm off all day tomorrow.' Sally grinned. 'I think Wendleton still feels bad about giving me that double watch, and seems to be trying to make it up to me. Anyway, I can do this alone. I'll see if I can hitch a ride to Kirkwall and back tomorrow – that'll be quicker than going by bus – and then I'll go to Bruna Camp.'

'What about this Gianni?' Mary looked worried. 'He might see you.'

'He should be at the docks. Don't worry – I'll keep out of sight if there's any sign of the Italians coming back to camp. I can't sit back and do nothing while Aldo's stuck there.' She turned to Iris. 'It was right, what you said after I found out about my dad. I don't know if Aldo and I are meant to be together, but it's wrong to do nothing while he's being falsely accused. I'm going to do everything I can to make sure Sergeant Frazer looks into the evidence more closely.'

Chapter Twenty-Five

Sally set out the next day as soon as breakfast was over and didn't have long to wait before she managed to hitch a lift with an army corporal who was taking supplies to Kirkwall. Less than an hour later, the corporal had dropped her outside the hospital, and she marched inside armed with the latest copy of the *Orkney Blast* and a scented soap she had managed to buy from the NAAFI. She had intended the soap as a birthday gift for her mother but thought Tessa's need was greater.

Her first obstacle came when the nurse in charge of Tessa's ward refused to let her in. 'Visiting hours are afternoons only.'

'Oh, please, I've come all the way from Stromness especially to see her. I don't get many days off.'

Maybe the same good luck that had got her the day off in the first place was still lingering. The nurse's gaze softened. 'Oh, well, I suppose it can't do any harm now rounds are over. She hasn't had any other visitors, poor lass. Go on, then, but keep your voice down, or all the patients will be demanding visitors.'

After thanking the nurse, Sally crept along the corridor to Tessa's room, doing her best not to draw attention to herself. She found Tessa sitting at the window in a high-backed armchair, gazing outside. A ball of pale blue wool lay on her lap, together with a pair of knitting needles, although there was no sign that Tessa had made any attempt to knit.

'Hello, Tessa. Can I come in?'

Tessa gave a little start and looked round. She had lost weight, making her eyes look too large for her face. 'Sally? I didn't think you would come again.' She pointed to the armchair opposite.

Sally wasn't sure how to answer that. After all, Tessa had done her best to make Sally feel small and unloved and could hardly expect Sally to be eager to see her. She took a seat in silence, and from this position she could see Tessa's face properly for the first time. She was still very pale, although her skin had lost the greyish tinge that had alarmed Sally when they had found her. The bandages were gone from her forehead, revealing a patch of cropped hair and a large scar. 'How are you feeling?'

'Much better, thanks.'

Sally couldn't stop her gaze from returning to the scar. Tessa couldn't fail to notice, and she pointed to it with a grimace. 'Not pretty, I know. The nurse tells me most of the scar will be hidden once my hair grows back, so I can live in hope.'

'How's your shoulder?'

'Painful and stiff but it'll be fine.'

Sally hesitated, unsure how to begin now she was here. Then she remembered her gifts and handed them over. 'I brought these for you.' She gave her the newspaper and the soap. 'I didn't know if you could get the *Orkney Blast* here, and it's just come out.'

Much to Sally's surprise, Tessa's eyes filled with tears.

'What's the matter? Do you feel ill? Shall I get the nurse?'

Tessa shook her head and cried all the harder, leaving Sally to sit in awkward silence. Not knowing what else to do, she patted Tessa's hand. 'Are you sure you're all right?'

'I'm fine. I just didn't expect you to be so nice after all the awful things I said. I'm so sorry.'

'You don't have to apologise.'

'Yes I do. I was horrible to you, and you deserve to know why.'

While Tessa paused to dab her eyes, Sally waited, not entirely sure she wanted to hear any explanation. Not if it involved hearing about whatever imagined faults had prompted Tessa's bullying. 'If you're too tired, I can come back,' she said.

Tessa tucked away her handkerchief, shaking her head. 'I'm not tired. Well, not more than usual, anyway. But I've screwed up my courage to say what I have to say, and I can't bear to put it off any longer.'

Now Sally was intrigued; her curiosity overtook her need to find out if Tessa had recovered her memory of the attack. 'I'm listening.'

'You must have wondered why I picked on you.'

Sally nodded, bracing herself. The reason was bound to be unflattering.

'Well, you see, I know I went on about my old posting a bit when I first arrived here—'

'That's putting it mildly,' Sally said, surprised at the unexpected turn of the conversation.

'The thing is, I didn't enjoy my last posting as much as I made out. No, that's a lie. I hated it.'

This last was said with a vehemence that shocked Sally, considering Tessa's listlessness until then. Sally leaned forward, waiting for Tessa to continue, her reluctance gone.

'I'm like you, you see, although I've tried so hard to hide it since I came here. I have my little superstitions that help me through the day. If I spill salt, I always have to throw it over my shoulder.'

'Your left one?'

'Of course. I won't step on the cracks in the pavement, and I try and avoid the number thirteen. Oh, and I never walk under ladders.'

'I never noticed any of that. Although I have to tell you that although Mary teases me about most of my superstitions, she tells me the ladder one is just common sense.'

'That's the problem I had with you, right there.' Tessa pointed at her as though pointing out a glaring fault.

Sally resisted the temptation to glance down at herself to check she hadn't spilt something down her front. 'I don't understand.'

'You have friends who tease you, but in a friendly way.' Tessa's chin wobbled, and she bit her lip and turned her face away for a moment. When she looked back, she had regained her composure, although from the tightness of her mouth, it was clear she was fighting to keep her emotions in check. 'The other Wrens at Harwich were awful to me. They would do things like invite me to go out with them on an afternoon, and I'd get my hopes up that they finally wanted to be friends, only for them to say we'd meet at *1300*.' Tessa put extra emphasis on the 'thirteen'. 'Then they'd all laugh like drains, and I'd realise it was just another joke at my expense. In the end, I requested a transfer, hoping to make a fresh start in a place where no one knew me. The first person from the Wrennery I met was you. You spilled some salt, remember?'

Sally nodded. She did have a vague memory of knocking over the salt cellar.

'Well,' Tessa went on, 'when you threw some over your shoulder, I hoped I'd found a kindred spirit. When Adam turned up... well, I thought he was good-looking and let myself get carried away. I didn't think you wanted anything more than friendship from him, though, or I wouldn't have come on so strong. I was just happy to be in a place where people weren't teasing me, and I let my excitement get the better of me. I really hoped we could be friends.'

'I don't mind about Adam,' Sally said. Then, deciding Tessa's honesty deserved the total truth in return, she added, 'Not any more, anyway. But what turned you against me?'

'You, Iris and Mary were such a tight group, I could see you didn't have room for another friend. And then I overheard them teasing you, but in a friendly way, and I hated you then. I hated that you could be yourself, and still keep your friends, yet I was forced to pretend to be someone else.' Tessa hung her head, addressing the next words to her knitting. 'And that's why I started bullying you. I thought if I couldn't be happy, I didn't want you to be happy either.'

Sally could hardly believe what she was hearing. 'I thought you were doing it because there was something wrong with me,' she said finally.

'It was because I could see so much of myself in you, and it felt so unfair to see you thriving when I had been practically hounded out of my last post.' Tessa toyed with the end of one of the knitting needles. 'Thank goodness the worst thing I did didn't work.'

'What was that?'

Tessa's answer was so quiet Sally had to lean forward to hear. 'I put itching powder in your boots. It must have been dud powder, though, because you never mentioned it. I'm really glad it didn't work now.'

After a moment's hesitation, Sally opted not to tell her the truth. Why distress her further? Then Sally remembered Tessa's request the afternoon of the attack. 'When you asked to speak to me, what was that about?'

'I wanted to apologise then. Your friend... Aldo. What he said at the tournament cut me to the quick. It was as though he had held up a mirror in front of me and I didn't like what I saw. I realised that I was causing you the same pain I'd been made to suffer. I was going to ask you to forgive me. I thought if you had room in your life for Aldo, as well as Mary and Iris, maybe you could find some room for me as well.'

Coming into this conversation, Sally could never have imagined that she could feel sympathy for Tessa beyond sympathy for her injuries. Now, however, Sally could see Tessa as an eager-to-please new Wren whose desire for camaraderie and to do well in her job had been slowly worn down by the bullies. More than ever, Sally was thankful that she had fallen in with Iris and Mary. 'I wish I'd known,' she said. 'We would have been only too happy to have another friend. What about Adam, though? Did you really like him?'

'I thought I did. Maybe it was simply because you liked him, and I wanted to be you so much. Or, at least, I can see that now. I didn't really understand at the time. But—' and now Tessa was twisting her hands, appearing more distressed than ever.

Sally hastened to reassure her. As hurt as she had been by Tessa's behaviour, she had now had a break from it for some weeks. Looking back on it, Sally was able to distance herself from the hurt. And, of course, she had never suffered to the same extent as Tessa. Tessa had faced her bullies alone. Sally had always had Iris and Mary's deep regard to reassure her that she was not unlikeable. 'It's all in the past now. You've had a far worse time of it than I have, and I'm prepared to let bygones be bygones.'

Tessa still twisted her hands in distress, though. 'That's not the worst of it.' Her voice dropped to little more than a whisper. 'When I tell you what else I did, I don't think you'll ever be able to forgive me.'

'Why – what did you do?' Sally couldn't imagine what Tessa could have done that was any worse than what she had already related.

'When you came to visit me at the hospital... you, Iris and Mary. I was so happy you'd all come to visit. And then I overheard you in the corridor. They were teasing you about Aldo, how in love you clearly were with each other. And I was so jealous. I forgot about making friends. I—' Tessa looked down at her hands and made the rest of her confession to them. 'I knew it wasn't Aldo who attacked me. When I heard he was a suspect, my memory had already returned. But I said I still couldn't remember because I... oh, I don't know. I suppose I couldn't bear to see you happy.'

Sally stared at her, aghast, thinking of how Aldo had suffered. She could forgive the slights against her, but this...

'Oh, I knew it was too much for you to forgive. I knew it was wrong at the time, and the very next day, I told the nurse I'd remembered and she said she'd tell Sergeant Frazer for me. He never came to see me, though.'

Tessa's distress broke through Sally's horror. Whatever she had done, Sally couldn't let her go uncomforted when it was clear she felt genuine remorse for her actions. She leaned forward and grasped Tessa's hand. 'It's... difficult for me to forgive, I admit. Not because of the hurt you caused me but to Aldo.' Then Tessa's words registered with her. 'Wait, did you say you tried to tell Sergeant Frazer the very next day?'

'Yes. I couldn't understand why he didn't think it important.'

'Oh, I know why.' And now Sally's anger had turned from Tessa. 'That's because he found the handkerchief Gianni – your attacker – had planted on you. It was Aldo's, you see. We tried to explain Aldo couldn't possibly have done it but he was determined to pin it onto him.' Sally felt a wave of helpless anger wash over her. 'He was suspicious of Aldo from the start – felt Aldo must be up to no good because he was *cavorting* with local girls, as he put it.'

The first smile Tessa had given in a long time put a little animation into her face. 'I've never pictured you as the kind of girl who cavorts with anyone.'

Sally couldn't hold back a wry grin. 'Try telling that to Mary. Frazer said it in her hearing, and she's never going to let me forget it.'

'I can't believe you're taking this so well. I thought you would be really angry.'

'I am angry, but not with you. That Sergeant Frazer should be shot. All it took was a bit of circumstantial evidence, and he was practically tying the noose around Aldo's neck.' Sally drew a breath to calm herself down. 'I'm glad you felt able to tell me, Tessa. I know this hasn't been easy for you. It took courage to admit to everything.'

Tessa still looked distressed. 'I wish there was some way I could be more help. Something to undo the mess I've made.'

'There is.' Sally clutched Tessa's hand in her excitement. 'Can you describe the man who attacked you?'

Tessa's brow wrinkled, and her gaze lost its focus. 'He was broad-shouldered. Very burly. Like a bull.'

Burly. Like a bull. That was exactly what Sally had thought when Enrico had pointed Gianni out to her. The only thing keeping her from whooping with jubilation was her awareness that she wasn't supposed to be in Tessa's room. 'Tessa, you're a genius.'

'Did I help?'

'You most certainly did. I could hug you, only I won't because I don't want to hurt you. If I hadn't forgiven you before, I would do so now.'

Even pale and injured as she was, Tessa had never looked happier. 'Then you won't mind being my oppo again when I return from sick leave?'

'I'll even treat you to tea and cake at the Beehive to celebrate when you come back.'

—

Sally left the hospital on the warpath. Any thought of enlisting the help of Captain Briars had gone out of the window. She marched straight to the police station and demanded to speak to Sergeant Frazer.

'What is this about?'

'I have new information about the attack on Ordinary Wren Bligh,' Sally replied and gave her name. For a fleeting moment she wished Iris could be there, with her posh accent that made her sound like she had the perfect right to stride up to any official and demand an explanation. But Iris wasn't there, and this couldn't wait. Sally could only pray that this time the sergeant would pay her attention.

She didn't have to wait long before the sergeant emerged from the inner office and beckoned her inside. 'I hope this won't take long, Miss Hartley,' he said. 'I'm a busy man.'

His dismissive tone made Sally's heart sink into her shoes. There was no way she was going to get him to listen. Iris could have done it, but not her.

She sat in the chair indicated, wondering how she was going to extricate herself from this situation without embarrassing herself further. As she sat, she felt the St Christopher pendant swing on its chain. It was a powerful reminder of Aldo and his predicament. It was also a reminder that while Iris might have got her way by making the most of her upper-class accent and attitude, Sally was very different from Iris. As such, she needed to approach the sergeant in her own way. Iris would have been direct and gone in for the kill. But Sally wasn't like that and knew if she tried to emulate Iris she would fail. She could only be herself.

She closed her hand around the St Christopher, and as she did so, inspiration struck. Tessa had bullied her because seeing Sally had brought back painful memories of being bullied herself. And Frazer was determined to think badly of Aldo because Frazer associated him with his own pain. Sally knew what she had to say; she could only hope Frazer would hear her out.

Clutching the St Christopher like a talisman, she began. 'I wanted you to know that I was very sorry to hear about your son. Archie Heddle told me.'

Frazer's expression froze. 'I… ah… that's good of you,' he said.

'The thing is, I know how tragedy and grief can cloud your judgement. I've seen it happen.' She was gradually accepting that her obsession with superstition was a result of Ted's accident, and now the letter from her mother showed how her father's violence had affected the way Annie had brought her up.

Frazer started drumming his fingers on the desk. 'Do you have a point? As I said, I'm very busy.'

'Oh. Right. Well—' Sally drew a deep breath. It was hard to concentrate with Frazer's finger's tapping out a tarantella. Only her sudden intuition that he was doing it from agitation rather than impatience gave her the strength to continue. 'I don't want to get you into trouble, which is why I'm saying this to you and haven't taken this up with your inspector. But although I understand that you must want to lash out at the Italians, Aldo Vanni is not guilty of the attack on Tessa, and deep down you know it.'

Frazer pushed back his chair and rose. 'We're done here. I don't have time for—'

'I know Tessa remembers that Aldo didn't attack her. You got that message, didn't you, Sergeant? Why didn't you act on it and release Aldo?' Sally didn't know where she found the courage to make the accusation, and stared at Frazer, inwardly cringing, waiting for the insults to pour out of his mouth.

They didn't come. Frazer sank back onto his chair, pulled a handkerchief from his pocket and mopped beads of perspiration from his brow. 'You know?'

He looked as though he had lost the power of movement. In front of her eyes, he shrank from the bullish sergeant that Sally had always seen and seemed to age twenty years in an instant. Now she could see the grief that he had been living with for so long.

'Yes, I know,' she said. She had to steel herself because now was not the time to show pity. Aldo's freedom depended on her. 'And I know that you wanted to lash out at someone for the terrible loss you suffered. But it's not Aldo's fault.'

Frazer stared at Sally, and the pain in his eyes was clear. 'My son had just got engaged,' he said. 'Then he was posted to the Mediterranean, and a few days later I got the telegram. I was looking forward to him having his own family, to having grandchildren. And then that telegram arrived, and I knew that I had lost everything that ever mattered to me. When the Italian POWs were freed, well, it brought it all back. And when I saw you together with… well, I felt I couldn't stand it.'

Sally did something she would never have dreamed of doing. She placed her hand over his. 'I know. It's not fair. If it helps, Aldo saw his brother killed in front of his eyes. The last remaining member of *his* family. You have more in common than you know.'

Frazer gave a helpless shake of the head. 'I don't think I can forgive them. Not yet.' He straightened his back, pulling his hand away from Sally's. 'I will inform Captain Briars that Aldo Vanni has been cleared of all suspicion. Although that means I need to start the investigation all over again.'

He looked so soul-sick that the last of Sally's anger melted away. 'I think I can help there, too.' And she told him about Aldo's suspicions and how Tessa's description of her attacker also pointed to Gianni.

'Well, that's certainly a start. It's all circumstantial, mind, but I'll be sure to question this Gianni. You have my word that I'll take this new evidence seriously.'

'Thank you.' Sally felt giddy with elation. She had actually done it! If she had known this morning that she would be facing down Sergeant Frazer in his own office, she would probably have turned around and fled back to Stromness.

She was about to stand when Frazer said, 'Why? You could have gone straight to the inspector. Why didn't you?'

'Like I said, I know grief can play funny tricks with your mind. You've lost everything. I didn't want you to lose your job too.'

'Thank you.' Frazer cleared his throat. 'I'll probably be driving to Stromness in a while. I can give you a lift if you like.'

Sally shook her head. Making peace with Sergeant Frazer was one thing; sitting in a car with him for over half an hour was quite another. 'Thank you, but I have some errands I need to run now I'm here.' Now she was confident Frazer would release Aldo, there was no need for her to see Briars, so she had time to go shopping in Kirkwall. She was going to buy a gift for Aldo to celebrate his release and maybe some treats for Iris and Mary to thank them for being her friends. After her talk with Tessa, she appreciated them all the more.

–

It was some time later that Sally stepped off the bus, armed with parcels from her impromptu shopping expedition. She couldn't wait to see Mary and Iris, so set off at a fast pace for the Wrennery. They would still be on watch, but by the time she had put her shopping away they would not be long in returning.

'Sally, Sally!'

Although she knew Aldo would soon be released, she couldn't have hoped it would be so fast. Yet there was no mistaking the deep, lyrical voice calling to her from some way behind her. She spun round, dropping her parcels as she did so. She didn't pay them any heed but jumped up and down on the spot, waving to Aldo who was running her way, blowing kisses as he ran. Sally only stopped bouncing when she saw they were attracting a lot of curious looks from passers-by.

'Sally!' he called again. 'I am free!'

'I can see that.' Laughing, she bent to retrieve her shopping. Aldo joined her and crouched down to help. A moment later they both stood at the same time and banged heads. The next thing she knew, Sally was sitting on the ground, clutching her head with her now rather battered parcels strewn around her.

Aldo helped her up. 'I am sorry. You must wish I was still shut in the camp.'

'No, never. I'm so happy for you. A bruised head is a small price to pay.'

'It is bruised? Let me see.' And then Aldo was brushing the hair from her forehead and exploring the tender bump with gentle fingers. He followed his fingers with his lips, and Sally's head started spinning for reasons other than the knock. 'How does that feel now?' he asked.

'Much better.' Although her knees felt so weak she gripped his hand to keep her balance. That was her excuse, anyway.

'I wish I could buy you a drink to thank you properly,' Aldo said, 'but I have work to do. Captain Briars told me I have you to thank for changing Sergeant Frazer's mind, although he didn't say why. Can I meet you tomorrow evening? You can tell me all about it. I might have even more news by then.'

'I'd like that. Meet me outside the church as usual? What time?'

'I am not sure yet. Wait for me at half past six, and if I cannot make it, I will send Enrico with a note.'

'Do you really have to work now? It seems a bit late.' After so long apart, she couldn't bear to wait another day.

'Not work exactly. I'll explain tomorrow. I have to go now or I'll be late.' He gave her a quick kiss on the cheek then ran off, leaving her feeling a little dazed. Then, smiling to herself at the prospect of a whole evening with Aldo the next day, she gathered her packages again and set off for the Wrennery. She had only taken a few steps when she passed a narrow lane that led down to the water. A movement caught her eye. She looked and saw a tall, burly young man in the brown uniform of the Italian labour battalion. She hesitated, thinking he looked familiar — a friend of Aldo's, perhaps. Then a chill ran down her spine when she realised where she had seen him before. He was the man Enrico had pointed out to her. The man Aldo had warned her against. Her heart hammering, she clutched her shopping to her chest and hurried away, stumbling over a cracked paving slab as she did so. Seeing a group of Wrens ahead, she strove to catch them up; there was safety in numbers. Once or twice she glanced over her shoulder, reassured when she failed to see Gianni again. By the time she had caught up with the group, her pulse had calmed a little. It had served as a warning, though. Although Aldo's name was cleared, she must remember to stay on her guard. The police had not yet caught the man who had attacked Tessa.

Chapter Twenty-Six

Sally was still on cloud nine the next morning. She was on watch with Mary, and even the weather matched her mood, with clear blue skies, warm sunshine and only a light breeze blowing through the open windows into the signal room.

'On days like this, I wish I could live up here and look at this view for ever,' she said, taking a deep breath of sea air.

Mary snorted. 'You might regret that on the other three hundred and sixty-four days of the year when the wind is howling round the building and you can't see a thing through the rain or fog. And don't forget the winters when it's dark most of the day.'

'Don't be a spoilsport. Aldo's out of trouble, the weather is perfect and we're being paid to look at the world's most beautiful view. What more could you ask for?'

'You want a list?'

Knowing she was unlikely to win Mary round, Sally stepped out onto the balcony so she could enjoy the view free from Mary's tart tongue. She hadn't been there more than a few seconds when a magpie flew by in a blur of black and white feathers and settled at the cliff's edge. There was only one, but Sally wasn't going to let herself get upset. As she had announced to her friends only the night before, when she had been delirious with joy, she was past worrying about silly things like blaming anything bad on whether a magpie had decided to make an appearance or not.

Then a second magpie swooped down to join the first and Sally gave a squeak of excitement. 'Two magpies!' she called to Mary. 'Something good is going to happen.'

'I thought you said you were past all that.'

'I know, but I can't help getting excited when I see two.'

'As long as you don't get upset each time you only see one. Anyway, I'm going to make some tea.' This was followed by the sound of Mary descending the metal ladder to the lower floor.

Sally leaned against the railing and gazed out at Hoy Sound. Crowned with sunlight, the hills on Hoy looked so close she felt she could reach out and touch them. Whatever Mary might say, today was special, and Sally intended to make the most of it. She regarded the two magpies again. While she was determined not to let superstition have such a hold on her, she couldn't deny it was also a part of who she was. She would try to view the world more rationally, yet she also had to admit that she couldn't change overnight. Her friends and Aldo accepted her, and that was the most important thing. She spared a thought for Tessa and decided that when she returned from sick leave, Sally would do her best to include her in the group. Last night she had told Iris and Mary about Tessa's confession, and they had been dismayed to hear how Tessa had been bullied by the Wrens at Harwich. 'If you can forgive and accept her, then we can jolly well try too,' Iris had declared, and she had made plans to visit Tessa on her next day off.

Sally snapped out of her reverie when she saw a ship approach from the north. She hurried to the telescope and sighted it, bringing the image into focus. It was a minesweeper. Halcyon class, by the look of it. Knowing she would soon get a call from the team monitoring the anti-submarine loop, she picked up the Aldis lamp and sent the standard challenge. The reply came back with the correct daily code and the ship's identification. Sally jotted the letters down on her signal pad. K... E... L... P

She had to grip her pencil to stop it slipping from her fingers in her excitement. 'Mary!' she shouted. 'Mary, get up here now!'

She didn't take her eyes from the ship, which was a good thing, as she saw another series of flashes from the signal deck: 'M... A... R... Y?'

'What about the tea?' Mary called.

'Leave it. You don't want to miss this.' Sally raised the Aldis lamp again and sent the signal to stand by. Behind her, she heard Mary climb the ladder muttering, 'This better not be another blasted magpie.'

'It's not,' Sally told her. 'You're wanted. I need to report a ship crossing the loop, so you must deal with the signals.'

Mary gave her an odd look but went to the window. After one glance out she gave a cry and dashed onto the balcony. Grinning to herself, Sally picked up the phone and reported the *Kelpie* about to cross the loop. Joe and Rob were back in Scapa Flow.

She finished the phone call quickly and hung up. She didn't go straight out onto the balcony, though, deciding to give Mary a moment to enjoy Joe's return. However, she could hear the shutters on the signal lamp clattering, and although she wasn't deliberately trying to follow it, she was able to make out the message Mary was sending: 'U took yr time.'

After a few minutes, Sally knew the *Kelpie* would be getting out of range, so she stepped out onto the balcony. Only to be enveloped in an enthusiastic hug.

'I'll never tease you about your magpies again. Two for joy is exactly right.' Mary's face was wet with tears but her smile was so bright the sun seemed dim in comparison. 'I can't wait to tell Iris the news. And guess what?'

'What?'

'Joe thinks he can come ashore tonight. I'm going to see him in just a few hours!'

What with Mary's joy and Sally's excitement about seeing Aldo again, they broke all records cycling back to the Wrennery after the end of their watch. While Mary sprinted up the stairs to find Iris, Sally went to the common room to see if anyone had brought a note from Aldo. Sure enough, Evelyn tapped her on the shoulder. 'Note for you, Sally.'

Sally glanced at it and her heart leapt to see Aldo's tall, spiky handwriting: *Meet me at six*. This had originally been 'six thirty', but the 'thirty' had been crossed out. That gave her five and a half hours to get ready. Sally went through to the mess feeling all knotted up inside. If anything, the long separation from Aldo had taught her how much she cared about him, and she was determined not to let the evening end without finding out how serious Aldo's feelings were. Although her experience with Adam had been painful, she had learned from it and was determined not to get in a relationship with Aldo if his feelings weren't serious. Of course she knew he couldn't promise they would be together for ever, not when he wasn't in control of his fate. But if he had already determined to return to Italy at the end of the war and break it off with her for good, she didn't want to go through that. Even if he told her he loved her and would do all in his power to stay with her, she knew she might still end up with a broken heart. Even so, she was going to guard herself against a relationship that had no hope. She knew she was falling in love with him, and as much as she yearned to be with him, she would rather break it off now than end up broken-hearted when he returned to Italy without looking back.

She was just going up to the hatch to see what food was left when Iris and Mary arrived. Sally grinned to see Iris's face was glowing as bright as Mary's. 'I take it Mary's told you the news?'

'Isn't it wonderful? I'm going to meet the drifter later, in case Rob has got leave too.' Iris linked arms with Sally and gave her a pleading look that any kitten would be proud of. 'Will you come with me?'

'But Mary will be there, and I'm meeting Aldo at 1800.'

'That still gives you time to come to the pier with us. Please come. If Rob can't make it, I'll feel like a complete gooseberry with Mary and Joe drooling all over each other.'

'We do not drool!' Mary, who had just picked up a sandwich, waved it in Iris's face.

'You did a jolly good impression of it the last time you saw each other.' Iris turned back to Sally. 'Please say you'll come.'

'But if Rob is there, then I'll be the gooseberry.'

'No you won't. You can go and meet Aldo.' Iris grinned. 'I know how much you enjoy cavorting with him.'

Sally considered it. 'On one condition.'

'Name it.'

'I can borrow your new red lipstick.'

'It's a deal.' A dimple appeared in Iris's cheek. 'Try not to smear too much on Aldo, though.'

—

It took all three girls longer than usual to get ready for the evening. Iris and Mary, understandably nervous and excited after a year and a half's separation from their sweethearts, agonised over what to wear and whether to put their hair up or leave it down. Sally, too, was jittery. This was the evening that would make or break her relationship with Aldo and she knew without doubt that she would be devastated if Aldo couldn't offer her some kind of commitment. On the other hand, she was building up greater heartbreak for herself farther down the line if she didn't get him to state his intentions, so she promised herself she would face the issue head on. Her hand shook as she applied the borrowed deep-red lipstick.

By the time she was accompanying Iris and Mary to the pier, she had worked herself into such a state of nerves that she was glad Iris had persuaded her to go. Hopefully, the walk would steady her nerves and help her mentally rehearse how to broach the subject of their relationship with Aldo. This proved to be the case. Iris and Mary's excitement was infectious, and Sally was entertained to see the usually down-to-earth Mary so flustered.

A drifter was already in sight when they reached the pier. 'Is it them?' Iris asked, craning her neck to try to see inside the boat.

'I don't know. I can't see.' Mary, a good two inches shorter than the others, was jumping up and down in her attempts to view the passengers.

As the drifter grew closer, it performed a slow turn in preparation for its approach to the pier. Now they could see the passengers more clearly, and one in particular, who was leaning perilously over the side, waving frantically.

'It's him, it's him!' Mary didn't stop jumping up and down and waved so enthusiastically that Sally had to step out of her way to avoid a slap in the face.

Iris was still craning her neck, looking this way and that. 'I can't see Rob. Maybe he couldn't get leave.'

Her expression was so crestfallen that Sally gave her hand a squeeze. 'He'll get leave another day if he's not here. At least you know he's safe and sound.'

Then the drifter bumped against the dock and men were swarming onto the pier; the air rang with cheers and laughter and voices discussing their plans for the night. 'Bloody Orkney,' one man's voice could be heard above the din. 'Knew we hadn't seen the last of it.' A moment later, Mary was being swung off her feet in Joe's arms.

Iris was still looking forlorn. Raising her voice over the hubbub, she said, 'It doesn't look like he's here. I'll just—'

She broke off with a wordless cry and barrelled into the crowd. Puzzled, Sally tried to follow but found it almost impossible to move in the opposite direction to the majority of the crowd. She caught sight of Iris just as she launched herself into the arms of a tall, auburn-haired man.

'Careful, lass, you'll have us both in the harbour.' Then Rob planted a kiss on Iris's lips which she returned with enthusiasm.

Smiling, Sally eased her way out from the throng, satisfied that Iris would not be requiring her company that evening. Anyway, it was only a few minutes before six, when she should be meeting Aldo. She hurried away from the docks, wondering a little wistfully if she and Aldo would ever have the kind of relationship that Mary and Iris had with their sweethearts. Remembering Aldo's kisses and his enthusiastic – if brief – reunion of the day before, she had to believe they could. Her heart beat a rapid tattoo against her ribs as she hurried towards their rendezvous.

She had originally chosen the church because it was easy to find, with its squat spire plainly visible above the crowded buildings of Stromness. Now she was glad of it for another reason: it was set back from the main street and the entrance was up a flight of steps from a side lane. This meant that it would be a secluded spot for a conversation. When she got there, she ran up the steps, pressing her hands to her stomach in a futile attempt to quell the quivering within.

Someone was waiting but it wasn't Aldo.

Gianni stepped out from the shadowy doorway, a wicked gleam in his eyes. 'You are Sally, yes? I am glad to meet you at last.'

Sally backed away with a gasp but before she could escape, a large, strong hand gripped her arm and she was pulled towards her captor. 'You and I will go for a walk down by the water. If you make a sound or try to escape…' He punctuated his words with a movement of his free hand towards her side. Sally choked back a cry when something sharp sliced through her dress and nicked her just below the ribs. Glancing down, she saw the glint of steel.

'This way.' Gianni dragged her down the steps and onto the main street. Sally glanced round frantically. Surely Aldo must be on his way? Too late, she remembered the crossed-out number on the note from Aldo, and it hit her what must have happened. Somehow Gianni had got hold of the note and crossed out the 'thirty'. Aldo wouldn't arrive for another half an hour. In growing despair, she tried to catch the eye of any passers-by. But there were only a few people visible, none of whom paid any attention. Sally supposed they must look like a courting couple. They only stayed on the main street for a short distance before Gianni dived into another lane, this one little more than a gap between buildings. It was empty. Not far ahead, wavelets lapped against stone, and Sally knew they were in a dead end, with nothing but water ahead. In desperation, praying Aldo would come looking for her, she yanked the fragile chain of her St Christopher hard enough to break it and flung it towards the entrance to the lane. It was her only hope.

Chapter Twenty-Seven

Aldo left the NAAFI bakery, swinging the paper bag containing the sticky buns he'd been handed at the end of his working day. He had Captain Briars to thank for getting him this job; the canteen staff had returned such a good report on his work that when news had reached the captain's ears that the NAAFI bakery was short-handed, he had sent them a message recommending Aldo. The manager had invited Aldo to talk to them about the job yesterday, which was where he had been going when he had seen Sally. If it hadn't been so important to him, he would have skipped the meeting, but this seemed like a step closer to his dream. The manager had been very welcoming and said that although the job would mostly involve cleaning and taking deliveries at first, he would see to it that Aldo got a chance to demonstrate his baking skills as soon as possible. Aldo was more than happy to accept, despite the early start that would be required from him some mornings.

He had finished a little earlier than expected and as he still had half an hour or so to kill before meeting Sally, he wandered to the docks to see if there was any sign of Enrico.

As it happened, Enrico was just emerging from working in a ship's hold all day. He was covered in dust, with trails streaked down his face where the perspiration had run. 'Come to bring me a treat to say sorry for deserting me?' Enrico pointed at the paper bag from which a delicious, yeasty aroma was escaping.

'I'll bring you something another time. These are for Sally.'

Enrico slapped him on the arm, leaving a smear of dust on his sleeve. Aldo cursed and tried to brush it away. 'You did that deliberately.'

'What do you expect? You're the one with a pretty girl and a cushy job.' But Enrico was grinning, taking the sting from his words. 'Anyway, I thought you'd be with her. Trying to play it cool by making her wait?'

'What do you mean? I'm meeting her at half past six.'

'The note you gave me said six.'

'No. I definitely said half past. I didn't know what time I would finish today, so I left myself plenty of leeway.' Then he stopped. 'Anyway, what are you doing, reading my notes?'

'It wasn't sealed, what do you expect? If you insist on making me your delivery boy, you can't expect me not to take a look. It definitely said six.' Enrico's brow wrinkled. 'Thinking about it, it did say six thirty, but the thirty was crossed out.'

'I never did that.' Aldo's mouth had gone dry. 'You didn't leave it lying around, did you?'

'No, I—' Enrico stopped. 'No, wait. I did, but only for a moment. I left it on the table when I went to return my tray. But I went and got it right away when I realised I had left it.'

Now icy cold dread settled in Aldo's stomach. He had given the note to Enrico at breakfast, to deliver during his midday break. He would have taken the note himself but he hadn't known what arrangements would be made for dinner so hadn't known if he would get a chance to deliver it himself. 'Gianni wasn't sitting anywhere near you, was he?'

'Maybe.' Enrico frowned. 'Yes, he was at the table behind. Why—?'

But Aldo was sprinting for the church.

It seemed to take for ever to get there; his lungs were bursting, and grey dots swirled before his eyes, but he didn't dare slow his pace. His every instinct screamed at him that Sally was in danger and he was the only person who could save her. When he reached the church he sprang up the steps, only to find it deserted. Putting his hands on his knees, he bent double, gasping for breath. Had Enrico been mistaken? Was Sally even now walking from the Wrennery in perfect safety, expecting to meet Aldo in a little under half an hour?

No. He hoped it was true, but he couldn't deny the strong sense of danger. Now he came to think of it, he was sure he had seen Gianni watch him that morning with an odd, triumphant gleam in his eyes. Gulping for breath, Aldo hurried down the steps. He wouldn't relax until he had found Sally safe and sound. When he reached the main street, he looked left and right. Which way? Right. Towards the Wrennery. If she was on the way, he would meet her. If she wasn't... Well, he would report Sally's danger to the Wren in charge. At least they would alert the authorities. He set off at a jog, not daring to go faster in case he missed any sign of Sally.

He hadn't gone many metres when a silvery glint on the pavement caught his eye. He glanced at it idly as he went by, dismissing it as a dropped coin. It was only when he had taken a few more paces that his brain caught up with what his eyes had seen. It hadn't been a coin but a silver pendant on a chain. He stopped and looked back. There it was, lying at the entrance to a shadowy gap between the buildings. It looked like the St Christopher he had given Sally all that time ago.

Keeping close to the wall, he ran on silent feet back to the pendant and picked it up. It *was* a St Christopher, the image worn from much wear. He could have drawn it in his sleep, it was so familiar. There was no doubt that this was the one he had given Sally.

Glancing around, he noticed that the street was deserted. No one to ask for help, and he couldn't delay. Peering around the corner, he saw a sight that made his blood freeze. Sally was backed against a wall, and looming over her, a knife to her throat, was Gianni.

'I'm going to use you to send Aldo a message,' he was saying. 'This will teach him to mess with me.'

There was no time to call for help. Aldo acted on instinct. He stepped into the alley, screaming in Italian, 'Get your filthy hands off her, you bastard!'

Gianni's head jerked around, his eyes wide in shock. Aldo used his one instant of surprise to land a cracking punch to his temple. The knife clattered to the ground, then Gianni's legs folded under him and he collapsed to the ground. Aldo had the presence of mind to kick the knife out of reach before pulling Sally into his arms. She was shaking and clung to his shoulders, burying her head in the crook of his neck. 'You're safe now,' he murmured. 'I'm here.' All the while he kept half an eye on Gianni in case he began to stir. How long they stood there, Aldo didn't know, but eventually he became aware of the sound of running feet and a voice – Enrico – calling his name.

'Over here!' he called.

Much to his surprise and relief, Enrico appeared, followed by Captain Briars, Sergeant Frazer and his constable. Frazer seemed to take in the scene at once and stooped over Gianni's inert figure, feeling his pulse before slapping a pair of handcuffs around his wrists.

'What happened here?' Briars asked. 'Tessa Bligh identified Gianni from a photograph earlier this afternoon, and we were on our way to find him when Enrico dashed up to us, babbling something about another Wren in danger.'

Sally freed herself from Aldo's arms, wiping her eyes. She appeared to be more composed, and she drew herself up to stand straight and look Captain Briars in the eye. 'That would be me. I don't know what would have happened if Aldo hadn't found us. Gianni tricked me into thinking I was meeting Aldo.' She glanced at Aldo. 'I'm not sure how.'

Aldo stepped in and explained what had happened. By the time his tale drew to an end, Gianni was stirring.

The sergeant pulled him to his feet. 'I'd better get this one into custody,' he said. Then, to Aldo and Sally, 'I'm afraid I'll need statements from you both, but it can wait until tomorrow.' Between the sergeant and Constable Hammond, they manhandled Gianni out of the alley and into the street. The others followed.

Aldo put an arm around Sally and found she was still shaking. 'I should take you back to the Wrennery.' Although he was disappointed that he wouldn't be able to open his heart to her as he'd planned that evening, it was clear she wasn't in a state to hear him.

'My staff car is parked just down the road.' Briars was looking at Sally in concern. 'I can give you lift to the Wrennery. Or perhaps you should get a doctor to check you over.'

Sally shook her head. 'No, thank you. I'm fine. He didn't hurt me. I think the walk will do me good.' She turned to Aldo. 'Will you walk me there?'

'Of course.' After what had just happened, he wasn't letting her out of his sight until she was safely inside.

—

Once they had parted ways with Captain Briars and Enrico, Sally clung to Aldo's arm as though her life depended on it. She kept reliving those horrific moments when Gianni had held the knife at her throat and told her exactly what he was going to do to her to get his revenge on Aldo. She could still hardly believe Aldo had shown up when he did. She wanted to thank him but didn't trust herself not to dissolve into tears again.

They hadn't walked far down Dundas Street when voices hailed her from behind. The next moment, Iris and Mary had run up, Rob and Joe in tow.

'Sally, are you all right?' Iris asked. 'We've just seen Frazer drag an Italian away in handcuffs, and there are rumours flying about him attacking you.'

And so Sally was forced to repeat the tale to the shocked exclamations of Iris and Mary.

'Thank goodness you're unhurt.' Mary pulled her into a hug when she finished. Then she turned to Aldo and kissed him on the cheek. 'Thank you for decking the bastard.'

Mary's choice of words combined with Aldo's look of shock made Sally giggle. Then she found she couldn't stop, and she doubled up, caught between laughter and tears.

Iris murmured in dismay and wrapped an arm around her shoulders. 'Come on, we should get you back to the Wrennery. It wouldn't hurt to get the doctor to look at you.'

Her words acted like the slap of cold water and helped Sally regain control. 'No. They'll only put me to bed, and I'll end up going over it all until I feel like I'm in a nightmare. I want to stay with you all.'

Iris and Mary exchanged glances then spoke at the same time. 'Curlew Croft.'

'Oh yes. That's the perfect place.' She didn't know why she hadn't thought of it before. In the soothing presence of Elspeth and Archie, surrounded by the scent of the peat-fired stove, she knew she would feel better.

'Come on then.' Iris turned to Aldo. 'You will come too? You're part of the group now.'

Aldo, looking delighted, agreed, and Sally shot Iris a grateful look.

They set out walking in a bunch, Iris and Mary wanting to hear from Aldo why Gianni had wanted revenge. By the time Aldo had finished explaining about how he had managed to overpower him in a fight, they were approaching the entrance to the Kyeness track. Once they were through the gate, the group naturally split into pairs, with Iris, Rob, Mary and Joe walking ahead. Sally, still feeling rather shaky, took Aldo's arm and didn't worry that she couldn't keep up. Soothed by the warm sunshine and the birdsong, not to mention Aldo's reassuring presence, slowly her shock melted away.

They had nearly reached the top of the hill when Aldo stopped dead. 'I just remembered something.' He pulled a silver chain from his pocket, and Sally was overjoyed to see the St Christopher dangling from his fingers.

'You found it.'

He nodded, his eyes grave. 'If I hadn't seen it, I would have walked past the alley without even noticing it. Did you leave it there deliberately?'

'Yes. I didn't know what else to do. I hoped you would come looking for me.' She reached out to touch the medallion. 'It really did protect me. Well, you protected me. But if you hadn't given it to me, I would have had no way to show where I was.'

'Then I will never stop thanking whatever power persuaded me to give it to you when I barely knew you.' He put it back in his pocket, saying, 'The chain is broken. I will give it back after I mend it for you.'

Sally couldn't drag her gaze from his. She felt she could drown in his dark brown eyes that were filled with such warmth. 'And I will never cease to thank God or fate or whatever impulse drove me to drop it there. But I will always be especially grateful to you for, as Mary so delicately put it, decking the bastard. It was brave of you to run at him when he had a knife.'

'I didn't feel brave. I only knew I had to stop him and save you.' He stooped and kissed her, and Sally thought she might explode from happiness. However, she forced herself to pull away before her swimming senses made her forget what she needed to say.

'Aldo, I—'

But Aldo started speaking at the same time. 'Sally, I know I don't have much to offer you. I am not even in control of my own fate right now. I don't know where I might be taken tomorrow. All I can offer you is my today. But as long as we are together in Orkney, I want to be with you. Because I love you. And if fate separates us, I will do all in my power to find you again.'

Sally blinked back tears, hardly able to believe that all her wishes had been answered. 'I love you too,' she said, as soon as she could draw breath to speak. 'For all I know, the WRNS could send me away from here tomorrow, but I want us to be together for as long as possible. I know Mary would laugh at me for saying this, but even if we are separated, I believe fate will bring us back together again.' Then she chuckled. 'And if it doesn't, I'll jolly well find you myself.' Then she wound her arms around his neck and kissed him, and they stood entwined in their embrace while the wind ruffled their hair.

Some time later they burst through the door at Curlew Croft, holding hands and giggling. They had long since lost sight of the others, and found them already sitting around the kitchen table, with cups of tea beside them.

'There you are,' Mary said. 'I was all for coming to look for you, but Iris was sure you wouldn't want to be disturbed. What have you been doing?'

Sally exchanged a look with Aldo then grinned. 'Cavorting.'

'Well, it does my heart good to see the six of you all together and looking so well,' Elspeth said. 'From what the others told me, Sally, I thought you might be needing a dram of whisky, but you seem to have found other medicine.'

'I have at that.' Sally pulled Aldo towards the table, where there were two empty chairs side by side. She still held his hand, not wanting to let him go, still bubbling over with happiness at the knowledge that he loved her and wanted to stay with her.

'As to that…' Archie rose and opened a high cupboard beside the door. 'There's more than one reason for enjoying whisky.' He lifted down a bottle. 'Let's have the special glasses, Elspeth. I want to make a toast.'

Once they were all holding cut-glass tumblers that sparkled whenever they caught the light, Archie raised his glass. 'True love never dies, even after those who hold our hearts have passed on. So I ask you all to raise your glasses and drink to the love of friends, family and sweethearts.'

'To the love of friends, family and sweethearts.' They all echoed the toast. Sally saw both Iris and Mary wipe away tears, and she knew Iris was thinking of her father, killed when his ship had hit a mine, and Mary of her fiancé lost when the *Royal Oak* had been destroyed. Elspeth also glanced at the shelf that held pictures of the Heddles' absent sons, one of them interned in Switzerland. Archie was right – love didn't die, and it would hold them together even if they should be separated for a while.

Sally felt Aldo squeeze her hand, and she smiled at him. Their future might yet be uncertain, but she knew that they would be together one way or another for the rest of their lives.

Epilogue

8 May 1945 – VE Day

'It's hard to believe it's over, isn't it?' Iris commented.

As they had done so often during the war when there had been something to celebrate, the group had gathered at Curlew Croft after the morning's thanksgiving service in Stromness. Miraculously, or so it felt to Sally, they were still all together. The *Kelpie* had remained in Scapa Flow after its return the previous year, and even Aldo was still there. Although the Italians in the camps on Burray and Lamb Holm had been sent to England, the Italians in Stromness were still in Orkney with no sign of them being sent away yet.

In addition to the usual gang, Tessa was also there. True to her word, Sally had made an effort to befriend her when she had returned from sick leave and gradually, a firm friendship had formed between them. Iris and Mary had been more wary at first but had finally come to accept her. Tessa had blossomed under their friendship and now even Mary admitted that she was a good friend and someone she would keep in touch with once they went their separate ways.

Sally looked at Iris over the top of her teacup. 'It might feel more festive if it weren't for this fog. What was the point of putting up bunting if no one could see it?'

There were murmurs and nods of agreement. No matter how happy everyone had been to celebrate the end of the war in Europe, standing out in the chill, damp fog had not been pleasant.

From the corner of her eye, Sally saw Mary exchange a glance with Joe, her brows raised in a question, and Joe gave a nod. Mary took Joe's hand, weaving their fingers together. 'Well, we've got something to celebrate.'

Iris beat them to it. 'You're engaged! You sly thing, when did that happen?'

Mary grinned. 'On the walk up here. It turns out the fog was our friend, after all.'

Sally felt a warm hand squeeze hers and she shared a lingering look with Aldo, remembering their own walk to Curlew Croft when they had managed to lag behind the others. Aldo had been true to his word, and the months since his name had been cleared had been some of the happiest of her life. Although she knew he was still in no position to offer her a future, she was secure in the knowledge that he would as soon as he was free, and she was able to offer her congratulations to Mary and Joe with a heart full of joy for the couple. Iris was slapping Mary's back, the light catching the beautiful opal on her engagement ring. Iris had been ecstatic when Rob had proposed on Iris's birthday, presenting her with a ring that had once belonged to his grandmother.

'Well, now, that is something to celebrate. A good thing I saved up our rations to make this cake.' Elspeth placed a plate holding an enormous fruitcake on the table and handed the knife to Mary. 'How about the two of you cut the cake?'

Sally bit into her slice and closed her eyes in ecstasy. 'This is delicious. Even better than the cake we had for Mum and Harry's wedding celebration.' For, much to her delight, Sally had managed to get a week's leave soon after her mother had become Mrs Rowbotham, and the whole neighbourhood had gathered to celebrate in as lavish a style as rationing permitted. If she had entertained any doubts about Annie's wisdom in marrying Harry, they would have been dispelled by her mother's radiant smiles and the way Harry looked at her as though he still could not believe his good fortune.

With their stomachs full of cake and the room ringing with laughter and happy voices, the talk turned to their futures, as was inevitable.

'We're sorted, of course,' Iris said with a nod towards Rob. 'We're not going to marry until we've been demobbed, and who knows how long that will take? But we're going to come back here to live. I'm setting myself up in Stromness as a dressmaker, and Rob's going to get work repairing boats until he can save enough to start his own boatyard.'

'It'll be lovely to have you both here,' Elspeth said. 'And I know plenty of people who will be queuing to have their old clothes remade even before clothes rationing ends, so you won't be short of work.'

'And there will be plenty of folk needing to get their fishing boats back in working order,' Archie added.

'Does anyone else know what they're going to do yet?'

'Joe and I were discussing it just now,' Mary said.

Sally laughed. 'What? You didn't spend the entire walk cavorting, then?'

Mary gave a mock scowl. 'As I was saying before I was so rudely interrupted, we haven't decided where to live yet, but we'd like to set up a gallery eventually.'

'That's a wonderful idea. I think your work will sell really well,' Sally said.

'The light in Orkney is a famous draw for artists,' Elspeth said. 'You should consider staying here.' It was clear she was reluctant to say goodbye to the youngsters that she had taken in over the years.

'We've certainly considered it. Joe's going to take on some accountancy work to help pay our way, so it depends if he can find enough work in Orkney. Otherwise we might go to Pembrokeshire, to be near my family.'

'What about you, Tessa?' Sally asked, trying not to feel jealous that her friends had their futures decided.

'I'm going to go back and live with my parents,' she replied. 'They're getting on a bit and I want to help support them. I thought I'd get a typing qualification and get a clerical job. It might be nice to work in an office after all those watches in the freezing cold signal station.'

'It's not over yet.' Mary's tone was dark. 'We could still be facing another winter up there.'

'I don't mind. I'm going to miss you all so much when I leave, I'm happy to stay here as long as I'm needed.'

Then came the question Sally had dreaded. 'What about you, Sally?' Iris asked.

'Well,' Sally shot a sideways glance at Aldo. 'It's hard to say until we know what's going to happen to Aldo.'

'Captain Briars spoke to me this morning,' Aldo put in.

Sally stared at him. 'He did? What about?'

'Well, I'd asked him earlier if there was a way I could stay in Britain and not be sent back to Italy with the others, and he said he'd find out for me.'

Sally caught her breath. 'And?'

'This morning he told me I might be able to stay but I have to get permission from the prime minister.'

'Well, you helped build his barriers,' Mary said. 'The least he can do in return is let you stay.'

'I hope so.' Aldo squeezed Sally's hand. 'Captain Briars said he would write a personal recommendation and do all in his power to help me. That makes me very happy because I want to stay with Sally.'

Sally had to turn away briefly to blink back tears. Then something Aldo had said before hit her. 'Wait. You said something about the other Italians being sent to Italy.'

'Yes. What of it?'

'You said Italy, not home.'

Aldo's expression softened. 'I do not think of Italy as home. I heard an expression the other day – home is where the heart is. My heart is with you, Sally. Always. I want my home to be with you.' Then, to Sally's complete shock, he slid off his chair and dropped to one knee beside her. 'Sally, I do not yet know how long it will be before I am free, but when I am, will you marry me?'

Sally flung her arms around his neck with an incoherent cry. She was dimly aware of Mary laughing then saying, 'I think you can take that as a yes.'

'Oh yes, it's absolutely a yes. I can't believe it. And I didn't even see two magpies today.'

Aldo wrapped his arms around her and held her close. He murmured in her ear, 'I am sure they were there, but they were hidden in the fog.'

'Of course.' Sally sat back and let Aldo rise from his knees. 'The fog has a lot to answer for.'

'And, I have more news,' Aldo told her. 'Captain Briars said it would be easier for me to stay if I had a job, so he has been making enquiries for me. And he says there is a baker in Kirkwall whose son was killed two years ago, and he has lost heart in the business. He is looking for another baker to gradually take over his role. Captain Briars has put in a good word for me, and the man says the job is mine as soon as I am released from the labour battalion. That is,' he gave Sally an anxious look, 'if you would be happy to stay in Orkney?'

'Would I?' Sally flung herself back into his arms. 'I would have suggested it before, but I thought you might not want to, what with you having come here as a prisoner.'

Aldo shrugged. 'The Orcadians have been very welcoming. I think I would be happy here. I know I will be happy if you will. And also, I put so much effort into cutting the stone for the causeways, I want to stay to make the most of my hard work. Oh, and to make a home for one very special Orcadian who befriended me.'

'Who?' Sally couldn't think who he meant and wasn't sure how she felt about sharing her home with a stranger.

'Nero the cat. I can't bear to think of him all alone after I leave Bruna Camp.'

Sally laughed. 'Of course. Our home wouldn't be complete without him.'

'This calls for another toast.' Archie retrieved his bottle of whisky and poured a generous amount in each glass. 'To friends and family, near and far, and to Orkney, the place that unites us.'

Her heart brimming with joy, Sally raised her glass and joined in the toast. 'To Orkney!'

Aldo tapped her arm and pointed at the window, now shorn of its heavy blackout blinds. There, on the stone sill outside, peering in, was a pair of magpies. 'What did I tell you?'

And Sally raised her glass in a second, silent but heartfelt toast. To Orkney, the place where she and her friends had found joy.

Author's Note

Although whole books have been written about the lives of the Italian prisoners of war based in camps on Burray and Lamb Holm, I could find frustratingly little information about the group who were moved to Stromness. After a brief mention that about sixty men were sent to Bruna Camp (sometimes also called Bruno Camp) near Stromness in the autumn of 1943, the record goes silent until the *Orkney Herald* notes that these Italians finally left Stromness in the first week of December 1945, the last group of Italians to leave Orkney. However, the article does also mention that the Italians were fine craftsmen, which gave me the idea for Aldo's carvings.

The article also notes that they played football to a high standard. As there are several accounts of the Italians in Camps 60 and 34 playing football with British teams once they were given more freedom, I thought it likely that the Stromness Italians would also have taken part in football matches. While I couldn't find evidence of a tournament such as the one in my story, that doesn't mean it didn't happen!

It wasn't until April 1944, seven months after Italy's capitulation, that the Italian prisoners were finally given the option to form volunteer cooperatives. Those that agreed would be paid and allowed greater freedom if they obeyed certain regulations. One of these regulations was that they were not to form relationships with women. Considering I was writing a story based around a romance between a British woman and an Italian prisoner of war, this fact caused me considerable angst when I first read it. You can imagine my relief when I found several accounts that stated that this rule was impossible to enforce and was universally ignored.

Finally, to anyone wondering why I refer to the Pioneer Corps instead of the Royal Pioneer Corps, it was only granted its Royal prefix in 1946.

Acknowledgements

To all the readers who have followed the adventures of Iris, Mary and Sally from the start and have been kind enough to leave reviews – thank you for your kind words which have encouraged me to keep writing.

A huge thank you to all the friends who have cheered me on along the way. Firstly, to the WHS girls who helpfully posted pictures of all the fabulous places they were visiting while I was locked in my room, desperately trying to hit my deadline. Thanks. But as you also sent me shelfies of my books in the wild, all is forgiven. To the Botswana crew, who were my very own 'found family' and a big reason why friendship is central to my books. Also to my writer friends who have helped keep me sane(ish), especially the Apricot Plots writers, my RNA Birmingham Chapter friends and the Wrekin Writers.

To the best agent ever – Lina Langlee of the North Literary Agency. Thanks for all your hard work and support. Last but not least, to my brilliant editor, Emily Bedford, and the whole team at Canelo, thank you for all the work that goes into making each book the best it can be.